A *Wedding* at Mulberry Lane

ROSIE CLARKE was born in Swindon, but moved to Ely in Cambridgeshire at the age of nine. She started writing in 1976, combining this with helping her husband run his antiques shop. In 2004, Rosie was the well-deserved winner of the RNA Romance Award and the Betty Neels Trophy. Rosie also writes as Anne Herries and Cathy Sharp. Find out more at her website: www.rosieclarke.co.uk

By Rosie Clarke

The Mulberry Lane series

The Girls of Mulberry Lane
A Wedding at Mulberry Lane
Mulberry Lane Babies

The Workshop Girls series

Lizzie's Secret
Lizzie's War
Lizzie's Daughter

Standalone titles

Jessie's Promise
The Runaway Wife

ROSIE CLARKE

A *Wedding* at Mulberry Lane

First published in 2017 by Aria, an imprint of Head of Zeus Ltd
This paperback edition published in 2018 by Aria,
an imprint of Head of Zeus Ltd

9 7 5 3 2 4 6 8

A catalogue record for this book is available from
the British Library.

ISBN (PB): 9781788546201

Typeset by Divaddict Publishing Solutions Ltd.

MIX
Paper from
responsible sources
FSC® C020471

Printed and bound by CPI Group (UK) Ltd,
Croydon, CR0 4YY

Head of Zeus Ltd
First Floor East
5–8 Hardwick Street
London EC1R 4RG

WWW.HEADOFZEUS.COM

A *Wedding* at Mulberry Lane

Chapter 1

'Where did that come from?' Tommy Barton demanded of his younger brother Sam. He took hold of Sam's wrist and twisted it so that he dropped the half-eaten bun into his hand. 'This is from the baker's round by the market. Where did you get a penny for a sticky bun?'

The stench of burning still held in the air and smoke drifted over some bombed-out buildings a few streets away. Here in the lanes of Spitalfields there was considerable damage to houses and to other buildings, because the heavy bombing had been continuous for the past month or more. It was January 1941 and freezing cold and both boys were wearing thin jackets over their shirts and worn-out trousers with patches over the knees. Their boots were down at heel and the toe of Sam's right boot had a hole in it.

'Give it back; I'm 'ungry.' Sam's thin face was sullen, his dark eyes glinting with temper. 'Weren't no need to do that,' he grumbled. 'I earned it round the scrapyard if yer must know.'

'What were yer doin' there?' Tommy demanded. 'Bert don't give money away fer nuthin'. If you've been selling pinched stuff, Ma will tan your backside.'

'What she don't know won't 'urt her,' Sam said defiantly,

swiping his dripping nose with his sleeve. ''Sides, I collect scrap fer Bert. He pays a lot of the kids to collect bits and pieces fer 'im.'

'And 'e don't care whether it's found honest or pinched,' Tommy said, but returned the half-eaten bun to his brother. 'Ma told yer not to go round there – and it's dangerous on the rubble of those bomb sites, Sam. Some of the bombs don't go off when they drop and if yer trigger an unexploded one they'll never find all the bits...'

Sam grinned, showing a gap in his front teeth. 'I'll give yer tuppence if yer don't tell Ma.'

Tommy cuffed his ear, but declined the offer. 'I ain't takin' no bribe, Sam. I shan't tell Ma this time, but I'm warnin' yer – keep orf them bombed-out 'ouses. Fer one thing it's looting and yer could be shot. Ain't yer seen the warnin' signs?'

'Nah, the bloody coppers just give yer a clip of the ear and tell yer to 'op it. Some of 'em would nick from the ruins themselves if they got the chance; it ain't doin' no 'arm.' Sam grinned at him. 'I ain't takin' nuthin' important, Tom; just bits of old metal – exploded shells and junk. I don't take what belongs to folks like us...'

'If yer want a job, knock the doors and ask if yer can clean the winders or somethin',' Tom said. 'I cleaned Mrs Tandy's winders this mornin' and earned sixpence fer Ma – and Peggy from over the road says she'll give me a shilling to clean 'er gutterin' out.'

'I asked round like yer told me, but they all said they didn't want kids muckin' about – Bert was the only one who offered me anythin'. He said to collect anythin' metal lyin' around, so I did...' Sam pulled a face. 'You're older than me and they trust yer.'

'Well get orf in then,' Tommy said, accepting his brother's excuses. 'Tell Ma I'll be 'ome fer me dinner after I've finished cleaning the gutterin'.'

Sam went, muttering and grumbling, but he usually did what his brother said in the end. Tommy couldn't blame him for trying to earn a few pennies for himself, because their mother never had enough money to feed them, let alone give them pocket money, and Tommy had been touting for work on Saturday mornings and whenever he got a chance in the evenings, because without the extras he earned, they would all go hungry.

He wished that Maureen Jackson were still at the shop. She'd always given him a few bargains or paid him to do small jobs, but her father was a skinflint and refused to give anything away. His wife Violet just looked down her nose and told enterprising lads to go away, but some of the other residents of Mulberry Lane were kinder. Alice Carter would give him tuppence for bringing in her coal and chopping a pile of wood, but Tommy knew it wasn't enough. At nearly fourteen he felt capable of doing a man's work and wished he could convince his mother to let him leave school after his birthday in April, but she wanted him to stay on and take his higher exams.

'You're a bright lad, Tommy,' Tilly Barton had told her son just that morning. 'Brighter than your brother, your father and me – so stay on for as long as you can and make something more of yourself. God knows, you don't want to live like this for the rest of your life.'

Tommy hadn't answered her but he knew what he wanted. He was tall for his age, an energetic, rangy lad, with big hands and feet, who looked older than he was, but he'd already been down the Army enrolment office and tried to persuade them he was eighteen; the sergeant had laughed and told him to come back in three years or so.

'I'd 'ave yer if I could, lad,' he'd told Tommy, 'but they'd 'ave me guts for garters.' He'd reached into his pocket and given Tommy a shilling. 'In the old days if you'd took me shillin' you'd be in the Army, lad, but there's rules these days, see; you've got ter be eighteen. Buy yerself a hot pie and mash and look after yer ma...'

Tommy's encounter with the friendly sergeant had made him keener than ever to join up, but he couldn't even leave school until the start of the summer term, even if his ma would let him then, so the best he could do was to find all the odd jobs he could in the lanes – and he always liked working for Peggy Ashley at the Pig & Whistle, because he usually got something good to eat as well as a few pennies in his pocket.

Whistling cheerfully, he walked across the road; the sign was creaking in the wind, its comic pig dancing to the tune of a penny whistle bringing a smile to his face. Tommy went under the arch to the pub yard and knocked at the back door, which was painted dark green and split in two like a stable door. Peggy often had the top open to let in some fresh air as she worked, but today it was shut tight. She opened it and smiled at him, nodding as he told her he was about to start on the job she wanted done.

*

'You've made a good job of that gutter,' Peggy Ashley said when Tommy had finished a couple of hours later. 'Here's your shillin', and I made a fatless sponge with strawberry jam for you to take home. I wish you were a bit older, Tommy. I'd give you a job in the bar servin' drinks.'

4

'Bet I could do it as good as anyone.' Tommy grinned as he pocketed the shilling. 'I reckon Ma could an' all if she wanted...'

'If your mum wants a little job washing up at lunchtimes tell her to come and see me. I'll give her two bob a session,' Peggy said and smiled as Tommy went off whistling. He was such a willing young man and whatever he did, he did well, and that guttering had wanted cleaning for ages. Laurence had talked of having it done for months before he went off to do whatever he was doing for the military. Peggy frowned as she thought of the husband she'd once loved, who had betrayed her trust by having an affair but dismissed it as unimportant: Laurence was no longer truly a part of her life. Her life was here in Mulberry Lane with her friends, her children and her granddaughter.

Her thoughts turned to Tommy again. Peggy wasn't the only one in Mulberry Lane who thought Tommy Barton deserved a break. His mother struggled to bring up two growing lads since her husband had been sent to prison for robbing a corner post office somewhere up the West End. Tilly Barton tried her best, taking on the job of scrubbing out offices down the Docks for two hours every morning, which meant her sons had to get themselves off to school, often without even a slice of bread and dripping in their stomachs. Peggy sometimes needed an extra pair of hands in the bar, but Tilly wasn't cut out for that sort of work, though she could help with washing the dishes if she accepted the offer.

'Was that Tommy Barton I just saw leaving the yard?' Nellie, her friend and daily help, entered the kitchen as Peggy put a batch of lemon curd tarts into the oven. 'They look good – haven't seen any lemon curd for ages...'

'I was lucky to get this,' Peggy said. 'Yes, it was Tommy; he cleaned my gutterin' out. It used to make a mess every time it rained, but it should be fine for a while now.'

'It's a pity his brother hasn't got as much sense...'

'What do you mean?' Peggy smiled at the woman, who was like a member of family these days. 'What has Sam done?'

'I saw him on the ruins of those houses up by the market, Peggy. He was with some other lads pullin' the rubble over, lookin' fer scrap metal. It's stupid but a lot of them do it in the hope of earnin' a few pennies.'

'That could be very dangerous.' Peggy frowned. 'He could injure himself on broken glass, sharp metal... I read in the paper about a boy who fell through a concealed crater into a cellar and was killed. Do you think Tilly knows what he does?'

'She would give him a hidin', but I doubt if she can stop him. It needs a man to control lads that age. He could end up in trouble with the law if he takes stuff from the bomb sites. What Sam needs is his father's belt on his backside a couple of times.'

Peggy was thoughtful. 'I feel I ought to tell Tilly what Sam's doing, but it might just make things worse for her.'

'I'll 'ave a word if yer like,' Nellie said. 'I knew Tilly's mother well – she might take it kinder from me.'

'Yes, all right,' Peggy said. 'I'm going to take these pasties through to the bar. Keep an eye on the tarts for me, will you – and put the kettle on...'

*

'That was good of Peggy,' Tilly said as Tommy handed her the sponge cake. 'I've mashed some potatoes and cooked carrots

6

and greens for dinner but there's no meat – unless you can pop over the road to the shop and fetch me a tin of Spam?'

'I already did, Ma,' Tommy said and put the tin of processed meat on the kitchen table. 'Sorry it's only the small size, but Mrs Jackson served me and she never gives me anythin' extra like Maureen used to.'

His mother eyed the small tin of meat, which was hardly enough for the three of them. 'It's a pity Maureen left her father in the lurch is what I say. I don't know what got into her, going off like that: years she stood behind that counter, day in and day out – and then all of a sudden she's gone orf somewhere.'

'Maureen is goin' to be a nurse,' Tommy said and smiled. 'I like 'er, Ma. She's all right. I reckon 'er father took her fer granted – but she always had a smile and a word fer everyone what went in there. Alice says she's thinkin' about changing her ration card to the shop in Bell Lane. She don't like 'em at the corner shop now.'

'Alice Carter! Take no notice of her.' His mother sniffed and he turned away. Ma was never happy these days, no matter what Tommy did to please her. He knew she had it hard, but then so did others. Alice Carter didn't have much but she was always cheerful, laughing and cracking jokes, even though she'd been a widow for years.

'Well, call yer brother in from the yard and wash yer hands,' Tilly said, tucking a wisp of mousey-brown hair behind her ear. Her face was pale and thin and her eyes a faded grey. If she had ever been pretty, it had all gone now, replaced by lines of worry and discontent. 'I've got to look fer another job this afternoon, because they're cuttin' me hours down the Docks. So when you've eaten you can wash the dishes and do a few jobs fer me.'

Tommy nodded, understanding her mood. No wonder she was so miserable. It wasn't much of a job scrubbing offices out, but the money she earned just about held them together, and what Tom earned bought a few extras like the tin of Spam: if she didn't find more work to replace the cut in her hours they would struggle to pay the rent and would lose their home.

'Peggy said she could do with some help washin' up at lunchtimes,' he offered over his shoulder as he went to the back door and signalled Sam to come in from the yard. Like most of the back yards this side of the lane, it was square with an outside toilet, a place to put the dustbin and enough space to run a double line of washing on when the sun shone.

'I'll 'ave a word if I can't get anythin' better then,' Tilly said and gave him a rare smile. 'I know yer try, Tom – but we need a man's wage comin' in. I'll never forgive yer father fer shamin' us all the way he did...'

Tommy didn't answer. His dad was a good bloke but he'd got desperate and made a mistake – and now they were all paying for it...

Chapter 2

One morning towards the end of January, the rain was coming down with a vengeance in the pub yard, the sky a threatening grey that had made the last few days seem dismal. Little puddles had collected between the old-fashioned cobbles, which were muddy and slippery, and belonged to a long-ago time and ought to have been replaced with flagstones. Inside her big kitchen, Peggy Ashley was warm as she worked, her fair hair sticking to her damp forehead as she prepared the food that kept customers coming to the Pig & Whistle even in these dark days of war.

The folk of the lanes knew that a warm smile and good home-cooked food would await them, even though Peggy might not be able to provide all the marvellous cakes and pies she'd been known for before the hostilities. Peggy's pub was at the corner of Mulberry Lane, close to the market and not far from Frying Pan Alley and Artillery Lane, where her stepfather Percy Ambrose and her mother had lived until their last days.

Local people often used the lane as a shortcut to Spitalfields Market, rather than get lost in the maze of little alleys and courts that were a leftover from ancient times. Perhaps for that reason she'd never known the pub to be empty during opening hours; there was always someone popping in for a beer, a drop of whisky or, these days, quite often a cup of tea with a slice of her famous apple pie. Sometimes they came simply for a chat, because the Pig & Whistle and its landlady were at the centre of life in the lanes, bringing everyone together in these dark times.

'While this place is still standing it's a symbol that life goes on,' Jim Stillman told her as he brought in a box of vegetables from his allotment and was given an apple and blackcurrant tart to take home. 'Alice Carter was tellin' me how you took 'em all down to the cellar again the other night when the siren went. She reckons she's safer in your cellar than in some of them bleedin' shelters the council put up...' More than one air raid shelter had collapsed under a direct hit during the Blitz, causing terrible injuries and loss of life, which meant a lot of people didn't trust them and preferred the underground stations, where they congregated in large numbers every night.

'Well, she's welcome to come, and so are you if you're near the pub,' Peggy said, smiling as he took his leave.

Seeing her daughter hurrying through the yard, Peggy opened the door and beckoned her in. 'I thought you were never coming, Janet. Was your train late again?'

'We stopped three times because there was a blockage on the line,' Janet said and shivered as she dumped her wet coat on a peg over the door. 'It's so cold I thought it would snow – in fact it was sleeting when I got off the train, but it's turned to rain now...'

One look at her daughter's pinched face told Peggy Ashley that the news was not good. She went forward and brought Janet closer to the warmth, taking her cold hands and gripping them firmly as she urged her towards the large comforting armchair by the kitchen range, which was freshly polished, made up with coke to last the day, and gave off generous heat.

'Sit there and tell me all about it,' Peggy said. She glanced round as the door opened behind her and Nellie made to come in, but on seeing Peggy's warning look she nodded and backed out, mouthing that she would finish in the public bar. With her husband Laurie away, Peggy relied more and more on her friends to help her keep this place running. 'What has happened to make you look like that, Janet love?'

Janet had bent to look at her daughter asleep in her carrycot. She'd left the child with her mother while she went to visit her husband in hospital. Janet stroked her daughter's head, blinking hard to hold back her tears. 'Has she been good?'

'Maggie is never any trouble,' Peggy said, 'but you're upset – what's wrong?'

'It's Mike,' Janet said, her eyes drenched with tears as she spoke of her husband who had been wounded while on duty with the Navy, and thought lost for months, before being transferred to a British hospital. 'He just stared at me as if I was a stranger and… I don't think he liked me. I tried telling him about Maggie and he shook his head, didn't want to know.'

'The hospital did warn you that it was still too soon. Mike almost died of his wounds, Janet. Perhaps the only way he can cope with his illness and the horror of what happened is by shutting everything else out of his mind – and it must seem strange to be told he has a wife and daughter he doesn't know.'

'Oh, Mum, I can't bear it,' Janet sobbed, because after two days visiting at the hospital, Mike's attitude towards her was worse not better. 'We were so much in love. Mike was always desperate to touch me and kiss me – and when I tried to kiss him yesterday afternoon before I left, he asked me not to...'

Peggy's heart convulsed with grief for her beloved daughter. Janet was a lovely girl, both in looks and nature, and she didn't deserve this on top of all she'd gone through. Her fight to get married, before Mike left to join the Navy at the start of the war, had pulled the family apart, and then Janet had suffered the loss of her home and months of not knowing if her husband was alive. Peggy believed one of the main factors in the breakdown of her own marriage was the quarrels with Laurie over Jan's behaviour. She'd taken her daughter's side, especially when she'd confessed that she was having Mike's baby before they were wed. Janet's confession had finally forced her father's hand and he'd had to give in; he agreed that Peggy could sign the necessary forms, but he'd vowed he wouldn't see her again. Laurie had since relented, but it was too late to restore what had been – at least for Peggy.

'I know it's hard,' she said, kneeling down on the rag rug in front of the stove where she did all her cooking for both her family and the pub, which she and her husband had run together for nearly twenty years, before he went off to some secret location for military training. He'd told her nothing about his work for the War Office on his brief visit home at Christmas. All Peggy had learned in those few days was that Laurie had been unfaithful to her and that it had meant more to him than a fling. She reached for her daughter's hand, looking intently into her face. 'When you lose something as precious as you had with Mike it hurts terribly.'

Janet looked blindly at her through the tears. 'How could you know? You've got everything – Dad, the pub, Pip and me, and Maggie, to fuss over. You don't know what it feels like to have your heart broken...'

'You don't know everything; perhaps my life isn't all roses,' Peggy said and stroked her cheek, kissing her softly and looking into her eyes for a moment. 'I do understand, darling, believe me.'

'Do you?' Janet looked into her eyes, something in her tone alerting her. 'Has Dad been unfaithful to you, Mum – is that why you've been so unhappy?'

'It doesn't matter about me; my troubles are nothing compared to yours, Jan...' Peggy avoided her gaze, because she hadn't allowed either of her children to see that things were wrong between her and Laurie.

'No, tell me the truth. I want to know – has Dad let you down?'

Peggy hesitated, feeling she didn't want to make her daughter's burden heavier, 'Your father has someone else – someone younger, I think...'

'Mum, he wouldn't!' Janet exclaimed, eyes opening wide with shock. 'Is it my fault... because you quarrelled over me?'

'Of course not,' Peggy said and got to her feet as the delicious smell from the oven told her the latest batch of scones was ready to come out. 'I'm not sure when it started – but things hadn't been right between us for a while.'

'I always thought you two were a perfect match – happy and still in love, still behaving as if you were lovers sometimes...'

Peggy sighed as she stood with her back to her daughter, her shoulders tense. 'I thought so too but then... oh, it doesn't matter.' Peggy forced a smile. 'Don't worry about me. I'm more concerned about you and Mike.'

Janet shook her head. 'How could Dad do that to you? You're still young and attractive – and you've made this pub the success it is. It wouldn't do half as well without the lovely food you cook…'

'Especially these days when we're continually running out of beer,' Peggy agreed. 'Which reminds me – I've got to ring the brewery and chase them up about our delivery. It's already two days late…'

'Are you content to go on working here, knowing that he's carrying on?' Janet shook her head in disgust.

'Don't look like that, darling.' Peggy laughed softly. 'It isn't the end of the world. Yes, it hurt, and I was angry, but it's been happening slowly this breaking apart, little by little… and besides, I have an admirer.'

Janet's shock was written all over her face.

Peggy was pleased that she'd managed to divert her daughter's thoughts from her own tragedy, even if only for a little while.

'Mum, are you serious?'

Peggy pretended to be affronted as she started slicing bottled pears for an upside-down cake. 'And you were just telling me how attractive I was – anyone would think I was in my dotage…'

'I didn't mean that – you know I didn't,' Janet smiled a little uncertainly at her. 'It's weird thinking your mother might be having an affair…'

'Now you're going too far,' Peggy said primly. 'It's one thing to have a young admirer, and I must admit he has helped me get through some dark days since Christmas, but having an affair… I couldn't! I never looked at another man while Laurie was away in the last war.'

'That was different back then when Dad was away at war,' Janet said. 'I wouldn't have dreamed of being unfaithful to Mike while he was away... but if you and Dad don't get on, perhaps...' She drew a sobbing breath as her grief returned, sweeping her own problems to the fore. 'Oh, Mum, I know I've got to be brave. The hospital told me it will take a long time to heal his physical wounds, though he'll walk and get back to normal given a chance to heal – but they can't be sure if, or when, his mind will heal.'

'You still love him, don't you?'

'Yes, with all my heart – what makes you ask?'

'I just wondered...' Peggy hesitated. 'Because of that man who sent you those lovely things for Maggie after your home was destroyed...'

'You mean Ryan Hendricks?' Janet's cheeks flushed slightly as she looked at her. 'He was just a friend, Mum. You know he thinks the world of his wife and children...'

'He thinks quite a bit of you, Janet. I sensed there was something between you. He went to so much trouble to find out about Mike, didn't he?' Ryan had used all his contacts to find Mike for her when he'd been lying in a hospital bed and no one knew who he was; it was his enquiries that had brought them the news, much swifter than if it had been left to the War Office.

'Yes...' Janet hesitated. 'I know Ryan likes me, perhaps more than he ought, but I love Mike. I always shall.'

'Not even a little bit of doubt there?' Peggy looked at her intently. 'Are you sure there isn't a little bit of you that wants to see Ryan again?'

Janet was silent for a moment, her pretty face torn with indecision and worry, and then, 'Not if I can have Mike back as he was...'

'And if you can't?' Peggy's eyes were very blue as they looked into her daughter's.

Janet closed her eyes for a moment and then looked at her. 'It isn't fair to ask that sort of question, Mum. How can I know?'

'Well, I think you do know in your heart,' Peggy said and washed her hands in the big stone sink. 'I should be telling you to stick by your husband to the last, but I don't think I need to, because I know you to be loyal and loving, my darling. You and your brother are my consolation, my hope for the future. If I didn't have you and Pip, I might run off to America and live forever with my young lover in the land of plenty...'

Janet smiled sadly and shook her head. 'I know you're trying to cheer me up, Mum. You wouldn't dream of doing anything of the sort. And I shall stick by Mike and try to believe in a future for us as a family: Maggie, her father and me.'

'It will come right,' Peggy said, and glanced through the back window. 'And here comes Anne to help out in the pub, so I'll take these scones through to the bar and you can tell her where I am, love.'

'Do you want me to do anything for you?' Janet asked.

'Just look after Maggie,' Peggy said, because the baby had begun to grizzle in her little Tansad pram, which folded up and could be used as a carrycot on buses and trains. 'She's sensed you're home and she wants a feed...'

Leaving her daughter to look after her baby, Peggy went through to the bar, which smelled of polish because Nellie had been hard at work rubbing the wooden surface of the bar and the little oak tables set at intervals about the large room. The Pig & Whistle was an old-fashioned pub in style, built more than a hundred years earlier, with dark oak beams holding a rail above the bar from which Peggy had hung horses' brasses that gleamed in the lights. The shelves behind were also made of oak that had gone dark with age, but Peggy had persuaded Laurence to have mirrors set behind them so that the bottles and glasses were reflected and it made the bar seem even bigger.

'You've got this looking lovely, Nellie,' Peggy said. 'If you put the kettle on I'll come through for a drink once Anne has her coat off...' She broke off as the door opened with a ping and right on cue their first customer of the day arrived. He was a travelling salesman with flat feet, which he made much of because it was the reason the army had refused him. 'Good morning, Mr Symonds. How are you?'

'Very cold and my feet are giving me hell,' he said. 'Have you a nip of whisky for me, Peggy? Just to keep the chill off my chest...'

'I'll 'ave a sit-down and a cuppa,' Nellie said cheerfully. 'Then I'll go up and give the bedrooms a clean...'

'Yes, please.' Peggy was thankful for her cheerful helper as she served the customer with a measure of whisky from under the bar. Because it was only so far the stock Laurie had so providentially stocked in the cellars before the war would stretch, Peggy had worked out that the regulars who always came to her for whisky should have their own bottles, which she kept out of sight. For the moment, she was still able to provide a drink of some sort even for casual visitors, but as the shortages began to bite harder, she'd known she must make sure that her regular customers didn't go without. 'Only a third of the bottle left, sir.'

'Can you put another one by for me?' Mr Symonds asked. 'I'd be happy to pay up front if you wish?'

'You know I don't ask for that,' Peggy said. 'I'll see what I can do, but it depends whether I can get more deliveries. They're very hit and miss...'

Peggy didn't want to reveal that there was still quite a stack of boxes stored in the pub's cellars. She hadn't even known they were there until Pip had shown her the secret hoard Laurie had put by without telling her – one of his secrets, like the money in the post office bankbook that he'd told her about at Christmas, just in case he didn't come back.

Once, Peggy had considered they were close, and she'd certainly been head-over-heels in love with Laurie when they married, because he'd been handsome and fun to be with. He was still attractive, but the laughter had come less often over the years, Laurie seeming to touch her only when he wanted sex. The spontaneous cuddles and kisses had been missing for years, and, without realising it, Peggy had allowed the friendship of her customers and neighbours to fill the empty spaces in her heart.

'You're the best, Peggy Ashley,' her customer said and winked. 'Give me one of those scones, will you?'

'I'm afraid there's only margarine today,' Peggy said. 'You can have jam as well – but most people just like them plain because they've got an almond flavour.'

'I'll have a little marge then,' he sighed. 'This rotten old war – it's a rum thing when we can't even get a bit of butter on a scone...'

He took his drink and the small plate off to a table in the corner and sat down to open his briefcase. Anne entered from the kitchen and Peggy nodded to her.

'I wasn't sure if you would be in today...'

'I'm free for the next week or so,' Anne told her, tucking a stray wisp of hair back into her severe style. 'The school board is trying to locate some children who ran away from their billets in the country and came home. When they're found, I've got to take them back and help settle them into their new schools.'

'It's a bit of an upheaval for you,' Peggy's ready sympathy came to the fore as she looked at her friend. Anne was attractive, her light brown hair drawn back today into a swirl at the back of her head, but she had beautiful soft-grey eyes and could have been really lovely had she taken the trouble to make more of herself. Peggy often thought Anne tried to look plain in her dull tweed skirts and hand-knitted jumpers, as if she had made up her mind to be an old maid and didn't want any offers from men; perhaps because she'd had an unhappy affair once before. 'Why don't they give you a proper settled job?'

'It's because they need supply teachers at a moment's notice. We've lost so many schools, either because they've been taken over by the War Office or they've been bombed. We've had to set up temporary schools where we can, and a lot of the young teachers are leaving to join the women's forces...'

'You thought of it at one time, didn't you?'

'Yes, when I was feeling miserable; that's why I've done some voluntary ambulance work, but I'm glad I stuck to my teaching – besides, you get moved around even more in the services. Maureen has just been told they're sending her down to Portsmouth...'

'She won't be happy about that now Rory has been transferred to a convalescent home nearer London.' Peggy shook her head over the news. For years Maureen had been virtually a prisoner in her father's little shop at the other end of Mulberry Lane, but Mr Jackson had suddenly remarried and Maureen had walked out on him and joined the Women's Royal Voluntary Service, opting to train as a nursing assistant. The man she loved had been wounded in the war and sent to a specialist burns hospital, but recently he'd been transferred back to London.

Thinking about Maureen's situation made Peggy frown, because she wasn't sure what her friend saw in Rory Mackness. Personally, she wouldn't trust him any further than she could throw him.

'No, Maureen isn't pleased, but she doesn't have much choice,' Anne said, turning to look as the door opened and a man in the uniform of an American captain entered. His chocolate-brown eyes went straight to Peggy, his face lighting up as he saw her. 'I think this gentleman has come to see you, Peggy...' Anne whispered and busied herself with setting out some clean glasses on a tray as the young officer walked up to the bar. He looked very handsome in his smart uniform, his dark hair slicked down as he removed his cap, and Peggy caught her breath as she saw the way he looked at her.

'Good morning, Peggy,' he said cheerfully. 'It sure is cold out today...'

'Yes, almost cold enough for snow,' Peggy replied. 'What can I get for you, sir?'

She was aware that Janet had just walked in from the kitchen and was carrying something that smelled good, fresh from the oven.

'Ah, Peggy, you promised me you'd call me Able,' he said. 'I thought we were friends?'

'Yes, we are, Able,' Peggy said and her heart took a giddying tumble in her chest. 'What may I get for you today?'

'I'd like coffee and a slice of that pie, whatever it is...'

'It's an upside-down cake,' Peggy said and glanced at Janet, who was trying to hide her grin as she covertly studied the young officer. 'I put it in the oven earlier and my daughter has kindly brought it through for me...'

That should put him off if anything would, Peggy thought. If he'd thought her younger than she was, it should dispel any ideas he'd had of romancing her. However, after a brief glance at Janet, he was looking at Peggy again, his eyes warm with admiration.

'You must have had her when you were fourteen,' he said and the intention to flirt was unmistakable now. Peggy breathed deeply as she saw the sparkle in those dark eyes and knew that she was far more interested than was good for her. At most, the young officer could want only a brief sexual fling, something that would be pleasant but would last for exactly as long as he was based in England. 'Hey... was that the siren? Hitler's thugs are starting early this morning...'

'It's probably a false alarm,' Peggy said, 'but if you'd put the lock on the door, Able, I'll take everyone down to the cellar. We'll be safe enough there...'

'I shan't stop if you don't mind, Mrs Ashley,' Mr Symonds said and got up in a hurry. 'I've got an important appointment this morning – I'll be on my way...'

Peggy watched as he went out and then Able closed the pub door and locked it behind him. Peggy picked up the coffee pot and Anne took the scones, Able followed with the freshly baked cake, and the three of them trooped through the door at the side of the bar to the cellar stairs; Nellie joined them at the top as the wail of the siren grew louder.

'They can't really be attacking us at this hour, can they?' Janet moaned as she rushed in last of all with Maggie in her arms.

The cellar had been set up for use as a shelter since just before the war began, long before the Luftwaffe started bombing London every night. Peggy had gradually brought down mugs, glasses, blankets, cushions and a few chairs as well as a single mattress. She had a paraffin stove to boil a kettle and several large stone jars filled with water, which were refilled daily, and both candles and kerosene lamps to use if the electricity went off, but at the moment it was still on.

'I'm sorry it's on the rough side,' Peggy apologised, mostly for Able's benefit. He was looking about him with interest at the boxes and barrels stored there. From this part of the cellar it was impossible to see Laurie's secret hoard of wines and spirits bought before the war. There was nothing illegal about them, because they'd been bought long before the war was announced, but even so, Laurence Ashley would almost certainly have been accused of hoarding if the authorities knew about his stores. Anyone hoarding these days could earn a stiff fine if it were discovered. 'Please make yourself at home and have some coffee...'

The coffee was hot and black and was the real stuff only because Able had supplied them with enough ground beans at Christmas to last for a couple of months. No one had thought about milk, though Peggy had some tins of condensed milk stored down here.

'This makes it sweet and not so strong,' she explained to Able as she opened a small tin and poured it into the coffee mugs for Nellie, Anne and Janet.

'I can drink it black, but I must have my sugar...' He took half a dozen sugar lumps wrapped in a twist of paper from his pocket. 'I carry these because most places don't have much and I need at least three – anyone else like some?'

Peggy said yes please and took two, preferring the taste of the coffee black with sugar, as he did, to the sticky sweet taste of the condensed milk. That was something she used all the time now in cakes and puddings, because it took the place of both sugar and cream. Although Peggy qualified for extra rations because she catered for the paying public, she still couldn't buy enough of what she would like to make her food as tasty as pre-war. Like every other housewife in the country she had to improvise, and it was surprising what you could do with dried egg powder and condensed milk if you had to; it was just a case of adjusting the quantities until you got it right.

Peggy cut the cake and passed it round, and they all tucked in, laughing and talking instead of listening for the sound of bombs. Janet said she thought she could hear explosions in the distance, but it was quite a way off and must have been the other side of the river or even further away. Peggy thought it might be the East India Docks.

Able entertained them, telling a story about how he'd been in a light aircraft with his general and forced to land in the desert somewhere because the fuel ran low. None of them knew the place he was talking about but they all laughed at his story and enjoyed listening to his rich southern voice and his quaint English.

It was over an hour before they heard the all-clear. Peggy went outside once they were on ground level, and sure enough she could see smoke rising from the area where the East India Docks were situated. Shivering in the cold air, she ran back inside the bar, telling Janet that she'd been right; it hadn't been a false alarm but a brief daylight raid.

The pub was opened again and a couple of lunchtime customers came rushing in. The rain had stopped and everyone was complaining about the cold as they gathered in front of the fire that Peggy kept going with logs and any kind of old wood she could find.

More people were entering the pub, as if taking the chance to enjoy themselves because it wasn't likely there would be another raid now, and Able paid for his slice of cake; though Peggy refused to charge him for the food offered in the shelter, he'd insisted on paying for coffee and cake before leaving with a promise to visit her soon.

She watched him leave with mixed feelings. It was nice to feel admired and wanted, but she would be an idiot to let it become anything more – wouldn't she?

Peggy was busy serving until after the lunchtime period and it wasn't until they were eating their own meal of corned beef hash that Janet teased her about the American.

'Able really fancies you, Mum,' she said. 'I think you should have a bit of fun if you get the chance, but don't think of it as permanent…'

'Is anything ever?' Peggy asked wryly. 'Are you taking Maggie to the children's clinic for her routine checks this afternoon?'

'Yes, I am – do you want to come with me?'

'I think I'll have a sit-down before I start the evening food,' Peggy said. 'Maureen did say she might pop in after three, because she's leaving for Portsmouth this evening and I shan't see her for a while…'

Chapter 3

Maureen had spent most of the morning at the nursing home talking to Rory. He wasn't happy that she'd been transferred out of London and had sulked for almost an hour. Rory was still trying to work out if his hasty marriage to Velma some years ago was legal or not, because he didn't trust her not to lie over it again. He'd been drunk when he'd tumbled into bed with her that first time, drunk and miserable because of his break up with Maureen. Velma had lied when she told him her first child was his, tricking him into marrying her, and she'd hidden the fact that his daughter had died of a fever soon after he left for service overseas; he knew she was capable of pretending to have been married to someone else before their marriage if it suited her. Velma would say anything to get her own way; she twisted and turned the facts to please herself, and he could never be sure when she was actually telling the truth.

'I have to go, Rory,' Maureen said and kissed him softly on the lips. 'I'm not sure when I'll get to see you again, but I'll write, and when I have a phone number I'll send it to you.'

'I don't know why you had to join the Volunteer Service,' he grumbled, but as she withdrew he grabbed her again and kissed her fiercely. 'Sorry, Molly, I know I'm being mean, but I'd hoped we'd be together at last.'

'If I'd known before I joined…' Maureen shook her head as she saw his expression. His sullenness wasn't attractive, but she put it down to his frustration at being stuck in hospital all this time. When she'd first met Rory it was his smile and the way he was always teasing and full of fun that had made her love him, but sometimes now it was difficult to remember what it had been like then, before they'd split up. 'I just wanted a worthwhile job after all those years of being stuck in Dad's shop and I wasn't sure if you would ever want to see me…' A look of sadness was in her soft-brown eyes, because the break with her father had distressed her. She'd always loved him and done everything she could to please him, including giving up her hopes of marriage to the man she loved, but he'd repaid her by remarrying and driving her from her home.

Rory reached out and took her hand, claiming her attention. Maureen shut out the tears that threatened. She'd fallen hard for Rory when they first met and she'd blamed herself for hurting him when she broke off their informal engagement to stay home and take care of her father. So although it had broken her heart when Rory married six years previously, she hadn't blamed him; it was her fault for refusing to desert her father, and, because she still cared for him, Maureen felt that it was only right she should give him the love and support he needed after his severe injuries. Besides, Velma had no intention of visiting him. She'd made that clear when Maureen asked her which hospital he'd been taken to when he was brought home injured after serving overseas.

'I wouldn't have joined the Service if I'd known you wanted me, Rory,' she said softly, a single tear escaping to trickle down her cheek.

'That was my fault,' he said and gave her his sweetest smile; it wrenched at her heart, making her remember the first time they'd met and he'd told her straight out that she was beautiful. 'My hands were painful the first time you visited the hospital and I thought I'd never be able to work again, but they've made such a good job of me that I feel like a man again. I'll be able to do some sort of job when I get out of here. Besides, I couldn't be sure I'd be free to marry you...' The smile left his eyes. 'If I get my hands on that bitch, I'll thrash her... letting my kid die like that. I don't care how many men she sleeps with but she shouldn't have neglected the kid.'

'I'm sorry about your little girl, because you would've made a good dad, but Velma isn't cut out for motherhood,' Maureen said, avoiding his gaze. She hadn't told him what Velma had confessed to her in the shop: how she'd cheated on him, giving birth to another man's child after he was sent overseas. She reached for his hand and held it. 'I love you, and one day I hope we'll have our own babies. I know it doesn't make up for...'

'Of course it does,' Rory said and gripped her hand so hard that she almost protested. 'I would've done my duty by the kid – but it has always been you I love, Molly. I want us to be married and have our own kids one day... if I'm ever able to provide a decent home for us...' For a moment, uncertainty and doubt showed in his face once more.

'You'll work again.' Maureen put all her love and trust into the smile she gave him. 'I hope they won't send you back out there, because you've done your share, Rory – but I'm confident that one day you'll find work you can enjoy...'

Rory looked anxious and she knew he was worrying about the eye that had been injured while he was fighting in France. His sight was still blurred and, though he could see well enough with his right eye, his left might never fully recover. The doctors had done wonders for the burns on his face, and his hands were healing well, though he would always bear the scars, but neither of them cared about that – Rory because he'd never been vain and Maureen because she loved him.

'Yes, I'll find something,' he said and kissed her cheek. 'You'd better go, love, but I'll be waiting for a letter – and they let us have phone calls in the day room so ring me in the afternoons if you can.'

'Depends what shift I'm on,' she said and kissed him again. At the door of the ward she turned and waved to him, her heart breaking as she saw his shoulders droop. She knew the news of his child's death and the callous behaviour of the woman he'd thought was his wife had first distressed and then angered him, but what she was seeing in him at this moment was sadness and disappointment – disappointment that his injuries had put him out of the war. He felt useless and redundant, as if his life were somehow over. Maureen wished she were going to be closer to Rory so that she could help him fight back and make a new life, but she'd taken on the job of auxiliary nurse at a time of loneliness in her own life, and she couldn't just walk out on her employers.

A part of her wanted to run back and tell Rory that she would get out of it somehow and return to him, but another part of her knew that she was needed at this time, when the hospitals had more patients than they could deal with. The wards were so full that the hospitals had had to spread out into prefabs or take over large houses that could be turned into convalescent homes. Besides, she wanted to prove she could hold down a job other than working for her father, and she needed to earn a living. Her father had never paid her a proper wage so she had very little money saved. Perhaps the war would be over by the time Rory was fit enough to leave the hospital and she could come back to help him find work and a home for them.

Gran would take them in for as long as they needed it and Maureen was certain Rory would settle down once he left the hospital. He was still having small operations and ongoing treatment, which she knew he found irksome, but at least while he was there he didn't have to do anything dangerous – like going back out to the Front.

Maureen hated the war and everything to do with it. She read the newspapers every now and then, but the reports of defeat and casualties only depressed her and she was aware that things were not going well for the Allies. It was unthinkable that they could actually lose the war, but she knew it was the unspoken thought at the back of everyone's mind. No true Brit would admit it, but the constant bombing of cities and ports was getting them all down, and the news of setbacks and defeats overseas was worrying. The one good thing was that Franklin D. Roosevelt had been installed as President of the United States of America for an unprecedented third term, so at least Britain still had an ally in that powerful country. With threats from all over and the war costing eleven million pounds a day, things looked dire.

Maureen pushed the gloomy thoughts to a tiny corner of her mind. She just had time for a quick visit to Peggy and then she must collect her stuff from Gran and get on that train. She'd never been away from London in her life, other than for a day trip, and it was going to seem very strange living away from all those she loved and cared about...

'What yer, Maureen!' a cheerful voice accosted her as she crossed the road to enter Mulberry Lane. Glancing towards the source of the cry, she saw a young sandy-haired lad standing atop a pile of rubble where a second-hand book-shop had once stood. 'How yer doin'?'

'What are you doin' on that rubble?' Maureen answered with a frown. 'That's dangerous, Sam. You want to be careful up there. You could fall and hurt yourself.'

'Nah, it's all right,' he said, throwing her a cheeky grin. 'I know what I'm doin'.'

Maureen hesitated, but it was almost impossible to make lads of that age take notice, especially when their father was in prison and their mother simply couldn't cope.

'Just be careful then,' she said and walked on, entering the lane and crossing the road to avoid passing her father's shop. She didn't want to speak to him or Violet just now, though she supposed she would have to go in briefly before she left for Portsmouth.

Mulberry Lane consisted of two facing rows of houses and shops. On one side was her father's grocery shop; a small wool shop came next and after that the hairdressers' salon, double-fronted with two big windows, which had opened up only just before the war in what had been a bookmaker's premises. Next to that was the lawyer's office, but it had stood unused for more than a year and no one knew what had happened to the dapper little clerk who had run it for ages; the rooms over the top had been empty for as long as anyone could recall. Then came a large double-fronted building that had once been a bakery but closed down some years previously when the owner died suddenly of a heart attack. It was a shame to see it so neglected but no one knew what was happening about it, because the baker had only a brother who lived in America. Between the disused bakery and the pub was a tiny window that fronted the cobbler's shop and then came the larger premises of the pub.

On the other side of the lane were two groups of terraced houses, with little arched entrances that led to the back yards, all of which were quite small the paths were paved but uneven and the cobbles in the road had holes between them, making carts rattle when they drove over them. Peggy had been on to the council several times but no one ever came to repair them.

Maureen waved to Mrs Tandy at the wool shop, who was dusting the inside of her window, and stopped to have a word with Alice Carter and some of her other neighbours, who all wanted to know when she was leaving.

'Later this afternoon,' she told them. 'I'll have to get on, because I promised Peggy I would pop in and see her...'

Passing the hairdressers', she noticed Ellie outside looking at a notice in the window and waved to her.

Ellie came rushing up to her, waving her left hand under Maureen's nose. 'I'm engaged,' she said. 'My Peter's got leave at last so we're havin' a small do at the church next Saturday and he's booked a little party at a posh hotel up West – can you come?'

'I'd love to, Ellie,' Maureen said, 'but I'll be gone by then. I'll send you a card and a postal order so you can buy somethin' nice...' She smiled at the young girl, who couldn't have been more than seventeen, and admired her ring. 'Lovely. I like rubies and pearls. 'I'd better go...'

'Yes – and I can see my perm on the way so I'd better get back inside...' Ellie grinned and dashed back into the shop to prepare for her next customer, the strong odour of waving lotions and ammonia drifting out into the lane as the door opened.

Maureen went under the archway into the pub yard at the back of the Pig & Whistle. There was an outside toilet and a large shed where old barrels were stored until collected by the brewery, and the cobbles were in slightly better condition than those in the lane. Peggy had a row of black cast-iron hooks either side of the door and in the spring she hung out baskets of spring flowers to brighten up the yard.

The top half of Peggy's back door was open and the smell of baking delicious, making Maureen feel hungry. She walked into the large comfortable kitchen, too used to the oak dresser with its array of blue and white china to take much notice, though she did notice that Peggy had some plants on her windowsill, which made it look bright and cheerful.

'Ah, there you are, love,' Peggy greeted her with a smile. 'Just in time for a cuppa and a piece of apple pie...'

'Lovely,' Maureen said and smiled as she sat down at the long pine table on which stood the results of her friend's hard work. 'I'm really going to miss this, Peggy...'

'You'll miss seeing Rory too,' Peggy suggested as she fetched cups and saucers from the dresser.

'It's awful havin' to leave him now he wants to see me,' Maureen said. 'He wasn't very happy this mornin'.'

'I guessed Rory wouldn't be too pleased,' Peggy said as they shared a pot of tea. 'I expect he'd hoped to see you more often when they told him he would be in London...'

'He was pretty fed up,' Maureen admitted. 'I think he's worried about what sort of job he'll find.'

'He needn't be. I know there are plenty of jobs around if he looks; people like me who could do with a man around for a few hours. I'm sure lots of shopkeepers would be glad to give a hero of the war a few hours' work.'

'Yes, I am too,' Maureen said, 'but Rory wants more than that for us – he always was ambitious. I think he thought he would come out of the Army with a trade or some sort of job offer…'

'He's not blind, love. People can still work with one eye and do lots of things – and maybe his sight will return.'

'I pray it does,' Maureen sighed. 'All those years I was tied to Dad and now I'm free and able to marry Rory, if Velma was telling the truth about their marriage being bigamy, but…' She shook her head and Peggy reached out to squeeze her hand.

'He's alive, Maureen, and he knows you, and he loves you. Just keep believin' that things will get better. Mike is rejectin' Janet at the moment and she's desperate, but I've told her that if she loves him she just has to keep hopin'…'

'Oh, poor Janet,' Maureen said and her eyes felt wet with tears. She flicked back her dark hair, which had a natural bend; she'd allowed it to grow a little so that she could put it up in a knot out of the way under her nursing cap. 'I'm so sorry for her – and him. It's an awful situation to be in. Compared to Mike and to other men at the hospital, Rory is lucky. Once they've finished all his treatment there's nothing to stop him comin' down to Portsmouth and findin' work there. I'll have a look round and see what's goin' and suggest it to him.'

'Yes, you do that,' Peggy said and picked up the empty teapot. 'Shall I make some more? Or we've still got some of the coffee Able gave me at Christmas – and I like sharin' it with my real friends…'

'Sorry, I have to get home. Gran is cookin' my tea and I have packin' to finish,' Maureen said, getting to her feet. 'I'll write and phone when I can. I've told Shirley Hart to come to you if she needs help while I'm away. You don't mind?'

'Of course not,' Peggy said. 'I've always liked Gordon Hart and, as I told you when he asked you to look out for his daughter when he was called up, we all help our own round here. I think her grandmother will keep goin' for years and there won't be the need, but if it happens I've plenty of room to put her up.'

'Gran would have her some of the time, but I thought it might be too much for her to have a young child around the whole time – besides, Shirley is safe enough on the farm as long as she has her gran. Gordon didn't want her in London because of the risk of bombing and her gran is related to the farm owners. Unfortunately, Shirley didn't like the people that own the farm much – Mrs Hunter is a stern, no-nonsense sort.'

'Shirley wasn't used to that,' Peggy agreed. 'When you offered to look after her, you didn't expect your father to get married, of course, or that you would be working away.'

'No, I thought I'd be here in the lanes. If Shirley does come to you let me know. I'll arrange somethin' – try to get relocated to London…' Maureen bit her lip. 'I'd like to do that for Rory's sake, but I've only just been assigned to Portsmouth and I wanted to help not cause bother…'

'You should set your mind to your work,' Peggy told her. 'Rory understands, even if he doesn't like it, Maureen. Besides, you couldn't fight the battles going on in his head, even if you visited every day. He has to come to terms with his life and to accept that things are different now. Laurie was quite a while gettin' over his ordeal in the last war... I'm not sure that he ever did manage to subdue his memories.'

'War is awful,' Maureen said. 'I didn't really know how bad it was until I met that troop train with the volunteers and saw the wounded arrivin' – and that's why I want to do what I can... but I feel guilty because Rory needs my help too.'

'You're a woman.' Peggy laughed gently. 'We never stop feeling guilt, love. It's a part of our being and we can't avoid it. You're not Rory's keeper or his mother. You didn't neglect his child and let it die – and you were not to blame for his injury. We all have to make sacrifices to do the right thing, and it would be wrong for you to waste the chance you've been given.'

'Yes, I know.' Maureen smiled at her friend. 'But it makes me feel better hearin' you say it. I'm going to miss poppin' in for a chat.'

'And I'll miss you, love,' Peggy said, 'but you're not goin' to the ends of the earth. You'll get home sometimes...'

'Yes.' Maureen stood up and they embraced. 'I'll write and tell you how I'm gettin' on, Peggy.'

'And I'll tell you what's happenin' here – and I'll visit Rory and let you know how he's doin'...'

'Thanks. I'd better go then...' She picked up her basket and left.

Maureen was grateful to Peggy for saying none of it was her fault, but she still felt guilty about deserting Rory. Yet there was nothing she could do just yet. Perhaps he would be released sooner than he thought and then he could come down to her; they could be together and he could look for work in the area...

Just as she was leaving the pub, Maureen saw a soldier wave to her from the other side of the road. She hesitated, surprised at seeing Gordon Hart in London, and surprised at the pleased feeling it gave her to see his tall figure walking towards her. He was attractive and his time away in the Army had given him a slight tan and a look of strength and determination he hadn't had before. She was very aware of the smile in his soft eyes and the way his dark hair was slicked back from his face; it was shorter than she'd remembered, but it suited him.

'Peggy and I were just talkin' about you.' Maureen smiled as he came up to her. 'Have you been down to see Shirley?'

'I brought her up to town for a treat,' Gordon said. 'I've got two weeks' leave, before they send me over there, wherever that is; they never tell us where we're goin' – Shirley was hoping you would come to the zoo with us and have tea at Lyons...'

'I would've liked that but I'm leavin' for Portsmouth this evenin',' Maureen said. 'I start my nursing trainin' this week.'

'Yes, I got your letter,' Gordon said and frowned. 'Are you pleased with the change, Maureen?'

'Yes, I am,' she said. 'You mustn't worry about Shirley, you know. Peggy and Gran would look out for her if necessary – and I'll always be around for her...'

Gordon smiled and nodded. 'I know. Shirley tells me about all the cards and little gifts you send her. She thinks of you almost as her mum these days...'

'Oh...' Maureen's cheeks heated, because Gordon had made it clear once or twice that he would marry her if she said the word. 'Well, she misses you, Gordon, and I thought it might help her a little to get letters, and of course I'm fond of her. Now, I must fly or I'll miss the train. I'll write to you – and remember to tell Shirley I haven't forgotten it's her birthday soon… She'll be seven this year, won't she?'

'You'll spoil her,' Gordon said as he nodded and leaned forward to kiss her cheek. 'You're a lovely girl, Maureen. I know you'll make a wonderful nurse.'

'Thanks…' Maureen smiled. 'I really must go…'

She walked quickly away, knowing that Gordon's gaze followed her. The first time he'd asked her to marry him, he'd just wanted a mother for his little girl, but his smile told her that his feelings were warmer these days. Maureen liked him and she was fond of the little girl, who had changed from a spoiled brat since she'd felt Mrs Hunter's hairbrush on her bottom. If she'd married Gordon, the child could've lived with her… but then she wouldn't have got back with Rory…

Maureen put thoughts of Gordon Hart and his motherless daughter to one side. After years of being virtually a prisoner of her father's shop, she was free to work where she pleased and at last it looked as if there might be a chance of happiness for her and Rory… Surely that was what she wanted? Yet a small nagging doubt was there at the back of her mind.

Chapter 4

'Get me another cup of tea, love,' Henry Jackson said to his wife as he sat down in his chair by the fire that evening. 'I've been on the go all day in the shop. That thankless daughter of mine! Popped in to tell me she's leaving London and then she was off without a care in the world...'

Violet passed him his cup. 'Well, Maureen is twenty-six this year. She leads her own life now, Henry, and you should be grateful she came in to see you... That ungrateful son of mine hasn't been to see me for years. I don't even know if he's still alive. It's ages since he sent me so much as a birthday card.'

'That's different,' he replied, frowning, because he'd wanted sympathy and his wife wasn't offering it. 'Your son went off years ago, but I gave that girl a good life. Why did she go and leave me in the lurch? I can't manage the shop without help, and you never go in unless you're forced.'

'I've got my own business, and it brings in more profit than yours does, Henry,' Violet said and gave him a hard look, because she'd made it clear more than once that she'd expected more of their marriage. 'I work hard as it is and you expect to be waited on hand and foot – let me tell you, I'm not your slave. Maureen may have put up with it, but I shan't. I've told you to get someone to help with the shop –

and I need a hand with the housework too. Just the scrubbin' and polishin'. I can manage the rest...'

'If you want help you can pay for it,' Henry muttered, glaring at her back as she went off to the kitchen. It had annoyed him when his daughter breezed in looking as if she hadn't a care in the world. She'd told him she was off to train as a nurse and he'd hunched his shoulders and refused to wish her good luck.

When he married Violet he'd thought Maureen would probably live with her gran but come into the shop and help him with the stock and keeping things straight. She might have cooked for him sometimes, because Violet wasn't much of a cook, and he'd discovered she had a sharp tongue. He'd tried having a girl in the shop years ago and it hadn't worked, but he'd thought Maureen would always be there, grateful for what he gave her – and in his opinion he'd always been good to her, keeping her and giving her a few shillings' pocket money. She just didn't know when she was well off.

'Henry, come and give me a hand with the washing up,' Violet called from the kitchen. 'I've got a customer coming for a corset fittin' later this evenin' and –'

'Sorry, love, I've got to do my warden's round,' Henry said and heaved himself out of the chair. He'd hoped for a nice peaceful sit-down, but it looked as if the only place he would get that was down the warden's hut. One of the younger men would brew tea for them and most likely they'd get an hour or two of peace and quiet before the siren went. 'I might be late back...'

'Henry...' He heard Violet calling him impatiently as he walked down the stairs, but he didn't look back. He was a fool to have got married. If he'd been sharper, he could have kept Violet waiting: there for him when he chose to visit her and his daughter at home to keep house. He'd made a bad mistake and he didn't think there was a chance of getting Maureen to come back now she'd got a taste of freedom.

*

Maureen looked around the room she'd been told she was sharing with two other trainee nurses. It had three single beds separated by small cabinets and each of them had a locker at the far end of the room, and there was a table with three chairs where they could sit to write letters or drink a cup of tea. She noticed that a tiny gas ring had been provided and there was a kettle, but no sign of cups or any other utensils.

'Hi. You must be the new arrival,' a pleasant voice said behind her, and Maureen turned to see a pretty young woman with black hair caught up under a uniform cap and bright blue eyes. 'It's a bit dire at first, but you'll get used to it...'

'I was just wonderin' how we made ourselves a drink...' Maureen said and went forward with her hand outstretched. 'I'm Maureen and I've just this minute got here – are you one of the girls I'm sharin' with?'

'Yes, there are three of us. My name is Sally Barnes,' the young woman said and took her hand in a firm grip. 'I'm glad you've come, Maureen. We can certainly do with another pair of hands. Our other sharer is called Pam and she comes from Devon. I'm from London, same as you, but south of the city...'

'Are we allowed to make tea?' Maureen asked, liking the friendly girl immediately. 'I brought some tea, sugar and a pint of fresh milk, also some condensed, but I only have one mug – and I didn't think about a pot...'

'That's all right; Pam and I both have our own mugs and we use an infuser to make it in our mugs. We put everything in our lockers, because we have things called spot inspections. Sister Roberts descends like a god from the heavens with an avenging light in her eyes every so often and woe betide us if we've left dirty cups about. We nip to the toilets to wash the mugs and spoons in the morning, but there's often a queue, so we keep a bowl under my bed and use the extra water from the kettle if it's dark outside.'

'Oh dear, it sounds rather spartan,' Maureen said. 'I wasn't sure what to expect, but I sort of thought it would be a guesthouse with proper plumbin', not a wooden hut...'

Sally laughed. 'Welcome to the war, Maureen. I was surprised too, but they told us it was temporary – that was several months ago, mind you...'

'I don't suppose it will kill me,' Maureen laughed, feeling that she'd already made a friend. 'Which is my bed?'

'I'm afraid you're in the end one,' Sally said apologetically, 'up against the wall. Last in gets what's left...'

'It's fine,' Maureen said. 'And is my locker the end one too?'

'Yes, number three, and I've got the key,' Sally took it from her uniform pocket and handed it to her. 'Pam wanted to use it until you got here, but I wouldn't let her. She always seems to have so much stuff and she'll pinch your space if she can.'

'I didn't bring much,' Maureen said. 'I was told I'd be given my uniforms and I don't expect to go out often...'

'Oh, we get invited all over the place,' Sally told her cheerfully. 'The lads invite us to dances, picnics, tea or the cinema all the time, once they're feelin' better – and of course we meet men from the naval base as well. I keep some of my stuff in a case under the bed. Sister doesn't much like it, but most of the girls do the same and she has accepted it – but woe betide you if she finds any dust there...'

'Oh, well, I shan't be going out with the patients or sailors,' Maureen said and smiled. 'I've got someone in London. He was in the Army and he's been wounded and I shan't let him down by goin' out with other men.'

'Oh, poor you,' Sally said compassionately. 'The girl who was here before me had someone in the Army too. He was badly injured and she went home to be with him, but I heard he died...'

'That's awful. Rory is gettin' better, but he'll be havin' treatment for a while yet, perhaps months...'

The door opened just then and another girl entered. She had blonde hair which was short and springy with natural curls, and she'd taken off her cap. Flinging it onto the middle bed, she sat down and kicked her shoes off, rubbing her toes and grimacing. She was plumper than either Sally or Maureen and immediately the tidy room seemed to be more crowded as her things just spread out everywhere in an unsightly mess. Her apron was slung on the end of the bed and slipped to the floor as she lay back against her pillows.

'Hi,' she said, belatedly realising that Maureen was there. 'Sorry. I'll talk to you later, but I'm bushed. We had a manic shift and I've got to sleep...' And closing her eyes, Pam appeared to do just that, her gentle snores making Maureen look at Sally, who was trying not to laugh.

'That's Pam for you. Come on, I'll take you to the canteen,' she said. 'I can rest later, because I have a day off. I'll show you where to get your uniform and introduce you to some of the others.'

'I've got to report to Matron in two hours...'

'Plenty of time to get your bearings,' Sally assured her. 'It will save you getting lost when you come back later. You'll probably be on night shift after you see Matron, and it's hell getting back here in the dark if you're not sure where to go...'

'Thanks,' Maureen said. 'Are there any lights at night or do I need a torch?'

'Are you joking?' Sally arched her brows. 'We don't have lights outside any of the buildings, because if we did we'd probably be toast by morning. I'll show you the remains of the nurses' accommodation that was... Hitler's lot made a right mess of it and some of the girls inside at the time were killed.'

Sally wasn't teasing now, her face tense with strain. The bombing was bad enough in London, but the realisation that nurses and injured men were at risk was somehow more upsetting. War was horrible at a distance, but Maureen was about to see it at first hand and she felt her stomach tighten. The reality was likely to be far worse than anything she'd imagined.

*

Maureen had never worked so hard in her life. She'd been on her feet for twelve hours straight with only short breaks for a cup of tea and a sandwich, and now all she wanted to do was sleep.

She was just about to switch off her light and curl up in bed when the hut door opened and the girl she'd seen briefly a couple of nights previously entered.

Pam smiled at her and sat on the bed next to her. 'You look whacked,' she said. 'It's Maureen, isn't it? I'm Pam. I'm sorry if I seemed rude the other night but I was exhausted – the way you look now.'

'I thought I worked hard at home,' Maureen groaned, 'but this… it's more tiring than working in a shop.'

'I worked in a dress shop.' Pam grinned. 'I must have been mad to throw it up and come here.'

'I'd have liked to work in a dress shop,' Maureen said and yawned. 'Sorry.'

'Don't let me bother you. I've been off duty and I have to change into my uniform. It was lovely meeting you, Maureen. I hope we get a chance to go out together soon… I think it's nice to have friends…'

'Me too…' Maureen murmured and fell asleep before Pam could answer.

*

She was woken by a series of loud explosions. Shocked, Maureen glanced round the hut and saw that she was alone; she jumped out of bed and pulled on the clothes she'd worn the night before. As she left her hut, a string of young women were heading for the hospital. Like her, they'd pulled on used uniforms and looked less immaculate than their daytime selves. She rushed into the hospital but, before she could even decide which way to go, a senior nurse directed her to a ward on the second floor.

'We need to get all the patients who can move down to the shelters in the cellar,' she said. 'Go straight to Ward Seven and take your orders from whoever is in charge. The hospital has been hit on the top corner and several people have been hurt, but your job is to help move our patients.'

Maureen nodded, not hesitating. She knew the drill and even now she was hurrying up the stairs like so many others;

lifts were out of bounds unless you had an injured patient. If you were young and strong you could walk.

When she got to the ward she could see that chunks of the ceiling had fallen, some of them onto the beds, even though it was the floor above that had taken the hit.

'Nurse, help me get these patients into the lift and go with them down to the shelter.'

'Yes, Sister.'

Maureen had no idea who she was obeying but for the next two hours she helped organise the movement of patients, some able to walk, others in chairs, down to the cellars, and when their ward was clear, she was detailed to help care for those men who had been so rudely pulled from their beds in order to be rushed to safety.

Drinks, medicines and changing patients' bandages took up the first hour and then, when the all-clear sounded, Maureen was drafted in to help change beds, clear up debris and get patients back to their beds.

'You look dead on your feet,' the senior nurse told her with a smile. 'Stirling work! Get some sleep or you will never get to work this morning – and if you're a little late tell your senior to ask me why...'

Maureen thanked her and then hesitated, 'Have you heard what happened on the top floor, Sister?'

'I understand a patient was killed and also a couple of nurses... You will be informed tomorrow, but I think one of them was a probationer like you...'

Maureen nodded, feeling anxious as she walked slowly down the stairs and out of the hospital. She'd just left and was making her way towards the accommodation huts when she heard Sally's voice call to her and she stopped, waiting until she caught up.

'Glad you're all right,' Sally said. 'I heard a couple of nurses were killed as well as a patient, and others were slightly injured...'

'You don't know who it was?'

'No,' Sally said. 'I hoped it wasn't you or Pam...'

'I'm all right,' Maureen said. 'I just hope it wasn't Pam...'

Chapter 5

'It's great, Mum,' Pip Ashley said and dumped his kitbag on the kitchen floor. He laughed as she eyed the bulging bag. 'Full of dirty washing, just like I promised. Honestly, I knew flying was what I wanted to do, but even in my dreams I didn't know how good it would be once I went up.'

'Are you flyin' already?' Peggy asked, because although he'd joined the RAF as soon as he was old enough, she'd expected he would be having lectures and taking the theory for ages yet, but the sparkle in her son's dark eyes told her that she was wrong. His hair was cut very short and controlled with Brylcreem so that it no longer stood up at the front in a quiff or was waved. 'You're not flyin' on your own yet?'

'Not yet,' he confirmed, 'but it won't be long. We have to do so many hours with our trainer and then we get to go solo. I can't wait...'

'How many hours do you have to do before you're considered a pilot?'

'Oh, a lot,' Pip said vaguely, picking up on her anxiety. 'Don't worry, Mum. It will probably be months before I get a pop at the Luftwaffe – more's the pity.'

'Don't be in too much of a hurry, darling. Let your instructors teach you all you need to know before you start volunteering.'

'It wouldn't do me any good if I did,' Pip said and kissed her cheek; squeezing her waist, he lifted her off her feet and laughed as she protested. 'Light as a feather. How do you stay young and pretty, Mum? Got a picture in the attic?'

'Idiot,' she said, 'Dorian Gray was a wicked, evil man...'

'Yeah,' Pip grinned meaningfully. 'Where's Janet and my niece?'

'They went shoppin' for me,' Peggy said and put a cup of coffee in front of him. It had been made with the last of the American beans and he smiled appreciatively as he sipped it.

'Better than the muck they serve us at the base,' he said. 'Everyone drinks beer rather than the coffee and tea they serve up – unless we can get into the village. They've got a nice pub there, Mum, and the landlady serves food and a decent cuppa. She isn't as good a cook as you, but it's better than we get in the canteen.'

'Do you want me to send you some food parcels?' Peggy asked, but her son shook his head.

'We're all in the same boat, Mum,' he said. 'We exist on chips and bread a lot of the time, although the bacon sandwiches are fine. A girl comes in mornings and cooks the breakfasts and you can rarely get a table then, because she makes lovely eggs and bacon – and she's a looker. Nearly as pretty as you.'

'You won't starve then,' Peggy said and smiled at his flattery, thinking how grown up her son sounded. A youth of eighteen had gone off to learn to fly and a man had returned. She could see a faint stubble on his cheeks and realised he was shaving regularly now; he was becoming an adult and would grow away from her as he became more confident in his new life, and yet she believed he would always come home.

'Are you hungry?'

'I wouldn't say no to a slice of that apple pie,' he said and finished his coffee, turning as the back door opened and Janet entered with Maggie in the pram. 'Hi, Sis. You look frozen...'

'It's bitterly cold out there,' Janet said and parked the pram close to the range without it being in her mother's way. 'The price of food is getting stupid. It's a good thing the government brought in controls or they'd want two bob for a pound of sausages! I was tempted to buy some of the veggie ones for eightpence a pound...' She walked over and bent to aim a kiss at her brother's ear and give him a hug round the shoulders. 'How's life in the RAF then?'

'It's great,' he said. 'One day you'll have to come down and I'll take you up for a spin...'

'Do you think I'm mad?' his sister derided with a grin. 'I'm not takin' my life in my hands. Maggie needs her mother.'

'Cheek,' Pip said, but was unruffled by his sister's mockery. 'Mum's not scared, are you?'

'No, I'll trust you... once you get your pilot's licence,' Peggy said and turned away to wink at Janet.

'Letters...' Nellie said and brought in a handful of envelopes, which had been delivered to the bar. Their usual postie had been off for a few days and Peggy was concerned because he'd been regular as clockwork for years and he hadn't told her he was going on holiday. 'One for you, Janet – and the others are yours, Peggy.'

Janet took her letter, glanced at the handwriting and slipped it in her pocket without a word. Peggy flicked through hers, realising that they were all circulars or bills, except for one, which she knew was from Laurie. It was the first time he'd written since Christmas and she wondered what had made him bother, because when they parted the situation between them had been distinctly cool. She decided to leave it for later. Nothing he had to say could truly interest her any more. Their marriage was over and if it were not for the war she imagined she might even now be looking for a home and a job as a cook, because she didn't think she could go back to the way it had been between them.

'I'd better go and open up,' she said. 'If you want anything more to eat, Pip, your sister will cook it for you...'

She left them and went through to the bar, unlocking the front door and then going over to the bar to set up some clean glasses. They'd had three days when she'd had no beer to offer her customers, but the delivery had finally arrived and she was expecting a bit of a rush. Her regulars came whatever the situation, many of them drinking tea or a cup of coffee, and sometimes even Bovril if there was nothing else. They stopped for a bite to eat and a gossip, because life had to go on whatever the shortages, and then, when she put the notice in the window that beer was available again, she always got an influx of customers.

'Morning, Peggy.' One of her regulars put his head round the corner. 'It's a bit early, but I'll have a half of bitter please. I've got a long day ahead and you might be sold out when I get back.'

'I don't think so, Bert,' she said to the rather disreputable-looking man who entered. Dressed in a rusty-black jacket, trousers held up with a piece of string, and heavy hobnailed boots, he ran a rag and bone yard just off Gun Street in Three Farthings Court, which consisted of three large derelict houses, in various stages of decay, and he'd managed to earn a good living before the war. She wasn't sure how business was for him these days, but he always seemed busy. 'I'm glad things are goin' well for you...'

'Not so bad, love,' he said and grinned. 'I've got an army of lads collecting scrap fer me and I reward 'em with chocolate bars. Me and the missus never eat sweets, so we save our rations and pay the kids in penny bars – sometimes 'ave to give 'em a copper or two extra if they've done well, but they like the chocolate best.'

'What do they bring you?' Peggy asked, but he tapped the side of his nose with his finger and shook his head.

'All sorts,' he said and chuckled to himself. 'Anythin' they can find – includin' empty shells. One of the brats brought a live 'un the other day. I put it in a bucket of sand quick. Might have blown us all to kingdom come...'

Peggy frowned because that was dangerous and not a source of amusement in her opinion. The boy who had brought in the live ammunition could have killed himself and other people, but of course he would only have thought about the chocolate bar he'd been promised. 'I hope you told him to be careful in future?'

'Aye, I gave him a cuff round the ear and told him to make sure it was empty next time or to call the cops – that's what I had to do and they brought the bomb squad out. Cost me a fortune in cups of tea to get it dealt with...'

Peggy nodded, but her customers were coming in faster now and she turned her attention to their requests, mainly for beer, but sometimes for food and soup to keep out the cold. Ellie Morris was back at work in the hairdressers' after a short honeymoon and looking down in the dumps because her new husband had returned to his unit and she was discovering that being married at seventeen wasn't much fun when your man was in the Army. She ordered a cup of coffee and a slice of hot toast, taking it to sit in the corner alone.

No one was particularly cheerful because the news had been worrying for weeks, and the bitterly cold weather didn't help. Peggy didn't feel it so much herself, but Janet was always cold and she fussed over Maggie, wrapping her up and constantly anxious that her baby should not get a chill.

Nellie came through to the bar to give Peggy a hand with serving until the rush died down, and then did the washing up. She'd slipped into the habit of staying to eat with Peggy and sometimes brought in meat or eggs she'd managed to buy in the market. Peggy had refused to take her coupons, but Nellie insisted on contributing her share and she couldn't refuse her friend, because she knew it meant a lot to her to stay with them for much of the day. Nellie found it lonely when she went home to her empty house and had talked about taking in a lodger of late.

'Be careful who you choose,' Peggy warned. 'We've had one or two in the past I didn't care for. Laurie could deal with them, but I wouldn't want some of them now he isn't here.'

'I'm not sure what to do,' Nellie told her. 'A woman might be a bit of company at night, but I don't know I could share my home with a stranger. I certainly wouldn't want a man I didn't know.'

'Well, I expect there are some lovely girls in the hospitals and volunteers needin' rooms,' Peggy said. 'Why don't you get in touch with someone who places them in temporary accommodation? They wouldn't want to stay on once the war is over...'

'That's not a bad idea,' Nellie agreed and nodded to herself. 'I might just do that...'

What Nellie really wanted was to have her son and daughter back home, but she knew it wasn't likely to happen, because they'd both joined the forces when war became imminent, and she was obviously lonely at home now. She'd been a widow for a lot of years and it was unlikely she would marry again... Thinking about Nellie's problems made Peggy remember the letter from her husband.

It was quiet in the bar once the first little rush was over and she took out his letter and read it through. He'd covered one small sheet and, although it was penned in a conciliatory tone, Peggy wasn't sure what to make of it.

My Dear Peggy,

I just wanted to tell you that it's over with her. I know that doesn't make everything right, but I am sorry I hurt you. It's war and all the stress of everything – but I'm not going to make excuses. I just hope that you can forgive me and try again. I may be home sometime around Easter, but I can't be sure because sometimes things get a bit manic here. I'll let you know when I'm sure of leave – if you want me to come?

I meant it when I said I wanted to keep the family together, but I don't expect you to forgive me just like that. Know that you are often in my thoughts and think of me with kindness if you can.

Affectionately yours, Laurie.

Peggy folded the single sheet, replaced it in its envelope and slipped it back into her pocket just as the door opened and a man walked into the bar. He came straight to her, smiling and seeming to bring a breath of fresh air into the room. His eyes lit up when she smiled at him, and the eagerness in his face caught at her heart, making her feel like a giddy lamb in spring.

It was so long since Laurie had looked at her like that.

'What can I get you, Able?'

'A cup of coffee and some pie,' he said. 'I'm on duty; just waiting around until my colonel is ready to leave London.'

'Are you going away?' Peggy knew he must have seen her disappointment because he laughed softly.

'Just for a couple of days...' He hesitated, then, 'When I get back, would you allow me to take you somewhere nice? I thought dinner and a show one evening, if you can get someone to take care of things here?'

Peggy drew a sharp breath because the invitation had caught her off guard. Her heart raced and for a moment she felt as if she couldn't breathe. It was on the tip of her tongue to deny him, because after all she was married – but then she realised that Laurie had let her down and betrayed her. Despite her husband's conciliatory letter, there was no reason why she shouldn't go out with this handsome man who made her feel so good about herself just with his smile.

'My daughter would probably manage or I could ask a friend,' Peggy said a little shyly. 'Yes, I'm sure something could be arranged. Thank you, Able.'

His smile was dazzling and her heart jumped, making her feel like a young girl on her first date. She was probably making a big mistake, but Laurie's letter had confused and annoyed her. He seemed to think all he had to do was say sorry and she would forget that he'd broken the promises he'd made years before on their wedding day. Saying sorry couldn't heal the hurt he'd inflicted or give her back the trust she'd had in him.

'That's great, Peggy,' Able said. 'We've got a dance coming up at the Savoy next month – our officers are giving it for our British friends. Perhaps you could manage that as well?'

'As long as the two events aren't too close together,' Peggy said. 'It isn't easy to find help I can trust, but I should love to come out with you sometimes...'

She felt a little surge of excitement, because in the midst of all the sorrow and worry there was a small spark of happiness beginning to grow inside her. Peggy didn't know what she wanted or expected from the future, and the way things were these days no one knew how much longer that future might be, but there was surely nothing wrong in taking the chance of a bit of fun? Laurie had apologised for hurting her, but she wasn't sure she'd forgiven him. Besides, why shouldn't she enjoy herself for a while? After all, Able hadn't said anything about an affair, he just enjoyed her apple pie and wanted to take her out because he was a stranger in a foreign land... No, Peggy wasn't going to pretend: there was every likelihood that she might end up making love with him, but somehow she didn't feel in the least bit guilty at the thought.

*

Maggie was sleeping peacefully in her cot when Janet sat down on the edge of her bed and took out Ryan's letter. It had given her quite a jolt when she saw the handwriting and knew it was his, because he'd said he wouldn't be in touch unless she contacted him. Janet had battled to keep her thoughts from straying in Ryan's direction, because it confused her. She was in love with Mike and felt certain that if he'd been injured physically but was still aware of her, still the loving man she'd adored, she wouldn't have even thought of straying. It was the rejection in his eyes when she'd told him that she loved him, explaining how they'd married and that they had a young child that had stung her, and when he turned his head from her kiss and told her not to touch him it had broken her heart.

She was sure her kiss couldn't have caused him pain, but it was as if he couldn't bear her near him and she didn't understand how he could forget her – surely there should still have been the same attraction, even if he couldn't recall all the details? How could love just vanish like that? And then, before she left, he'd asked her not to visit him. Janet hadn't told her mother that bit, because it had hurt too much.

'Please, if you love me, as you say you do, just stay away. Let me get over this in peace. I can't handle a wife and daughter I don't remember...'

'But, Mike... what about me? Don't my feelings matter?' Janet had asked as the despair swept through her. It was as if he were a stranger, as if the man she'd loved so much were lost – dead to her. 'We are married, even if you don't remember and I have every right to visit.'

'Not if I refuse to see you. I'm asking you not to come until I can handle it – if you care about me please accept it...'

Janet had hurried away, tears trickling down her cheeks. As she was leaving the ward, the sister in charge had caught her arm. Janet had tried to pull away, but the nurse had drawn her into a small office and made her sit down.

'Mike isn't the man you knew,' she said unnecessarily. 'You have to make allowances and forgive him if he says things that hurt. Once he's come to terms with his injuries he will need you, because it's going to take several operations and a lot of treatment to get him well again – months of suffering – and he does need you, even if he doesn't know it at this time.'

'He doesn't want me,' Janet said, anger surfacing because she didn't like the nurse's attitude, as if this were her fault. 'Mike can't remember me. He doesn't want to remember – he's shut me out and asked me not to visit again until he's ready.'

'We did tell you it was too soon to visit,' the nursing sister said gravely. 'I know it's hard, Janet – but a lot of women don't have their husbands back at all. You should try to accept his illness. Don't come down for a few weeks. We'll contact you as soon as Mike shows some improvement. Once he stops rejecting what has happened to him, he will probably begin to remember – and then he'll need you.'

Janet had wanted to shout at her and tell her to mind her own business. What right did she have to dictate what Janet should and shouldn't do?

'I can't stop you coming down, but my advice would be to wait for a while,' the nurse went on.

Janet had somehow managed to answer her politely and leave. All the way home she'd nursed her bitterness at the cruelty of war and the destruction of her happiness. Her mother's advice was given more sympathetically, but was basically the same – be patient and wait for Mike to come back to her.

Supposing he didn't?

Janet shook her head and read the letter from Ryan. He began with an apology. He had meant to stay away and not contact her. He knew that Mike was in hospital and needed her – but...

I can't stop thinking about you, Jan. Remembering how brave you were when your home was bombed. I know I don't have the right to ask, but I'd like to see you one day. Perhaps we could just go out for tea...

Janet screwed the letter into a ball, her knuckles white because she was so tense and tight. Ryan shouldn't have written; he shouldn't tempt her – because, despite it all, she was Mike's wife and she couldn't just be friends with Ryan as he asked. He didn't want it either. She knew he wanted more, despite his telling her he was in love with his wife. If Janet agreed to see Ryan – even if it were just for tea sometimes – it would be the start of something that would lead to the destruction of her marriage and his. Janet wouldn't do it. She was stronger and better than that, she thought, and raised her head. She would write to Ryan and tell him that Mike needed her now – even though he didn't...

Chapter 6

'The government want us to save paper, Mrs Ashley,' Tommy Barton said when he poked his head over the split door in her kitchen. 'I'm collectin' orf everyone who can spare anything – newspapers, old letters, anythin' will do…'

'Have you got a trolley?' Peggy came to the door and looked out. Tommy had put four wheels on a large wooden vegetable crate and used a strong rope to pull it. 'You can do a job for me and collect some paper at the same time.'

'Anythin' you want,' Tommy said hopefully, his nose twitching at the smell coming from her oven.

'I'll just take these jam tarts out of the oven and then we'll go up to the attic,' Peggy said. 'There are piles of old magazines up there. A lot of them were up there when we came. Laurie was going to clear the attic but he never got round to it. I'll pay you sixpence an hour to clean it out for me – and you can take all the old magazines and newspapers, and I'll give you somethin' to eat when you've finished.'

'You're on,' Tommy said and grinned at her, because it was just the kind of job he liked. He could really get to work on clearing out the attic, earn some money for his mother and collect much-needed paper. There was a competition in the lanes for who could collect the most. Sam had told him about it and the prize, and he'd decided to help his brother win it.

Peggy led the way. The Pig & Whistle was an older building, with an attic accessible by a narrow staircase; it was a leftover from the days when servants had slept in the attics and it made them easier to get into. She snapped on the light, illuminating the loft and showing all the trunks and packing cases stored there. The piles of old magazines were easy to pick out, because there were so many of them.

'I hadn't realised there was so much stuff up here,' Peggy said, looking round. 'A lot of it hasn't seen the light of day for years. I'd like you to go through the boxes, Tommy, and tell me what's in them. Some of it might be of use to other people and we'll decide what to do with it later, but a lot of it could probably go to the tip.' She smiled at him. 'It looks as if you've got a job for the next few Saturdays and Sundays.'

'I'll have a half term too and then it will be Easter,' Tommy said, and Peggy realised he was relishing the idea of getting to grips with her junk. 'I'll take them magazines out of yer way first, Mrs Ashley, and then start on the boxes.'

'Just call me Peggy,' she said and saw the appreciation in his eyes. 'You're a young man now, Tom – the man of your family...'

'Yeah, reckon I am,' he said. 'Ma thinks I should stay on at school until I'm sixteen, but I want to work for meself one day. When the war is over, I'm goin' into a trade or business where I can be my own boss, but I'll join the Army as soon as I can.'

'A jack of all trades,' Peggy said. 'I reckon you could do most things if you tried, Tom. You just need to learn a few things and then you'll be away.'

'Yeah, that's me,' he grinned and started to gather the paper into bundles. He had a roll of string and a pen-knife in his pocket and was soon making bundles that he could easily carry. The way he set about it had purpose and Peggy was openly smiling as she went back down to the kitchen.

She'd wanted that attic cleared for years. It was just one of many jobs Laurie had promised to do when he had time. If Tommy were set on starting up for himself, Peggy might be his first customer, with a list as long as her arm...

'Who does this belong to?' Janet said, coming into the kitchen with her basket full of shopping and eyeing the trolley doubtfully.

'It's Tom Barton's,' Peggy said. 'He's collectin' paper and he's clearin' out the attic for us. I think that should keep him busy for a while...'

'I saw his mother just now,' Janet said. 'She was having an argument with a woman from Gun Street. Something to do with her Sam and Mickey Jones from Gun Street being carted off down the police station for pinchin' off a bombed-out house...'

'Oh no,' Peggy said. 'I wish I'd told her myself what Sam was up to now, but she didn't come for the washing-up job and I thought she would tell me to mind my own business... Besides, I'm sure Nellie had a word with her about it.'

'Well, she was blamin' Mickey Jones for leadin' her son astray and his mother said Sam was the culprit; the two mothers were goin' at it hammer and tongs just now.' Janet picked Maggie up from her pushchair and set her down in the playpen.

'I blame Bert Higgins from Three Farthings Yard,' Peggy said and frowned. 'He's been encouraging the kids to take scrap there for chocolate – and kids see no danger in climbin' on rubble. They don't realise what could happen.'

'Well, I expect the police will let Sam off with a warnin', but his mother will give him a hidin' and it serves him right. It's looting, Mum. The police have told people they could be shot for stealin'. I know they're only kids, but it's still wrong.'

'Well, if he were my son I'd make sure he had plenty of chores to do at home and that would stop him gettin' into trouble,' Peggy said and then looked up as the postie came to the back door and looked in. She smiled, because she saw it was Reg and he hadn't been for a while. 'You're back then?'

'Did yer miss me?' Reg grinned at her and came into the kitchen. 'I 'ad a boil on me unmentionables, Peggy. They took me in the infirmary for a couple of weeks and it was mighty painful, but I'm all right now.'

'Good to see you back,' Peggy said. 'What have you got for us today?'

'There's a letter for Janet,' he said. 'Looks as if it's from the 'ospital – let's hope it's good news – and there's one from Maureen for you, Peggy. I'd know 'er 'andwriting anywhere. How is she gettin' on down there? Her father never stops moanin' about her goin' orf and leavin' him, but I reckon she'll make a good nurse.'

'Yes, she will.' Peggy smiled. 'Would you like one of these rock buns, Reg? They're fresh out of the oven...'

'Don't mind if I do.' He grinned at her as he took one. 'This will keep me goin', love. See yer tomorrer...'

'Doesn't that annoy you, the way he always tells you who the letters are from?' Janet asked, tucking her letter into her pocket as the postman disappeared into the yard.

'Sometimes,' Peggy admitted, 'but I've known him for years and he's a part of our lives.' She turned as Tommy came down with several bundles of magazines. 'That should fill your trolley...'

'Yeah, I'll be back for the rest soon. Bye for now...'

'Take one of these to keep you goin'...' Peggy gave him a rock cake and he smiled, slipping it into his jacket pocket.

Peggy looked at her letter from Maureen. She tore open the envelope and began to read. After a moment or two she gasped, 'Oh no...'

'Something wrong, Peggy?' Nellie asked as she entered the kitchen. 'Not bad news?'

'Well, yes,' Peggy said. 'Maureen has written to me and it seems as if there was a terrible raid on the hospital a couple of nights after she got there. One of the girls she shares accommodation with was killed tryin' to save the life of a patient...'

'That's terrible,' Nellie said. 'I read about somethin' like that the other day. They can't always move the patients and this nurse stayed to protect hers, but both she and the man were killed by them murderin' devils...'

'Maureen says she and the other girl she shares with have been cryin' their eyes out...'

'I'm not surprised,' Nellie said and sniffed into her large handkerchief. 'It gets yer 'ere...' She tapped her chest. 'And I don't even know the poor girl...'

'Maureen says she didn't know her well, but she liked her – and it's an awful thing to happen.'

'Yes, it is,' Nellie sighed, 'but it's 'appenin' all over, love. We none of us knows these days...'

*

'What's fer dinner then, Violet love?' Henry Jackson asked when he walked into the room above the shop and sat down. 'I've been rushed orf me feet and I'm dyin' fer a cuppa...'

'I haven't had time to cook,' Violet said, coming out of what had been Maureen's bedroom with a pale-pink corset in her hand. 'My customer is booked for a fitting this afternoon and this isn't quite ready.'

'Damn!' Henry muttered. 'I was hopin' you would go into the shop fer an hour or two, Violet. I've got to get to the wholesaler today and my mother refuses to come in. She says she's too old – and I should've thought what I was doin' before I pushed Maureen out of her home.'

'Your mother doesn't like me much,' Violet said and pursed her red lips. 'Well, my fitting should be done by four. If you can wait until then, I'll have an hour in the shop for you – but I shan't cook tonight. We'll either have fish and chips or you can take me down the café for a nice plate of steak and kidney pie.'

'Violet...' Henry protested. 'I've been on my feet all mornin' and I'm 'ungry.'

'Make yourself a corned beef sandwich,' Violet said over her shoulder. 'I bought some pickle down the market. I've no time for cookin' and we live over a shop. It's time you learned to get yourself somethin' to eat, Henry...'

He glared at her back as she returned to Maureen's old bedroom. He wished his daughter were still here. She'd always had a decent meal waiting for him, and she made her own pickles. Henry sighed as he got up to put the kettle on. He was beginning to realise that he'd picked a woman well able to stand up to him in Violet. She was every bit as determined to have her own way as *he'd* always been.

For a moment his thoughts dwelled on his daughter. Perhaps if he phoned her at the hospital and said his chest was bad... but no, she'd gone and he didn't think she was coming back.

Chapter 7

'You just back?' Sally said as she slipped her nursing cloak around her shoulders. 'I'm on duty this evening.'

'Are you all right?' Maureen asked, because Sally looked dreadful. They'd both been devastated by the news of Pam's death, but proud too when they were told later that Pam had tried to protect a bed-ridden patient with her body, but in vain because the falling debris had killed them both. Although she'd hardly known the girl, Maureen felt as if it were a member of her family that had died. Both she and Sally had been shocked and disbelieving, even though they knew that similar incidents were happening all over the country. Brave nurses refused to leave the side of patients who were too ill to move, and if their ward took a direct hit they were injured or died amongst the falling debris, but of course they weren't the only ones. People were dying in air raids and the resulting chaos all over the country.

'As right as I shall be.' Sally shivered. 'I can't get it out of my head.'

'I know. I feel the same…'

'She didn't deserve it… Those bastards bombing a hospital…' Sally caught back her sob. 'We're helping people – we've even got some Germans in here. They needed patching up and we took them in – and then those bastards bomb us...'

Maureen sighed and gave her a hug. Sally had known Pam longer than she had and was hurting a lot. 'I hate this war,' she said. 'I helped wash one of the German patients the other day and he's just a boy, Sally, cryin' for his mum because he's lost his legs and he's in pain – just like our boys. He didn't want to kill people, he told me so... It's that bloomin' Hitler and those men in high places who think it's a good idea to have a war.'

Sally nodded. 'I'd better go or I'll be late. Is it cold out?'

'Freezing,' Maureen said. 'At least the heating is working on the wards. It's a darned sight colder in here.' She hesitated, then, 'We can't do anything, Sally.'

'I know. I'm all right,' Sally said and went out.

Maureen slipped off the heavy rubber-soled shoes she wore for work and sighed as she lay back on her bed. The mattress was hard but at that moment she felt as if she were floating on clouds. She was so damned tired! She'd been working since a quarter to seven the previous evening and it was now five-thirty in the afternoon; almost twenty-four hours with barely a break for meals and a drink. Maureen had thought she was on her feet long hours at the shop, but that had been a picnic compared to her working days now.

Normally, she worked about fourteen-hour shifts, but yesterday had been like Bedlam on the wards. Over a period of several nights the hospital had come under fire from enemy planes; they flew over and strafed the building with their guns, and the bombers had done some damage to a part of the older building, which had collapsed. During that time all the nurses had been on double duty and they were all exhausted.

'I'm going for a drink tonight – comin'?' Sally asked that Saturday night. It was the first time they'd both had the same evening off for ages. 'Come on, Maureen. You never go anywhere...'

Maureen hesitated and then agreed.

She went out occasionally with the girls from work, though she said no to all the offers of dates with young servicemen. That night, though, she'd wanted a few stiff drinks and it was a good thing she'd gone, because she had to help Sally back to their hut. Sally had had one too many and kept falling over. When they managed to reach the camp, she passed out just after they went through the gates, and one of the young guards on duty laughed and hoisted her over his shoulder.

He winked at Maureen. 'Too much celebrating?' he said.

'Hardly. Our friend died in the raid the other night. She needed a few drinks to help her get over it...'

'My big mouth,' the guard cursed and then apologised. 'Sorry, love. I didn't realise.' He'd carried Sally into the hut and then hesitated before leaving. 'Look, I wasn't being nasty just now – and I am sorry.'

'It's fine,' she said. He looked to be a nice young man and she gave him a fleeting smile. 'You couldn't have known. Thanks for helpin' us.'

'You're welcome. I hope your friend doesn't feel too bad in the morning.'

'Thank you.' Maureen smiled at him and shut the door of their hut. Looking down at Sally as she snored, oblivious to the grief and sorrow that had driven her to drink too much, Maureen felt her eyes sting with tears. It was all so damned horrible.

The next day Sally apologised. She was on duty first thing and went to work with a thumping headache, vowing she would never drink again, but Maureen understood. The work they did every day on the wards was hard, often dirty and smelly, and sometimes you had to let go or it would drive you mad, but that was nothing compared to learning that a friend had been killed by a stray bomb.

Sister Matthews talked to the nurses and auxiliaries a week after her death, gathering them together in the lecture room. She was strict and gave the juniors a hard time if she caught them slacking or smoking on her ward. Pam had been in trouble more than once for sharing a crafty fag with one of the patients, but underneath she'd been hard-working and honest and she'd given her life for her patient.

'We all regret the untimely deaths of Staff Nurse Wendell and our trainee nurse Pam Morton. I know some of our trainees shared accommodation with Pam and must feel her loss terribly. She was brave and selfless and an example to us all – as was Jill Wendell. We miss them and mourn them, as we do the patients we sometimes lose – but the work goes on. If any of you have problems with carrying on as normal, please come and talk to me. A transfer might be arranged if necessary.'

'The old trout has feelings after all,' Sally told Maureen as they left the lecture room later. 'Pam would laugh her head off if she heard herself being held up as an example to all of us. She was forever in trouble with Sister Matthews and broke all the rules – and she didn't care.'

Maureen nodded, smiling because at least Sally could talk about it now without tears in her eyes, and it seemed that Sister's little talk had done some good after all. It had helped Maureen, because she would think about Sister's softer side when she was being told to scrub the bedpans again because they weren't up to Sister's standards. Sometimes at the start she'd felt resentful of the senior nurse's stern lectures and the way she always seemed to pick on Maureen to do the dirtiest jobs; scrubbing floors and bedpans, disinfecting beds and trolleys and remaking beds that weren't quite right at the corners had seemed such tedious and, at times, un-necessary work, when what she wanted to do was to help nurse the men.

It had been a great day for Maureen when Sister asked her to go and assist Nurse Petty with changing bandages. Of course, her role was just to fetch and carry and hand things to the competent nurse, but it was a step up from the menial tasks she was normally given, and Nurse Petty had asked for her again. So Maureen was spending more time helping with the patients, often just filling water jugs and straightening beds, but she got to talk to the men and that made everything else worthwhile. They were always so grateful for the slightest favour: the seriously ill ones acknowledging her presence with a faint nod or a glimmer of a smile, but the ones on the mend grinned and asked her to be their girl, teasing her about where they were going on their honeymoon and all sorts of nonsense.

Maureen didn't take the teasing seriously, because it was the same for all the girls. Even Sister got teased by some of the cheekier lads, but she just gave them one of her no-nonsense looks and told them to be good boys, which soon quietened even the most riotous of the recovering men.

It must have been about two weeks after Sister's talk, and Maureen was returning from her recent stint on the wards in the early hours. The sky was just beginning to get light and she realised that it felt a little warmer after weeks of bitter-cold nights and that it must be nearly Easter. She never looked at a newspaper, unless one of the patients showed her something specific, and time just went by in a blur; one day it was Saturday and then it would be Thursday night. There was no such thing as a day off, because Sister was always asking for volunteers to do extra shifts and if she looked directly at you that was it.

'Hi,' a male voice said as she approached the field where the accommodation huts stood in dark rows. 'I thought I recognised you – how is your friend now?'

Maureen stared and then realised it was the guard who had helped her the night Sally got drunk. He was wearing naval uniform but carrying a kitbag, as though he were off duty. 'Sally is fine,' Maureen said, because her friend wouldn't want her to tell a stranger that she was a mess and fighting her grief by working until she was so exhausted that she fell asleep the moment her head touched the pillow. 'Thanks for askin'...'

'Sally – nice name,' he said and offered his hand. 'Harry Ransom. Will you tell me your name?'

'It's Maureen,' she said. 'I apologise, Harry, but I've just worked twenty hours and I need to sleep...'

'Poor you,' he said and smiled in a way that appealed to Maureen because it was honest and sincere. 'I know how it feels. I'll see you around – unless you have a day off soon?'

'What's that?' Maureen said and yawned. 'Sorry. I need to sleep... Bye, Harry. Maybe see you around...'

'Maybe...' He stood aside and let her go, and she sensed he was watching regretfully as she walked to her hut and went inside. Maureen wouldn't have gone out with him even if she'd had a day free, because there was Rory. He was waiting for her and as soon as she got a couple of days off she intended to take the train back to London and visit him. In fact, she would finish the letter she'd been writing to him for the past couple of days and send it on her way into work that afternoon. She was due back on at four so that meant she had time to catch up on a few chores and get some much-needed sleep.

*

Maureen tried to write to Rory but the words wouldn't come. She placed the half-finished letter back in her notecase and saw Gordon Hart's latest letter. He wrote most weeks just to ask how she was and if she'd heard from Shirley, and Maureen looked forward to getting his letters.

She drew a sheet of paper towards her and began to write:

Dear Gordon,

I should've replied sooner, but it's been awful here. The hospital was bombed and one of the girls I shared a hut with was killed trying to save her patient. Sally is really miserable and keeps crying. I didn't know Pam that well, but I liked her and it has upset me. I know it's happening all over, but it's always worse when it's people you know.

Sorry to be a misery. I hope you're all right and not having too bad a time out there, Gordon. Shirley is fine and seems happy at her school. She wrote to thank me for a drawing book and some sweets I sent her two weeks ago. I hope to get down and see her one day – and perhaps you'll be back on leave again soon. Please take care and come back to your friends who miss you.

Best wishes, Maureen

Folding the letter and putting the stamp on the envelope, Maureen smiled. If only it were as easy to write a nice, cheerful letter to Rory, but he hardly ever wrote to her and when he did it was always to complain that she hadn't been to visit. He just didn't seem to understand that her job was important and she certainly couldn't tell him about Pam.

*

Maureen was woken by the sound of crying. At first she was feeling groggy and couldn't make out where she was, but as her vision cleared she became aware that she was in the hut she shared with Sally. As yet, another nurse had not been allocated to their hut and she thought Sister was being sensitive to their feelings by not replacing Pam too quickly.

'Sally, what's wrong?' Maureen threw back the covers and went over to the other girl's bed. Sally was sitting on the edge and she had a letter in her hand. Wordlessly, she thrust it at Maureen. She hesitated, then took it and read the single page. Despite the sympathetic terms of the letter it carried devastating news and Maureen felt stunned. Sally's older and much-loved brother had been killed on active service and her mother wanted her to go home for a service of remembrance.

We haven't got our darling Billy back to bury, because he's lost at the bottom of the sea, but we're going to mourn him in church just the same. Please come home and help your father bear this, Sally, because if you don't I think he will just sit there and die of a broken heart...

'Oh, Sally love, I'm so sorry,' Maureen said, because Sally often talked about her brother and she'd heard an awful lot about Billy, who was clearly the darling of his family. Sally adored him, wrote to him frequently and sometimes read bits of his letters aloud, so it almost felt as if she knew him – and it hurt her to see the devastation in her friend. Sally had found it difficult to cope with the loss of their friend Pam; how she must be feeling about this Maureen could hardly imagine. She put her arms about her friend's shaking body to try and comfort her. 'Is there anything I can do for you?' It was all she could think of to say, because sorry never helped and nothing would bring Billy back to life.

Sally sat with the tears running down her cheeks for a moment or so longer and then turned to look at Maureen. She hesitated for a moment, then, 'Will you come home with me? Please? It will be just for two days – a forty-eight-hour pass and then we'll return to work...'

'I'm not sure Sister would let us both go...' Maureen was doubtful on two counts, because surely Sally's parents wouldn't want a stranger in their home at such a time. She looked at Sally intently. 'Won't your parents mind? They don't know me... Surely I'd be in the way.'

'Sister can't refuse, and I don't care what my parents think,' Sally said, a mutinous look in her eyes. 'Please come, Maureen. I don't think I can face them if you don't. You don't know what it's like for me at home. Billy was everything to them – he was the prince of their lives and I came a long way down the list. I loved him too, but they worshipped the ground he walked on. If I have to face that alone...' Her voice trembled with emotion and Maureen knew she was at breaking point. Sally needed her and she couldn't refuse her.

'You won't,' Maureen assured her and held her tighter. 'I'm coming with you, love. I can't pretend to know how you feel, but I've known hurt and pain and I'll help you all I can.'

'I didn't think it could happen to him too – he was the golden boy and I thought he would come through it unscathed like he always does.' A sob escaped her and the effort to conquer her grief collapsed. 'It's so damned unfair...'

Maureen held her, rocking her as she sobbed out her pain. Sally convulsed with grief: it was just too much, too soon after Pam's death, and her friend was like a broken doll.

They stayed with their arms wrapped around each other for some time and then Sally quietened. She looked up at Maureen and attempted a wry smile.

'You must be wishing you'd never been landed with me as your hut mate?'

'Never,' Maureen said stoutly. 'I wouldn't change you for the world, Sally. When I first came down here I expected to feel homesick and was planning to ask for a transfer back to London, but since we became friends I've been content to stay.'

'I was thinking of asking for a transfer before Pam was killed,' Sally said, 'but after that it would have seemed as if I were running out on her.'

'Yes, I know what you mean,' Maureen said and offered her a clean hanky. 'Wash your face and let's go grab a cup of tea and whatever's going. I'm starving.'

'Yeah, all right,' Sally said. 'I could do with a stiff drink, but I'd better not start because I might not know when to finish...'

Chapter 8

Peggy looked at herself in the dress she'd had made for the dance Able was taking her to that evening. The material was a heavy quality silk and she'd found it at the back of a second-hand shop just off Commercial Road. It had been under a pile of old curtains and the shop assistant had clearly never seen it before.

'That must have been there years,' she said as she looked at the ticket price of five pounds ten shillings and eleven pence. The roll cost more than most families had to live on a week for rent, clothing and the lot. 'It's a bit expensive for most of our customers, but it looks good quality and would've sold these days if anyone had seen it.'

'Yes, I was lucky to find it,' Peggy said and paid quickly because she'd seen the envious looks the assistant was giving the roll of material and knew if she'd tried to knock the price down she would've lost it. 'It's exactly what I want...'

The colour was a shimmering crimson and Peggy had known it would make a sensational evening dress the moment she'd spotted it. Yes, it was far too much money to spend on a dress, but now, as she smoothed it over her hips and looked at the clever shaping which made her waist look narrow and emphasised her generous hips and breasts, she was almost afraid to wear it, because she looked... voluptuous.

Oh dear, she thought, *I'm not sure I dare go out in it.* Staring doubtfully at herself, Peggy was wondering what else she could wear when the door opened and Janet walked in behind her.

'Mum! You look stunning,' Janet said and the sincerity in her voice made Peggy feel easier. 'Fifteen years younger and really... beautiful.'

'I thought it might be a bit, well, you know... provocative?'

Janet studied her and then nodded. 'I've got just the thing – Mike bought it for me last year...' She went into her own room and came back moments later with a large black Spanish lace shawl, which she draped over Peggy's bare arms. Immediately, it softened the silhouette a little and made Peggy feel vastly more comfortable.

'Yes, that helps,' she told her daughter with a smile. 'But are you sure you don't mind my borrowing it if Mike gave it to you...?'

Janet's smile flashed out at her. 'I trust you not to lose it,' she said. 'Honestly, Mum, that dress suits you, and the shawl makes it... gives you the decorum you prefer, though you could wear it just as it is, believe me.'

'Thank you, darling,' Peggy said and kissed her, leaving a trace of deep-crimson lipstick on her cheek. 'What did I do to deserve such a wonderful daughter?'

'You're a great mum,' Janet said. 'Besides, I know you. You were thinking of putting on your old black dress, weren't you?'

Peggy laughed and nodded. 'I'd better go down. Able will be here shortly – are you certain you and Nellie can manage here, love?'

'Stop worrying, Mum,' Janet said. 'We'll manage just fine – besides, Anne got home this afternoon and she said she would pop in and give us a hand if we need it and just have a chat if we're not busy.'

Trade was up and down these days, because the shortages meant Peggy didn't always have beer, and customers couldn't order their favourite drinks. Even the food depended on what coupons she had left and what she could find in the shops. Thankfully, the government had put the lid on price inflation on food, making it illegal to charge more than a certain amount for all kinds of food. She tried to produce both savoury and sweet pastries but the fat wasn't always available, and, although she improvised, even her cooking couldn't always disguise the lack of good ingredients. Normally, she was able to buy margarine in sufficient quantities and a lot of customers were happy with hot toast and tomatoes or sometimes sardines, but that evening she'd provided both apple pie and treacle tart, as well as a tasty vegetable pie, which she called her wartime special. It was made of root vegetables, and topped with potatoes, but she'd spiced it up a bit with onions and topped the crispy potato layer with melted dripping from the weekend joint; browned under the grill, it tasted good.

'I know you will manage,' Peggy said and smiled at her daughter. She picked up her black evening purse and left the room, followed by Janet.

Able was already waiting for her downstairs in the kitchen, looking so handsome in his smart uniform. He'd come round the back rather than going into the bar, which she knew was deliberate, because some of Peggy's customers might have been shocked to see her leave with an American officer for the evening. Peggy knew local people liked Laurie and respected him; they could have no idea that he'd let her down, and in any case would not have approved of her going out with another man even if they had known her husband had been unfaithful to her. So Able was discreet and Peggy ignored the frowns of a few people who had guessed something was going on. She didn't feel she was doing anything wrong by letting him take her out occasionally. Able behaved like a perfect gentleman, respecting her as a married lady and so far – despite the looks he sometimes gave her – he'd done no more than give her a peck on the cheek after escorting her home. Peggy wasn't sure whether she wanted him to make a more amorous advance or not, though she couldn't help feeling attracted to him. His smile made her toes tingle and her body responded like a young woman's.

However, the look on his face when he saw her in the red gown made Peggy draw her breath sharply. He seemed stunned for a moment, but then he came forward and took her hands, gazing at her in a way that she could only describe as hungry.

'You're beautiful,' he said in a deep, gravelly voice she hadn't heard from him before. 'Stunning! I shall have to fight the other officers off this evening, Peggy. They will all want to dance with you.'

Peggy glowed with a warmth that filled and lifted her. It was so long since a man had looked at her like this... desire, wanting and pride. She smiled, feeling shy all of a sudden, because something told her that Able wouldn't just kiss her on the cheek and walk away tonight...

*

Perversely, they were busier that evening than they had been for weeks, Janet thought as she served a customer with a half of beer and a slice of her mother's fatless sponge. She put the money in the till, making sure that she made a note of the price of the sponge. That money belonged to her mother, and Janet hadn't forgiven her father for being unfaithful to Peggy. Her anger against him for his intransigence over her marriage and then his behaviour to her mother had made her encourage Peggy to go out with Able. He was a really nice man and Janet liked him, and she didn't see why her mum shouldn't have a little fun once in a while. It wasn't as though she was having a torrid affair, though after Able saw her in that dress… Janet considered her own feelings if Peggy did have an affair and decided she wouldn't mind. She loved her mother and thought she deserved to be happy.

Janet's gaze moved round the crowded bar. It was ages since she'd seen as many people in. Ellie from the hairdressers' was having fun. She seemed to have picked up a couple of young Army chaps, who were buying her drinks and vying with each other for her attention. Janet wondered what Ellie's husband would think if he walked in and saw her knocking back gin and orange like a trouper; she normally only drank a small port and lemon. Still, it wasn't Janet's business, even though she suspected the girl was getting in over her head.

She served a regular with half a pint of beer, but as she turned from the till to serve the next customer, her heart skipped a beat.

'Ryan…' she said and caught her breath. 'You didn't say you were coming…' Janet had replied to his letter and told him it would be better if he didn't visit, but seeing him here had knocked the breath from her body and she hardly knew what to say. It was only after the initial shock had worn off that something in Ryan's eyes warned her that he was under a great deal of stress. 'Is something wrong?'

'Yes,' he said tersely. 'May I speak to you alone?'

'Yes, of course.' She lifted the hinged counter for him to come through. 'Go to the kitchen and wait. I'll be there in a few minutes. It's the call for last drinks so I can't desert Anne at this time...'

Ryan nodded grimly and went through the door at the side. He knew his way and Janet tried to ignore the desperation she'd seen in his eyes as she served the customers with last drinks for the evening.

Once the rush was over, the bar started to empty and she looked at Anne. 'Can you manage to lock up now?'

'Yes, of course,' Anne smiled at her. 'We're nearly done here. I'll go out the back after I've put the lock on the pub door, Janet.'

'Yes, thanks a lot, Anne. You're a pal. I'll come through and finish clearing up later – and Nellie will wash up anything we leave in the morning...' She left Anne to it and went through the side door to the kitchen. Ryan was standing in front of the range, his back to her, and she could see the anguish in the set of his shoulders. 'What's wrong, Ryan?' she asked softly, and when he turned to face her she saw the tears trickling down his cheeks. 'Oh, my dear, something bad has happened, hasn't it?' She went to him, her arms going about him and holding him as he suddenly started to sob. 'Your family...?'

'Dead, all of them,' Ryan said in a muffled voice against her hair. 'My wife had fetched the boys home for the Easter holidays and... It was a direct hit on the house.' He raised his head and she saw the hell in his eyes and felt an intense rush of pain – his pain – because he'd adored his wife and his sons, even if he did feel more than he should for *her*. 'It's a punishment...' he said at last. 'It's my fault because I wanted...' he choked and couldn't finish. 'It's my fault.'

'No, my dearest; it's this damned war,' Janet said and stroked the back of his neck to comfort him, forgetting in the overwhelming sadness and sympathy that she was married to a man she loved and feeling only the forbidden ties that were drawing her in closer to this man. 'It couldn't be. You loved them, you still love them – we didn't do anything wrong: nothing that could hurt them.'

His eyes were drenched with tears as he met her look of kindness. 'But I wanted to, Jan. You know that – and so did she. She sensed it somehow and we'd had a tiff over it. I was angry with her and told her she was foolish, but she'd seen your letter in my pocket and she knew...'

'But there was nothing between us.'

'She knew I wanted there to be,' he said brokenly. 'I felt such guilt, Jan – as if I'd been having a love affair, which of course in my mind and heart I had.'

'No...' Janet shook her head. 'It was just a few foolish thoughts. You would never have done anything to hurt her.'

'Wouldn't I?' Ryan looked at her sadly. 'I think you knew I would, if you gave me the chance. You were the loyal one, Jan – you were the sensible one. You stuck by your husband.'

'Don't think it was easy to write that letter,' Janet told him. 'I know there's something between us; I've felt it too.'

Ryan gave a moan and then his lips fastened on hers and her arms went up around his neck. Their kiss was long, passionate and with all of Ryan's desperation in it. He spoke her name over and over against her hair as he continued to hold her close, his whole body shuddering. Jan held him until the shudders passed and then gently pushed him away as she felt the quickening of his need. For a moment she was tempted just to give into his need and her loneliness. It was such a long time since she'd felt the warmth of a man's love and known the satisfaction of physical love, but then she thought of Mike in hospital and her resolve strengthened. Mike was her husband and she couldn't betray him.

'No, Ryan, not like this – and not now,' she said softly. 'Please don't think me uncaring, but it shouldn't happen this way. You're grieving and I'm not sure – I don't know what I want yet, and I don't want it to be like this...'

Ryan stared at her and mutiny flared in his eyes, but then he inclined his head. 'Yes, I know, it isn't right – but you're not sending me away for good?'

'I'm saying we should wait and see,' Janet said and touched his cheek. 'I do care for you very much, Ryan, but I have a husband and he needs me too, even if he doesn't know it.'

'I'll go...' he said and turned to leave, but she caught his arm.

'No, stay and sleep here on the couch. You shouldn't be alone. I'll make a hot drink with some brandy in it and we'll talk. You can't be alone tonight, Ryan. I'll talk to you and sit with you, and we'll share this terrible thing and perhaps it will ease the horror and grief.'

'No wonder I love you,' he said. 'We'll have that hot drink and we'll talk, but then I'll go, my dearest. I don't want to take advantage – though I was ready to just now, but I'm sane again. And that's because of you.'

Janet looked at him, and then nodded. She'd known Ryan liked her and fancied her but loving was something more and she didn't really know how to answer him. Perhaps it was best that she didn't, because it would be easy to stray and she had to keep faith with Mike, even though he didn't remember her and seemed not to want her near him.

Chapter 9

Peggy opened her eyes and stared in bewilderment at the plush surroundings. Where on earth was she? This wasn't her room at the pub... Suddenly, she realised that she was in one of the best bedrooms at the Savoy Hotel, where the American top brass had given their dance for British friends. Able had taken her to the lavish affair, where champagne had flowed as freely as it had before the war – however that was possible – and Peggy had got more than a little tipsy on both vintage wine and flattery.

Able hadn't been joking when he'd told her all his friends would want to dance with her. She'd been complimented, called beautiful and swell, and a lot of other flattering things that had made her laugh in a way she hadn't for ages. It was as if the years had rolled back to when she was young, before she'd met Laurie – except that she'd never been to a place like this or had a dress that made her look like a film star. At least that was what several young officers had told her. Peggy was normally a sensible, level-headed woman, who took compliments in her stride, but either the excitement or the wine went to her head and she'd giggled and teased Able in a way she would never normally have done – and this was where she'd ended up. In bed with a man she hardly knew and feeling rather foolish and a little regretful. It seemed that she'd behaved like an immature girl...

'Hi, beautiful,' Able's voice said teasingly and she saw him come in from the adjoining bathroom. 'How's the head this morning?'

'Rather delicate,' she said, realising that she was wearing nothing but the lace French knickers she'd worn under her evening dress, because it had been structured so that she didn't need a bra. 'I think I must have had a little too much of that wonderful champagne last night.'

'It was good, wasn't it?' Able said and sat on the edge of the bed. 'I've ordered some coffee to be sent up when we're ready – and it will be drinkable, because we supplied it, as we did the wine last night.' He leaned in to kiss her on the mouth. 'You look good even in the mornings, and you taste nice too.'

'I'm sure I look a fright,' Peggy said. 'I'm sorry if I made a fool of myself last night. I rarely drink more than one glass of wine in an evening, but it was all so gorgeous, the food and the champagne – and after months of managing on so little, I'm afraid I indulged a little too much...' She gave an embarrassed laugh.

'You did nothing of the sort,' Able said and touched her cheek. 'A lot of you English folk are buttoned up and stand-offish, you know? My friends thought you were natural and lovely – and they all envied me.'

'Oh, Able...' Peggy sighed. 'What happened last night? I don't mind if we made love – but I would rather have known what was going on the first time.'

He laughed delightedly, and flicked her hair back from her face with his fingers. 'I wouldn't do that to you, darling Peggy. I want us both to know all about it when it happens, believe me.'

'We didn't?' She looked at him shyly, hardly believing that it hadn't happened.

'You thanked me very nicely for a lovely evening and then went to sleep like a little kitten. I carried you up here, because you fell asleep on a sofa in one of the rooms downstairs. I must admit I'd hoped for a different ending – but seeing you sleeping so peacefully was kind of cute.'

'After all the trouble you went to, hiring this room and bringing me here...'

'I wanted to give you a nice evening and you were happy; that's kinda nice, Peggy. I've wanted to give you lots of things: food, coffee, stuff we can still get – but I didn't want it to look as if I was trying to buy your favours.' He reached out and touched her hair, letting it slip like silk through his fingers. 'I think you know I don't come to the pub just for your great apple pie. I want you – and I think I've fallen in love with you, Peggy, but I knew you were married and I didn't expect you to risk all you have for me, because I don't think things could stay the same if we became lovers.'

'Oh, Able,' Peggy said and smiled at him. 'You're so nice – no, don't pull a face. A lot of men don't have your scruples, and I love your manners.'

'But you still love your husband and you think I just want an affair?' He arched his brows, half mocking, half in entreaty.

'I'm not sure about either of those things,' Peggy told him truthfully. 'Laurie went away on government business; you knew that, of course. I can't talk about it, even though I know so little – but I do know he has someone else... a younger woman who means something to him.'

'He's a fool to throw away your love,' Able said. 'Men are often fools. Yet I don't think I would have let you go if you were mine.'

'I'm over forty,' Peggy said. 'You've seen my daughter and my son, and of course my granddaughter... You're younger and there will be lots of women in your life, Able. If-if we did have an affair I wouldn't expect it to last forever...'

'Would you mind if it did?' he asked, looking deeply into her eyes. 'Supposing that I asked you to leave everything here, and come back home with me when I go? Would that be asking too much, Peggy? I don't live in a grand mansion, but my pa left me a property in town; it's just a small country town in Virginia, but OK. It isn't a pub, but I guess we could turn part of it into an eating house if you wanted... or we could sell and start a new life over here?'

'It's too soon to ask a question like that,' she said. There were a lot of questions she wanted to ask, but this was the first time Able had mentioned his family. She hadn't liked to probe, but she was going to have to talk to him seriously one of these days. 'Why don't you get us that coffee? I need to wash and go home. I have a business to run.'

'You didn't answer my question.'

'Because I can't yet,' Peggy replied and leaned in to kiss him on the lips. It was pleasant and she enjoyed it, just as she enjoyed his company and his compliments. 'We need to know each other a lot better before we think about the future. We have to talk, tell each other things...'

'Yeah, I guess,' he said and grinned. 'My mom says I always did grab the shiniest toy the moment I saw it. She's still alive, but lives with her cousin in Wyoming. I never see her or any of my family since my pa died. Will you come away with me one weekend, Peggy? Go somewhere we can be alone – find out whether we like each other? It doesn't have to end with us sleeping together, but it might.'

'Yes,' she said and this time she had no hesitation. 'Yes, I will, Able. I said yes when you asked me out, because I felt resentful of what Laurie had done – but this is different. I didn't realise how much I was going to like you. I should like to get to know you much better.'

'Great. I'll let them know we're ready for coffee and then I'll take you home in a taxi.' He grinned at her again. 'If the neighbours see you walking up the street in the dress you wore last night you'll have no reputation left...'

*

In the end it had got too late and Ryan had fallen asleep on the kitchen sofa. He was still there when Janet came downstairs to see to the fires and make a cup of tea. She warmed a bottle for Maggie, who had been weaned from the breast for some time and now took some soft foods, but still liked a bottle of milk first thing in the morning. Just as she was about to take it upstairs to feed her daughter, Ryan stirred, opened his eyes and looked at her.

'God, is it morning? How much brandy did you give me last night? I must have gone out like a light.' He sat up and looked at her ruefully. 'I'm so sorry, Jan. I never meant to stay all night.'

'It doesn't matter. No one needs to know about it,' she said. 'I don't think Mum came home last night anyway. I looked in her room before I came down and the bed hasn't been touched since she left.'

'I'll go,' Ryan said in a rueful tone. 'I'm sorry about last night. I was desperate and I had nowhere else to go.'

'You've lost your home as well as your family,' Janet said. 'I know how that feels, Ryan. I'm not going to let you go off just like that. You can use the bathroom upstairs and one of the guest rooms. You're not far off my father's size. Some of his older shirts will fit you. I'll lend you one – but his trousers would be too big...'

'I've got a few things at the office and I'll get myself whatever else I need on the way to work, if you're sure your mother won't mind?'

'Of course she won't,' Janet said. 'I'll take you upstairs so you can have a wash and shave. I'm sure there's some kit in the bathroom, either Dad's or Pip's, and then I'll get you some toast and a cup of tea before you go. I just have to give Maggie her bottle and change her.'

'I'm such a nuisance. I shouldn't have come here...'

'Of course you should; we're friends,' Janet said and led the way upstairs. She showed him the bathroom and the spare room, which was opposite, and then fetched one of her father's shirts from the wardrobe in her mother's room, leaving Ryan to freshen up while she fed and changed Maggie.

Ryan was just emerging from the guest room when she carried Maggie down to the kitchen and put her in the playpen while she filled the kettle and set it on the range, which was heating nicely.

She'd made toast and provided some of Peggy's home-made marmalade, and Ryan had begun to eat when the back door opened and Peggy walked in. She looked startled and then a little flustered.

'Oh – I didn't realise,' she said. 'I'm not sure what to say...'

'It isn't what it looks like,' Janet said quickly, because she could see Ryan's embarrassment. 'Ryan had some bad news last night, Mum. I made him sleep on the couch and he's borrowed one of Dad's older shirts – because his house was bombed and everything went in the fire...'

'I'm so sorry,' Peggy said. 'That is awful for you. I've just come from up West and I've seen some of the fires are still smouldering this morning. We had a little one in the yard when an incendiary hit our shed once, but apart from replacing the windows in the pub a couple of times, we've been lucky.'

'Mum…' Janet glanced apologetically at Ryan, because it wasn't like her mother to babble on, but he shook his head.

'I'll just go up and change my dress,' Peggy said and now she was the one to look embarrassed. 'I'm afraid I had a little too much champagne last night and I'm told I fell asleep. If there's anything we can do, Ryan, please say. You're welcome to stay here. It isn't easy to find a room these days. Folk are always asking me for a room, but I don't want a permanent lodger – however, you would be very welcome to stay for a while…'

'Thank you, Peggy. That is kind of you. If I really get stuck I might take you up on the offer.' He swallowed the last of his tea, picked up his half-eaten toast and rose to his feet. 'I'll get out of your way, Jan. Thanks for the brandy and sympathy. I have to get to work.'

He left the kitchen, taking his toast and eating it as he went.

Peggy looked at Janet and then they both smiled awkwardly.

'I don't have a leg to stand on,' Peggy said. 'I'm not going to play the heavy-handed mother when I've just got home at this hour – but people do talk…'

'Let them,' Janet replied. 'My conscience is clear – and Ryan was in a bad way last night, Mum. He lost his whole family as well as the house. His sons were home from school for a holiday and they all died; he can't understand why they didn't go to the shelters and he was devastated.'

'Oh, my God, no!' Peggy went white and sat down on the nearest chair. 'There was me wittering on about broken windows – I had no idea that...' Tears trickled down her cheeks. 'The poor, poor man! Jan, I'm so very sorry. No wonder you made him stay here. I would've done the same thing.'

'That's what I thought, Mum,' Janet said. 'Ryan came to me for help and I couldn't let him go wandering off late at night knowing he had nowhere to go. He helped me – I should probably have died in the plane crash that destroyed the cottage; if it hadn't been for him taking me to tea I would have been there making Maggie's bottle...' A little shiver went through her as she remembered the German bomber that had been hit in a dogfight over Portsmouth; it had made for the sea but came down on the cottage she'd been renting from her friend Rosemary, only a few minutes from the pilot's goal, resulting in a fire that destroyed her home and took the crew's lives.

'No, of course you couldn't let him down,' Peggy said. 'Is there any tea in that pot, love? I could do with one. That news has made me feel sick – to think I was out gallivanting while you had to cope with all this...'

'Maybe you had too much wine last night?' Jan teased.

'I'm assured nothing happened last night. Able is a gentleman,' Peggy said a little defensively, and then raised her head, meeting her daughter's eyes. 'Something may develop quite soon, Janet. He's asked me to go away for a few days, and if Anne is around to give you a hand...'

'I could probably manage with Nellie,' Janet said, 'but if Anne is here all the better...' She looked at her mother oddly. 'You're sure this is what you want, Mum? Going to a party is one thing – but a weekend away sounds more serious?'

'Able seems serious,' Peggy confessed. 'He thinks he's in love with me, Jan. I'm not sure what it means or how I feel about it, but I do know that I'm ready for something different. I want a little fun and excitement before I'm too old to stand a chance of finding love. Is that wrong of me?' She shook her head. 'My head keeps telling me I'm too old for him and I know I should forgive Laurie, accept he was unfaithful and get on with things – but I can't.'

'You're angry with Dad and I don't blame you. I'm angry with him too.'

'But you don't think I should get too serious about Able?'

'I don't know, Mum,' Janet admitted. 'I understand how you feel. The next bomb could drop on us so why shouldn't we take what we can from life while we have the chance? And yet, if it all falls apart, you might get hurt and I don't want that. This pub has been your life. You have so many friends here. Supposing Dad found out and demanded a divorce – would you be happy leaving everything you know to make a new life elsewhere? And what happens if you discover you made a mistake?'

'I honestly can't answer that,' Peggy said. 'I could cook anywhere and I think I could find my own living – but it would hurt both you and Pip if the family broke up. That would upset me...' Peggy sighed. 'Is it so wrong to feel happy because a young man thinks I'm beautiful and wants to be with me?'

'No, Mum, it isn't. In a way I know just how you feel. You're not the only one to be tempted – but I'm resisting, because I still love Mike. At least, I love the man I married...'

'Oh, Jan,' her mother said and sighed. 'My problems are nothing compared to yours. I shall think about it carefully, but when a marriage falls apart there isn't that much left.

Laurie hasn't valued me for a long time. I know it happens to lots of people, but I believed that at heart we were still one, still the people who fell in love and married, but I don't think that any more. Laurie changed and I think perhaps I have too. I think I may be the one asking for a divorce.'

'Oh, Mum... I'm so sorry,' Janet said. 'But you know I'll always stand with you whatever you decide.'

'Thank you, my darling.' Peggy finished her tea and got up. 'I'm going to change out of this dress and get on with some cooking, but I don't regret agreeing to go with Able and if that means change then so be it...'

Janet watched her mother leave the kitchen and was pensive. She'd thought it was dangerous for her mother to get too involved with the young American because it could lead to the break-up of all their lives, and perhaps there was an element of selfishness in that; the pub was Janet's home and she didn't know where she would go if she had to leave.

It was a sobering thought, because Janet knew she couldn't work full time and look after her daughter, and Mike was going to be in hospital for a long time yet. She wasn't sure that she would ever have a home with him again, and that hurt so much.

'It's all this damned war,' Janet said as she looked at her daughter crawling round her pen and trying to stand to peer through the bars. Maggie could walk a few steps now, even though her attempts usually ended with her sitting down abruptly on her bottom. Tears stung Janet's eyes. 'Your daddy has to get better and come back to us – he has to because otherwise...'

Janet felt as if a black cloud were hanging over her. Her own marriage was in peril and her parents were on the verge of splitting permanently. She wondered if her father knew

how much he'd thrown away and realised she'd never truly
known him.

*

Laurence had been labouring over the code for several days
and it wasn't working as he'd intended. Something was
missing in him – the spark that had been there when Marie
was around.

Damn it! He missed her. He missed her like hell and he
was having difficulty in concentrating his mind on the words
in front of him. Pushing back his chair, he got to his feet,
reached for his jacket and shrugged it on. He needed to walk
to clear his mind… to give himself a chance to work out
where he was in his life.

It was wet and dank in the lanes about the large country
house in which they were based. When the sun shone and
the mist cleared there were the most beautiful views over the
Scottish hills and he'd often walked with Marie when they
were together… He would never regret having that time with
her, even if it did lead to the wreck of his marriage. If he were
truthful, he knew it already had. Peggy had instinctively
realised that he'd been unfaithful and she was too proud a
woman to simply accept it. Laurence had always known that
about her; it was one of the reasons he'd admired her from
the start.

His mind went back to the beginning, when they were
courting and the first big war was tearing Europe apart.
She'd seemed so beautiful, bright and clever – the best chance
he would ever have of making the kind of marriage he
wanted: a woman who was passionate about life and loving;
a woman who would help him build up a business and

become a successful man – and she had. Peggy had worked hard, bringing up their children, being a loving wife and a wonderful cook. The pub was busy all the time because of her – and he was a damned fool to have thrown it all away.

Yet his content had eroded over time, long before he'd met Marie and fallen under her spell. He wasn't sure why – perhaps because Peggy had so many friends. He'd resented the time she gave to others, her stepfather included. Percy had been a bit of a lecher in his time, though he'd managed to keep that from his wife and stepdaughter. Peggy had made such a fuss of him when he was ill that it made Laurence angry; he'd even wondered if they were having an affair, which he knew was stupid. The man was feeble, dying, and if he'd ever had ideas about Peggy they were long forgotten – replaced by gratitude for her kindness in his last months and weeks. Even though Laurence's mind told him he should pity the man, he couldn't, and he knew he'd given Peggy short shrift over the hours she'd spent there looking after him.

Was that the start of the rift? Laurence shook his head. No, it was earlier, deeper, more fundamental. He thought it was just that he'd grown bored with his life, bored with the sameness of every day and the same woman in his bed. He'd never been unfaithful to Peggy until he met Marie. Of course he'd thought about it. Some of the girls who came to the pub in the lunch hour were flirtatious and gave him the eye, but he didn't have time for an affair, and it was too much of a risk. He didn't want to lose his family or the pub – but then he'd been forced to leave, to come to Scotland to this training centre, and everything had changed. Life was exciting, new, and challenging, and Marie was like no one he'd ever met.

Their relationship had lasted only a few weeks. He'd gone home for Christmas and she'd gone over there – risking her life somewhere in France or perhaps even Austria or Germany. Laurence didn't know. They were never told exactly where their operatives went, but they knew it was somewhere close to danger – somewhere they could be discovered and killed at any time.

The thought of all that vitality and passion being wiped out by a German gun made Laurence sick to his guts. He wanted her so desperately at times that he could hardly keep his mouth shut when he was told that Marie had sent an important message. Although he'd known her so well, he wasn't her radio partner and all he heard were snippets. He wasn't sure how he would feel if he heard she'd been killed, although he accepted that their relationship was very probably over. Marie had told him before she left and she'd never pretended it was for life, just for now, for pleasure – for satisfaction.

She'd certainly given him that, he thought with a smile on his face: the best sex he'd ever had, but she'd also made him feel young, important and special, and for that he'd adored her. Marie was everything he'd wanted to give him back the hope and ambition he'd lost over the years, but now she'd gone, and even if she survived and returned to England, he knew it was over. Now it seemed that he had little choice but to save what he could of his marriage. If Marie had agreed he might have been willing to jettison the lot for her sake...

'The boss wants to see you...' Laurence was told as he entered the house and made his way to his office. 'He's in a bit of a bother so don't keep him waiting.'

'OK, thanks,' Laurence said and turned towards the major's office, knocking and entering when he was invited.

Major Harris glanced up from a sheaf of papers and stared at him, then inclined his head. 'Ashley, thanks for coming. We've had some bad news I'm afraid – a couple of our people have been arrested by the Gestapo. I think they may have our latest codes. Is that new one you're working on ready for me?'

'Very nearly,' Laurence replied. 'I was struggling for something but I took a walk to clear my head and I think I've cracked it.'

'Good. Get it to me as soon as you're certain. We'll be sending someone out early next week and I want him to have the latest codes. Until then we need to be on our guard in case of false messages...'

'Yes, sir. I'll work on it all night if necessary...'

'Good man...' Major Harris hesitated, then, 'I believe you were quite close to Marie?' Laurence nodded, not trusting himself to speak. 'Yes, I thought so – never a wise thing in the circumstances. She's one of the two that have gone missing. We're not sure, but you understand the position. Once the Gestapo get them... Well, I thought you should know. Crack on with the code, there's a good chap.'

Laurence hesitated. Every nerve in his body was screaming and he wanted to beg for more details, to force his superior to send him out there, but he knew it was useless. He would be told the minimum necessary, and, if he offered to go out there, be informed that he wasn't qualified and would make a mess of things. What hurt most was that it was true; there were others much better equipped to lead the double life necessary for an operative in the field.

Biting back the torrent of emotional words, he left the officer and went back to his own desk. He was filled with a bitter anger against the enemy – against the men who were even now beating or torturing the woman he cared for so much that it made him feel dizzy with anguish. At that moment he wanted to fight; he wanted to be given a gun and sent out to shoot Germans, but they wouldn't let him be a soldier because he was too old and they wouldn't let him be a spy because, as Marie had once told him, his French would get him hanged – if not by the Gestapo by the French themselves. As far as his superiors were concerned, he had one skill they were interested in and one only.

Bending his head to the task, Laurence discovered the solution was jumping out at him. Perhaps it was his sense of grief and despair that made what had seemed a boring task half an hour ago become vital and necessary.

'You can do it, my Laurence.' He felt Marie's breath on his cheek and heard her husky voice in his ear. 'My beautiful man. You are so clever and I want you – kiss me now...'

Laurence felt the pain strike into his heart because he knew with a certainty beyond question that Marie was already dead. Tears stung his eyes but he brushed them away impatiently. Marie had told him that they must live for the moment and she'd given him the sweetest memories, but there would never be any more. Maybe she'd known even before she left that she would not return...

Chapter 10

'That's over then,' Sally said as they returned to the bedroom they were sharing at her parents' home. The funeral had been bleak and hard for everyone; Sally's mother sobbed into a large handkerchief all through the ceremony and the reception afterwards, her thin face gaunt with grief. Sally's father, a tall sallow-complexioned man, had remained stony-faced, greeting his daughter with a stare that did not acknowledge her and refusing to notice that she'd brought a friend with her: he hadn't spoken to her once. Maureen understood why her friend had begged her to go home with her, because the atmosphere was so tense it was almost unbearable. Sally was stripping off her dark clothes with hands that trembled in their haste. 'Take those clothes off, Maureen. I need to get out of this house for a while...'

Maureen changed out of the black dress she'd borrowed for the funeral with relief. It belonged to Sally's mother and, though it was all right pulled in tight on the waist, a cloying scent of lavender water clung to it. She was glad to get back into her own purple tweed skirt and pink twinset.

'Will your mum mind us going off without a word?' she asked as Sally led the way down the stairs and out the front door. Maureen was feeling uncomfortable because Sally's parents had made it obvious that she wasn't welcome in their house. Sally's mother was in the kitchen putting away all the china and glassware that the two girls had washed up between them, and they made their escape before anyone saw them. 'I had the feeling that she wanted you to talk to your father now it's all over...' Maureen ventured.

'It will never be over for either of them,' Sally said and made a wry face. 'I've tried talking to my father, and he ignores me. I don't exist as far as he is concerned. Whatever I say or do I can't bring Billy back and they don't care about anything else.'

Maureen looked at her uncertainly as they walked away from the neat semi-detached house. Sally's parents were relatively well off, compared to the people she'd grown up with, and they had a nice house in the suburbs with four bedrooms and a small car standing in the drive. Sally's father was head of the accounts department in a large store and wore dark suits all the time. In the house everything was in its place, shiny and pristine, and it had felt like a morgue to Maureen, and not just because they'd been to Billy's funeral. She imagined Sally must have had a hard time growing up in such a home, and understood perfectly why her friend had begged her to go with her. Even though the hostility of Sally's parents made her uncomfortable, she was glad she was there to support her friend.

'Where do you want to go?' Maureen asked.

'I don't know. Somewhere there's life, and friendly faces. I just have to get away from *that* for a while...'

'Shall we go to Peggy's pub? We can get the underground and then walk. She's always got a smile – and she does good food too.'

'Sounds wonderful,' Sally agreed, slipping an arm through hers. 'I'm so glad you came, love. I couldn't have got through it without you.'

'You're coming back to Portsmouth with me tomorrow, aren't you?'

Sally nodded. 'Yes; we're on duty the day after. Matron didn't want us to have that long... Is there anything else you have to do before we leave?'

'I'll pop in and see Rory in the morning, because I don't manage to visit him often enough. I saw him this morning for an hour before we got ready for the church, and he was really fed up.'

'Does he want you to marry him?'

'Yes, one day,' Maureen said vaguely. She didn't want to explain the awkwardness of their situation. If she told Sally that, after their break-up some years previously, Rory had gone straight off and married someone else, she would think Maureen was mad to stay with him, but she couldn't understand that Maureen still clung to the memory of how sweet their love had been before she'd had to end it for her father's sake. Rory blamed her for what he'd done and, in fairness, perhaps she was a little to blame. Perhaps that was the reason that she'd let him back into her life, but for the moment she wasn't sure what that meant or whether they would ever be together.

Until Rory could find proof that Velma wasn't actually his wife because of a previous marriage, he couldn't legally marry Maureen. Besides, she was in no hurry, because it would mean she would have to apply to be posted to London and Matron wouldn't be happy about her leaving. Marriage was still frowned on amongst the nurses and trainees, though some matrons turned a blind eye if they needed the nurse.

Even if she could remain with the service, once she was Rory's wife he wouldn't be happy about that, especially as it was unlikely that he would be able to return to a fighting unit. Maureen knew he was apprehensive about the future and felt guilty that she wasn't there for him more, but he didn't make it easy.

'I'm never going to get married,' Sally said firmly. 'I didn't tell you about Mac, did I?' Maureen shook her head. 'We were more or less engaged but he was in the regular Army and was killed in the first battle over there... I don't think it's worth caring about anyone. When you see what it's done to my mother and father... I don't want to love anyone, even a child.'

'Oh, Sally...' Maureen's throat felt tight. No wonder her friend had got so upset when Pam was killed. It must seem to her that anyone she cared for died or stopped caring for her. 'Let's go and see Peggy,' she said. 'She's a really good friend and I know she will like you, love.'

Maureen saw the headlines on a newsstand and stopped to buy a paper. 'It looks as if we've been pushed out of Greece,' she said. 'The news gets worse – and only last month the Bismarck sunk *HMS Hood*...'

'Why you even bother to read it I don't know,' Sally said. 'Throw it away, Maureen, I can't take any more bad news.'

*

'Your friend is knocking the gin back a bit isn't she?' Peggy said to Maureen as she fetched another round of drinks. Maureen had stuck to fizzy orange after one small gin and orange, but Sally had swallowed several gin and tonics quickly. 'I know it was her brother's funeral, but... I don't like to see a young woman drink too much. If she has any more she'll never get home tonight.'

'She has a rotten home life,' Maureen said. 'I don't think she can bear going back to that house.'

'Poor girl,' Peggy said and looked more sympathetic. 'It's a good thing she has you, love.'

'I'm not sure I could've stuck it the first few months at the hospital if it hadn't been for Sally. I think anyone is entitled to let go after so much bad luck – she lost someone she cared about right at the start of the war...'

'This damned war!' Peggy said fiercely. 'This round is on me, Maureen – and if your friend can't walk out of here, you can both stay the night...'

Even as she spoke they heard the siren wail and Peggy groaned. It was the second attack they'd had that day – the first was on the Docks in the middle of the afternoon – and it meant she had to take as many customers as she could down to the cellar. Some people decided to leave their drinks and make a dash for the shelters, others moaned when she insisted that they all go down into the cellars, but most picked up their glasses and carried them down.

Peggy, Janet and Maureen took some of the food and the coffee pot, which Janet had refilled in the kitchen.

It was crowded down in the cellars and someone suggested a sing-song, which Sally joined in with enthusiastically if not very tunefully. She'd brought her glass, but it was empty and she shook her head at the offer of coffee, mooching around the cellar until she found a dusty bottle of wine, which she bore back to Peggy triumphantly.

'Can you open this for us? I'll pay...'

'I don't have a corkscrew with me,' Peggy said, and then a huge bang made them all jump and Sally dropped the wine. It smashed and the rich red liquid spread out on the floor.

'I'm sorry,' Sally said and suddenly burst into tears. 'I'm so sorry...'

'It doesn't matter, love,' Peggy said and put an arm about her, drawing her away from the curious eyes into a shadowy corner. 'It's only a bottle of wine...'

Sally shook her head, saying between sobs, 'It's me. Nothing I do is ever right. Billy always protected me and took the blame, but it's my fault. I should be dead – he should be here, because everyone loved him.'

'It's not your fault,' Peggy soothed, letting the girl weep into her shoulder and holding her close. 'You didn't force him to join up. He had to go and even if you were dead it wouldn't bring him back...'

Somewhere close at hand there was another loud bang and then the sound of glass shattering. Peggy felt the girl shudder and knew that she was terrified, like most of them. It was the closest the bombs had come to the pub and she wondered what would be left when they went back upstairs.

Sally stopped crying as Maureen put an arm about her shoulders and squeezed. She looked subdued as she took the hanky Peggy offered.

'I think you should stop here tonight,' Peggy told her. 'You and Maureen can share a room. When the all-clear goes, I'll take you up and get you a warm milky drink...'

'Yeah, we'll be all right together,' Maureen said. 'We're safe enough here in Peggy's cellar – besides, the Germans daren't bomb Peggy's place. She'd give them what for...'

'I believe you.' Sally gave her a watery smile. 'I wish you were my mum, Peggy. Maureen is lucky to have you as a friend.'

'Well, now you're my friend too,' Peggy said. 'You're welcome to come here whenever you need a bed for the night – and I'll help you in whatever way I can.'

'Thanks...' Sally looked at the soggy handkerchief. 'Shall I wash this or do you want it back?'

'Why don't you keep it for now?'

Suddenly, they all heard the signal that the raid was over and everyone started to make their way back up the cellar stairs. Peggy was shocked when she entered the bar and saw the damage. Every window in the pub had been shattered and the floor was covered with glass from broken drinking glasses and bottles. She groaned as she saw how many bottles had smashed, because they were irreplaceable these days and it wasn't just the loss of profits they represented, but the fact that she had to tell people they couldn't have their favourite drinks. She'd stored as many as she could under the counter in old wooden crates and those were mostly intact, but everything on the back of the bar had gone down in the blast, and the front door was off its hinges. Even as she tried to take in the devastation, the door swung back and an ARP warden wearing a tin hat entered.

'Everyone all right here?' he asked, looking around him at the devastation. 'It looks bad, but a few houses down from you they've taken a direct hit, and there's a whole row gone over that way...' He pointed over his shoulder.

'No...' Peggy looked at him in horror. 'Nellie lives there – my friend. She helps me out in the pub. Oh no! Did you say the whole row has gone?'

'Sorry, love, but they caught several hits – but we're not sure if anyone was inside. She might have been in the shelters...'

'I'll pop round and see if she's about...' Janet said and grabbed her coat, but at that moment the front door lurched open again and a familiar figure walked in. 'Nellie! Thank God...'

'I thought I'd best come round, love, and let you know I am all right. Your pub sign is hanging by a thread and there's a great hole in the road just down the lane. That lawyer's office next door to the hairdressers' is a right mess: half of the building has gone and the rest is burning, but the fire brigade has it under control; it's a good thing no one lives there. The hairdressers' and Mrs Tandy's place are all right though; I saw Mrs T puttin' her cat out,' Nellie said, looking about her. 'Cor blimey! By the looks of things it's just as well I did come. We shall be all night clearing this lot up.'

Peggy rushed to her and hugged her. 'You'll stay here until you get sorted,' she said, 'and we'll find you some clothes to wear, love – don't you worry about anything...'

'Lord bless you, Peggy,' Nellie said cheerfully. 'I'm not bothered about my few bits. I always take me papers and me photos down the underground wiv me of a night just in case. Weren't nuthin' else as mattered – and I've got me post office book in me bag...' She beamed cheerfully at Peggy. 'I think you'd best call early hours, Peggy. You can't carry on in the middle of this lot; they could come back again yet, 'sides it must be long past closing...'

'Yes, you're right. Can everyone please leave?' Peggy said. 'I'll try to be open tomorrow but it may take a while...'

'I'll stop and give yer a 'and,' one of her regulars offered. 'And my son 'ere will get them winders boarded up for yer, love.'

The offer to help clear up was endorsed by several others, and the warden warned her to be careful and give him a call quick if she smelled gas, in case there might be a leak in the area.

'I'll be in again before long to keep an eye on things,' he said. 'I should take that offer, Mrs Ashley. My men will be run off their feet tonight and I'm not sure when we'll get to you – we've got worse to deal with...'

He went out and Peggy realised that it was quite light out there – and then she guessed that the bright red and gold of the sky was from fires all over London. She thought it might have been one of the worst nights of the year and shuddered as it suddenly came home to her that it could have been the pub that had gone up in flames. Everything she and Laurie had worked for all these years would have gone just like that; it made her feel thankful they'd got off so lightly and she set to work clearing up with a will. This sort of damage could be put right and, although she'd suffered a loss, she and her friends were still alive – still defiant and determined to get on with their lives despite all that Hitler's Luftwaffe could throw at them.

'I'll put the kettle on when we've done,' she said. 'I've got some bubble and squeak and a bit of bacon. I'll do a fry-up with fried bread, tomatoes and the lot. This deserves a celebration – celebration of life and good friends...'

A little cheer went up from the people still busily carting broken glass to the bin someone had fetched in from the yard, and although one or two refused the offer, most of them accepted gratefully. After a night like the one that had just gone, everyone felt glad to be alive and amongst friends...

*

Sally smiled and hugged Peggy before she left the next morning. 'I'm glad I was here last night, and I feel so much better. I want to thank you for everything you did for me, Peggy.'

'I didn't do anything, except feed you and send you to bed when you were nearly out on your feet,' Peggy said and laughed. 'I was glad of an extra pair of hands. Take care of yourself, love – you and Maureen. Keep in touch and come and see me when you visit London...'

'Yes, I shall,' Sally said and impulsively kissed her cheek. She smiled as Maureen gave Peggy a hug and then they left together.

They were shocked by the devastation they saw in the lanes. Peggy's pub sign had fallen off now and debris from someone's roof was strewn across the path. A large hole was in the road in front of what had been the lawyer's office and that was just a blackened shell, its door blown off and the windows gone in the blast. A pall of thick smoke still lingered over it and Sally could see nothing inside but charred ruins and realised they were lucky that the fire hadn't spread to other shops and houses in the lane.

'We were lucky the pub wasn't hit,' Maureen said, because several of the houses had suffered damage. She shivered because they'd all been closer to death than they'd realised. Peggy and her customers had made light of it, but seeing the awful devastation that morning brought it home to the girls as they arrived at Maureen's bus stop and parted. She was off to visit Rory again before meeting Sally at her home so they could travel back to the hospital together.

'See you later,' Sally said as they went their separate ways.

*

When she walked in the front door, Sally's mother rushed out of the kitchen wearing an enveloping floral apron and clutching a tea towel.

'Where have you been all night?' she demanded. 'We were worried to death. Your father was very angry with you, Sally – surely you could've let us know where you were?'

'I was caught in a raid in the East End,' Sally said a little uncertainly. 'I was in a cellar with a lot of other people, Mum, and I didn't have access to a phone, because the lines were down for the rest of the night...'

'Well, I still think you could've made an effort to get home,' her mother grumbled. 'I don't see why you were even there. I suppose you went somewhere with that girl you brought home. I can't think why you brought her here at such a time – when you knew it was a service for Billy...' She sniffed into her lace hanky that smelled heavily of lavender water. 'Your father was furious. How could you do such a thing? And then just go off without a word to either of us.'

'Maureen is a good friend and I care about her. We help each other and I don't think it matters that she comes from the East End – we're nothing special...'

'Your father is a professional man and he has certain standards to maintain. He told me to ask you not to bring a girl like that here again...'

'Couldn't he say it to my face?' Sally was furious but trying not to show it. 'Where is he?'

'He went to work as usual,' her mother said. 'Where would you expect him to be at this hour of the day?'

Sally stared at her, no longer able to hide her disgust. 'Surely he didn't go back to work straight after Billy's funeral?'

'It was a memorial service not a funeral,' her mother said primly. 'Your father has never been given to displays of emotion; he finds them unseemly...'

'Yes, I'm sure he does,' Sally said and turned away. 'I'm going upstairs to pack, Mum. I'll be taking everything I care about and I shan't be coming back to this mausoleum...'

'Sally! How dare you?' There was both shock and anger in Mrs Barnes' voice as she spoke. 'I don't know how you can say such things to me – not come back? This is your home...'

'No, not any more,' Sally said and turned to look at her. 'It was a home while Billy lived here, but without him it's an empty shell. He was the only one here that ever cared about me, and I doubt you'll even miss me...'

Sally walked upstairs and began to pack her clothes. Maureen's stuff lay where she'd left it the previous day and, when she'd finished her own packing, Sally did Maureen's as well, checking that everything had been retrieved from the wardrobe and chest of drawers. She checked her watch. Maureen would be here in half an hour. By the time she got everything downstairs, she wouldn't have long to wait and the sooner she could leave the better.

'Sally – Sally, you can't mean what you said...' her mother said from the doorway as she saw the various cases and bags. 'You've got nowhere to put all that stuff...'

'I'll put what I don't need in a lock-up somewhere. They've got them on the station – and there's a storeroom at the hospital.'

'Sally, please, I don't want you to go like this – you're my daughter and I've got no one else...' There were tears hovering on her lashes, but she blinked them away.

Sally looked at her and felt a twinge of sympathy for her. She'd lost her precious son, and her husband had never been a warm and loving man, though he'd smiled when Billy won his scholarship and when he'd seen him in his naval uniform.

'I'm sorry if you're lonely, Mum. I am too, but I can't come back to this house. I don't want to see Father – I can't stand it here. I loved Billy as much as anyone else, but life is for the living. I have a job where I'm needed and even appreciated. I passed all my first exams with flying colours – did you even bother to write and congratulate me? No, but I didn't expect it, so I wasn't disappointed.'

'I'm sorry you feel so bitter...' Now the tears were on her cheeks, her eyes seeming to beg Sally to relent.

'I'm not bitter, just angry. Maureen has shown me more love and affection in the short time I've known her than you or Father ever did – and so I'll be staying elsewhere if I come to London, and I probably shan't bother much...'

'I'll come and see you...' her mother said, clutching at her arm. 'Don't go like this, Sally. I'm sorry about what I said concerning your friend. I'll talk to your father – you can bring her if you really want to...'

Sally gave her a pitying look and picked up the first of the bags. 'I'll write now and then, if I have some news – and if you really want to come down that's up to you. You're my mother and I shan't refuse to see you, but I never want to see him again as long as I live...'

Sally's mother shook her head and picked up two of the bags, following her downstairs. She stood for a moment in the hall, watching as Sally went back up for the rest, but when Sally returned she'd gone into the kitchen.

Sally remembered that she'd left a scarf in the kitchen and went in search of it. Her mother hardly looked at her as she hunted in vain, speaking with her back turned to her.

'If you're looking for your scarf I washed it. I'm afraid it is still wet. I'll send it to you…' She turned then and stared at her. 'Surely you will have a cup of tea and a sandwich before you go?'

Sally heard the door knocker. 'That will be Maureen, Mum. I'll let her in and then we'll go… We can get some food on the way down…'

'Here, have this…' A parcel of cake wrapped in greaseproof paper was shoved into her hands. 'We had a lot of stuff left over from the reception. I'm sure you girls are always hungry.'

'Thanks…' Sally gave her a quick kiss on the cheek and then ran to open the door to her friend. 'I've got everything packed,' she told Maureen. 'Come on, let's go…'

'Sally…' Her mother came into the hall. 'I'll be expecting a letter…'

'All right,' Sally said and thrust Maureen ahead of her into the street. Her friend looked a bit startled and Sally smiled wryly. 'I wanted to get away. We had words and then she turned on the tears. It's emotional blackmail and she always does it, because I'm daft enough to give in – but not this time…'

'Oh, I know all about emotional blackmail,' Maureen said. 'My dad did it all the time to get his own way. Every time I said I was going out with friends, he was ill. I don't know how he managed it, but he would work himself up until he collapsed or couldn't get his breath…'

Sally nodded wryly. 'Mum has the headache or feels unwell, but she doesn't ask the doctor to call. Father just stares at you until you wilt. I was always in trouble as a kid, because I was clumsy or too noisy or I upset my mother. Billy used to protect me as much as he could, but even if I didn't get the strap I got the cold stares and the tears…'

'Oh, Sally love,' Maureen said. 'It sounds as if we've got more in common than we realised...' She sighed deeply. 'I walked out when my father got himself another wife, but it didn't stop me feeling guilty.'

Sally nodded and squeezed her waist, because she understood so well what Maureen had gone through all those years.

'How was Rory?'

'He was having treatment this morning so I only got a few minutes with him.' Maureen looked sad. 'He wasn't happy because he wants me to ask for a transfer back to London – or better still give up my job...'

'After all the training we've done?' Sally cried. 'Not bloomin' likely! My father never wanted me to work. He thought I should stay at home and help my mother, but I couldn't have lived there alone with them after Billy joined up – and now I can't even bear being in the house with my father.'

'I don't think he liked me. I think he was annoyed that you took me home, Sally.'

'Next time we come we'll go and stay with Peggy. She said we could – if she meant it...?'

'Of course she did,' Maureen laughed. 'I told you Peggy would love you, didn't I? She's always been the same – has lots of friends and she makes them all welcome.'

'That was obvious last night,' Sally said. 'I was frightened during the raid but afterwards – well, it was lovely the way everyone got together to help. Peggy cooked us that lovely breakfast and everyone stood about her kitchen, eating their food with a fork. It was a nice atmosphere, almost like Christmas despite what had happened.'

'You must come to her Christmas party next time,' Maureen said and then the smile left her eyes, because it was months away and who knew what might happen in the meantime? 'I just hope the pub will still be there. It was close last night, Sally. That house in the lane – just smouldering rubble when we left this morning. It was a lawyer's office, though no one ever seemed to use it, but it could have been anyone's home: Dad's shop or the cobblers' or Mrs Tandy's wool shop. I can't imagine life without Peggy's pub; it has always been there...'

'Yes...' Sally nodded grimly and shifted her parcels. 'I've had enough of this. Come on, I'm getting us a taxi...'

Chapter 11

'They've given me a grant down the council, to buy a few bits,' Nellie said as she entered the kitchen that morning, bringing a blast of cool air with her. It was spring but an easterly wind was blowing and it felt cold out, or perhaps that was because Peggy's kitchen was so warm. 'You're like a furnace in here...' Nellie peeled off her coat and scarf.

'Yes, I know. Sometimes I think I should've let Laurie put the gas cooker in for me, but the range is reliable – and it's too cool outside to have the door open for long.'

'I see they've got the glass back in the pub windows again,' Nellie said. 'I sometimes wonder if we shouldn't just board everything over for the duration.'

'I was tempted to just leave the boards up, but people kept asking me if we were open,' Peggy said and laughed. 'I can't replace the coloured glass in the door for love or money. That was Victorian and Laurie was so proud of it...' she sighed. 'He thought about having it removed and stored safely but he didn't get around to it and now it's gone – such a shame.'

'Yes, that was a lovely bit of work,' Nellie agreed. 'I went down the housing too, Peggy, and asked what chance I had of getting a house and they said none at all. If the kids were at home they would put me higher on the list, but as it is all

I can hope for is a room. I'll start looking when it turns a bit warmer; it's cool for May, isn't it?'

'Very, but the forecast says warmer tomorrow.' She smiled at Nellie. 'I know you want your own home, love, but you're welcome to stay here for as long as you like...'

'If you're sure. They've got me name on the list if an empty 'ouse becomes vacant, but there's too many piles of rubble where 'ouses used ter be, and there's only one of me these days. Them with a family need it more...'

'You've plenty of time to find somewhere else,' Peggy said and bent to take a pie from the oven. 'I feel awful because this is the first time I just haven't had anything to offer as a sweet but a jam tart. Maureen used to put me some golden syrup by whenever she got it in, but now I have to queue when they've got some and, unless Janet goes for me, I don't have the time...'

Nellie smiled and reached for her bag. She withdrew a large tin of the precious syrup and placed it on the table. 'I just happened to see the notice going up in the window and I was first in. Violet Jackson was serving and would only let me have the one, but if Janet goes down this afternoon she might get another...'

'Bless you,' Peggy said. 'I'll ask her if she's goin' shoppin'. If not, I'll pop along myself and see what's on offer...'

'Mum...' Janet's voice from the doorway drew their attention. 'Your American friend is here and he's got something for you – his friends are carting it in now...'

'What on earth do you mean?' Peggy was startled. Able had been in twice since the bomb had caused so much devastation and he'd hinted that he might be able to replace some of the stock they'd lost, but when she hurried through to the bar she was astonished to see that four large boxes stood on the wooden counter and another two on the floor. 'Able... what's all this?' she asked.

'My pals and I had a chat with a few others and decided to see what we could find for you, Peggy. I hope you can use some of this stuff...'

Peggy smiled at the two young men with him, thanking them for their gifts. She received a big grin in return as they left.

'Able, you shouldn't have done all this...' Peggy said as she discovered that some of the boxes had bottles of wines and spirits, all with American labels, as had the bags of coffee beans and the tins of food, and the black treacle, jam in professional-size tins and sugar in strong brown bags. 'Where on earth did it come from?'

'From our stores,' Able said easily. 'We all get extra over here – they tell us we can give some to British friends; of course we're not allowed to sell it, but this wasn't all mine. I had some help...'

'I can't thank you enough,' Peggy said. 'You must invite your friends here and I'll give them a few drinks and some food one night – I can't believe what you've done...'

'I knew it must have caused you a problem when I saw the damage,' Able said. 'You're not offended or annoyed with me, hon?'

'How could I be after such generosity?' Peggy went round from behind the counter and kissed him softly on the lips. 'You're a lovely man, Able, and I'm very grateful – but I'm not sure I can take all this stuff...'

'Sure you can,' he said and grinned, and reached for her as she moved away. 'Don't think this was a bribe, but I have to go away this weekend – and I wondered if we could go somewhere tonight?'

'Yes, I'm sure I can swing it,' Peggy said and laughed as she realised she was using his language these days. 'Anne is home for the next month or so. I was thinking we might...' she broke off and blushed.

'Maybe go away ourselves next weekend?' he asked and she nodded. 'I'd like that fine, Peggy. Do you want me to carry some of this down to the cellar?'

'Yes, I think that's the safest place for it,' Peggy said. I'll take these tins through to the kitchen and then I shall have to open the bar...'

*

Peggy looked at her full shelves and knew she had the ingredients to make tasty pastries and cakes for her customers for a couple of weeks or more. Able's gift was a huge help to her, because it was getting harder and harder to find the things she liked to buy; he was so generous and she really appreciated that he'd gone to so much trouble for her. British convoys were taking a battering on the Atlantic run, many of them being sunk by German U-boats because there just weren't enough escort ships to protect them, and the shops often had very little to offer these days other than home-produced goods. A few of the ingredients Able had given her were strange to Peggy, but she'd read the labels and knew she could make something out of them, even though peanut butter and blueberry jelly sounded very different to her English ears. She was a little concerned about the bottles of spirits and wines that Able had brought. The papers were filled with warnings about black-market goods now, and, though Peggy hadn't done anything illegal, she might have difficulty in explaining where they'd come from if she had a sudden inspection.

She'd dragged the boxes behind the partition that had hidden Laurie's secret stock. He'd had invoices for his wines and spirits, bought long before the war, so Peggy had never worried that someone might find them, but the American stuff might be frowned on. Perhaps it might be a good thing to keep her empty bottles from the bar and refill them down here rather than take the risk of someone noticing the different labels and reporting her.

Peggy knew that most of her customers were loyal, but the war had hardened attitudes and people were now telling on those they suspected of selling black-market stuff: something no one round here would have done before the war. Everyone was finding life hard and Peggy understood that some found it more difficult to produce anything worthwhile with the rations they all got. She'd had one or two women ask her how she managed to cook something that tasted so good with what was available, but they didn't know how many hours she spent experimenting before she introduced a new dish.

Able's gift was very useful, because she'd lost so much in the raid, but not if it brought the law down on her head, because she was sure they would never believe that he'd given her so much. She would be accused of trading on the black market and she would be fined – she could even be arrested and might end up serving a few days in prison. Peggy decided that she would have to make certain that Able's generous gesture wasn't repeated...

*

'I found this in one of the tea chests,' Tommy said, bringing Peggy a fine cup and saucer and tea plate later that morning. 'There's a set of twelve of everything, a teapot and stand, a milk jug and covered sugar – and I reckon there's a nice dinner service in one of the other tea chests. Do you want me to bring it all down and wash it for you?'

'Yes, please,' Peggy looked at the tea service. 'This is so pretty – I think it's Shelley ware. Yes, it is. I remember my grandmother had a set once, but half of hers got broken. I had no idea this was up there.'

'I think there's a lot more good stuff too,' Tommy said. 'I've only unpacked three of the chests yet, but I think there's more china – some of it looks real bright colours and there might be some silver too. I ain't sure cos it could just be silver plate.'

'Even that would be nice,' Peggy said. 'All these years and we never had any idea what was in those boxes. They belonged to Laurie's uncle's wife's family I think. Laurie looked in one and it was just books.'

'Yeah, I found the books an' all, but I reckon they're all spoiled – they smell damp and the pages are spotted.'

'We'll sort the china out first. I can always use more of that, and Janet could do with some things if she ever gets her own home – Nellie too.' Peggy smiled at him. 'You're doin' a really good job up there, Tom. Found anythin' else of use?'

'Well, there are some rolls of wallpaper – enough to do one of the bedrooms I should think...'

'Ah yes, that pretty pink floral pattern. I bought it two years ago but Laurie didn't like it...' Peggy was thoughtful. 'I wouldn't mind havin' it up in my bedroom now if I could find someone to do it – better than wasting it.'

'My dad showed me how. I helped him paper Ma's front room before he got banged up,' Tom said. 'I reckon I could do it, Peggy – and I saw some sweeps' brushes up there. I thought I might clean Ma's chimneys if I could borrow them.'

'Quite the handyman,' Peggy smiled. 'You can paper my bedroom and I'll need my chimneys done soon. Practise on your ma's first and then you can do mine.'

Tommy laughed. 'Ma was moanin' about hers, so I reckon she'll be glad fer me to have a go.'

'Just remember to put plenty of paper down everywhere,' Peggy said. 'Soot makes a lot of mess...'

'Yeah, I remember when me dad did it last time,' Tommy grinned. 'I shan't make much worse mess than he did. Ma gave him 'ell over it fer weeks.'

'Well, just make sure she doesn't take her stick to you,' Peggy teased. 'Fetch that tea service down then, and I'll give you a slice of pie and a glass of squash...'

*

Janet sighed as she looked at the letter that had just arrived. It had come from the hospital and she'd hoped it was from Mike, but instead the ward sister had written to her. Brief and to the point, it said that he was improving health-wise, but as far as his mental state was concerned he had not changed.

I realise this is a terrible period for you. However, I must ask you to be patient and wait for a little longer before coming down. Doctor did suggest a visit, but when Mike was asked he became angry and confused. Therefore, may I please ask that you refrain from visiting again this month? Yours sincerely, Sister Monica James.

Janet placed the letter in the file she'd kept. At first she'd felt like throwing the letters straight in the bin, but something had made her save them. She didn't know why, because it hurt like hell to be told Mike hadn't wanted to see her... again. Surely he must have come to terms with the fact that he had a wife and child by now?

What should she do about the situation? Mike seemed to be trying to push her away, and the nurse at the hospital was blaming her for his distress. Would it be better to just walk away and move on with her life for all their sakes or should she fight for her marriage and the man she loved?

Feeling restless, Janet reached for Maggie's warmest coat and put it on her. The pram was downstairs in a little cubbyhole off the kitchen and she would wrap the child up warm and take her for a walk. The warden's men had been round to repair the pavements recently, because it had been difficult to walk after all the bomb damage. Now it was possible to take the pram out again and she would walk down as far as the church, where there was a small green space known as Itchy Park, because the down-and-outs had once gathered there and locals said the kids picked up fleas if they played there.

Her mother was in the kitchen preparing to take some food through to the bar. She asked if Janet would fetch a couple of things from the shop on her way back and gave her the ration cards, warning her that Nellie said there was still a chill even though the sun was inviting.

'We'll both wrap up warm, Mum,' Janet said and looked at her lovingly. She was lucky to have a mum like Peggy Ashley and knew it helped to make up for the pain of Mike's latest rejection, though she didn't know how much longer she could stay away when she needed to see him so badly.

Janet felt better for being out in the fresh air and for getting some exercise. She met some other young mothers and stopped to have a chat about each other's babies and how difficult it was to get new clothes for children in the shops. Janet felt a little guilty because of all the wonderful baby clothes Ryan had sent her, though Maggie had grown out of most of them and Janet needed to make new ones.

Lingering in front of a fashionable clothes shop, she saw a display of new Viyella dresses in the window. They were all very much alike with a collar, short sleeves, buttons down the front bodice and a belt. However, there was one that looked rather smart in a green and red tartan and Janet was very tempted. Perhaps she would come back tomorrow and try it on... For the moment she wanted to visit the market and see if she could find any toys for Maggie.

She wanted to make sure her daughter had a happy life – but surely she needed her father. Janet's mouth tightened into a determined line. Mike was her husband and Maggie's father and she wasn't going to let some nurse who hardly knew him tell her what to do!

Chapter 12

Maureen sat down at the canteen table to drink her tea and eat a bacon sandwich. She picked up a discarded newspaper; it was more than a week old, but Maureen read with satisfaction of the sinking of the Bismarck on the 27th of May; it was revenge for the loss of *Hood* and the paper was making the most of the event. Someone had told her about it when it happened but it was satisfying to read the report, because so much of the news was dismal with nothing to convey but setbacks for the Allies.

Maureen had just collected three letters from the office, which she flicked through eagerly, hoping for something from Rory. One was from Shirley; her childish scrawl was easy to pick out, even though her new school had improved her writing. She was seven now and seemed happy enough, her brief letter mostly a thank you note for some sweets and crayons Maureen had sent. The second letter was a cheerful one from Gran and the third from Gordon. He'd written to tell her that he was now overseas with the British troops, but the exact location had been heavily scored out in blue pencil.

It's pretty awful here, Maureen. I expected it to be basic, but the conditions...

The next few words had been scored by the censor.

Still I suppose we manage all right; at least we get fed regularly and your letters are a godsend. Thanks for the cigarettes you sent and the mint humbugs. You shouldn't spend your money on me and Shirley, but if I'm honest I don't think I'd keep sane without them. You darling girls really don't know how much a letter from home and a gift means to us out here.

I dream of being home again and I often think of that day we took Shirley to feed the ducks... and then the car broke down on the way home. I think of you an awful lot, Maureen, and I wish I'd let you see how much you've come to mean to me. I know there's someone else but if he ever lets you down... But I know it isn't likely. Any man who is lucky enough to have your love would be a fool to let it slip.

God bless you, my dearest girl. Know that I think of you constantly. You are the kindest, sweetest person I've ever met and I'm lucky to count you as my friend. Take care of yourself and write whenever you can. Love from your friend, Gordon. xxx

Tears stung Maureen's eyes. Gordon sounded as if he was finding it hard out there, and from what she'd read in the papers she knew it must be terrible. The reports were conflicting, as talk of advances here and retreats there gave a confused picture as to what was going on in the rest of the world. In Britain and particularly London there had been a fresh blitz throughout the spring, culminating in the night that almost broke Londoners' hearts, though just recently it seemed to have eased a little.

Maureen tucked her letters away, finished her meal and rose. It was time she started work again. At least for her the next few hours would be too busy to think about the war or to worry why Rory hadn't replied to her last two letters. Gordon's letters came regularly and she would reply to his that evening when she'd finished her shift, telling him about something she'd found for Shirley. She'd managed to buy a skipping rope with wooden handles and a pretty hair slide, which she was sending his daughter as a gift. She smiled at the thought of the little girl's pleasure and knew Gordon would be every bit as pleased when he heard, because he wasn't able to send Shirley anything for the moment and she knew he worried about her.

Maureen walked across the compound into the hospital proper, greeting several nurses that she knew by sight and exchanging a few words as she made her way to the ward.

'Ah, so you've decided to grace us with your presence at last, Nurse Jackson?' Sister Martin said coldly as she paused at her desk.

'Am I late?' Maureen glanced at the little silver watch pinned to her uniform and gave a little cry as she realised she was five minutes late. Sister Martin was even stricter than Sister Matthews had been and Maureen was finding it hard on her ward. 'Sorry, Sister. The canteen was busy...'

The excuse was futile. Sister made the expected reply and banished her to the sluice room for another morning of scrubbing bedpans. It was another black mark against her and Sister looked as if she was in one of her bad moods. For a moment Maureen wished herself back in the shop serving her customers, but then she remembered that it wouldn't have been the same. Violet had taken over and she no longer had a place at the shop.

Sighing, she set the scrubbed pans aside and dried her hands. Hopefully, Sister would be in a better mood now and might even give her a little time on the ward. Maureen cheered up at the thought, because those few precious times when she was able to help care for the wounded were worth all the sore hands and the scolding she got from Sister.

*

'Is that from Maureen?' Henry asked as Violet placed some letters and cards on the table in front of him. 'Has she remembered my birthday?'

'I expect so,' Violet replied sourly. 'There's one from your mother and one from me, but that's all. I've bought you some new pants, vests and socks. I couldn't find a decent pullover anywhere; the shops just don't have anything suitable.'

'Maureen always knitted me one in two-ply wool,' Henry said. 'She bought the wool from Mrs Tandy. You're not much of a knitter, are you, Violet love?'

'I don't have time to waste on knitting,' Violet said. 'Besides, you've got several pullovers; it was underwear you needed.'

'Yes, thank you, dear,' Henry said meekly. He didn't raise his eyes, because she would see his disappointment and know that underwear fell far short of what he'd been expecting; a few bottles of beer would have gone down a treat.

He ate his toast and marmalade and drank a cup of tea, opening the cards from his mother, wife and daughter. Maureen's was of a man sitting in a red sports car with the roof down and waving to everyone as he lifted his glass of wine; and it wished him, *Happy Birthday Father*. She'd enclosed two white handkerchiefs with his initials in the corners. He smiled and took up the letter she'd written. It told of her busy life as a nurse and said she hoped he was keeping well and not to eat too much fatty stuff.

Henry grunted. Maureen didn't change much. It was ridiculous because he'd always taken her for granted when she was here, but now that she was living at the other side of the country he missed her. She'd been a good girl to him but he hadn't realised how much he relied on her.

Chapter 13

'I never expected this...' Peggy looked round the lovely country cottage in delight. Able had told her he was taking her to a friend's house for a couple of days, but she hadn't thought it would be like this... furnished with expensive antiques in rich dark mahogany with beautiful shining surfaces set with silver, glass and porcelain; large Persian-style rugs on wooden floors, a huge inglenook fireplace in the spacious sitting room, and vases of fresh flowers everywhere – even in the bedrooms. 'Your friends must be rich, Able?'

'I guess Wilf is OK for money,' Able shrugged his shoulders. 'He inherited this place from his English grandfather and most of the time he lets it out to people he trusts. Not that he's charging me a penny...'

'Well, I love it.' She smothered a sigh because it was a long-held dream of Peggy's that one day she might have a cottage like this... when she and Laurie retired. Of course it would never have been furnished like this, but she could've made it nice for a lot less money. However, it wasn't likely to happen now. Laurie hadn't written recently, and Peggy still didn't know whether she could ever live with him again. 'Thank you for bringing me here, Able. I like this much better than a hotel.'

'I thought you would, and I wanted you to be happy,' he said and put his arms about her, looking into her eyes. 'Wilf says there are a couple of decent places to eat nearby. One does really good seafood and they're still managing to get supplies of most things...'

'It's being so close to the sea I suppose,' Peggy said. The bedroom window was open and she could hear the sea as the waves broke against the cliffs. 'I've never been to Devon before. It's so beautiful down here, Able. I don't know how you managed to get enough fuel to bring us here, but I'm so glad you did.'

'You're a beautiful person, Peggy,' he said, and she turned to see him looking at her in a way that made her stomach clench and her breath come faster. It was so long since a man had looked at her with so much hunger in his eyes and it was very seductive. 'You know I love you – don't you?'

'Yes, I do,' Peggy said without hesitation. She walked to him, smiled and leaned into his body, feeling it leap with anticipation. Her arms slid up about his neck and she moved in as he bent his head to kiss her, his mouth cool and soft at first until the kiss deepened and filled with passion. Her need and wanting overflowed and she moaned with pleasure as Able bent and lifted her effortlessly, carrying her to the bed.

'You are ready to move on?' he asked in a husky voice. 'I want you so much, Peggy, but you can say no – we can just have a lovely visit...'

'I want you to love me,' she said and held her arms out to him. 'Hold me, kiss me; tell me you love me again. I want to be loved, Able. I want you to make love to me...'

'Peggy, hon,' he said gruffly, 'Never doubt it. I want you like hell, but I love you too and I always shall – you're the woman I've been looking for all my life.'

Peggy laughed softly as he joined her on the bed and they kissed hungrily, looking into each other's eyes as if they couldn't believe how wonderful everything was all of a sudden. War, differences in age, and the difficulties that might lie in the future were forgotten as, somehow, amidst laughter and passion, their clothes were first unbuttoned and then discarded piece by piece, each enjoying undressing the other, teasing and kissing as intimate places were revealed and worshipped in suitable fashion.

Able seemed content to tease, touch and lavish with his mouth and tongue for what seemed to her much longer than she'd expected, and by the time they were both naked and lying close on the bed, she was in a state of high expectation and need. When finally they came together in the slow, sweet rhythm of love that gradually became urgent thrusting, ending at last in an explosion of pleasure that had Peggy pulsating with such joy, she knew that she'd never – not even once – come close to such fulfilment in her life. Afterwards, as she lay with her head on his breast, she wept gentle tears and thanked him.

'I didn't hurt you?' He looked down at her anxiously, wiping away a tear from her cheek.

'It was so good – so lovely,' she whispered, feeling shy and rather like a young girl. 'I've never felt quite like that before – thank you, Able. I didn't know it could be like that...'

'Nor me, hon,' he said and grinned, clearly pleased with himself and with her for telling him. 'I guess it's because I've never loved a woman before. I've known women, not going to deny it, but none of them ever meant anything – not like this anyway...'

Peggy wondered what she'd done to deserve this, but she didn't say, just kissed and stroked the sprinkling of dark hair on his firm stomach. He had a fantastic body, hard and supple, and a lot of stamina. The thought made her smile, especially when her touch made him begin to harden again. Her lover was young and strong and would take a lot of satisfying. He wouldn't grunt and roll over as soon as the sex was finished, falling asleep before you had time to talk.

She felt lucky and happy and there was no guilt or regret about coming here with Able. In fact she wished that she might stay here forever...

Forever was a long time, even in Paradise. Peggy laughed as she felt the urgency in Able and moved to climb on top of him, looking down at him with mischief. She saw an answering leap of passion and fun in his eyes and his strong hands circled about her waist possessively as she came down on him.

Peggy bent her head to kiss him and his hands caressed her breasts, cupping them and gently squeezing. She lowered herself so that he could kiss and lick at them and then sat back, lifting herself and coming down very slowly so that he gave a shout of pleasure and his hands encircled her waist once more, lifting her and driving so that once again they became lost in the fierce passion that engulfed them both. She laughed as he rolled her over so that they lay side by side, still entwined, and he finally had her beneath his body again as they reached an awesome climax once more.

When they were satiated they lay still, just enjoying being close, warm and happy. Neither of them wanted to move but eventually Peggy needed the bathroom and decided on a shower to freshen herself up. When she returned, Able was smoking a cigarette, still naked and sprawled back on the bed.

'Want to go out for some food?' he asked as his eyes went over her. 'You smell gorgeous and you look wonderful...'

'I had a shower with the soap I found in the bathroom.' Peggy moved towards him, discovering that she wasn't in the least bit self-conscious of her nakedness. Able looked at her as if she were beautiful and she felt beautiful because of the way he saw her. 'I'd love to go for a walk on the beach first,' she said. 'Maybe just get something light later...'

'Great,' he said and put his long legs over the side of the bed. Peggy saw a deep scar on his right thigh that she hadn't noticed before. He saw her looking at it and grimaced. 'It was an accident a few years back...'

'It looks as if it must've hurt,' Peggy said. 'Is it OK now?'

'Throbs a bit sometimes,' he said and forced a grin. 'Long time ago...' He hesitated, then, 'I don't want secrets between us, Peggy, so I'll tell you... When I was fifteen my mother had an affair and my father discovered what was going on. He was so furious that he got his shotgun and threatened to kill her. I ran between them and in his fury he knocked me flying. I landed on the sharp edge of a plough. We were smallholders in Virginia then and this was on the property...'

'Oh, Able...' Peggy looked at him in shock. 'What happened?'

'My leg was cut deep and the blood sure brought Pa to his senses. He picked me up and rushed me to the doctor's in his truck. They thought I might die, but I recovered with just this scar to show for it.'

'Thank God...' Peggy closed her eyes briefly. 'That was awful, Able.'

'Pa thanked me later; he wept and told me he would have killed her if I hadn't intervened. He sold the land then and bought a place in town, working as a mechanic until he died of pneumonia. I rarely see Ma now or any of my family because I chose Pa and they cut me out...'

'I'm sorry you were hurt and I'm sorry your pa died,' Peggy said. 'Family is important.'

Able smiled down at her. 'You're important to me,' he said. 'All I want is a future with you, hon...'

Peggy went into his arms and let him hold her. His story had made her love him even more and her heart ached for that boy who had acted so bravely and almost died because of it. She closed her eyes, breathing in the scent of him and praying that this lovely closeness between them would last forever.

Smiling, she held her hand out to him. 'Let's go for that walk. Let's make the most of this, Able. I want to savour every moment of our time together...'

*

Like all good things their idyll was over too soon. Able had put their things into the car on the morning of the third day, locking the cottage after him. He put an arm around Peggy's waist as she paused to look back at the gardens and the red-bricked cottage with its thatched roof and small leaded windows.

'We'll come back one day,' he promised. 'Maybe for short breaks – maybe we'll live here when the war is over... I like your country, hon, and I'd like to make a life here with you.'

'Yes, maybe we could have a pub in the country and run it together,' she agreed, because she was still in the land of the possible where happiness lasted and love was all. Life would intrude once they were back in London, but that wouldn't be until the following day, because they were going to drive slowly and stay at a hotel for one night. Able had wanted to make the most of their holiday, and Janet had told her to stay for as long as she wanted.

'Anne, Nellie and I can manage,' she'd said. 'Enjoy yourself, Mum. You don't know when you'll be able to do it again.'

'We'd better go, hon,' Able said, his arm about her waist as he nuzzled her neck. 'I promise it isn't the end. We'll have the rest of our lives together... Somehow I'll make it happen. I promise...'

'Yes,' Peggy said and hugged him, because she wanted to linger in the dream that this weekend had been. Able was sincere; she knew enough of him now to know that he meant what he said, but life had a way of mocking you and Peggy couldn't help a slight fluttering in her stomach as they got into the car and moved away. 'I've had a lovely time, Able. I've loved being with you here – and I want it to be like this again one day...'

'It will be,' he said and smiled, and she saw that he believed it and wished that she might too.

For his sake, Peggy laughed and teased, making the most of every minute they spent together. They stopped several times on the long drive home, having a drink in a lovely old inn, and then lunch at a pleasant café they saw advertised from the road, following the signs down country roads and pulling into a large courtyard covered with crunchy gravel.

The woman promised them a meal of gammon steaks, red cabbage and mashed potatoes with her own special honey sauce, followed by gooseberry crumble.

'Them's all us own grown,' she told them with pride. 'Reared that porker, did us, from a young 'un and them berries are out of the garden – tatties too.'

'It's the best ham I've ever tasted,' Able told her in his strong American accent, and she looked at Peggy, puzzled.

'Your husband be a Yankee I reckon, missus – don't he know the difference between 'am and gammon?'

Peggy hid her smile as she saw the question in Able's eyes. He was having trouble with understanding the woman's accent. 'Able says a lot of his friends call fried bacon "ham" – I suppose it all comes from the same source...'

'Ah, thass right, my lovely,' the woman said and laughed. 'No tellin' with some folk is there? Don't know proper English like what we do, eh?'

Peggy struggled to hold the laughter inside until they were clear of the little café and couldn't be seen and then she almost doubled up as it came burbling out of her.

Able grinned and caught her to him in a hug of love and happiness. 'Taught us a proper lesson that has, my lovely...'

'Yes, you really must learn to talk proper, Able.'

Laughing, they set off again, the window down, enjoying the warm sunshine and the slight breeze. Peggy turned to look at Able's profile. She was so happy. She thought that she would never forget this time even if something happened and she never saw Able again.

But of course she would see him again. He'd told her he might be away for ten days or so but then he would come to the pub and they'd make plans for the future. He looked so happy and so sure of his ability to make it happen and she was caught up by his enthusiasm. Peggy reached across to kiss his cheek. He shot a glance at her.

'What was that for?'

'Because I love you,' Peggy said. 'You're a lovely man, Able. I'm so glad we met...'

Able had to get back to work, so he didn't come in when they reached the pub. Peggy went round the back, stopping to look at the motorbike propped up against the back wall and wondering who it could belong to. As she went in, she heard the sound of voices she knew arguing and guessed it must be Pip who'd arrived on the bike.

'Don't be such a prude!' Janet was saying as Peggy approached the door, which was opened at the top to let in the sunshine. 'Why shouldn't Mum go away with a friend? Grow up, Pip...'

Peggy leaned in and unbolted the door, causing her children to look at her. Janet looked harassed and there was anger in Pip's eyes as he saw her. She felt coldness trickle down her spine, because her son had never looked at her like that in his life.

'You're back then...' Janet said as Peggy walked in and put down her suitcase.

'Yes, I'm back. Able had to report for duty otherwise I might have stayed longer. It was a gorgeous place and I really enjoyed myself...' Peggy looked at her son deliberately, because she wasn't going to shy away from this, even though the look Pip was giving her was slaying her.

'You've been away with that bloody Yank,' he said and there was such disgust in his voice that for a moment Peggy's nerve failed. 'I couldn't believe you would do such a thing... You must be ten years older...'

'Not quite,' Peggy said, meeting his furious look. 'Even if I were it wouldn't make any difference. Able is in love with me – and I feel the same...'

Her son made a sound of disgust in his throat. 'I think you've lost your mind. He only wants you for sex and he'll drop you when he's ready...'

Peggy flinched as if he'd hit her. 'I don't think he will and even if he does it won't matter. I'm enjoying my life, Pip. I feel loved and wanted – and that means a lot to a woman of my age.'

'What do you mean?' he asked in a belligerent tone. 'You've always been loved and wanted. We all love you...'

'You and Janet may love me as your mother.' Peggy was determined not to raise her voice or get angry. After all, he was shocked and entitled to his opinion. 'One day both of you will have families of your own and I'll be alone with my memories – why shouldn't I have some good ones? It doesn't stop me loving both of you...'

'What about Dad?' Pip looked like a sulky schoolboy again. 'Where does he fit in?'

'I wish I knew,' Peggy replied. 'Your father has his own life – and he hasn't been in love with me for a long time. We rubbed along all right until he went away, but he...' She shook her head, because she didn't want to shatter his illusions about his father. 'We might stay together for the sake of you and Janet and the business – but we might not...'

Pip stared at her for a few minutes, then, 'Janet says he's got someone else – is that true?'

Peggy sighed. 'I don't know much about it, Pip, and that's the truth. I believe he's in love with her, whoever she is, and he doesn't want me, despite what he said in his letter. He wants his pub and I'm a part of that but there's very little between us these days...'

'So you went with the Yank to pay him back for cheating on you?'

'No,' Peggy said. 'It's hard to explain. At first I was just flattered and then when I found out about the other woman at Christmas I was very angry – but now...' She allowed herself to smile. 'I love Able. I know it may not last, but I could be killed in an air raid at any time, Pip – as any of us could. Able is a soldier. He's assigned to a general at the moment but he could be sent to fight if America comes into the war...'

'Pigs might fly...' Pip said scornfully, but his expression had softened. 'I'm sorry – I'm sorry I was rude and I'm sorry Dad hurt you, but I was angry and I didn't know...'

'Of course you didn't,' Peggy said and shook her head. 'How long have you been here? Have you had anything to eat?'

'Yes, I had some toast and dripping,' he said and grinned at her. 'Why not? I like it and I'm a growing lad...'

'Yes, perfectly old enough to eat what you choose,' Peggy said. 'How long have you got?'

'I had forty-eight hours but I arrived yesterday and I'm going to meet someone this afternoon, so just a few hours really. I thought I would miss you when Jan said she didn't know when you would get back...'

'Have you brought lots of washing?'

'Not this time,' Pip said, a faint flush in his cheeks. 'I couldn't manage it on the bike and – someone said she would do it for me...'

'Found some friends down there, have you?'

'There's a girl I like. Her mother has some of the chaps to stay when they've got a few hours off and don't want to rush home. She does their washing and cooks decent food for us – and I like Sheila. She works in the local pub behind the bar. She's the same age as me and she's going to join up as soon as her uncle can replace her – she wants to join the Wrens...'

'Is Sheila pretty?' Peggy asked, resisting the impulse to tell her son he was far too young to get serious.

'Yeah, she's OK,' Pip said carelessly. 'Not as beautiful as you were when you married Dad – but nice. I like her because she's serious and reads the kind of books I like...'

Peggy drew a sigh of relief. It didn't sound as if he was passionate about the girl or having a mad fling – and who was she to object if he were? She turned away to busy herself making sure the stove was hot enough to cook on, before looking at Janet.

'I'll go and change and then I'll start on the cooking,' she said. 'Oh – Able gave me a pair of silk stockings for you, Jan. I'll give them to you later...'

'Silk stockings!' Janet squealed with delight. 'Thank him for me. I haven't had any for months.'

'He thought you should have something nice for lookin' after things here,' Peggy smiled. 'Is there anything I should know about in the meantime?'

'No...' Janet hesitated, then, 'Dad rang last night. He says he may be coming home soon for a few days, but he wasn't sure when exactly. I told him you were out with a friend. He didn't seem bothered...'

Peggy frowned over the news that her husband might be coming back for a few days. She wasn't sure how she felt about seeing him after her wonderful time with Able. Peggy couldn't make promises to her husband for the future but she wasn't ready to walk away just yet either. 'Nothing else – no calamities here?'

'None,' Janet said and smiled. 'I'm glad you had a good time, Mum.'

'Thank you, darling...' She glanced at Pip. 'We'll talk again when I come down. You'll stay for lunch – won't you?'

'Might as well,' Pip said. 'To tell you the truth, I've got a bit of a head this morning – had a few too many drinks last night.'

'He found that American stuff in the cellar and took a bottle of bourbon to his room and drank the lot,' Janet said. 'It serves you right if you feel sick, you idiot. Mum lost a lot of stuff in the raid and she can't replace it – we were lucky that Able brought us some replacements.'

'What did you do with the bottle?' Peggy asked.

He shrugged. 'Chucked it in the rubbish this morning. Why?'

'I always soak the label off first,' Peggy told him with a frown. 'I don't want to be arrested for dealing on the sly.'

Pip laughed. 'They were a gift from a friend, Mum. You don't need to worry over that – American brands aren't what the government are after. I should think they're only too glad for whatever our American friends can provide.'

'Able says they are doing all they can for us without antagonising the Germans – not just food, but all kinds of stuff, things he couldn't tell me about.'

'Ships and arms, I should think,' Pip said. 'We can't build them fast enough to replace all those the Germans are destroying. I don't know why the Yanks don't just throw down the gauntlet and get stuck into the war with the Allies. It might make the Germans think again...'

'Able says that's what the majority of the American people want, but there are factions and lobbies to satisfy, and at the moment the president has to go carefully.'

'Yeah? Well, one excuse is as good as another,' Pip sneered, still angry even though he'd half forgiven her. 'The chaps say the Yanks like to come in with flags flying when it's nearly over.'

Wisely, Peggy ignored that last crack and left her children. It was time for her to get back to her work...

Chapter 14

Maureen sighed as she looked at her hands; they were red and cracked between the fingers and felt very sore. She applied cream every night but it was only a temporary relief, because the next day she was back on bedpan duty and the hot water and disinfectants made it start up all over again. Sally said she should go to Matron and ask to be put on other duties, but Maureen didn't want to go over Sister's head. Something she'd done had upset Sister Martin and since she'd been moved to her ward Maureen had been given all the dirty jobs.

'Nurse, haven't you finished those pans yet?' Sister's voice made her jump and she turned sharply, almost upsetting a pile of pans cleaned and waiting to be placed in the sterilising unit.

'Just finished, Sister,' Maureen said and wiped her hands on a towel. She noticed a smear of blood as she discarded it and hid her hands behind her back.

'Is that your blood?' Sister Martin demanded. 'Show me your hands, nurse.'

Wordlessly, Maureen held them out for inspection and heard Sister give a snort of disgust. 'You young nurses have no idea of how to keep your hands properly. Have you no creams?'

'I use Pond's, Sister...'

'Ridiculous! Report to my office this evening before you leave and I will give you something to protect your hands – and in the meantime you'd better go on ward duties. Get someone to put a bandage on those fingers. I can't have you bleeding all over my patients...'

Maureen swallowed hard. 'Yes, Sister. Thank you, Sister...'

'You've been here long enough now to have learned a few things. I'll give you this much, Nurse Jackson, you have stamina and courage. A lot of girls would have run for home if they'd been suffering as you clearly have. What made you stay?'

'We're needed here to do the menial jobs, because the staff nurses can't manage all the extra jobs,' Maureen said. 'They need to look after our patients, because they're suffering far worse than I was...' She looked down at the floor, amazed at herself for speaking out.

'It appears I misjudged you,' Sister Martin said thought-fully. 'I imagined you were just here for a job, but we might make a proper nurse of you yet – if that's what you want?'

'I should like a chance to learn...'

Sister nodded her approval. 'Very well, I'll put you down on my list to attend extra lectures and we'll see – and don't forget to get those hands attended to please.'

'Yes, Sister – and thank you.'

Sister Martin nodded and walked off, looking pleased with herself. Maureen stood without moving for a moment. She'd thought the sister one of the meanest on the staff and yet she'd known that the best survival rate for the men was on this ward. It fired a new flame in her. When Maureen joined she had intended just to find work for the duration of the war and since then she'd considered giving up and going back to London, because Rory's latest letter had begged her to go back and marry him. A part of her had come close to giving in recently, but for some reason another part of her was waiting. She hadn't been sure what she was waiting for until Sister had spoken to her and now she knew. She wanted to be able to bring comfort to men in pain and for that she needed to become a proper nurse.

*

'Are you coming to the pub this evening?' Sally asked when they sat in the canteen after their long shift was over. 'A group of us are going in a truck – all out together and all back together...'

'I was thinking I might stay here and do some revision,' Maureen said, looking up from her newspaper. The headlines were proclaiming that Hitler had made his worst mistake of the war so far by invading Russia, and opening another front. 'We've got some more exams soon and I want to get decent marks...'

Sally looked at her. 'You know you're the best friend I have, Maureen. I'd like us to have some fun together. We deserve it!'

'Yes, we do and I thought we might get a weekend off soon and go up to Peggy's together. We could shop and see the latest flicks...?'

'Bless you for thinking of it, love,' Sally said and gave her a quick peck on the cheek. 'Sure you won't come tonight?'

'I really do have to work...'

'All work and no play...' Sally quoted and sighed. 'I've been revising for weeks and if I fail after that it will not be my fault...'

'You're cleverer than me,' Maureen said and folded the paper, drawing her notebooks towards her. 'After exams I'll go out all you want, love. Besides, I'm tired. I've been running around after the nurses all day and my feet are sore.'

'OK – you don't mind if I go?'

'No, of course not,' Maureen said and smiled. 'Enjoy yourself, Sally. I don't grudge you a minute of it...'

Sally nodded, 'OK, I'll shut up and eat – this shepherd's pie isn't too bad for once...'

After they'd eaten, the girls returned to their hut. Sally had a wash and changed into a clean dress before going off to meet the others. Maureen washed and changed into her nightclothes before sitting down to write some letters. She wrote Gordon a long letter telling him what Sister had said to her and describing the day-to-day happenings at the hospital, then a short cheerful one to Gran, another similar to Peggy and a brief message to her father and Violet – and then lingered over a letter to Rory.

She told him that she'd been put on the ward and encouraged to think about becoming a full-time nurse, and that she was going to try to pass the exams.

I should like to prove myself by becoming a staff nurse. I know that means we can't marry while I remain in the service, but you don't know whether Velma is your wife or not anyway. Perhaps one day they will allow nurses to get married – I know some places make the exception these days, but they're very strict about it here... Once you leave hospital you could find a job down here and we can see each other whenever I'm free – that's if you want? I do love you so much, Rory, but I don't want to give this chance up. It's a way of proving I'm worth something. My father said I'd crawl back and beg him to take me in, but that I'm determined never to do. I don't want the shop even if it were mine, which Gran says it will be one day.

Hearing the first loud bangs of the evening, which seemed to come from out at sea, Maureen turned her light down and shaded the lamp. She went to lie on the bed, wondering whether she needed to dress and run back to the hospital. Most of the off-duty nurses volunteered if the hospital was attacked, but as far as she could tell the bombs were dropping further away, over the sea and perhaps the town. Besides, she was very tired and it wouldn't be any use volunteering if she couldn't keep her eyes open. She would just shut her eyes. If the raid came nearer it would wake her and then... She fell asleep before she could finish the thought.

*

It was morning when Maureen's alarm clock woke her and she jumped straight out of bed, knowing she only had half an hour to wash, dress, grab a piece of toast and get to the ward for the start of her shift. She was on early this morning, but Sally was luckier: she could lie in – but Sally wasn't in bed.

Maureen stared at the bed, which was neatly made. How had Sally managed that without waking her? And why hadn't she woken her? Sally's scarf and nursing bag were still lying on the top, just as she'd thrown them down before she went out last night. She hadn't been back all night!

Where on earth was she? It wasn't permitted to stay out all night without a pass, and Sally didn't have the right pass.

Maureen frowned as she hurriedly dressed and went down to the canteen to join the queue for toast and coffee, but there was no sign of her friend. She noticed a few of the girls looking at her oddly, but no one spoke and she didn't take much notice. She couldn't ask if they'd seen Sally without landing her in trouble so she chose not to talk, hoping that Sally would turn up before she was due on duty.

The queue took so long that she grabbed her buttered toast and a cardboard cup of coffee, eating and sipping the hot drink that tasted of nothing much but was wet and warm as she walked, and disposing of the remains in the bin as she approached the hospital. She walked up the stairs to the landing where Sister Martin's ward was situated, knowing she was on the verge of being late.

'Nurse Jackson...' Sister's voice stopped her in her tracks and she turned slowly, expecting a telling-off, but the senior nurse looked anxious and upset. 'Would you come to my office please?'

'Yes, Sister.' Maureen followed her, heart racing, hardly knowing what to expect. What had she done that warranted a visit to Sister's office?

'Sit down, nurse.'

Maureen sat, because her knees had suddenly turned to jelly. Was she going to be dismissed? What had led to this? She had no idea.

'I'm very sorry to be the bearer of bad news,' Sister Martin said, sitting herself. She looked white and almost on the verge of tears and Maureen shivered. 'I wanted to tell you personally if you hadn't heard – fifteen of our staff, nurses and porters were killed in the raid last night...'

'Oh no...' Maureen felt faint and sick. No wonder people had looked so strange this morning. 'I fell asleep. I didn't realise the hospital had taken a hit or I would've reported for duty earlier...'

'We were not hit here. It was in a pub just outside the town centre. Several of the staff had gone there for a night out. I understand there was a band of some kind and – well, the pub took a direct hit. Everyone inside was killed – the staff, landlord, his family and our nurses and one junior doctor.'

'No!' Maureen half rose from her seat and fell back as she realised what Sister Martin was telling her. 'Sally was with them...'

'Yes, so I understand,' Sister said gently. 'I believe you were good friends...'

'She's dead?' Maureen swallowed hard. It was hard to accept that the girl she'd come to love almost like a sister had been killed while out relaxing and enjoying herself. 'First Pam and now Sally...'

'Yes, your hut mates have both gone now. I shall either have to assign new inmates or move you, Nurse Jackson. Which would you prefer when you return from compassionate leave?'

'I'd like to stay where I am, Sister.'

'You don't feel that it's cursed?' Sister frowned. 'Someone said as much to me this morning, but I dismissed it as rubbish.'

'It is rubbish,' Maureen said firmly. 'Neither of them was killed at the hut – it isn't the hut, it's the damned war...'

'I couldn't agree more.' Sister smiled in approval. 'My opinion that you have the temperament for an excellent nurse has been confirmed. I am sending you home for two weeks – and then I shall expect you to return ready for work.'

'Thank you,' Maureen said. 'The funeral...?'

'Sally's parents have been informed. What remains will be collected and a service may be held to commemorate her life. From what I hear, there isn't much left of anyone to bury.'

Maureen felt the vomit rise in her throat. She'd guessed something of the sort, but to hear it put into words was horrifying.

'You may go, nurse,' Sister said and handed her a pass. 'I am sorrier than I can tell you. It is most unfortunate to lose two good friends in this way.'

'Yes...' Maureen's eyes stung with tears.

She walked away quickly because she couldn't trust herself not to break down. Sally was gone – and what would that mean to her parents? Sally's father might be a cold, hard man who didn't care, but his wife had cared. Even though Sally's mother had loved her son most, she'd cared for her daughter – and now she had lost them both.

Outside in the compound, Maureen spewed out the vile vomit she'd held back in Sister's office. Her chest felt as if it had a ten-ton weight sitting on it, and her throat was raw with grief, but she couldn't cry yet. It hurt too much. Maureen would telephone Sally's home when she got to London, because she wanted to attend the funeral – the church service anyway. She knew Sally's father would not want her at any reception they might hold.

Feeling numb with grief, Maureen went through the motions of packing her things. The last time she'd been to London was for Sally's brother's funeral and now Sally was dead too.

It was almost more than she could bear. She avoided looking at Sally's things, because it was too painful. They'd become so close and now it was over. Sally was dead and Maureen felt as if she'd been turned into stone...

Chapter 15

Peggy had a bit of a struggle to do her skirt up that morning. It was all the bread and pastry she ate these days, because there wasn't much of anything else. She managed to close the zip at last, but realised it looked awful and took it off again, putting on a dress with a pleated skirt and short sleeves, which fitted much better. Satisfied, she went downstairs and got on with her work, leaving Nellie to take the last batch of pasties out when she went through to the bar to open up. She'd only just taken the cloths off the pumps when the door opened and someone walked in.

'Maureen, love...' Peggy's smile slipped as she saw the look in the girl's eyes. She put the bar flap up and came round to offer a hug, which Maureen accepted gratefully. 'What's happened?'

'It was a bomb...' Maureen choked as Peggy led her behind the bar and through to the kitchen, leaving Janet in charge of the bar. 'Sally and some others – fifteen of them – went to a pub for a night out and they were all killed in a direct hit.'

'Oh, my God!' Peggy felt the tears sting her eyes as she took her friend into her arms and held her, and for some minutes they just wept together. It was such a shocking thing to happen that she would have felt like crying even if she hadn't known any of them personally, but she'd really liked

Sally and thought of her as a girl she would love to know better. 'That poor, tragic girl...'

'She asked me to go with them, but I wanted to study for my exams so I said I wouldn't...'

'Thank goodness you didn't,' Peggy said. 'I would've lost another friend and I just can't bear it...' She took out her handkerchief and wiped her face, blowing her nose. 'Do you remember Jim Stillman – he always brought me a box of vegetables from his allotment every week?' Maureen nodded. 'He was killed two weeks ago. He was helping clear some rubble from one of the bombed-out sites and there was another device no one knew about. It went off and killed two of the volunteers...'

'This bloody war!' Maureen said, anger bringing her head up fiercely. 'I thought after that night in May, when half of London looked like it was on fire, the Germans had had enough for a while, but it seems they've transferred their attentions elsewhere. We're not the only ones catching it now. Coventry, Liverpool, Birmingham and a lot of the industrial towns are getting it worse.'

'I think they thought if they could destroy London it would break us, but when that didn't work they decided to hit areas that are crucial to the war effort, factories and shipping – besides, our boys in blue gave them a bloody nose when they thought to invade us...'

'I know we expect them to try to hit the factories and the ports and airfields,' Maureen said, 'but it makes me sick to my stomach when they hit the hospital or just drop their damned bombs on random targets...'

Peggy nodded, because she felt the same way. 'I expect we're doing the same to them; according to the papers our raids on Germany are killing thousands,' she said, 'but killing innocent men, women and children doesn't help anyone...'

Maureen swallowed hard. 'I'd like to telephone Sally's parents and find out when the funeral will be...'

'You can use my phone,' Peggy offered. 'I'll make you a cup of tea and you can ring them now. Go into the hall...'

She busied herself about the kitchen, bringing out a fat-less sponge filled with her own strawberry jam, and setting the large brown pot on a tray. She'd just filled it with boiling water when Maureen walked in looking distressed.

'They must be terribly upset...' Peggy said. 'It was awful for you, having to ask about the funeral...'

Maureen looked fit to burst. 'Sally's father answered. He said it would be a small service for family only and then he put the phone down. She didn't have much family and I know she'd want me to be there...'

'He really is a horrid man,' Peggy said. 'It's no wonder Sally didn't want to be at her home more than she had to. Don't worry, love. I'm sure we can find out where it is somehow – and we'll go together. They can't stop us attending the service even if we're not invited to the reception.'

'I wouldn't go to that anyway,' Maureen said. 'I just thought I'd like to attend the funeral, but now...' She lifted her head proudly. 'No, you're right, Peggy. They can't stop us going to the funeral even if they ignore us – and it will be Christ Church in Southwark; it was for her brother...'

'Sit down and have a cup of tea,' Peggy suggested. 'We've all lost friends in this awful war. I just don't know where it will end...'

'I hope we win,' Maureen said fiercely. 'I hope they make that bloody Hitler pay for what he's done...'

'We'll win,' Peggy said confidently, even though the newspapers were busy spreading gloom and doom. 'If you read what he's doing to the Jews you can't doubt he's an evil man. We're in the right, so we've got to win haven't we?'

'It makes you wish you were a man so you could go and shoot them...'

Peggy shook her head. 'We have the worst of it, love. We're the ones that have to wait and worry. I reckon we're doing a good job now, especially you working all hours as a nurse.'

Maureen sighed. 'I just want to hit back for Sally...'

'Yes, I know. Alice was in here yesterday and she said the same thing about Jim Stillman, but all we can do is pray and hope, Maureen. We'll pray for Sally in church and perhaps that will ease your pain a little.'

*

The church was almost empty: just Sally's parents, an elderly woman who might have been her grandmother, and two young women who had probably gone to school with her. Peggy and Maureen sat a few rows behind them, and when Sally's father turned to look at them, Peggy stared him down. He was glaring at first but then he dropped his eyes and turned away as the service began.

It was short and there was only one hymn that no one but Peggy sang. Her sweet, pure voice rang out above the mumbled grunts which were all that came from those in front. Peggy looked at Maureen, saw the tears in her eyes and squeezed her hand, her voice clear and somehow all the more poignant for being the only one. She saw the vicar nod at her approvingly as they sat once more and he concluded the prayers.

Peggy and Maureen had agreed previously that they wouldn't follow out to the graveyard.

'I can visit and take flowers any time,' Maureen said, 'and I don't want to intrude.'

They left as the small party of mourners shuffled out behind the coffin-bearers. Maureen looked round the rows of neat graves and took note of where her friend was being buried, but they didn't wait. They'd had to catch a bus to come here and they went quickly to the stop and waited until another came along.

'Thank you for singing that beautiful hymn,' Maureen said. 'It was lovely. I think Sally would have appreciated it...'

'It was all I could do for her,' Peggy said. 'She was a lovely girl, Maureen, and I feel sorry that her life was cut short like that. So many folk are losing people they care about, but it was all so cold and clinical – and Sally deserved more.'

'Yes, she did, but I don't think people like her parents understand love...' Maureen said, and Peggy agreed. Sally's parents seemed cold, unfeeling people who didn't deserve a warm and loving daughter like Sally had been.

However, two days later, Peggy was serving in the bar when the door opened and a woman entered. She was well dressed in a smart black coat with a grey felt hat and it was a few minutes before Peggy realised that she was Sally's mother.

'Mrs Barnes?' Peggy asked as the woman approached the bar rather tentatively. 'Can I help you? Have you come to see Maureen?'

'Yes – but I also wanted to thank you, for attending my daughter's service, and for singing the way you did. I couldn't sing a note that day and my husband never does, but it was so lovely – and my daughter was worthy of more...'

'Sally was a wonderful girl and she didn't deserve to die the way she did.' Peggy lifted the flap. 'Would you like to come through to the kitchen so that we can talk?'

'Can you leave the bar?'

'My daughter Janet will come through...'

Peggy had felt anger against Sally's family, but she could see that Mrs Barnes was grieving. Obviously, her husband ruled her life and he'd wanted the small service, but Sally's mother had felt it wasn't right.

'Thank you – you're very kind. You don't know me and I dare say you've heard nothing that makes you think I deserve anything other than what I've got...'

'Now why should I think that? I have no right or reason to judge you, Mrs Barnes.'

Sally's mother blinked and brushed at her cheek with her hand. Clearly upset and emotional, she was barely holding herself in check.

Janet went straight through to the bar, leaving Peggy and her guest in the kitchen. Maggie was building bricks in the playpen and Peggy saw her visitor look at her with what was obviously envy.

'You're so lucky to have a grandchild. I'd hoped I might – but it won't happen now...'

'I'm sorrier for your loss than you can imagine,' Peggy said. 'Maggie is a joy and I adore her, as Janet does. Her husband was injured at sea and he's in hospital so that makes the child even more precious to us...'

'I'm sorry to hear about her husband,' Mrs Barnes said. 'Do you run the pub on your own, Mrs Ashley?'

'Please call me Peggy,' she said with a smile. 'I have help – Nellie does a lot of my cleaning for me and I have friends who come in and help with the bar. Maureen isn't here much, but she will give me a hand when she is – and there are others...'

'I have so few friends...' Mrs Barnes sighed. 'My husband was never very sociable, but now... it's as if he's closed right down and won't speak to anyone. He hardly speaks to me some days – I've lost the friends I once used to ask in for dinner...'

'I'm very sorry,' Peggy said. 'I expect he is grieving...'

'Is he?' Mrs Barnes shook her head. 'He seems to be angry rather than grieving, as if he thought the children did it on purpose – especially Sally. He never wanted her to be a nurse and he was furious when they told us she was in a pub. My husband isn't fond of public houses...' she faltered. 'If he knew I'd come here he would be angry.'

'Then don't tell him,' Peggy said. 'Men shouldn't think they can dominate our lives in every respect, Mrs Barnes. A woman needs some freedoms.'

'Your husband doesn't help in the pub?'

'He's away workin' for... the government,' Peggy said, unsure of how to describe Laurie's job. 'Even if he were here, I shouldn't allow him to control my life. I never have...'

'Mr Barnes is so difficult. If I try to object or be independent he makes my life intolerable. It isn't just the silence or the reproachful looks. He pushes his food away and shuts himself in his office – he has many ways of punishing me...' Tears were rolling down her face. 'I'm not sure why I told you that – I've never spoken of it to anyone, even the children, though I think my son knew. He tried to protect me many times and he said I should leave Mr Barnes...'

'Why don't you?' Peggy asked. 'It's never been easier for a woman to find work than it is now. Why stay with a man like that when you could have a different life?'

'I suppose I've always been too timid. I have nothing of my own – he gives me only the housekeeping money. Everything else is paid by him...'

'Find a job and somewhere to live,' Peggy advised. 'Have you nothing at all you could sell?'

'I suppose the silver candlesticks are mine. My father left them to me and I have a valuable cameo brooch that belonged to my grandmother...' Mrs Barnes was clearly considering the idea of leaving her husband.

Peggy gave her a measuring look. 'If you decided to leave you could come here. I have a room you can use – and I always need help in the bar. I dare say it isn't what you're used to, but it might be a way to make the break and then you could find more suitable work. Did you work before you married?'

'I typed letters and accounts for my father...'

'Well, then. Come here while you take a course to refresh your skills and then look for a job as a typist...' Peggy smiled at her. 'What should I call you?'

'My name is Helen...' she smiled tremulously. 'You're so kind and caring. I've never met anyone like you, Peggy...'

'Well the offer is there,' Peggy said. 'Now, could you do with a teaspoonful of brandy in your tea? I certainly could...'

*

Peggy smiled as Helen thanked her and left the pub. Maureen, who had recently returned from visiting Rory, had brought her through and seemed thoughtful as she watched Sally's mother leave.

Raising her brows, Peggy invited her friend to talk. 'What did she actually come for?'

'She wondered if I would like any of Sally's things. Apparently, she has some nice clothes and Helen wondered if I could make use of them – it being so difficult to find anything decent in the shops. She probably just wanted to apologise for the way her husband spoke to me when I rang...'

'Yes, I expect so,' Peggy said. 'I think she's very lonely – she might leave her husband and come here for a while...'

'Never! I wouldn't have thought she would ever leave him. She has a posh house, and her clothes are good, though not very fashionable...'

'Even if she has all you say and more, she's very unhappy and I think she's frightened of Mr Barnes...'

'I'm not surprised. Sally was too, even though she stood up to him. Well, I hope Helen does walk out on him; he deserves it. Only, if she does, he might come here and drag her back...'

'No, I don't think so,' Peggy said. 'Bullies are usually cowards. If he tries anything with me he'll be sorry...'

Maureen burst out laughing. 'I believe it. Oh, Peggy. I'm so glad I've got you and Gran...' Tears were hovering beneath the surface and she smothered a sob.

'What's wrong, love?' Peggy asked.

'It's Rory,' Maureen said. 'We had a row. He demanded that I give up my job and come back and marry him – and I said I was going to train to be a proper nurse, take all the exams, and he said some awful things...'

'Oh dear...' Peggy put an arm about her shoulders. 'Is he sure he isn't still married to Velma?'

'He managed to get confirmation of her prior marriage to someone called Fred Brown and he reckons that makes it all right for us to marry...' Maureen drew a deep breath. 'I don't know what to do, Peggy...'

'He'll get over it,' Peggy said. 'He has to have a lot of treatment yet – besides, I'm not sure you could just walk out of your job like that. You must have signed a contract...'

'I would have to give notice or just get married. They would probably throw me out then – that's what Rory says...'

'What do *you* want, love?' Peggy looked at her. 'Are you sure he's the right one for you?'

'I love Rory; at least, I think I do...' Maureen sighed because recently she'd begun to wonder if she'd been deceiving herself. Rory knew how to turn on the charm when he chose and she'd been swept off her feet as a young girl, but then he'd married Velma. Now his marriage was over and he seemed to think he had a right to dictate to Maureen. She didn't like his moods or his sullen manner when he wasn't getting his own way, yet her conscience pricked at her, making her feel it would be mean to walk out on him when he'd been badly injured. 'It's just... I've begun to enjoy my work, Peggy. I feel it's worthwhile and I don't want to give it up. I begged him to wait, but he says if I loved him I'd want to be with him. He says he needs me here...'

'He probably does,' Peggy said fairly. 'It's your choice though, Maureen. I think you have to consider your options carefully. You know what happened before and if you don't do as he asks...'

'He'll find someone else like last time?' Maureen lifted her head. 'If he loved me, surely he'd wait. There's nothing stoppin' him gettin' a transfer to another hospital – one near me – why should it be me who has to give in all the time?'

'I can't answer that,' Peggy said. 'You're the only one that knows what you really feel – but if it were me I'd make it clear that I wasn't going to give my job up. If you let him dominate you, he might become a tyrant.'

'Yes, and I've had enough of that...' Maureen bit her lip. 'I'll have to think carefully, won't I?'

'Just take your time, love.'

Maureen nodded and walked out of the kitchen, leaving through the back door and making her way from the pub yard.

Peggy watched her go and her heart ached for her friend. Loving was never easy and Maureen had had more problems in her love life than most – but, if it were down to Peggy, she would think very carefully before throwing up the job she liked to marry a man who seemed to think she was there just for his convenience...

*

Maureen walked back to Gran's, enjoying the warm sunshine. The streets around her looked dingy and forlorn: so many derelict buildings like skeletons against the sky, waiting for demolition, and the evidence of the heavy bombing everywhere. Grass was beginning to push its way through on some of the derelict sites, and billboards reminded them it was illegal to buy on the black market and exhorted women to go into the factories. When would this awful war end? According to the papers there was no end in sight, nor did it look good for the Allies; resources were running low and the country was staggering under the heavy burden of war. Maureen felt as if they were all trapped in an ongoing nightmare from which there was no escape. Her heart was heavy because she hated being at odds with Rory and it made her unhappy when they had a row. However, Rory was becoming very demanding and she'd begun to wonder whether she would be happy as his wife. She'd always worked and, even when she'd been tied to her father, she'd clung to a measure of independence. Once she was married, Rory would expect her to be there all the time and if children came along it would be an end to her dreams of doing something different with her life, being more than her father thought she could be.

Why did life have to be so difficult? Maureen was frowning as she ran across the street during a lull in the traffic, heading towards Gran's. Sister Martin had given her two weeks' leave, but after eight days she'd had enough of shopping and doing nothing much. Gran liked having her there at night, but she would understand that Maureen felt she ought to be back at the hospital, where she was needed. Lost in her thoughts, she didn't notice the young man who was staring at her until he put out a hand and touched her arm.

'Maureen…' She turned and gasped as she saw herself looking into Gordon's smiling eyes.

'Oh, Gordon,' she said, and the swell of emotion nearly made her cry. 'It's so good to see you. I had no idea you were back home on leave.'

'I've been given a few days before I go on a new training course,' he said and looked at her intently. 'They'll be shippin' me out again after… but it doesn't matter about me. Somethin' is upsettin' you, love.'

'Yes…' She blinked hard. 'How long have you got?'

'As long as you need,' he said. 'I'm going down to see Shirley tomorrow but I have all afternoon and evening...'

'Can we have a coffee and talk?' she said. 'I wrote to you about Sally but you probably haven't got it...' She swallowed a sob and took his arm. 'It's just so lovely to see you...'

'Let's have that coffee and this evening I'll take you out for a meal,' Gordon said and smiled at her. 'You know I'm always there for you if you need me?'

'Yes...' Maureen smiled, feeling a little shy. She did know that Gordon cared for her and she'd learned to trust him, and through his letters to like him more and more. 'It's about whether I should give up my job...'

*

'It's not my place to tell you whether you should marry Rory or not,' Gordon told her, looking at her a little sadly as they sat over their coffee. 'Only you know if you love him – but I would just ask you to be certain before you give up a job you enjoy. Nurses are needed badly just now and I think he should try to be a little bit understanding... but whatever happens, remember you have friends.'

As she lay in bed later that night, Maureen's thoughts returned to the talk they'd had and then the pleasant few hours she'd shared with Gordon that evening. They'd settled on fish and chips at a café and it had been lovely, just talking about Maureen's work and Shirley, as well as all the gossip from the lanes. Gordon had walked her home afterwards. He'd given her a kiss on the cheek and looked into her eyes.

'Don't let anyone make you unhappy,' he'd said and held her hand for a moment longer. 'And don't forget I'm always your friend.'

Maureen sighed as she turned over in bed. Her emotions were tangled and twisted this way and that, unable to settle. If only Rory were as gentle and considerate as Gordon, how happy she would be...

Chapter 16

'You're looking happy this morning,' Peggy said as Anne entered the pub and came over to the bar. 'Did you win the football pools?'

Anne laughed and shook her head, her light brown hair falling attractively across her face because she'd had it cut shorter in a shaped bob. She was wearing a pretty yellow and white cotton dress and some strappy cream leather sandals with Cuban heels and looked very attractive.

'No, something better than that – I've been given the task of setting up a new school. Well, the building isn't new; it was an old warehouse, but it's been tidied up and made habitable for the kids – and we're hoping to open in time for the autumn term.'

'Are there enough children in London to make it worthwhile?' Peggy questioned.

'More than you might think,' Anne said cheerfully. 'Most parents sent their children away before the bombing started, but it looks as if the Germans have forgotten about London for the moment. We may get the occasional raid, but not that awful blitz night after night. I think they're busy on other fronts now, particularly in Russia – though a lot of the coastal towns are catching it instead of us.' Anne looked thoughtful. 'Quite a few children have returned to London, some under their own steam; others have been fetched back by parents who aren't comfortable with their children being away from them... so we're going to get this temporary school going...'

'Right, that will keep you busy...'

'I'll be in London permanently and that's what I want,' Anne said. 'I can still help you sometimes in the evenings – and there's another reason I'd like to be here more...'

Peggy nodded, a smile flicking at the corners of her mouth. 'I thought there was something else... Come on, you have to tell me now. I'll ask Janet to cover while we have a cuppa and a chat in the kitchen...'

There were only two regulars sitting quietly in the corner and it was unlikely they would have a rush, because the beer delivery was late again and Peggy had a sign in the window to say there was none available. She sometimes thought if it were not for her food and the coffee Able supplied from time to time, she might as well close up for the duration. She wouldn't be the first. Several public houses in the district had boarded up their premises and the landlords had retired or gone away. Peggy was determined to hang on to the bitter end, and her reasoning was that if others gave up there would eventually be more beer for her and her customers.

Leading the way through to the kitchen, Peggy settled her friend with a cup of tea and a coconut bun she'd made that morning, having been fortunate enough to purchase some desiccated coconut at Maureen's father's shop. Peggy still kept it as her regular supplier, even though the service wasn't as friendly and sometimes they seemed to run out of everything she needed.

'Now tell me all of it...' she said, because she could see that Anne was bursting to pass on her news.

'I met him at the railway station,' Anne said, bubbling over. 'The train was packed and he gave up his seat for me and stood in the corridor until there was a vacant seat – and then we got talking...' Her eyes sparkled. 'He works for the Ministry of Food and he travels a lot, inspecting farms and abattoirs...' Anne laughed. 'I know, it sounds awful, but, as John said, someone has to enforce the laws or we might not have enough to go round; then we would have riots and people fighting each other on the streets. Poor man, he says that he feels he's public enemy number one – but it's not his fault that rations are continually being cut. We've got to live within our means, Peggy – and there's only so much our farmers can do...'

'Yes, I know,' Peggy agreed. 'I sometimes curse the government for making it so hard these days, and I don't know what I'd do if...' she shook her head, because it wasn't wise to talk about Able's gifts too openly, even with a friend. 'Well, as you say, it's no one's fault. We've all got to manage as best we can.'

'Yes, it's the only way.' Anne looked thoughtful. 'John says some people are making a fortune on the black market from stuff they've hidden from his ministry or stolen goods, but they're going to crack down on the people who trade in goods like that...'

'Well, I suppose they have to.' Peggy felt vaguely uncomfortable, because some people might say that she was guilty of using black-market goods – except that hers were a present. In her heart she knew that if she got caught selling American bourbon she would probably be in for a heavy fine at least. Thank goodness there were only a couple of bottles left in the cellar... She would have to make sure that Able didn't repeat his generous gesture in the future.

Anne stopped for an hour and then went out the back way, leaving through the yard. Peggy frowned as she watched her friend walk away. She was sure Anne had no idea that Peggy had been using goods that might come under the heading of illegal. Morally, she felt no guilt at all at taking the gift, because Able had done it out of the goodness of his heart, to make up for the stock she'd lost when the bomb hit, but Peggy could just imagine what people would think if she got had up for trading on the black market. Some of them might wink and tell her they didn't blame her, but others would definitely stop coming in.

Able hadn't been in for a couple of weeks and she was a bit anxious about him. He'd told her he would be away for a while, but she had an uneasy feeling that things were not as they should be. Yet she knew she was probably just being silly and overanxious. It was because he'd become so important to her and she wanted him around all the time.

Peggy smiled to herself. At first she'd been nervous of giving up what she had, even though it was far from perfect, but since she had spent those few days with Able she knew what she wanted – and that was to be with the man she loved for the rest of her life. It was just finding a way to do that without ripping her children's lives apart...

*

'What yer, Mr Ashley. Are yer home fer good?'

Laurence paused in the street as he saw the youth pulling a wooden crate on wheels that was just now filled with vegetables. It took a moment for him to recognise the lad, because he'd shot up in the past few months and looked older than his years.

'Tommy Barton?' he said. 'Where did you get that lot from?'

'Jim Stillman's wife let me take over 'er 'usband's allotment,' Tom said and smiled his satisfaction. 'I used to 'elp 'im sometimes and so his missus said if I give her some of the veg each week, I could keep the rest – I'm sellin' this lot, and then I'll take some 'ome fer Ma.'

'Well done you,' Laurence said. 'I imagine Peggy will buy some from you if you ask her.'

'She already has, thanks,' Tom said. 'This makes a big difference to me, Mr Ashley. I'll be able to keep Ma in veg and sell the surplus – if they let me hang on to the allotment.'

'Yes, that's the problem,' Laurence said. 'You're a bit young yet – but perhaps if Mrs Stillman agrees to keep it in her name, you can give her the rent for it.'

'Good idea. Thanks,' Tom said and grinned at him, before starting off down the street to knock on doors and ask if anyone wanted any veg from his cart.

Laurence paused outside the pub and looked at the door, noticing that it showed signs of damage and the beautiful stained glass had gone. He knew that the pub had suffered some damage in a raid in the spring and cursed himself for not having had the rare glass taken out and stored below in the cellar, where it would have had more chance of surviving.

As he pushed open the door and went in, he saw that a few regulars were sitting at the tables, but there was nowhere near the busy rush that had been the lunchtime norm before the war. Janet was serving a woman, wearing a turbaned headscarf, with a cup of tea and one of Peggy's pasties. She glanced at him and frowned but then offered a slight smile when he approached the bar.

'Hello, Dad,' she said. 'Does Mum know you're coming today?'

'I didn't ring because I wasn't sure until the last moment,' he told her. 'I was coming home a few weeks ago but then we had a flap on and all leave was cancelled. I've only got three days, but I thought I should make the effort...'

'I should've thought you'd be pleased to come home, even if only for a few days...' Janet threw him a challenging look. 'Mum's in the kitchen. She managed to get some fruit in the market and she's making jam and crumbles...'

'I'll go through and surprise her,' Laurence said. 'I've got a box of stuff which I think she'll find useful in the car outside...'

'Did you come by car?' Janet questioned, her brows rising. 'Where did that come from all of a sudden?'

'I borrowed it from a friend,' Laurence said. 'He wasn't using it for a few days so he said I could take it if I liked.'

'That was good of him,' Janet said and turned away to serve another young woman with a tomato and paste roll.

Her tone sounded sceptical so Laurence ignored her and walked through to the kitchen, because although he'd forgiven her, there was still some resentment towards his daughter. Peggy wasn't there; nor was she upstairs, so he went out to the car and fetched in the farm foodstuffs he'd managed to buy. Two hares, fresh salmon, line caught by the same friend that had loaned him the car, some farm butter and a large punnet of gooseberries. He hoped to put a smile on his wife's face with the gifts, because he'd come to a decision. The pub might not be doing so well while the war was on, but it was a good business and he didn't want to lose it – or Peggy. She was an asset that he couldn't afford to throw away, and now that he was feeling less bereft over Marie's loss he knew he had to make it up with his wife.

Just as he had finished unpacking the box, Peggy entered carrying two whisky bottles. She started as she saw Laurence. Placing the bottles on the kitchen table, she turned to look at him, her expression puzzling him. He wasn't sure whether he was welcome or not and frowned. Noticing she'd had her hair cut shorter, he thought she was looking younger, brighter.

'Laurie, this is a surprise – when did you get back?' She looked at him uncertainly. 'You didn't say you were coming.'

'I couldn't let you know because until the last minute I wasn't sure…'

'It doesn't matter,' Peggy said. 'You don't have to ask; this is your home.'

'Is it?' he asked and saw her frown. 'Have I turned you against me completely, Peggy – or is there still a chance for us?'

'Do you want the truth?'

'Yes, of course.'

'Well… it depends on what you're hoping for…'

Laurence nodded, sucking in his breath and then letting it out slowly. 'I'm hoping we can go back to being husband and wife – and when the war is over I thought we might have a few holidays, maybe think about moving to a country pub like you always wanted…'

'I'm not sure what I want at this moment,' Peggy said, and he saw that it was costing her to put her thoughts into words. 'It's too far off and too uncertain to talk about at the moment, but it's over as far as our marriage is concerned. We might manage friends for now…'

Laurence nodded, realising that he was pushing her too far too quickly. Peggy had been hurt and perhaps he was taking too much for granted. 'Yes, I know you must think I've behaved badly...'

Peggy shrugged but didn't answer.

He wondered what was behind the guilty looks at the bottles she'd brought up from the cellar and then he realised that the labels were American.

'Where did this come from?' he demanded, suddenly angry. 'You damned fool! If you've been buying black-market stuff you could lose me my licence...'

'Able gave it to me,' Peggy said defensively, 'after we took that terrific hit on the pub. There was glass everywhere – bottles and glasses were lost. Able brought a whole load of stuff over but I don't use it in the bar in those bottles. I take the labels off and decant it into one I've emptied...'

'You should've refused it,' Laurence said. 'It might be construed as dealing even if no money changed hands... especially if there was a lot. Just how many bottles did he give you?'

'About four boxes... as well as some foodstuffs,' Peggy answered reluctantly. 'I've already decided I'll tell him not to do it again, but we'd lost a lot and he was just being thoughtful... considerate of me...'

His eyes narrowed as he saw the guilt in her eyes. 'Why should an American we hardly know be considerate of you?' he asked, his anger mounting. He'd been thinking she was hurt because of what he'd done and he'd felt a bit mean, but now he understood that she'd retaliated in kind and it stung. He'd expected Peggy to be waiting for him to come back to her, not having an affair of her own. 'You may not have paid him in money, Peggy – but what else have you given him?

Surely you haven't been that stupid? The man's years younger than you; he'll be laughing with his friends over how easy you were – just another silly English woman too ready to slip off her knickers for a few favours...'

'That is a rotten thing to say to me,' Peggy said, flushed, and walked over to the sink to start splashing water on the label of an empty bottle.

'What are you doing?'

'Removing the label before I put them in the rubbish...'

'Where's the sense in that? It just makes us look as if we're doing something underhand. Leave that and put the full bottles in your store cupboard. You can use them for cooking – that way if we were searched the story about them being a gift would ring true.'

'I can't use whisky in cakes and stuff when we could do with it in the bar...'

'Well, this is still my pub and I'm telling you. I don't want that stuff being sold over the bar. You'll do as I tell you or I'll smash them both and throw the contents down the sink...' Laurence approached her, grabbing her arm roughly and glaring at her. 'I know you thought you were entitled to get back at me – but you've had your fun and now it stops. Do you hear me?'

'Able was just...' Peggy looked up and he saw the change come into her face: defiance, pride and anger. 'Yes, all right, we have been lovers – but that still has nothing to do with Able's gift to me. He's in love with me and he wants me to leave you when I'm ready and go away with him... and I think that might be quite soon.'

For a moment Laurence was fit to murder her but something in her eyes stopped him. She looked young and proud, very like the woman he'd married – the woman he'd thought he was in love with until time and life got in the way. He'd taken her for granted and maybe she'd felt hurt and neglected – and he'd wanted Marie. If she walked back into his life, Laurence knew he would probably wish Peggy good luck and walk away, but he also knew that he would never see Marie again.

News had filtered through that the Germans had tortured and then killed her, and Laurence had wanted to die of the pain; it was the reason he hadn't come back for months, and now he realised that he'd taken too much for granted. He'd expected he would have to make a fuss of his wife to get her on side, but now he saw it would take a lot more than he'd imagined. Peggy loved the pub and her friends, but it wasn't enough for a passionate woman like her; she wanted more of life. And at the moment she didn't want him.

'Mum...' Janet's voice from the kitchen doorway broke into his thoughts. 'Is everything all right?'

Peggy looked at her and nodded, a grim little smile on her lips as she shook off Laurence's hand. 'I'll come back now – are you busy or something?'

'No, Mum, there's a couple of people to see you... friends of Able...'

'Able's friends... Why would...?'

Laurence saw the colour stripped from his wife's face. In that moment he knew that the young American serviceman had meant more than just a fling to her. Whatever was between them it was serious.

Peggy went through the kitchen and the hallway into the pub's bar. Laurence followed her, waiting just inside the door where he could see and hear but not be noticed.

'Yes, gentlemen,' Peggy said. 'What can I do for you?'

'Mrs Peggy Ashley?' one of the servicemen asked. 'My name is Tony Rivers. Able Ronoscki was a friend of yours I understand?'

'Yes, Able is a friend...' Peggy's face was ashen and Laurence saw her clench her fists. 'Is something wrong?'

'I'm very much afraid I have bad news, ma'am,' Captain Rivers told her. 'Able's plane took off during rough weather in Belgium and it didn't arrive at its destination. It was a small two-seater and he and his pilot are eleven days overdue with no contact.' He handed her a letter. 'We found this amongst Captain Ronoscki's things and it's addressed to you... It also appears that he put you down as his next of kin. If his death is confirmed we shall be sending his things to you in time, but I thought you should be informed that he is missing, believed lost...'

'No...' Peggy swayed and fell backwards. Laurence shot forward, but Captain Rivers got there first and caught her, supporting her to the nearest chair. Janet poured water into a glass and as her mother came round she took it to her. 'Oh no...'

'I'm very sorry to upset you, Mrs Ashley...' the American said, distressed.

'No...' Peggy sat up straight and swallowed hard. Her hands were shaking and she looked on the verge of collapse. 'Has Able's family been told?'

'He may have had some relations, but no one he wanted contacted in the event of an emergency – yours was the only name he gave us as his next of kin...'

'I see...' Peggy was blinking, struggling against her tears, which were trickling down her cheeks. Laurence went forward and offered her a handkerchief.

'I think you should go to bed, Peggy. You've had a shock – I'm sure these gentlemen will excuse you…'

'No, no, I'm fine.' She pushed his hand away impatiently and looked at Captain Rivers. Her face was very pale as she said, 'You will keep me informed – if there is any news?'

'Yes, of course, ma'am,' the American said. 'Able was not a close friend of mine, but I'm sure some of his friends will call… anything we can do, of course…' He looked awkwardly at Laurence, who glared at him.

'Thank you, I'll be fine now. It was just the shock.'

'Go and sit down for a while in the kitchen,' Janet said, slipping an arm about her waist. 'Dad can look after the bar for once.'

'Yes, thanks, darling,' Peggy said and walked past Laurence without looking at him, but he could see the grief in her face and he felt a pain strike him in the chest, but wasn't sure whether it was for his wife's distress or his own. Clearly, she had loved the young American and his loss meant more to her than the rupture in their marriage.

The American officers took a rather hasty leave. Laurence guessed they'd known something was going on between Able and his wife and he felt a surge of anger and of humiliation. Common sense told him that he'd brought this on himself and he felt regret. He'd thrown away years of working together, love and laughter for… Marie. Yes, their brief liaison had been exciting and satisfying, but was it worth all he'd lost?

Perhaps he and Peggy would make things up in time, especially now that her young lover had been cruelly taken from her – but could it ever be the same?

*

176

Peggy was conscious of a dull ache all over her body as she lay in her solitary bed that night. She'd lain crying for hours, feeling as if she'd been mortally wounded; the happiness she'd been glowing with ebbed away, leaving a desert in its place. How could she go on living now that Able was gone? The pain of his loss was like a knife wound, causing her heart to bleed. She remembered his smile, the look in his eyes as he'd told her how much he loved her and the feel of his mouth on hers, the way their bodies fitted and the agony curled up into a ball inside her. No one had ever loved her the way Able did and she didn't know how she could get through life without him.

Able's letter was unopened under her pillow. Peggy couldn't bring herself to read the words, because it would be like turning a knife in the wound. She wanted him here beside her, holding her close, and she knew it most likely would never happen again.

Yet missing wasn't confirmed dead... Peggy tried to take comfort from the thought. Men did go missing and turn up again, but she knew in her heart that something was badly wrong. If Able were alive he would have contacted her somehow. His first thought would be for her. Peggy knew without a shadow of a doubt that if it were possible he would let her know... which meant that the most probable outcome was that he was dead.

She'd missed him and looked for him, but it had never occurred to her that something might have happened to him. He wasn't at war. Why should he be killed?

Once or twice she'd wondered why he hadn't been in; she'd even wondered if, as Laurie had implied, Able had tired of her once they'd had their weekend of love – but in her heart she'd known that Able's love for her had been so much more. She'd just believed he would visit when he could. He had truly been a blessing in her life, coming to her at a time when she really needed it, but now he was gone and she felt dead inside.

Laurie had taken his suitcase into the spare bedroom. He was being considerate, as though he understood what she was suffering. Peggy had acknowledged his care in her mind, though she said nothing. She wasn't sure about the future. Even before the terrible news, Peggy hadn't been certain that she dare rip her life apart for her own selfish desires, but now she knew that if Able walked in the door and said 'come', she would go. Except it was never going to happen. Her lover was dead and her youth had flown. All she had left now were her children and grandchildren...

Chapter 17

'I've got a bit of a pain in me chest, Violet love,' Henry Jackson said to his wife that morning as she put a plate of fried bacon, fried potato, fried bread and fried egg in front of him. He poured brown sauce all over it, because his wife's cooking wasn't anywhere near as good as Maureen's and he found her food a bit greasy these days, but grumbling never did any good. 'You've spoiled me, but I'm not really that 'ungry.'

'You're not goin' to waste good food after I've spent all that time cooking it especially for you?' Violet said and pulled a sour face. 'Honestly, there's no pleasing you these days. Eat it up, Henry, and then get out of my way. I've got an important customer comin' in soon and I don't want you cluttering up my sittin' room...'

Henry muttered under his breath as she poured a cup of tea and then went off into Maureen's bedroom. It was coming to something when he couldn't sit down in his own house; she was lucky he wasn't feeling up to giving her a piece of his mind. The only trouble was that Violet's tongue was sharp and these days he usually came off the worst.

It was no good, he couldn't stomach all that grease. Pushing back his chair, Henry left the room and went down to the shop. He rubbed at his chest as he fetched the papers in from the alley where the delivery van dumped them each morning. Humping them into the shop, he bent down to cut the string that tied them and for a moment the world went black.

'Are you all right, Mr Jackson?' a youth's voice broke through the fog after a few moments, and Henry stared groggily up at Tommy Barton.

'What 'appened?'

'I think you passed out for a moment,' Tom said, looking concerned. 'I came in to get a box of matches and a tin of corned beef and found you slumped over the papers, sir.'

'I was going to sort them...' Henry pulled himself up into a sitting position. 'Came over dizzy of a sudden. Can you give me a hand up, lad?'

'Yeah, all right. Do yer want me to tell yer missus – or fetch a doctor?'

'No, I'll be all right in a minute...' Henry puffed and moaned a bit as he got up, but then sighed with resignation. 'I think I'd better go up and 'ave a lie-down for a while. Do you reckon you could sort the papers for me, lad? You could look after the shop for an hour or two, couldn't you?'

'O' course I could, Mr Jackson – if you'll trust me to go to your till and take people's money.'

'I ain't got much choice,' Henry muttered and then shook his head as the lad frowned. 'No, I do trust you, Tom. I ain't always said as much, but everyone knows you're honest. Hang on 'ere until I sort meself out and then I'll give yer half a crown.'

'Yes, all right,' Tom said. 'I'll stay 'ere and serve folk until you come back.' He tipped his head to one side, considering. 'I reckon you miss your Maureen more than yer thought, Mr Jackson.'

'No business of yours,' Henry muttered. 'Don't give any credit and watch the kids don't pinch stuff – and if yer do all right, I'll give yer a regular job on Saturdays.'

'I'll need five bob for a Saturday,' Tom said. 'I've got a lot of customers these days, Mr Jackson, and I'll 'ave ter see if I can fit yer in...'

Henry gave him a dark look but he was still feeling a bit light-headed so he ignored the lad's grin and walked past him and back upstairs. He was going to have a lie-down, whether Violet liked it or not...

*

'Where 'ave yer been?' Tilly Barton demanded when her son walked in at half past eleven that morning. She was up to her elbows in hot water and soda in the sink and glared at him. 'I asked you to fetch some matches so I could light the copper hours ago...'

'Mr Jackson was took bad and 'ad to 'ave a lie-down,' Tom said, dodging as his mother aimed a wet slap at him. 'He asked me to look after the shop for him and he gave me half a crown and a tin of Spam cos he was pleased wiv me.'

'You were supposed to go to school this mornin',' his mother said crossly. 'I shall have the man from the School Board round 'ere after me if yer don't go to school – and that will cost me more than you earned this mornin'.'

'You can give me a note tomorrow, say I'd got the toothache,' Tom said and looked round for any sign of dinner. 'What's to eat today, Ma?'

'Get yerself a bit of bread and drippin' if yer 'ungry,' she said. 'I'll be cookin' teatime when yer should be 'ome. Why can't yer be sensible, Tommy? You'll end up 'avin' ter wait in line fer jobs like yer father did – and follow in his footsteps to the nick, I shouldn't wonder.'

'No, I shan't do that,' Tom said. 'Until they take me in the Army, I'm goin' ter work for meself, Ma. I've got three chimneys to clean this weekend, and Mr Jackson wants me to work Saturday mornin's fer 'im, but that only pays five bob – and Peggy pays me more to do jobs for 'er. I ain't sure yet whether I'm goin' ter oblige 'im. Like I said, I got a lot of customers now, Ma.'

His mother made a tutting sound and shook her head. 'Don't get too big fer yer boots, lad. Pride comes before a fall. That Peggy Ashley's been givin' yer work, but what yer goin' ter do when it runs out?' She gave him a cuff round his ear.

'I'll find more jobs,' Tom said. 'It's only until I'm eighteen and then I'm orf to the Army. I'd go now if they'd 'ave me. At least then I might get a smile or word of praise now and then...'

'Where are yer goin'?' his mother asked as he walked out of the back door.

'Alice asked me to chop some wood fer her,' he called over his shoulder. 'And I've got to measure her back windows and get some new glass to replace the windows that got blown out the other night. She's got cardboard up at the moment and she wants it done proper...'

'Go on then,' his mother said. 'Maybe you'll have time to chop some wood fer me when yer get back...'

*

'You've made a lovely job of them winders,' Alice Carter said as she admired Tom's handiwork. 'I wasn't sure if yer could do it, but yer've done well – as good as Mr Timms done fer Peggy when 'ers got blown out...'

'Thanks, Alice.' Tom smiled, because he liked doing jobs for the elderly woman who was always grateful for his efforts and paid him what she could afford. 'It cost seven shillings fer the glass and I'll charge yer a bob fer doin' them...'

'You'll take this and thank you very much,' Alice said and pressed a much-folded ten-shilling note in his hand. 'It would've cost me twice as much if the builder came out, lad. I'm very pleased so don't say no or I can't ask you again.'

'Thanks, Alice,' Tom said and pocketed the money. 'I'll just fetch in the coal fer yer and then I'll get orf 'ome.'

'Thanks, lad.' Alice hesitated, then, 'I don't know whether to tell you, Tommy lad – it's about your Sam...'

'What's he done now, Alice? If he's been teasin' yer cat I'll give 'im a slap.'

'No, it's somethin' more worryin',' Alice said. 'I went round to see Uncle Joe yesterday, popped me Auntie Myrtle's teapot again. He lets me pay a shillin' a week until I get it back...'

Tom nodded, because Uncle Joe was the pawnbroker in Artillery Lane and people often took their things to him for a loan, paying it back a bit at a time and a few pennies interest until it was repaid.

'What was Sam doin'...?' he frowned. 'He wasn't sellin' somethin' there?'

'I don't know for sure – but he came out with money in his hand and I saw a gold weddin' ring on the counter...'

Tom whistled, because there was no way his brother could've come by such a thing honestly. 'Thanks fer tellin' me, Alice.'

'I wasn't sure if I should – I don't like tellin' tales and I wouldn't tell anyone else, but 'e's been on the bomb sites again. I saw 'im meself and so did Peggy.'

'Right, I'll sort 'im. You did right, Alice. If Ma finds out she'll go crazy.'

'Yes, that's why I've told you,' Alice said. 'You're a hard-working lad, Tommy Barton, and it's a pity your brother isn't more like yer.'

*

'What are yer doin'?' Sam asked when he walked into the bedroom they shared that afternoon after school. His brother had got a tin box on the bed and he'd taken up the loose floorboard where Sam stored his treasures. Several pieces of gold and silver were spread on the white candlewick coverlet. 'Those things are mine.'

'Where did you get them, Sam?' Tom frowned at him. 'Or should I know? These came from the homes of dead people – or people who've been bombed and lost everythin'. How could yer? I've told yer and the police 'ave warned yer. A bit of scrap metal is one thing, even though you could be killed – but these things belong to someone else – and that's stealin'…'

'No one claims them,' Sam said. 'They're either dead or gone away. It takes a lot of searchin' ter find this stuff and I reckon it belongs ter me.'

'You've got ter 'and it in down the nick,' Tom said. 'I'm tellin' yer, Sam. Yer can't keep this stuff – not weddin' rings and jewellery, personal stuff. It's not right. If yer don't 'and it in I'll tell Ma – and she'll go to the coppers. Yer know what she's like over pinchin'…'

'It ain't nothin' ter do wiv yer,' Sam yelled and dived on the gold, swooping it into his trouser pocket. 'It ain't just me. Others are in it and I 'ave ter share...'

Tom shook his head at him. 'You'll end up in prison like Dad did,' he said. 'I've warned yer, Sam. Take that stuff down the nick and tell 'em where yer found it. That belongs to someone...'

'Yeah, me,' Sam said. 'You think yer so high and mighty, but I'm earning more than yer ever will wiv yer little jobs. I'm in with some people now and I'll be goin' somewhere; they told me to stick by 'em and they'd look after me. I ain't goin' ter be like you or Dad. I'll 'ave money and be someone – so just keep yer mouth shut or somebody might shut it fer yer. There's a lot of people keepin' an eye on me, so just yer be careful...'

Sam turned and shot out of the room, leaving Tom staring after him in frustration. It was impossible to deal with his brother. Their father might have been able to keep him in order but he was in prison and Sam ignored him and Ma. Apart from the danger of unexploded bombs, Sam was digging a hole for himself that could only lead to trouble in the future. Tom could just imagine what sort of people his brother had got in with and there was nothing he could do except hope that Sam came to his senses before the police discovered what he was doing.

Chapter 18

Maureen was filled with trepidation when she approached the noticeboard. Most of the young nurses were clustered around it, trying to see where their name was on the list and giving squeaks of excitement or walking away with a look of disappointment in their eyes, their heads down. Unable to get to the front of the crowd without shoving, Maureen saw some of her friends' names mid-list and looked further down. She couldn't see her name anywhere.

'You clever thing, you!' A girl called Rita tapped her on the shoulder. 'Look where you came – talk about a dark horse!'

'I haven't seen...' Maureen craned. 'I hoped I might come halfway...'

Rita gave a crack of laughter. 'You're only second from top... Bettina, the swot, is top of course, but you're second. Well done, you!'

'Second...' Maureen felt as if all her breath had been squashed out of her. 'I can't believe it...'

'You can truly call yourself a nurse now,' Rita said. 'Just a few more exams and you'll have half a chance of knowing what you're doing...'

Maureen giggled, feeling a rush of excitement. 'I think that's going to take years,' she said. 'But at least I'm getting the hang of what they actually let us do… and I never thought I'd get past scrubbing pans.'

'You'll be Sister's pet now,' Rita said. 'Several of us are going out for a celebration this evening – are you coming?'

'Are you sure they want me along?' Maureen asked, because she knew that some of the nurses thought of her as a Jonah and sometimes tried to shut her out of group conversations. A few girls like Rita were friendly, but many of them looked at her and whispered about the two hut mates who had been killed. 'I know some of the girls think I'm cursed or somethin'.'

'That's just nonsense,' Rita said. 'I've been living with you for weeks and I'm still around…'

'Don't challenge fate!' Maureen said and squeezed Rita's arm. She was the only nurse who would move into the fated hut and they had a beginner in with them too. Carol was terribly shy and hardly spoke to any of them, but so far she hadn't actually shunned Maureen, and both she and Rita were trying to help the girl through the dark days of her initiation as a probationer.

Maureen still felt the pain of Sally's loss. In a few short months they'd become so close and there was an aching void when she looked at Rita in Sally's bed and knew she would never see the girl she'd loved like a sister again.

She sighed as she walked away from the noticeboard and the thinning crowd of excited girls. Rory's latest letter was still in her drawer. Maureen hadn't been able to bring herself to open it, because she knew that once again he would demand she gave up her job to marry him. Sometimes as she tossed and turned on her lumpy mattress and felt every bone in her body ache she thought she must be mad. How many times had she wished that Rory were free to marry her? Now he was begging her to get married and she wanted to wait.

'It makes no sense you being down there,' he'd told her before she left London to return to her job. 'I'll be out of here once I have my last little op and then I'll find a job and we'll get married...'

'No, Rory, not yet,' Maureen had told him. 'I'm doing well in my nursin' now and I want to stay and pass my exams and be a proper nurse. Nurses can go on workin' forever if they want and I'll always have a job.'

'What you're sayin' is that you don't trust me to look after you,' Rory had said, looking sulky. 'The Army won't send me back out there after this lot... I can ask for a job here in London and...'

'But you could come down to Portsmouth if they discharge you and find work there. I'm sure there are plenty of jobs where I am...'

'I'll still be in the Army, but probably workin' as a mechanic, which is what I'm trained for after all. I still have to go where they send me...'

'You could try, couldn't you? Ask for somethin' down that way...'

'You've changed,' Rory accused and scowled at her. 'You were always such a gentle, obligin' girl...'

'I had years at Dad's beck and call and I want a chance to please myself for a while...' Maureen said.

'What you're really sayin' is you don't want to marry me.' He'd glared at her, but she'd seen the hurt in his eyes. 'I don't think you ever did. If you had, you would have told your father we were gettin' married.'

'That isn't true,' Maureen had said. 'Please don't be angry, Rory. I do love you and I want to marry you one day – but not just yet...'

Rory had hunched his shoulders and turned away from her. She'd landed a kiss on the side of his face even though he pulled his head away, but in the end she'd had to leave him with their quarrel unresolved. It had lingered with her since she'd returned to duty, though she didn't have time to worry about it when she was on the wards.

There was a constant flow of wounded men in the hospital as the casualties mounted. They were primarily from the Armed Forces, but when there were casualties in the town or factories they had civilian patients, which meant that the wards were always filled to capacity.

Maureen worked the equivalent of one and a half normal shifts before Sister Martin told her that she looked dead on her feet and should go to bed before she did something stupid. Even when she was being considerate she sounded grumpy, but Maureen knew her better now and they actually got on very well.

As she was leaving, Sister congratulated her on her exam results, which left Maureen with a little glow inside as she made her weary way back to the hut she shared with Rita and Carol. Both girls were sitting on their beds talking excitedly as she entered, and Rita burst out laughing, winking at Carol as though they shared a secret.

'What?' Maureen asked, bewildered.

'Who is the dark horse then?' Rita demanded. 'You didn't tell us you'd got a hero for a boyfriend...'

'What do you mean?' She looked at them in bewilderment.

'He's been here looking for you. The guards let him through because he was in uniform – he's obviously been wounded serving his country. He told us he'd been posted down here...'

'Rory...?' Maureen looked round the hut as though he might jump out at her. 'When – where is he?'

'He was here hours ago, when you should have been off shift – at least three hours ago. He said to tell you he's staying at the inn just down the road and he'll be here at nine in the morning outside the gates.'

'Rory's here?' Maureen felt bemused, because he'd been so adamant that he wasn't going to give in and that she had to come to him – and now he was here and it sounded as though he was impatient to see her. Her heart gave a little kick of joy, because it meant she would be able to see him more often. 'I didn't expect...'

'He's very good-looking, isn't he?' Rita said and winked. 'I know he's got that scar on his face where he was burned, but we thought it just made him more romantic – didn't we, Carol?'

Carol blushed bright pink. 'I thought he was lovely,' she said, 'and so brave. I asked him if he still felt the pain and he laughed and made out it was nothing. He said his injuries were light compared to some of the men – well, we know that, of course, because we see worse all the time... but I thought...' Carol collapsed in embarrassment, and Maureen guessed that Rory had worked his charm on her friends.

'Yes, he was brave,' Maureen confirmed, seeing that her friends wanted to know more. 'I was with the WRVS when the train came in full of badly injured men. Rory was with a friend and he wouldn't leave him, even though I tried to give him a drink and food: his friend died in hospital that night but Rory was luckier. He needed treatment for the burn to his face and injuries to his hands, but otherwise he's OK – he wants us to get married, but I want to do my nursin' trainin' first...'

'Surely you won't make him wait?' Carol said and the look of shock in her eyes made Maureen feel strange. 'You should marry him, before he has to go back to his unit...' She blushed and looked suddenly aware of what she'd said. 'If you want to, of course...'

Rita burst out laughing again. 'If you didn't have prior claim, I'd fight you for him,' she said and Carol shot her an agonised look that made Maureen stare at the younger girl. Carol wasn't much more than eighteen and Maureen suspected that she had fallen for Rory's charm. Rita was just teasing; she had a string of young men dancing after her, including three she wrote letters to...

Remembering Rory's letter, Maureen took it from her drawer and opened it, annoyed with herself for not doing so before.

He said he would be arriving today and would call in at the hospital and hope to see her when she'd finished for the evening.

She saw Carol watching her as she scanned Rory's letter. He told her that he'd been thinking hard and he didn't want to lose her. He'd arranged a transfer on his release from the hospital, and, fortunately, managed to wangle a posting as a mechanic at the naval base. She smiled because Rory had done what she'd asked and made arrangements to be near her. It must show that he cared for her despite all the arguments and the way he'd behaved in the past. She folded the letter and slipped it into her letter case in her bedside drawer, aware that Carol was watching her every move.

'Something wrong?' she asked.

'Oh... no...' Carol stammered and blushed when she saw Maureen looking at her, but Maureen smiled at her to reassure her. The trainee was young and shy, and very impressionable. It wouldn't take much effort on Rory's part to capture her imagination. Maureen just hoped her heart wasn't involved, because she'd been down that road herself and knew just how much it could hurt.

'You're on early shift, Rita,' she said. 'Give me a shake will you please? I don't want to miss him...'

Rita promised she would tip her out of bed if she didn't wake up, and Maureen threw her used uniform on the floor before crawling into bed in her underwear. She was too damned weary to do anything more...

*

'Maureen, I wasn't sure if you would come...' Rory looked at her uncertainly as she ran to him outside the gates. 'I was a bit of a pig to you last time, but I was sick of being stuck in that hospital for months...'

She looked up at him, noticing that the burn marks on his face had faded now to a brownish smear and didn't look anywhere near as bad as Velma had implied they would when she'd spoken to Maureen in the shop the previous year. If Velma had realised what a wonderful recovery Rory would make, she would probably not have confessed that their marriage was a sham and gone off with someone else.

'I know, darling,' Maureen said and kissed him. 'I know I'm not bein' fair to you, Rory. It's just that I feel I'm doing somethin' worthwhile for the first time in my life and...'

Rory stopped the flow with a kiss that went on and on and drew a whistle from one of the naval guards at the compound gates. He grinned as he let her go.

'It's all right, love. Your pals told me how well you did with your exams. I'm proud of you, Maureen – and we'll just get engaged for now. I reckon you've had to wait for me all this time and now I can wait for you until you're ready...'

'Oh, Rory!' Maureen threw her arms about him in delight, because the way he was looking at her made her feel as if she would burst with happiness. 'Yes, darling, we'll be together as much as we can – and then we'll get married. Once I've passed all my exams I can probably get permission to marry. It will take me a couple of years...'

Rory's kiss burned against her lips. 'I don't want to lose you,' he whispered into her hair. 'It's goin' to be murder wantin' you and not havin' you, but I'll manage...'

Maureen smiled up at him lovingly, because this was the old Rory and she adored him. She hadn't been sure of her feelings for the surly man who had tried to dominate her from his hospital bed, but this was the man she'd fallen in love with. 'If we were careful...' she said shyly and Rory caught her to him once more, his breath rasping hoarsely against her hair. 'I do love you so very much...'

'I adore you, my angel,' Rory said, smiling in the way that made her heart catch. 'I'll take care of you, love. There are ways...'

Maureen nodded and looked up at him trustingly. 'Yes, I know. We learn a bit about that sort of thing. You can find a room or somethin' for us and we can spend time together...'

'My sweet girl...' Rory said and looked at her as she stood back. 'You have to go already?'

'I'm on duty in fifteen minutes,' she said, 'but I can get away at seven tonight. I worked extra hours last night, so I'll tell Sister I have to leave on time this evenin'.'

'I'll pick you up at half past,' Rory said. 'I start work this lunchtime and finish at seven... so I'll be here by half past. Does that give you time to get ready? We'll go for a drink and somethin' to eat in town...'

'Yes, fine, lovely,' Maureen said and kissed him again before breaking from his arms and running back to the compound. She turned and waved to him but Rory was getting onto a motorbike and didn't look back.

*

'That was a lovely meal,' Maureen said when they'd finished eating and Rory had paid their bill. It was a warm evening and they went outside together, lingering in the shadows to look up at the moon, which was lighting up the sky.

'It's a bomber's moon,' Rory said. 'We'll catch it somewhere tonight; if it isn't here, it will be somewhere else – Liverpool or Coventry probably...'

'Yes, I expect so,' Maureen said and drew closer to him. He held her pressed against his side and she could smell the faint perfume of his hair oil. 'Why do men have to fight? I wish this war had never happened...'

'A lot of poor devils aren't around to wish anything,' Rory said and she sensed the tension in him. 'I feel guilty that I'm not out there with them.'

'You've done your share,' Maureen said quickly and put her arms about him, hugging him to her. 'I'm glad you're here, Rory. I want you to be safe now.'

'Don't worry, they won't let me fight again,' Rory said. 'I'm in reasonable shape, love, and I can work as a mechanic – but one of my eyes isn't as good as they need if I'm going to be part of a fightin' force, and my hands – I can still do my job, but I'd find it difficult to feel the sensitivity of a trigger. I was a bloody good shot too...'

'You're not regrettin' that you can't fight?' She gazed up at him, trying to read his thoughts.

'When I see things are goin' badly for us, I itch to kill Germans. A part of me still wants to be out there with my mates, but I wouldn't be much use to them in a fight,' he admitted and then grinned and kissed her. 'When can you get a weekend off? I thought I'd borrow a car and we'll go somewhere – book into a hotel as man and wife...'

Maureen drew a sharp breath, because he'd dropped it into the conversation so casually. She knew he'd expected them to be lovers if he came down, and accepted it was time. Rory needed proof of her love and this was him testing her. She turned to look at him, smiling up into his eyes.

'I'm due for a break next week. It's two days in the middle of the week though – Wednesday and Thursday, back on duty Friday lunchtime...'

'I'll change shifts with someone,' Rory said and looked down at her hotly. 'I want our first time to be proper, Maureen love. I'd like to give you a special treat, be together for longer. Really have a chance to talk and just go off wherever we please.'

'We've never done that,' Maureen said. 'Let me know, because I can get permission to leave on Tuesday evenin' if you can get away...'

'We don't normally work such long hours as you nurses,' Rory said ruefully. 'Once I start on full shifts I'll be back by six in the evening...'

'I never get away before seven and then it's a struggle sometimes,' Maureen sighed. 'If ever I'm late meeting you, you'll know we've had a rush of patients and Sister has asked me to stay late.'

Rory nodded. 'Your friend told me what it's like on the wards. I didn't realise what a good job you were doin' – I'm really sorry I behaved like a spoiled kid in London.'

'It's all right,' she assured him and hugged his arm. 'I know what you went through, love. I felt rotten about quarrelling with you over it – but I feel as if I'm needed here.'

'I need you too, don't forget that,' Rory whispered close to her hair. 'I love you, Molly. I really do. You'll see how much next week...'

'I can't wait,' she said and kissed him again. 'You're so special to me, Rory. It would break my heart if you stopped lovin' me now.'

'I've never stopped lovin' you,' he told her. 'Even when I married Velma I wanted you. She made a fool out of me and if I ever see her again I shall tell her just what I think of her for lyin' about her first marriage.'

'She isn't important now,' Maureen said and looked up at him. 'The past is the past, Rory, and we have the future to look forward to...'

Chapter 19

'These are Able's personal things,' the young American said and gave Peggy a cardboard box sealed with tape. She took it reluctantly, feeling that it was much too soon. Surely they hadn't given up on Able already? His letter to her was still under her pillow unopened, because she couldn't bear to read what he'd written. 'Anything to do with the American Forces has been removed, so there isn't that much…'

Peggy looked at him uncertainly, her heart racing. 'You've heard nothin' more of him? You don't know what happened to the plane?'

'No, I'm afraid not, but there are no reports of it having landed anywhere off course, so it's presumed that it went down over the sea,' he replied, unable to meet her eyes. 'I'm real sorry, ma'am. I know he thought highly of you – and I can see why, if you don't mind me sayin'? You're a nice lady…'

'Thank you,' Peggy said, a faint smile on her lips. 'You're very kind. I shall put Able's things away just as they are – in case he does turn up…' Her throat caught with emotion and she shook her head. Tears stung her eyes as he walked away. She'd been praying that Able's plane had landed somewhere abroad and he would simply walk in and tell her that it was all a mistake and he was fine, but more than a month had passed now since the plane had gone missing and common sense told her it wasn't going to happen.

She took the small box upstairs and slid it under her bed. One day, if Able never returned, she would open it, but not yet – Peggy wasn't ready for anything like that right now. It would feel intrusive, because they hadn't known each other long enough and she didn't truly know anything about his life before they met. All she knew was that he'd given her love at a time when she really needed it and she was grateful for the short time they'd had together.

Laurie had gone back at the end of his leave. He'd kissed her cheek, told her he was sorry for everything and that he hoped one day they could be friends again, and left it at that before taking his leave of Janet. Peggy had just nodded and told him to take care of himself. She was too raw with grief over Able to even consider that she might live with Laurie as his wife again.

'You've just missed Pip,' his daughter told him. 'He's comin' home on leave this weekend...'

'It's a shame we passed in the night,' Laurie had said and gave his daughter a peck on the cheek. 'I'm sorry for what I said to you now... when you wanted to get married...'

'It's all right,' she said gruffly. 'I know why you did it...'

Peggy looked at her after he'd gone. 'I'm glad you made it up with him, love. I don't want you kids to turn against him just because of me...'

'What are you goin' to do, Mum?' Janet asked. 'Will you stay with him now?' She faltered as she saw the pain strike her mother. 'I'm sorry. I shouldn't have asked...'

'It's all right,' Peggy said. 'I know Able has gone. I'm still numbed from the shock, but it will get easier to bear in time. Everythin' does...' She was silent for a moment. 'As for your father, I'm not sure. I'll stay here for the duration of the war, because I think that's best for all of us, but I'm not sure about anything yet.'

'I understand, Mum. You've been hurt too much…'

'I shall get over it in time.'

'Yes, I suppose everything eases in time…' Janet looked at her oddly. 'Will you look after Maggie this weekend please? I'm going to see Mike again and I'd rather not take her with me this time…'

'Yes, of course I will. She's no trouble to me, bless her,' Peggy said. 'Won't he want to see his little girl? He's going to miss all her baby times… it's such a shame.'

'He doesn't acknowledge her as his,' Janet said, a touch of bitterness in her voice. 'When I took her to visit, he wouldn't even look at her… he shouted at us and it made her cry…'

'I know it's hard to bear,' Peggy said, 'but try to remember how much harder it must be for Mike. He can't remember you and yet he's told that you're his wife – how must that feel?'

'I know how it feels to me,' Janet said. 'It makes me miserable – and I haven't done anythin' wrong, so why does he treat me as if I'm trying to cheat him or somethin'?'

'I'm sure he's simply lost and doesn't know what to think,' Peggy said. 'I think you just have to keep visitin' and hope that his memory returns soon…' She frowned. 'What time does your train leave?'

'Ryan is takin' me down,' Janet said and her eyes slid away from her mother's. 'He rang me and told me he has a couple of days free. I said I was visitin' Mike, so he asked if it would help if he took me down and I jumped at the chance. It's hard visitin' alone and being rejected, Mum – and the nurses don't help. One of them seems to dislike me and she told me not to come, but I'm goin' anyway. Ryan thinks I should…'

'Well, I agree with him,' Peggy said. 'You have to break down the barriers if Mike is goin' to come home to you, love. Have you any pictures to show him?'

'Yes, of our weddin', and one before we were married. I thought I would show them to him this time...'

'Give me a hug,' Peggy said and put her arms round the girl. 'We haven't had much luck recently, have we?'

'No...' Janet said, her voice muffled as she buried her face in her mother's shoulder. 'Sometimes, I feel as if I can't stand this any longer... I want to tell Mike that it's over...'

'Janet! You can't do that,' Peggy said. 'Supposing Mike recovers later, remembers you and how much he loves you, you would regret it for the rest of your life. Besides, he's ill and he needs you.'

'He doesn't need me, Mum. I think he resents me – and he wishes I wasn't his wife... He's pushin' me away the whole time I'm there.'

'Oh, Janet, I'm sure he doesn't mean to hurt you...'

'It does hurt. Sometimes I'm not sure I can bear it, Mum. It might be easier just to walk away as Mike wants...'

*

Janet hesitated outside the hospital, holding her breath and feeling a little sick. When she'd visited Mike the first time, the nurse who disliked her had told her she was thoughtless and her visit would destroy Mike's peace of mind, which he was gradually regaining, but Ryan had told her to ignore the woman's spiteful tongue.

'It's my opinion she fancies Mike herself,' Ryan said. 'He's your husband and, if you love him, go ahead and fight for him...'

Janet knew that in his heart Ryan wanted her to leave Mike and get a divorce, but he wasn't pushing her. Instead, he'd encouraged her to stand up for herself.

'Mike is your husband. Even if he has suffered in the war he has responsibilities and he has to accept them. Show him the pictures, Janet – make him acknowledge that you're his wife...'

'Yes...' Janet knew that he was talking sense, because Mike had had months to recover from the shock of being told he had a wife and it was time he faced up to it. They had to try and make a go of things. Otherwise, it really was over. 'Yes, I shall.'

'Good. You know how I feel about you, Jan – but Mike is your husband. He's Maggie's father and he deserves the chance to know her. If it doesn't work out, I'll be around...'

'You're a lovely man, Ryan,' Janet said and reached up to kiss his cheek. He'd told her he was going to fit in a call for his work while she was visiting Mike and they would meet for dinner at the hotel, where they had separate rooms.

She walked into the hospital and up the stairs to the wards where Mike was housed, stopping to speak with the nurse who so disliked her before proceeding to Mike's ward. He was in a small private room for the moment, because he'd had another operation that week and was recovering.

'You really should have warned us before you came,' Sister James said. 'I'm not sure he is up to having visitors...'

'I'm Mike's wife in case you've forgotten,' Janet said, 'and I have every right to visit him. I shan't upset him and if he's tired I can leave and come back later...'

The woman's face went pink with temper but Janet met her eyes and after a moment she dropped hers. Janet thought that perhaps Ryan was right and the nurse had become overprotective of Mike because she had feelings for him.

As she entered the room, she saw that Mike was sitting up in bed reading a newspaper. He looked at her for a moment in silence and then nodded, an expression of uncertainty in his face.

'You decided to visit again then. I thought you might not – after what I said to you when you brought the baby...'

'You're my husband, Mike. I've brought some photos...' Janet said and handed them to him. 'I've also brought some magazines you used to like and some fruit...'

'Thank you...' He took the pictures and looked at them and then at her several times before nodding. 'Yes, I've accepted that I am married to you, and that we have a child... but it still doesn't stir any real memories. I'm sorry, Janet. I know this must be awful for you.'

'It's as bad or worse for you,' Janet said and sat down on the edge of the bed, reaching for his hand. This time he didn't withdraw it immediately. 'I'm really sorry for all you went through out there, Mike. I love you and I want to take care of you when you come home...'

'They're talkin' about sendin' me home in time for Christmas. Do we have a home?'

'We had one in Portsmouth not far from your base but... a plane crashed onto it. It was a German plane and the crew were still inside. I think the pilot was tryin' to get to the sea to ditch but then he saw the field behind the cottage – if we'd been there both Maggie and I would be dead.' Janet gave a strangled laugh. 'It might have been easier for you...'

Mike's hand gripped hers so hard that it was painful. 'No! You mustn't say that. If we're married I must have loved you – and the baby is mine. One day I'll remember and then

I'll be able to love you again...' He looked at her and there was a hint of desperation in his eyes. 'You're all I've got to cling to, Janet. Without you and the baby it's a huge void of nothingness... Can you forgive me for not remembering our love?'

'It hurts me an awful lot, Mike,' Janet said but smiled, because at least he was acknowledging her now, even if he still couldn't remember her. 'It's not somethin' you need to ask forgiveness for, darling. You didn't ask to be like this – though you could have stayed safe in your job at the Docks...' She blinked to hold back the tears as she saw him searching for a memory. Even his job was lost to him, because he had no recollection of it. 'We'll be all right – as long as you don't shut me out. Let me help you remember. Let me visit more often so that we can talk about how it was before the war – the way my dad refused to let us marry and... we became lovers. I was having Maggie when we got married. Mum talked Dad round then and we lived in lodgings for a while until your captain's wife rented us the cottage. I'd made it nice for when you came home...'

Mike shook his head and looked sad. 'It sounds as if we were very much in love...'

'You were desperate to make love and you took me to a wonderful hotel for dinner and a dance up West and that was the first time and – it was so lovely...' Mike squeezed her hand as her voice caught.

'You're a really nice person, Janet, but...'

'You usually called me Jan,' she told him and kissed his hand, which was now free of bandages although still scarred and red. 'I loved you so much, Mike. It broke my heart when they told me you were dead – but then somethin' told me you weren't. I kept tellin' everyone that you were alive, but no one believed me.'

'They've told me I've got a piece of shrapnel in my brain,' Mike said suddenly, sending a shiver of apprehension through her as she saw the naked fear in his eyes. 'It's too deep for them to remove it, though at the moment all it does is cause me headaches. The doctor told me last night that I'll have to live with it for the rest of my life – which could be quite short if it moves…'

'Mike, no!' Janet exclaimed. 'Surely they'll be able to do somethin' in time?'

'It's very tiny, too small for them to go in after without causin' untold damage to my brain. If it stays where it is, the chances are it will just gather a kind of protective crust that will enable me to live with it – but it may be the cause of my memory loss; they don't really know what the future holds for me. If the shrapnel moved in one direction, I might lose my ability to move my limbs or I could suddenly lose vision – or I might die.'

'Oh, Mike…' Janet stared at him in distress. For a moment she was lost for words, because the prognosis was too awful to contemplate. 'What a thing to say to you – you might be all right. If it just stays there – for years…'

'Yes, I might and I might not,' Mike said ruefully. 'There are other options. I might turn violent and nasty – attack people or…'

'Don't!' Janet put her hands to her ears. 'Please stop, Mike. I don't believe this – I won't listen to it. I don't know why they told you such things. You're gettin' better. Why should this thing in your head move? If it was goin' to do all those nasty things surely they would already have happened?'

'The doctor said that as well – but he was obliged to warn me,' Mike said, 'and I felt obliged to warn you. If we're goin' to make a home together you have to know what could happen...'

'Nothing will happen,' Janet said stoutly. 'We love each other, Mike. I'm sure you will remember that in time – and things will get better for us. If we have love and affection then we can face anythin' together...'

Mike smiled and for a moment he was the old Mike, the man she'd loved so much. 'You're a nice person, Jan. I realised that after I sent you away last time – but there are moments when my head hurts so much I don't really know what I am sayin'. It all seemed so wrong. I couldn't remember a wife, and to be honest I didn't want a family – but now...' He sighed. 'It doesn't seem fair to you, but will you take me on? Knowin' that anythin' could happen, will you give me a home and a chance to live?'

'Yes, Mike, I will,' Janet said and leaned forward to kiss him on the mouth. A little to her surprise he kissed her back, holding her head as she would've withdrawn, and then he smiled as he let her go.

'That was nice. You taste good and you smell lovely. I like that perfume.'

'You bought it for me the last time you were home... It was Christmas 1940...'

'Is it French?'

'Yes – how did you know?'

'I'm not sure – I think I just guessed,' Mike said and looked odd. 'Don't get your hopes up too much, Jan. The perfume is familiar to me but that doesn't mean I'll remember anythin' else...'

'When can you come home?'

'In a couple of months I think,' Mike said. 'I believe there are two further ops to go – but I'm not sure where home is…'

'I've been living with Mum at the Pig & Whistle in Mulberry Lane in Spitalfields since the cottage was bombed,' Janet said. 'I'll look for somewhere for us, though I'm sure it would be all right for you to come there until we find a place of our own. Will the Navy give you a discharge?'

'I think I might be given an office job when I'm fit enough to return to work,' Mike said and grimaced. 'Not really my kind of work. I like…' He halted and looked at her in wonder. 'I'm good with my hands – or I was… I think.'

'You worked in the shipyards. Fittin' ships and engines and things…'

'I worked with the engines or the housing…' Mike frowned, as if a memory were disturbing him. He put a trembling hand to the side of his head. 'Sometimes it feels as if a nail is being hammered into my brain…'

'Mike, I'm so sorry, darling…' Janet leaned forward to kiss his mouth softly. 'Can I make it better – get you a hot drink or somethin'?'

'It's time for your medication.' A voice came from the door and Janet saw Sister James had brought in a white metal tray with a syringe. 'You'd better leave, Mrs Rowan – Mike needs to rest now…'

Mike's fingers closed over Janet's wrist. 'You will come back please?'

'Of course,' Janet smiled and bent to kiss his cheek. 'Do as the nurse tells you, Mike, and I'll visit in the mornin' – before I go back to London.'

'We'll talk some more then,' he said. 'Forgive me…'

'Nothing to forgive…'

Janet waved to him from the door just as the needle was plunged in his arm. She walked away, her feelings mixed. At least Mike had decided to accept the fact that he had a wife and child – but his news had chilled her and she knew he was haunted by it. The doctor had been honest with him but it had left a shadow over his life – over her life too, Janet thought as she left the hospital with its smells of disinfectant and carbolic behind and went out into the bright sunshine.

She took a deep breath of the fresh air, deciding to go for a long walk before she returned to the hotel. Mike was getting better in himself; she'd seen a big improvement since her last visit, but that metal in his head was causing him a problem and one that he had to live with, because it was never going to go away...

*

'So, you're goin' to visit Mike more often now?' Peggy said when Janet told her about the trip to the hospital. 'I'm sorry it has turned out like this for you, my dearest. I hoped you would be happy, and I was sure Mike would come to accept you and perhaps remember in time... I even wondered if you'd fallen for Ryan.'

Janet looked her in the eyes. 'If you're askin' – yes, I do care for Ryan, Mum, and it wouldn't have been hard to give in and have an affair, but we haven't – even though he stayed here overnight and we have kissed. Ryan wants me, but Mike needs me and he's my husband...' There was a little sob in her voice. 'I have to give us a chance to be happy again, don't I, Mum?'

'Yes, my darling, you do,' Peggy agreed. 'Mike has been through a lot – seen things we have no idea of – and we have to make allowances. You told him he was welcome here, of course?'

'Just for a start,' Janet said. 'I don't think I could cope alone. You don't mind?'

'I should've been upset if you hadn't wanted to stay,' Peggy said. 'All I want now is to see my children happy – and my little Maggie too, of course…'

'Have you heard from Dad since he went back?'

'He sent a card for my birthday and five pounds to buy myself a present…'

'He might have bought you a gift…' Janet looked disgusted.

'I can't recall the last time your father actually bought me a present other than food,' Peggy said. 'It was before you kids were born. He says he doesn't know what to get and it's best I have the money – and in a way that's good, because I can choose what I like…'

'But he should know after all this time,' Janet said. 'I should be disappointed if Mike gave me money…'

'He may not be able to give you anythin' this year,' Peggy reminded her and then apologised. 'Sorry love, but stuck in hospital like that it might not be possible, even if he remembered the date…'

'I know…' Janet faltered and looked sad. 'Ryan bought me a silk scarf on my last birthday…'

'Have you decided not to see Ryan again?'

'I shan't see him for a while, Mum.'

'And do you regret it?'

'Yes, in some ways, but not in others – and the longer we went on seeing each other the harder it would've been to part. I don't know how it's possible but I love both of them in different ways.'

'Ryan has been good to you. He's a friend and it's natural you should feel some affection for him...'

'It isn't just affection...' Janet said and sighed as she went to take Maggie from her cot.

Peggy watched her daughter change the little girl's nappy and her heart ached, because she knew what Janet was going through. She'd struggled when Laurie was away in the first war. He'd come home a changed man and for almost two years he'd suffered from nightmares – terrifying dreams that would cause him to start up in the night and sometimes he kicked and fought, and if she got in his way he hit her, but he'd been abjectly apologetic afterwards and Peggy had learned to leave him alone to come out of the darkness. In time he'd got over the bad dreams and put his war experiences behind him, but she knew it had scarred him inside. Perhaps even then they'd started to grow away from each other...

When was this damned war going to finish? Peggy couldn't see an end to the suffering and misery it had caused and sometimes she felt it was hardly worth getting up for, especially now Able wasn't here... And yet there was Pip and Janet and little Maggie.

Straightening her shoulders, Peggy gave herself a mental telling-off. She was luckier than some and she should stop feeling sorry for herself, even if Able's loss had left an empty space in her heart...

*

Feeling unbearably lonely, Peggy opened Able's last letter that night as she lay in bed. It had taken her a long time to get to this stage, but at last she felt that she could face the words she'd longed, and yet dreaded, to read:

If you're reading this, my own darling, it means I'm dead. I decided to put my feelings down on paper, because I know you worry about being a bit older, but I really don't see it, Peggy. You're lovely, sexy and the most loving lady I've ever known – and I do see you as a lady, my love. No other woman has ever come close to you in my heart and mind, and I wanted you to know that I hoped we'd have all our lives together.

I wouldn't have taken you away from your country. I like London and I think we could've found a place to be happy here, though I wouldn't have minded living in the country with you – maybe I could've run a country hotel and we could've made a new life somewhere.

Obviously, this is just dreams now, but I wanted you to know what was in my mind. You were always more than just a flirtation to me. You've given me more than you can imagine and I want you to have a good life, my love. I have some money in an account in London and it's yours, Peggy, for if you ever need to find a life of your own or just as a safeguard for whatever life throws at you. It isn't a huge amount but it might be useful.

I hope you will remember me with love in your heart and know that you were truly loved, and perhaps if Paradise really exists we'll meet there.

Your ever-loving Able.

P.S. There is a will, so my London lawyer will contact you in due course.

Peggy's eyes were wet with tears as she folded the letter and replaced it in its envelope. She would put it away with some other small things Able had given her and keep it always. It would lift her spirits when she was feeling miserable, though nothing would ever take away the emptiness his loss had created inside her. She might not have known him long, but he'd given her a taste of a different life, a life that might have been hers had his plane not gone into the sea.

'Oh, Able,' she whispered. 'Rest in peace, my lovely man. I shall never forget you or what you gave me.'

Chapter 20

Maureen finished changing a bandage on one of the less seriously wounded men on the ward. It was only the third time she'd been allowed to do it without supervision and she felt pleased with herself when the patient thanked her and told her it felt much easier now.

'You're a good nurse,' he said, 'careful and kind, and I reckon you don't get much thanks for what you do. That Sister never stops going on at you young nurses...'

'Sister's bark is worse than her bite,' Maureen said and straightened his bed, knowing that the minute her back was turned he would have the sheets out at the corners again, because like most of the men he didn't like being tucked in tightly, but Sister insisted and the nurses would catch it if sheets were hanging loose when Doctor made his rounds. Doctor's rounds were sacrosanct and the ward had to be spotless with nothing out of place or Sister would go on the rampage afterwards.

'Nurse Jackson...'

Maureen turned as she saw Sister coming towards her, a familiar lurch in her stomach. The formidable nurse was frowning and Maureen mentally reviewed her work of the last few days – had she done something unforgivable? Apart from going away with Rory for two days that was; Sister would not have approved of that, even though it had been heavenly for Maureen.

'We've had news of an accident on one of the ships in the port,' Sister Martin said. 'We have four seriously injured men coming in shortly, nurse. I want you to make up the beds in wards three and four. They have all been badly burned and will need special treatment – and I'm going to ask you to special one of them. He's a young lad and not as badly affected as the others, but he will still need watching. It means I shall expect you to stay longer this evening – until we can be sure he is out of danger...'

'Yes, Sister,' Maureen said and thought regretfully of her promise to meet Rory after she finished work. It would have been their first chance to go anywhere since their holiday – or honeymoon as Maureen privately thought of it. Rory had given her a gold wedding band to wear so that the hotel staff wouldn't be suspicious, and she'd still got it in her handbag. He'd told her to keep it in case they wanted it another time and the way he'd looked at her made Maureen's toes tingle, because she knew he wanted them to be together again.

Maureen wanted it too, very much, because Rory had been so sweet and tender and they'd made love over and over again. She'd been a little shy at first, but after the first time she'd really enjoyed herself, discovering her nature was more passionate than she'd ever dreamed. Rory was a wonderful lover and Maureen was happy that she'd given herself to him. Rory had told her that as far as he was concerned they were as good as married.

'I love you, Molly,' he'd said against her ear as he stroked her back with gentle hands, making her tremble with love for him and strain against him until they came together in the heat of desire.

They'd lain in bed late in the mornings, relishing the chance to get up when they liked and sending for breakfast in bed. When they did get up they went for long walks by a local river and ate at an inn situated in the bend of the river, returning to their hotel and sharing a bath before getting dressed for the evening. The hotel was a quiet country one and there was nowhere to go other than downstairs for dinner and a drink in the bar, but they didn't mind and went early to bed, spending their time talking and making love as they sipped the sweet wine Rory had taken up to their room.

'Are you listening to me?' Sister Martin's voice intruded into the pleasant memories and she jumped.

'Yes, Sister, you want me to watch over the patient and change his drip when needed – and talk to him if he wakes. Was there anythin' else?'

'Not for the moment. He will have had treatment for the burns before he arrives, but he's on strong medication, because there is a lot of pain, so you need to make sure that the right dose is administered every four hours...'

'Yes, Sister,' Maureen said and took her notebook out, making a few extra notes. She felt nervous as she set about making up the four beds, two to each room, because she hadn't been asked to special a burns patient before and she knew the young man was going to be in terrible pain when he came round...

Her patient arrived two hours later. His head, hands and one leg had been badly affected and were heavily bandaged. His eyes were closed and she could see burn marks on one side of his face, but didn't think they were as bad as some she'd seen previously. He had his eyes closed and she guessed he was sleeping, though he cried out once or twice in terror and

Maureen bent over him whispering words of encouragement, though she wasn't sure he could hear her.

'It's all right, George,' she said. 'It's over now. You're in hospital and I'm here to look after you...'

She couldn't touch him because she wasn't sure whether he was hurt anywhere else until Sister came to give her further instructions. All she'd been asked to do was watch, check the drips and make sure medication was administered when necessary, but her heart ached for him because he looked as if he couldn't be much more than sixteen. She'd read his notes and gathered he was an apprentice engineer. It seemed he'd been working to repair damage to a ship's engines when there was an explosion which quickly became a blazing inferno. Luckily, some of the older men had dragged him and the others out and there had been no fatalities, though she'd been told some of the casualties were in worse shape than her patient.

She saw the other patient assigned to this ward arrive, accompanied by a senior nurse. He looked to be very heavily bandaged, but Nurse Simmons told her that he was the next least serious of the four.

'We have the easy job, Nurse Jackson,' she said. 'The patients in room four are in much worse shape.'

'Poor devils,' Maureen whispered. 'Mine seems quiet enough for now – is there anything you need?'

'I can manage, thanks,' the nurse said and smiled. 'If you're worried just ask me. Sister put me in with you just in case. This is your first time, isn't it?'

'Yes...' Maureen drew a breath of relief. It was good to know an experienced nurse was just the other side of a curtain. 'I was wondering what to do if he needs the pan or anything – should I touch him, help him?'

'You will probably need to help because of his injury – but I don't think he has any burns to his body so don't be afraid to lift him. If I'm not busy I'll give you a hand, but otherwise fetch another nurse. Even though you're his special, you can't do everything alone, so don't be shy of asking for help.'

Maureen felt better then, and for several hours her patient was quiet, crying out only occasionally in his sleep. She needed to replace the drip bottle once, and to administer a painkilling drug to keep him sedated.

Nurse Simmons watched her and nodded approval. 'Well done, nurse. Just carry on like that and you will be fine...'

Maureen stayed with her patient until late into the evening when another nurse came to relieve her. She was reluctant to leave George even then and checked everything before she left, making certain she'd written down the drugs she'd given her patient.

He was in her thoughts as she walked back to the hut she shared. She'd asked Rita to meet Rory for her and explain why she couldn't see him that evening. When she got in, both Carol and Rita were asleep, though she thought Carol stirred as she took off her shoes and fell into bed fully clothed, but she didn't speak. Maureen fell asleep almost at once and didn't wake until she heard an alarm the next morning.

She sat up groggily, rubbing at her eyes as she saw that Rita was dressing. Carol was nowhere to be seen and her bed had been neatly made.

'Is Carol on early shift?'

'She didn't say anything much to me, but I didn't see her last night – she was asleep when I came home...'

'Did you see Rory and tell him I'd had to work...'

'Sorry, Maureen love. I had to rush off last night: my brother got an unexpected pass and wanted to meet before they ship him abroad – but I asked Carol if she would and she promised she'd give him the message.'

'Oh... Well, I expect he got it then,' Maureen said. 'It was a bit of a nuisance, but you can't refuse extra duty when it's for the sake of a patient...'

'How did you get on? Burns are bloody painful...'

'He was whimpering a bit in his sleep, but the drugs were keepin' him sedated, so I don't really know.'

'They will probably bring him out of it later today,' Rita said. 'Depends on what degree they are... Some of the worst are kept under for longer, until the pain becomes bearable.'

Maureen nodded, because Rita had been on the burns unit for a long time earlier in the year and knew what she was talking about. They walked to breakfast together, discussing saline baths and various treatments once the patient started to recover, and then parted after eating thick marmalade on crunchy toast washed down by large mugs of strong, lukewarm tea. Maureen was used to it now, though at home she would never have drunk her tea that way in a million years.

She collected her post and discovered a letter from Gordon, one from Gran and another from Rory. She put Gordon's to one side, feeling slightly awkward. Rory wouldn't like it if he discovered another man wrote her regular letters and Maureen knew that one of these days she would have to tell Gordon that she couldn't continue, but she also knew what a blow that would be to him. Rory's letter had been hand-delivered and expressed his disappointment at not being able to take her out the previous evening.

I took your friend for a drink, because she was a bit down, he'd written. *She's a bit of a little mouse, but I suppose she's all right. I missed you, Molly. I want to get a night away again as soon as we can...*

Maureen read the note and smiled. She slipped it into her pocket with Gordon's and Gran's, which she would read later...

*

Maureen was busy all day looking after her patient, who was still under the drugs for most of it, and helping Nurse Simmons change her patient's bed twice. He was still drugged too and he'd wet his bed a couple of times, but it was only to be expected and the two nurses helped each other to change the sheet under him, which was folded in two and easy to pull out and replace without moving him excessively.

'I'd rather have this job than see them in pain,' Nurse Simmons said. 'It's when they wake up that things get harder...'

George was allowed to wake just around teatime and when he opened his eyes for the first time Maureen saw they were bright blue. He stared at her for a while in silence before he spoke.

'Are you a nurse?'

'Yes. There was an accident and you were caught in an explosion...'

'Is that why I'm feeling so bloody groggy?'

'Yes, we've got you on painkillers to help you, but they do knock you right out...' Maureen bent over him and smiled. 'I can't offer you a cup of tea yet because you're still nil by mouth. You're receivin' food and drink through this tube in your arm.'

'I feel sick...' George said and turned on his side and spewed up dark bile, most of which went on the floor, splashing both the sheets and Maureen's shoes. 'I'm sorry...'

'It's fine,' she assured him. 'I'm goin' to wipe your face and you can rinse your mouth with water but please do not swallow – or you'll be sick again.'

He obeyed her, spitting into the bowl she held. Maureen wiped his face and then removed the sheet, replacing it with a spare which she'd fetched earlier, ready for the next change. Once he was settled, she wiped the floor and her shoes and had just finished cleaning up when the door to the side ward opened and a doctor entered, followed by Sister Martin.

'It stinks in here,' the doctor said and frowned. 'Get a window open and clean this mess up, nurse.'

'Yes, sir. I was just going to…'

Sister frowned at her and she gathered the dirty sheets and almost ran from the room, feeling like a scolded child. It was hardly her fault that the patient had been sick minutes before the doctor arrived. Dumping the soiled linen in the basket, she washed her hands at the sink and went back into the small side ward.

'What's this?' The doctor was staring at the glass of water. He glared at Maureen. 'Nil by mouth means nil by mouth. No wonder your patient vomited. It's a good thing he hadn't had surgery or his wound might have opened.'

Maureen opened her mouth to reply and then closed it when Sister shook her head. Doctor's word was law and you didn't argue; it was one of the first things she'd been taught – even though she was being unfairly accused, she had to accept it.

She was relieved when he nodded over her chart, wrote something on the bottom and then went through the curtain to Nurse Simmons.

'I'll speak to you later,' Sister Martin hissed at her and followed him.

Maureen made her patient more comfortable with an extra pillow, as she could see he was struggling to sit up. He looked distressed and she asked him if he was in pain.

George shook his head and whispered, 'I need to relieve myself...'

Maureen nodded. 'Bottle or bedpan?' she asked, and he whispered back that he needed the pan. She fetched one from a small cupboard at the side of the room and slid it under him, helping him onto it and settling the covers as the doctor emerged from behind the curtains. George gave her an agonised look and relieved himself; the pungent smell made the doctor glance at him and wrinkle his nose. He left the room immediately and Sister followed, casting an amused glance at Maureen's patient.

'Sorry about that,' George said as Maureen retrieved the pan minutes later and covered it with a white cloth. 'It's a bit embarrassing – especially after he got onto you about the smell when I was sick.'

'It's all right,' she said and laughed. 'When you've dealt with as many of these as I have, you get used to it. Is there anythin' else I can do for you?'

'Can I wash myself?' he asked, still a bit uncomfortable at having opened his bowels in the presence of two nurses and a doctor. 'I think some of it went over me – and maybe the bed...'

'I'll fetch a cloth and give you a bit of a wash when I've dealt with this...'

'Ahh!' George had discovered his hands hurt as he tried to pull back his covers. 'It bloody hurts...'

'Yes, I'm sure it does,' Maureen said sympathetically. 'Don't worry about anything yet, George. I'll change your under sheet if it needs it and clean you up...'

'I feel like a damned kid...' he said, looking acutely embarrassed. 'Sorry to be such a nuisance...'

'You're not and couldn't be,' she assured him with a smile. 'It's what we're here for...'

She went out and fetched some water and soap and returned to find that he'd rolled to one side of the bed, trying to find a way of escaping the mess, and in the meantime had caused himself more pain. His eyes were filled with tears, which he rubbed at with his bandaged hands.

'I'm a bloody useless idiot,' he said fiercely, but Maureen smiled and went to help him roll further away from the mess. She deftly removed the under sheet and placed a clean one underneath, then she wrung out her cloth in the warm water she'd brought with her and gently sponged his back, drying him and settling him back comfortably. By this time George was thoroughly exhausted and tears of weakness were trickling down his cheeks. 'Sorry, nurse, but it hurts – my hands feel as if a thousand bees are stinging them...'

'Is it very bad?' Maureen asked and he nodded. She checked his chart and saw that he wasn't due for any more painkilling medicines for another hour. 'I'm sorry. I can't give you anything more just yet.'

Nurse Simmons had been out of the room but returned with some fresh sheets for her patient. Maureen took her to one side and explained what had happened.

'I think changin' the sheets and washin' him was too much – should I have left him as he was?'

'We have to keep our patients clean,' Nurse Simmons said and looked at the patient and then his chart. 'Nothing you can do yet, Nurse Jackson. Speak to Sister when she comes and tell her the medication isn't lasting the full six hours. She will ask the doctor if he can go on more...'

It was late when Maureen finally got to bed. Rita was out and Carol didn't lift her head even when she asked if it was all right if she put her light on for a while. The little shaded lamp by her bed shouldn't disturb the other girl and Maureen really wanted to read Gran's letter. She hadn't had time to open it all day and she wanted to see what Gran had to say, because it was only a few days since her last letter and something made her wonder if her grandmother was all right.

Tearing the envelope open, she read her Gran's words.

I'm sorry to worry you, Maureen love, but I've had a letter from that lot at the farm in Essex; it seems that Shirley's grandmother died suddenly last month and they're finding it difficult to cope with the child. Mrs Hunter went on about all the work she has to do and I'm sure she's busy, but I think the trouble is she doesn't like Shirley. We both know she can be troublesome, but the poor kid will be feeling upset with her gran dead. They say you're responsible for her now, love, and they want you to fetch her as soon as you can – and I know that's not easy for you...

I know you can't look after her now you're working as a nurse and I'm willing to take her on here, at least for a while. You can write to her father and explain what has happened and he'll get leave and come home to make other arrangements when he can, but I can't fetch the child so you'll have to arrange that, Maureen. I'm sorry to put this on you but didn't know what else

to do. Can't leave the poor little thing with the misery
guts who doesn't want her, can we?
Love from Gran.

'Oh no...' Maureen stared at the letter for several minutes in dismay. She was concerned and upset for Shirley, Gordon Hart's little girl. She remembered the day he'd come in the shop before the war started and asked her if she would have the care of Shirley if anything happened to his mother – and to him out there – and she'd said yes, of course she would, never thinking what it would mean, because she'd expected Mrs Hart would live for years yet. Gordon had made Maureen her guardian if he died and now she felt the weight of that responsibility on her shoulders. Gran was willing to look after Shirley for a while, but she was getting on in years and it wasn't right or feasible for her to have the permanent care of her. 'Damn...'

'Is something wrong? Is it bad news?' Carol was sitting up in bed looking at her with an odd expression in her eyes.

Maureen sighed. 'In a way – a friend has died and there's no one but me or my grandmother to look after the child. Shirley's father is in the Army and I promised I'd look after her if anythin' happened – but that was before my father remarried and I signed on to become a nurse...'

'What will you do?' Carol asked. 'You can't give your job up for a child that isn't yours, especially after you wouldn't give it up for Rory...' Carol's cheeks went pink and she couldn't meet Maureen's eyes. 'I mean – you said that...' She stumbled and looked guilty, because Maureen hadn't told her anything of the sort, which meant it had come from Rory.

'Is that what Rory told you when you met him the other evenin'?'

The other girl's eyes avoided hers as she said, 'He talked about you all the time, said you'd been wonderful to him and how much he wanted to get married, but you wanted to finish your training and – I'd give it up in an instant if he asked me...' Carol was really red in the face now as she floundered. 'I mean, he wouldn't of course because he loves you, but...'

'You've fallen for his charm haven't you?' Maureen stared at her, half in anger, half in sympathy. She'd felt the same the first time Rory had smiled at her, telling her she was wonderful and the prettiest girl he'd ever seen. Carol wouldn't be the first or the last young woman to do that, she thought as the girl looked embarrassed. Even with the scars on one side of his face and the backs of his hands, Rory was still too good-looking, but more than that he had a way of smiling and looking at you that could melt any heart. His scars just made him look heroic, enhancing his appeal, and Maureen knew only too well how it felt to love a man who belonged to another woman. Sympathy for the young girl overcame the anger. 'Don't be upset, Carol. I know you don't mean any harm. Rory is very attractive...'

Carol raised her head then and looked her in the eyes. 'I'm in love with him,' she said defiantly. 'I don't care about you – you don't deserve him. You could marry him, but all you care about is yourself – and another man's kid. Well, one of these days Rory is going to get fed up waiting and I'll be there...'

Maureen was shocked, because it was a declaration of war and she felt hurt and bewildered that a girl she'd liked and thought of as a friend would say such a thing to her – and mean it.

'I think you may regret sayin' that in the mornin',' she said, holding her temper. 'I'm sorry you feel that way, Carol, but what I choose to do is my business and Rory's – and if he chooses you over me then he wouldn't be the man I think he is...'

Placing her grandmother's letter in her bedside cabinet, she snapped off her light and got into bed without bothering to undress. As far as Maureen was concerned she had nothing more to say to the girl in the bed next door. Yet she lay without sleeping for ages, puzzling over the problem Gran had set her and thinking about Rory.

*

'I've been given leave to go and fetch her and take her back to London this weekend,' Maureen told Rory. 'Gran is goin' to look after her for the time bein', but I think Peggy might have her at the pub if it's too much for Gran.'

Rory frowned. 'I don't see that it's up to you to worry over her future, Maureen. Gordon Hart is nothin' to you – is he?'

'No, of course not,' Maureen said, feeling uncomfortable. 'It was before the war. I thought I'd still be at the shop, so when he asked if I would look after her if anythin' happened I said yes – and he made me her official guardian until he returns...'

'Supposin' he doesn't?' Rory's voice was harsh. 'You'll be stuck with the kid for the rest of your life – and where does that leave us? I'm not prepared to work to keep someone else's kid – especially his. I don't like him. I saw the way he hung round you at that church social...'

Maureen was chilled by his tone and his looks. She'd known he could be selfish, but surely he wasn't so heartless as to abandon a child?

'Rory, we've only ever been friends. You can't be jealous?'

'I thought we'd go somewhere on your next weekend off,' he said, glaring at her. 'Now it will be ages before you get another one...'

'Perhaps we could go down together, perhaps spend the night somewhere on Saturday and then fetch her Sunday mornin' and take her back to Gran's – we'd be together all weekend, Rory...' Maureen heard the pleading tone in her own voice and hated it.

He hesitated and she saw the uncertainty in his eyes. A part of him could see the benefits, because they would have all Saturday alone, but he wasn't sure about fetching Shirley.

'I'll go down on the train if I have to – but you could borrow a friend's car like last time, couldn't you?'

'Yes, all right.' Rory relented and it was like the sun coming out when he smiled, making her want to melt in its warmth. 'I'll take you – but Hart better come home and arrange his daughter's future, because I'm not gettin' stuck with her. I want kids of our own when this lot is over...'

Maureen smiled, kissed his cheek and thanked him, but inside she felt as if she were carrying a dead weight. She loved Rory, but he could be very selfish and she was hurt that he hadn't taken her feelings into consideration. Rory was a charmer when he wanted to be but he also liked to dominate and that made her uneasy for the future. She pushed the doubts that had started to come into her mind to a far corner. Rory was entitled to his point of view and, naturally, he didn't want the burden of another man's child – though Shirley wouldn't be a burden to her.

*

'We shouldn't quarrel,' Rory said and stroked Maureen's hair as her head lay against his on the pillows. They stopped for the night at a small hotel on the way to Essex, Maureen wearing the wedding ring he'd bought her, and booking in as Mr and Mrs Mackness. 'I don't know why I do it, because I adore you, Molly love. I've been with other women, but none of them ever meant anything to me. You're the one I love – and I'm lucky you put up with my temper.'

Maureen leaned over to kiss him on the lips. They'd made love several times that weekend and it had been wonderful again. When Maureen was in his arms she felt as if everything were perfect. Happiness made her smile as she ran a finger down his cheek and kissed him on the lips. Rory could be thoughtless and selfish, but she did love him and she believed he loved her.

'I want to spend the rest of our lives together,' she murmured. 'You won't be cross tomorrow when we fetch Shirley will you? As Gran says, we can't leave her there, because they don't want her – and I did promise I would look after her. She's only seven and she hasn't had a happy time of it lately.'

'Her father should never have asked you,' Rory said and got out of bed. 'I don't mind fetchin' her and I've no objection to you sendin' the girl things and helpin' to look after her, but I don't want to be stuck with her forever. It's hard enough bringin' up a family as it is, Maureen. Just make sure Hart makes other arrangements for her if he gets killed over there...'

'With any luck he'll come home...'

'Yeah, but he may not.'

Maureen didn't answer, because she hated to think that Gordon might be killed out there, realising that she would miss him and his letters more than she'd bargained for. She didn't want to let Gordon or his daughter down, but Rory had a point. It wouldn't be fair to expect him to bring up another man's daughter (although Maureen would've been quite happy to contribute from her earnings), but obviously if she had kids and was at home looking after them the burden would be on Rory, and he was partially disabled – even though he never complained that his eyesight was troubling him.

'Yes, all right, I'll write and tell him,' she promised. 'Now come back to bed, because it will soon be time to leave for the farm...'

'Just going to the toilet,' Rory said. 'Keep the bed warm for me, love...'

Maureen turned over and sighed. She felt so awkward over this business of Shirley, because she'd given her word to Gordon, and she didn't want to let him down – but she didn't want to quarrel with Rory over it more than she already had.

*

'I could take her if your gran thinks it's too much for her,' Peggy offered when Maureen saw her on Sunday. 'You mustn't worry about the girl, love. You know I like havin' kids around. Anne is stayin' here with me at the moment and she'll know about fixin' up a school for her. They've opened a few of them up again, because a lot of kids are comin' back now the Blitz is over.'

'Oh good,' Maureen said, feeling relieved. 'I didn't want to ask, because I told Gordon I'd look after her...'

'Things change,' Peggy said. 'You're doin' a good job, love. I'm just here same as always, cookin' and cleanin', and one small girl doesn't make much difference to me. I'd enjoy havin' her.'

'Thanks so much, Peggy. I'll write and tell Gordon not to worry, though I expect he will have had an official letter about his mother, but he'll want to know if Shirley is OK. They might give him compassionate leave, but it depends how bad things are wherever he is…'

'Yes, of course. Now stop worryin'. I shall look forward to helpin' where I can, and so will Anne. We look out for each other here, love…'

'Yes, thank goodness for the women of Mulberry Lane…'

She felt much easier now, because Gran would have Shirley for a while and then Peggy would take her on to give Gran a rest now and then. It would work for the time being, but Maureen realised she was going to have to ask for a transfer back to London as soon as she'd passed her next round of exams – and she wasn't sure how Rory would feel about that. She'd told him he must wait but now she was thinking about transferring to London for the sake of another man's child. Rory was going to be angry…

Chapter 21

'Tommy!' Alice Carter hailed him urgently as she saw him leaving the yard of the Pig & Whistle that morning in July. 'I want a word with you, lad.'

Tommy ambled across the road to her good-naturedly. The sun was shining and he'd just earned five shillings from Peggy and all was right with his world. Alice was always wanting something and he was happy to help out where he could, but something about her manner made the back of his neck prickle and he realised she was upset.

'Is somethin' the matter, Alice?'

'It's your Sam,' Alice said. 'I was going to the market this mornin' and I saw the warden puttin' up notices on some of the bomb sites. I asked him what was wrong and he said they'd discovered an unexploded bomb in one of the ruins and were warnin' people to keep away because there might be more...'

'I've told Sam a hundred times it's dangerous...' Tom said and swore beneath his breath. 'Have you seen 'im?'

Alice nodded vigorously. 'He's up the other side of the market. I think he was headin' for what used to be a second-hand jewellery shop before it was bombed. The police 'ave put a cordon up round it, orderin' people to keep orf, but you know what the kids are like, Tommy. I've seen half a dozen of 'em diggin' around. I expect there's a lot of valuables there somewhere...'

Tom nodded, frowning as he realised that most of the stuff he'd found in Sam's things had most likely come from the second-hand shop. There was probably a gang of kids hunting for stuff, and, as Sam said, there would be men of the criminal type organising the search when so many valuables were there for the picking. They wouldn't risk their own lives, but would happily send kids in to do their dirty work and pocket the lion's share of the profits.

'Thanks, Alice,' he said. 'I'll see if I can find him. If he's there I'll give 'im a good hidin'; it's the only way to stop the little fool.'

'Yes, well, I don't know if there's one of them devices in them ruins, but you don't want nothin' to happen to the lad, Tom.'

'I'll make 'im wish 'e'd never been born!'

Tom set out grimly in the direction Alice had mentioned. He was angry, because he'd warned his brother over and over again, and he'd had enough of it. Sam thought he could get away with anything now that their father was in prison, but Tom was the man of the house and he was going to show Sam the error of his ways! Tom didn't want people thinking his brother was a dirty little tea leaf and labelling the whole family as villains. He marched quickly, his heart drumming in his chest as his anger mounted.

Tom was out of breath when he got to the area that had been badly damaged earlier in the year. Several houses were just piles of rubble, but a couple still had a wall or two standing, and one had half the wooden roof structure hanging precariously, ready to fall in the slightest puff of wind. Tom saw three young lads, one of whom was his younger brother, and a man in a navy striped suit talking to them. He looked like a spiv and, as he saw Tom approaching, he turned and walked quickly away.

The boys started picking over rubble, not even bothering to glance up when Tom yelled to his brother. Sam ignored him until Tom arrived at the pile of rubble where they were working, then glanced up in annoyance.

'What do yer want?' Sam muttered, clearly annoyed at the interruption.

'I've told you about pinchin' stuff,' Tom said, furious now. He charged up the rubble, grabbed his brother by the scruff of the neck and started to drag him down it, causing a shower of bricks to slide and pitching them both forward just as a loud explosion from the other side of the bomb site shook the ground.

Tom felt himself caught up and blown forward by the force of the explosion; he felt sharp pain in his left shoulder and then everything went black.

*

'What was that?' Peggy looked at her daughter as she was serving a pint of beer. 'I didn't hear the siren – but that was definitely an explosion.'

'Perhaps it was a gas main,' Janet said, rushing to the pub door to look out into the street. 'It's over by the market. There's a cloud of smoke rising...'

Now they could hear the sound of a police siren and shouting. Alice came running across the road, her face white with fear.

'It's my fault...' she babbled as she clutched at Janet's arm. 'If anythin' 'as happened to the lad I'll never forgive meself...'

'What are you talkin' about?' Janet said. 'Did you see what happened?'

Janet supported the elderly woman into the taproom and sat her down. Alice was trembling and clearly distressed. Peggy poured a drop of brandy into a glass and Janet put it into Alice's hands.

'What's wrong, love?' Peggy asked, kneeling down to take Alice's hand. 'What do you think has happened?'

'I sent Tommy Barton after his brother,' Alice said and took a gulp of her drink. 'They were puttin' up notices about an unexploded device and I saw young Sam goin' up that way – the young lads 'ave been diggin' for stuff on that bomb site where the jeweller's shop was...' Alice took another drink, her hand shaking. 'I sent Tom after the lad...'

'Take care of Alice,' Peggy said urgently. 'I'm off up there to see what's goin' on...' She grabbed her jacket and pulled it on as she ran out into Mulberry Lane. Several of her neighbours were outside and she saw Tilly Barton looking up and down the lane; she was wearing a flowered pinny and a snood over her hair, her feet still in worn house slippers.

''Ave yer seen my boys, Peggy?'

'Alice said Tom went after Sam when she told him there was an unexploded device in the rubble,' Peggy told her.

'No! Not my boys...' Tilly started screaming and set off at a run. Peggy went after her, following as they ran up past the market to an area where intensive bombing had left a whole row of houses and shops in ruins.

People were running and police whistles were blown. In the distance a siren could be heard. When they arrived at the scene, a police officer was trying to keep the small crowd back and they could hear the whine of an ambulance in the background.

'Is anyone hurt?' Peggy asked a man with a cycle. Dressed in a greasy boiler suit and a checked cap, he was just standing there watching as other people rushed to help. 'I think there were some boys from our lane up here...'

'Two of them are over there...' The man pointed to the far side of the rubble. 'I don't think there's much hope for them. They must have been on top of it, probably set it off – but there's a couple more where the copper is now. I reckon they're hurt bad, but I think they're still alive...'

Tilly had reached the policeman kneeling on the ground. Peggy heard a piercing scream as she flung herself down next to the prone figures of two youths. Her cries and screams were wild and despairing as Peggy went to her and took hold of her shoulders.

'Sam... My Sam...' Tilly cried bitterly. 'It's Tom's fault.'

'Tom came to fetch his brother away,' Peggy said and took her shoulders, half lifting her to her feet and trying to lead her away. 'The ambulance is here now – let the men through...'

Tilly shook her off and tried to fling herself on her younger son's body, but one of the men dragged her off. Peggy took Tilly's arms and forced her back as the ambulance men bent over the lads. Her throat was tight with fear and emotion as she watched them place a blanket over Sam, before he was carried into the ambulance, because she'd seen for herself how badly he was injured and expected the terrible outcome, but now Tom was being lifted onto a stretcher and placed into the ambulance as well, his face white and his eyes closed.

'Will he be all right?' Peggy asked the ambulance driver.

'Can't tell you yet, missus. His left arm is badly damaged and he has a head wound, but he's alive at the moment.

Sorry, love. See what you can do for the dead lad's mother. Can you tell me his name?'

'Sam Barton. His mother lives at number five Mulberry Lane...'

'Right, thanks. Do you know the other lad?'

'Tom is Sam's brother. He tried to make him come away because it was dangerous.'

'Well, he risked his own life for nothin',' the man said. 'They never learn, these lads. That's the second accident we've had this last month – but the last one wasn't as bad as this...'

'Oh, God...' Peggy caught a sobbing breath as she saw Tom's pale face. 'Pray God he's all right. He's a good lad...'

Tilly had stopped screaming as the ambulance door was closed. She pressed forward, begging to be allowed to go with her sons, but one of the policemen held her back.

'We'll let you know how the boy is once the doctors have had a look at him, Mrs Barton. There's no point in your goin' with them, because he will need surgery. You can visit him later...'

Peggy took hold of her arm. 'Come back with me, Tilly. I'll get you a cup of tea or a drink. They're takin' Tom to the London – and Sam... We'll make arrangements with an undertaker once we get the certificates. I'll help you. We'll all help you...'

'Can you bring Sam back from the dead?'

'No...' Peggy saw the despair in her eyes and couldn't find words that would ease her grief. 'Tom still has a chance, though...'

'What do I care about him?' Tilly said, her eyes wild. 'They've taken my boy – they've taken my boy...' She put a hand to her face and then crumpled to the ground in a heap.

'Perhaps I can help?' a voice asked and an attractive man with silvered hair came forward. He was wearing a smart dark suit and smelled of fresh cologne. 'I'm a doctor. She's in shock. Can you help me get her in my car please? I'll take her home and give her a sedative...'

'She would be on her own,' Peggy said. 'I think you'd better bring her to me. I'm her neighbour and I can take care of her until she gets over the shock.

'Are you prepared to look out for her for a few days?'

'Yes, of course. I run the pub at the corner of Mulberry Lane. I know the family well. Tom does a lot of little jobs for me...'

'Then she'll be in good hands...' He offered his hand to shake and Peggy took it. 'Doctor Michael Blake. I work at the London and heard the explosion as I was on my way to work, Mrs...?'

'Ashley. Peggy Ashley.' Peggy smiled. 'Thanks. It's only just down the road. If we can get her in the car...'

Tilly was only half aware as they manoeuvred her into the back seat of the comfortable Morris car, its worn seats smelling of old leather and polish. Peggy climbed in with her to hold her if she started to struggle or scream, but she was quiet and stared straight in front of her, not acknowledging Peggy or speaking. Even when some of Peggy's regulars volunteered to carry her upstairs and she was placed under the eiderdown, she didn't give any sign that she knew anyone.

'I'll give her a sedative and she should sleep for several hours,' Doctor Blake said to Peggy. 'If you need me, call this number and I'll come out in my own time. It will be in the evening or early morning – unless she would prefer her own doctor?'

'I doubt Tilly bothers with a doctor often and I doubt she pays into a doctor's panel,' Peggy said. 'I'm not sure she could afford for you to come out, sir.'

'I wouldn't dream of charging her,' he said and smiled. 'Just do what you can for her – because there's no telling how a shock like this will take her when she does come out of it.'

'Yes, of course. We all help each other in the lane, Doctor Blake.'

'You more than anyone I believe?' he said. 'Yes, I have heard of Peggy Ashley of the Pig & Whistle.'

He injected Tilly's arm, replaced his syringe in his bag and stood up.

'I'll call again tomorrow morning. I hope she won't be too much trouble to you, Mrs Ashley. Goodbye for now...'

Peggy gazed down at Tilly's face as she slept. Even in slumber she looked tortured, and, judging by her comments when they took Sam away, she would be devastated when the fact of her son's death really hit her. Peggy felt deep compassion, because the poor woman had been coping as best as she could with her husband's imprisonment and now this had happened – her life must be nothing but grief and hardship. It made Peggy realise how lucky she was to have the pub, her daughter and son, and Maggie – and to have known Able's love. She'd lost him but at least she'd had something wonderful to remember.

She would do whatever she could for Tilly. A collection would have to be made, because Tilly just didn't have the money to pay for a funeral. No one had very much to spare these days, but the people of the lanes helped each other and Peggy would put an empty cocoa tin on the bar, because whatever was donated would help to get the family through this terrible tragedy.

'How is she this mornin'?' Alice asked when she entered the bar the next morning. 'Mrs Tandy phoned the 'ospital last night and they said Tom 'ad come out of surgery and was 'oldin' his own...'

'Yes, I phoned early this mornin', and they told me the same thing,' Peggy said, smiling because it was good news. 'Tilly is awake. I took her a cup of tea and she drank some of it but just shook her head when I asked if she wanted some toast.'

'She's upset over them boys...' Alice nodded. 'She spoiled that Sam somethin' awful. Tom always got it in the neck, but Sam couldn't do no wrong – even though he was a little tea leaf...'

'We don't know he stole anythin',' Peggy objected, though she knew Sam was up to no good on that bomb site.

'I do,' Alice said grimly. 'I caught 'im in me purse once. That's why I wouldn't 'ave 'im to do me jobs. Tom is as honest as the day is long...' She gave a little sob. 'But that brother of 'is ain't much – and I know I shouldn't speak ill of the dead.'

'You're upset, Alice,' Peggy said. 'I don't mind you tellin' me the truth, but don't say anythin' like that to Tilly, will you?'

'Nah, 'course not,' Alice said. 'Feel sorry fer 'er wiv 'er husband banged up an' all...'

'Yes, very sorry,' Peggy agreed. 'But I feel more sorry for Tom at the moment. He has a nasty injury to his shoulder and he may not be able to use it properly...'

'No!' Alice looked aghast. 'What will the poor lad do if 'e can't work no more?'

'I don't know,' Peggy shook her head. 'I'd give him a job in the bar if he was old enough, but he was such an active lad – and so proud of what he was doin' and earnin'.' She blinked hard. 'It will break his heart and I think it will break mine as well...' Peggy felt the tears spill over as she could no longer keep her emotions in check. 'It's too much, Alice, it's just too much...'

'I know, love,' Alice said and put out a sympathetic hand to touch hers. 'I reckon there's got ter be somethin' good soon or we'll all go right round the bloomin' bend...'

Peggy struggled to fasten the waist of her favourite pencil skirt, but it was no use. It wouldn't close by almost an inch. She frowned as she took it off, because that was the third thing she'd tried on that was too tight but she couldn't imagine why she was putting on weight… unless it was what they called middle-aged spread? She looked at herself in the mirror and her eyes widened as she noticed the new fullness in her breasts. Now that she thought about it, her breasts were a little tender – and it was ages since she'd had a proper period. There had been just a few spots for a couple of days last month and she'd wondered if it was the first sign of the change, but it just hadn't occurred to her that she might be pregnant.

Peggy stared at herself as she counted back to the last time she'd had a full period. It was the week before she'd gone away with Able for that lovely few days in the country. What an idiot not to have suspected it before, but she hadn't felt in the least bit sick, which she had with both of her children – and after Pip's birth, which had been harder than the first, she'd been told it was unlikely she would conceive again. Laurie hadn't bothered to take precautions for years and she hadn't fallen… but now she was almost sure she was having a baby.

Sitting on the edge of the bed, Peggy felt numb with shock. She knew they'd been careless that weekend, making love over and over again with no precautions, but it hadn't bothered her, because she was sure her days of childbearing were over. It had disappointed her when the doctors first said it was unlikely she would have another baby, because she loved them and wouldn't have minded a bigger family, but that was when she was younger...

Peggy stared at her white face and felt her heart flip. How could she not have realised what was happening to her? She'd been in such distress over Able's disappearance and the arguments with Laurie and then Pip – and then there was Janet and Mike. Recently, Tom Barton's accident and his brother's terrible death had sent everything else out of her mind. Even though Tilly had recovered enough to go home, Tom's life was still uncertain as far as the residents of the lane knew, because the hospital wouldn't give anyone but his mother full details and Tilly wasn't bothered. Peggy had asked if she wanted to telephone from the pub but she'd refused.

Struggling to bring her mind back to her own problems, Peggy felt the tenderness in her breasts and accepted what she could no longer deny. She must be nearly three months gone and yet she'd experienced none of the usual symptoms, but she knew in her heart it was true.

She was carrying Able's child. Peggy drew a shaky breath, feeling light-headed. It was as if he'd reached out from beyond the grave to give her a precious gift and tears of joy stung her eyes. Her cheeks were wet, but all she could do was just sit there and let it sink in. She was having another child – she was going to have Able's baby. Peggy had thought he was gone from her, but now she would have him with her always: a child that looked like his father to love and cherish for as long as they both lived. Suddenly the world that had seemed so empty after they told her Able was missing was brighter. She crossed her arms over herself, hugging the knowledge to her.

It was only as the rush of joy was subsiding that she started to think about the consequences. Laurie needed to be told, because she couldn't deceive him if she tried – and she didn't want to. There was no way the child could be his, and he was going to be angry and resentful, which was natural – but would he demand that she leave his pub?

Peggy wanted to stay here where she had friends, but she had to face facts. Laurie would be entitled to demand a divorce, even though he'd been unfaithful to her first. Peggy didn't know how she felt about that – divorce wasn't something people she knew ever did. If couples split up, one went off and the other struggled on alone; it was very rare that they divorced and remarried, because it was just too expensive. Laurie had gone off, but he hadn't abandoned the pub and, although she was the temporary landlady, the lease was in his name. If he'd been a casualty of war she might get it made over to her, but in the circumstances he would win hands down – and she couldn't fight him for it anyway. It wouldn't be fair – no, it would be Peggy who would have to move out when Laurie insisted, but for the moment she was staying put.

This pub was her home and her children's home. Janet had nowhere else to go and she wanted to bring Mike here when he left hospital, because it was almost impossible to find a house in London now. The bombing had left a severe shortage of accommodation, and even a room was like gold dust. Peggy had told Janet it was fine; and although Pip was away with the Air Force, he liked to come home on leave.

What was Pip going to say when he discovered she was having another man's child? He'd been upset and angry when he realised she'd been away with Able for a weekend – she could imagine the disgust in his eyes if she told him that she was having Able's child. He would hate her for it and that hurt, but it couldn't be helped.

Both Pip and Laurie would probably say she should get rid of it, but Peggy would die rather than do such a thing. Worry started to niggle at the back of her mind. She was plenty old enough to be having a child, forty-one and a bit, and it could be dangerous for both her and the baby...

Peggy fought down her panic. She would visit the doctor and hear what he had to say before she started in with the worry beads... In the meantime she had to find something she could wear and carry on as usual.

*

It was confirmed! Peggy's head was spinning as she left the doctor's surgery two days later. He'd told her she was having a child after an examination and patted her kindly on the shoulder before she got dressed.

'Well, I don't think I need to advise you what to do, Mrs Ashley,' he said as she emerged from behind the curtain. 'Eat and drink normally and take plenty of exercise – but I imagine you already get plenty of that at the pub. In the last stages you may need to get help in, but I don't see why you should change your life just yet...'

'I'm over forty now, doctor...'

'Yes, but you've kept yourself fit and healthy, which can't be said for all my patients, Mrs Ashley. You will of course want to tell your husband, but there's no need for him to come rushing home. I don't foresee any problems at this stage...'

'Thank you...' Peggy picked up her gloves and put her hat on. 'Shall I get extra rations now?'

'Orange juice and milk I expect, but I'll give you all the relevant information...' He picked up some leaflets and offered them to her. 'I'm not sure if you will need to go into hospital for the birth...'

'I had the other two at home...'

'Yes, and it is what we hope for this time, Mrs Ashley. The hospitals are trying not to take in maternity cases where it isn't strictly necessary, for obvious reasons. However, in your case, it may not be possible for you to manage at home. I want you to come for your prenatal appointments – don't miss them just because you feel fine. Despite what I just said, we do need to keep an eye on you until the birth.'

Peggy thanked him and walked home. He'd taken it for granted that the child was her husband's, as would most people, unless things changed between her and Laurie. She was fortunate in having a little money put by and she would use it to go away to have the child, if Laurie insisted. She ought to be able to find work of some kind, cooking or as a housekeeper – her thoughts were so busy that she walked right past one of her customers until he called out to her.

'All right, Peggy – nothing wrong is there?'

'No, nothing at all,' she said and beamed at him. 'How are you, Mr Parish?'

'I'm fine thanks, love. I'll be round on Saturday night for a pint – so keep some for me, Peggy.'

'Yes, of course. We had a delivery this mornin' so you're all right,' Peggy said and smiled.

She smothered a sigh as she pushed her personal worries to the back of her mind. The first person she had to tell was Janet, but then she was going to have to write that letter to Laurie – and goodness knows what he would think of her then!

*

'Oh, Mum, you're not havin' another baby at your age!' Janet cried, staring at her with a mixture of anxiety and disapproval. 'Couldn't you have, well, taken precautions or done something to get rid of it?'

'We didn't think about it,' Peggy admitted, feeling a little foolish. 'Able was as careful as he could be, but once or twice we were careless – but I didn't think it mattered. I told him I couldn't have another baby... I didn't think I could – and although it was a shock at first, now I've thought about it, I'm delighted.'

'Isn't it dangerous for women of your age? I mean, there could be all sorts of complications.'

'I'm not in my dotage, Janet.'

'Of course you're not! You don't look more than thirty but you are forty-one – and I don't want to lose you. I love you, Mum...'

'Thank you, darling...' Peggy suddenly found it funny and started laughing. Janet looked bewildered and she shook her head. 'Sorry, love, but the doctor says I'm fit and healthy, more so than a lot of women half my age. He's goin' to monitor me, but he doesn't think I'll have too much trouble – though I may have to go into hospital to have the baby.'

Janet nodded, relaxing and smiling as she recovered from the shock. 'You're happy about it, aren't you?'

'Yes, I am. I loved Able so much, Janet – and I thought I'd lost him. Now I'll always have a part of him to love and that has given me so much to look forward to...' She saw the look in Janet's eyes and reached out to take her hand. 'Of course I love you and Pip, and Maggie, and I'm just as interested in your futures – but Able made me feel young again. Just for a while I knew what it was like to be in love and to know that a man felt the same for me – to be wanted in a way Laurie hasn't wanted me for years. I felt alive and really happy again and when they told me...' Her voice broke. 'It took everythin' for a while. I was comin' back from that when I realised I was pregnant and now I feel on top of the world again. Can you understand that and not feel slighted or less loved?'

'Of course I can, Mum. I'm a mother myself. Babies bring new love with them; they don't take it from anyone else – your heart just gets bigger to let them in...'

'Oh, darling,' Peggy said and they embraced, both with tears on their cheeks. 'It will make more noise and mess about the place – and a lot of work. I shan't have as much time for the pub...'

'You'll have to get someone in...' Janet frowned as she began to think of the consequences. 'What is Dad goin' to say about this? He said he didn't want a divorce – but he might change his mind now.'

'If he does I shall have to think about findin' a home and a job...'

'He can't turn you out. If he thinks I'll take over here I won't. We'll simply refuse to move until we can find somewhere for all of us – after all your years as a landlady, you should get your own lease. I've heard of women who've lost their husbands to the war and are applyin' to become the landlord, or should I say landlady? Ryan said it should be easy in your case if you ever wanted...'

'Well, that's for the future. If Laurie is goin' to be away for the duration, he might let me stay on here. Once the baby is born I can look for somethin' – even if it's workin' for someone else as a cook or behind the bar of another pub...'

'We should miss you, Maggie and me,' Janet said. 'I'll tell Dad he's got to be reasonable – after all, he's not blameless in this. You need time to sort yourselves out that's all...' She hesitated then, 'Are you goin' to tell Pip?'

'I think that's harder than tellin' your father,' Peggy said. 'Laurie will be angry, but he'll cope – your brother will hate me...'

'He couldn't, Mum. He really loves you, though he will be angry with you.'

'Yes, I'm afraid he will,' Peggy said. 'I think I'll tell him next time he's home...'

'Are you sure? Supposin', he hears about it from someone else first?' Janet smiled at her. 'Be brave, Mum. I'll write and tell him if you like...'

'I'd better do it myself. I thought it would be better face to face – but you're right, darling. Someone might tell him and he would hate that. I'll write to them both. Put the kettle on and I'll have a cup of tea to give me some courage...'

*

Laurence read the letter three times before he could believe it was true. His wife was having another man's child and she had every intention of keeping it. Reading between the lines, despite her apologies and her excuses, she was happy about it.

He'd thought she was past all that, though at the back of his mind he'd known she hadn't actually gone through the change, but they'd had regular sex for years and he'd never taken any precautions. He wasn't sure how that made him feel – as if he were the one who'd got old and couldn't have children. It must surely be that way or Peggy wouldn't have fallen just like that – unless she'd been lying about how long it had been going on, but even so... It couldn't have been more than a few months at most and Peggy hadn't even suspected she might be pregnant since Pip's birth.

Marie had made him feel like a young man again. For a while he'd forgotten about his old life, the pub and Peggy, and even the kids. Janet had her own family now and Pip was serving his country like a man. If he survived the war he would marry and leave home – but there would be another child in the house for years: a cuckoo in the nest. If he allowed Peggy to stay, that was – because he was well within his rights to throw her out.

He closed his eyes as the sick anger raged through him. If they'd been in the same room he thought he might have struck her, tried to beat the bastard out of her – but that was stupid and wrong. When he was younger he would have beaten her without a second thought if she'd cheated on him, but he was too old to bother these days. And tired. He felt ridiculously tired, as if life were just too much bother.

Shrugging, Laurence bent his head over his work. This was all that seemed real to him these days: the need to come up with better, safer codes to protect the men and women who risked their lives daily to save their country from defeat and invasion. Laurence knew it didn't look like it from the reports in the newspapers that spoke of defeats and setbacks for the Allies, but he believed they were winning the war, the men and women who worked tirelessly, some in uniform in constant danger, and others at a desk.

He would give it a few days before he wrote to Peggy. Let her sweat over it for a while; she deserved that at least, but to be honest he didn't see much sense in making trouble over this... She would have to pretend it was his child, of course. He wouldn't stand for anyone knowing, because he wasn't going to be mocked or pitied, and he didn't need to have a lot to do with the kid – but Peggy was a good mother and a good landlady. They didn't have to share the same bed, but otherwise they could go on as they always had – and if he felt like having an affair he would.

At the moment he hadn't found anyone to replace Marie, but there was a new girl just being trained to take messages in code and he'd seen her looking at him a few times. She was in her twenties, blonde and pretty, and she looked fantastic in uniform... He might just ask her out for a drink one night.

Chapter 23

'Are you sure you don't mind lookin' after Shirley when she gets in from school?' Hilda Jackson asked. 'Maureen said you wouldn't mind havin' her occasionally. Only I've promised I'll visit Eddie Miller – I don't know if you remember her? She used to be a close friend of Percy's, your stepfather – and she's in the infirmary. I got the message that she's dyin', poor woman, and asked for me special. Her family lived in Frying Pan Alley when she was younger – but she split wiv 'er 'usband and went orf wiv 'er fancy man. We all thought she was daft, cos it was as plain as the nose on me face that he was only after one thing…'

'Oh, poor Eddie,' Peggy said smiling at Maureen's gran. 'I think I remember her a little – didn't she have red hair?'

'Out of a bottle maybe,' Hilda said with a twinkle in her eye. 'She was blonde or red, whatever took 'er fancy. Messed around wiv your Percy fer a while, but that came to nothin'. So she went after this 'ere soldier and run orf – but he left her after a few months. Still, she 'ad a good 'eart did Eddie, and she'd 'ave give yer the shirt orf her back if she liked yer…'

'Well, I'll look after Shirley. It will be a pleasure to have her, Mrs Jackson.' Peggy hesitated, then, 'I'm goin' to see Tommy Barton in the London tomorrow. His ma hasn't been to see him once – and she told me it was none of my business when I said she ought – so I'm goin' tomorrow and you could come as well if you like.'

''Course I will, Peggy,' Hilda said. 'That boy has done me a good turn or two – and if his mum isn't lookin' out fer him some of us should.'

'Yes, that's what I think,' Peggy agreed. 'I'm goin' to be talkin' to a few people, Hilda, and I reckon we ought to try and do somethin' about gettin' his father home for a while – until Tom is on his feet again perhaps.'

'Do yer think it's possible?'

'We shan't know if we don't try – but Tilly is like a dead thing. She just sits in her kitchen and stares at the wall. I've spoken to a doctor about her and he says they might let her husband home on compassionate grounds – someone's got to bury Sam. Tilly won't even talk about it – but I'm thinkin' of gettin' up a petition. If enough of us signed it, they might give him a few months off for compassionate leave.'

'In that case, I'll do whatever yer want, Peggy. I'll talk to people I know – I reckon most folks round 'ere would sign in the circumstances.'

'Thanks. You get off now. You don't want to keep your friend waitin'...'

'Right, then I'll take a bottle of that stout for Eddie. She always liked it, so she might as well 'ave a drop afore she goes, if the nurses will let 'er...'

'Yes, why not?' Peggy handed the bottle over the bar. 'Take it as a gift from me. I remember Eddie visitin' my mother in hospital and takin' her some flowers. You give her this and tell her we're all thinkin' of her...'

'Right, I'll get her five Woodbines an' all – that might bring her round. She was always one for the fags and the stout – and if she's goin' out she might as well enjoy it.'

'You'll cheer her up,' Peggy said and laughed, then, 'Does Shirley know where to come?'

'Anne said she'd bring her,' Hilda said and grinned, because it showed she'd taken it for granted that Peggy would have the girl.

Peggy smiled inwardly. It was always the same in their little neighbourhood and she wouldn't have had it any other way. It was like being one big family here in this little community; the folk of Mulberry Lane and the surrounding alleys and streets all knew each other's business, and some of the women spent half the day gossiping. Yet in hard times they came together.

'Good, then I shan't have to fetch her myself,' Peggy said.

'I fetch her most days, but Anne brings her home sometimes; it's on her way when she's workin' at the school. Did you know that her uncle's bad again? Poor chap; I think it's his heart and he might not 'ave much longer.'

'Anne will be upset about that,' Peggy said. 'I know she's fond of him and if anythin' happens she'll miss him.'

'Yes, I expect so – it's time young Anne found 'erself a 'usband. Otherwise, she'll wake up one mornin' and discover the world's passed her by...'

'Anne is only thirtyish,' Peggy said and frowned. 'I think she may be courtin' now, but I'm not certain.'

'There was a chap,' Hilda said, obviously in the know. 'He was an inspector for the bloody government, but she fell out wiv 'im cos he told on the father of one of her schoolkids. He was done for dealin' in meat what fell off the back of a lorry – and now 'e's in prison and the family is sufferin'...'

'Oh, I hadn't heard that,' Peggy said, relieved that Anne's friend was unlikely to pay her a visit and so stumble on the fact that she'd been using American whisky on her premises, but sorry that Anne had once again suffered a setback in her personal life.

However, when Anne brought Shirley round that after-noon she seemed perfectly happy. She stayed to have tea with them all. Shirley was on her best behaviour, or that was how it seemed to Peggy, but later that evening, after Maureen's gran had popped round to fetch the girl home, Anne told her that Shirley was no trouble these days.

'If anything she's a bit on the quiet side,' Anne said as they took the clean glasses through to the bar together. 'I'd prefer to see a little more spirit in her, but she doesn't laugh much and hardly ever runs about in the playground. It's almost as if she's afraid to raise her voice or get into mischief like the other kids.'

'Maureen said she was shocked by the change in the girl,' Peggy told her. 'When she brought her home, they came to have their tea with me and Maureen said it was that woman at the farm. She thinks Shirley was bullied and made to work – apparently she spent all her free time from school doin' chores on the farm. She's only seven, Anne, and it's hard on her to be passed from one person to the next. Maureen was spittin' mad. She said if she'd known how Mrs Hunter was treatin' her she would've fetched the girl home ages ago.'

'But she can't look after her now she's nursing...' Anne said and frowned.

'She's goin' to ask them if she can transfer to a hospital nearer home,' Peggy said. 'I've told her she should stop where she is and that we'll take care of Shirley for her, but she feels responsible.'

'There's not the least need,' Anne said. 'I've been told I shall be based in London for good now, Peggy. I'll take my share of looking after the girl. I like Shirley and I liked her father, what I knew of him. I'm living in a small room now but I'm goin' to try to get something more permanent round here...'

'That might not be easy...' Peggy thought for a moment, and then nodded. 'Mavis Basset is considerin' takin' on a lodger. She lives right opposite to Jackson's shop at number twelve.' Peggy looked sad. 'She lost two sons to this war and a husband to the last, poor woman, though he didn't die *during* the war, but slowly afterwards of the mustard gas. I think she suffered through his illnesses for years – as he did, of course. There is a married daughter but she moved away and Mavis only sees her a few times a year. She asked me if I could give her a job and I said she could help me in the bar in the mornings, wipin' down tables and washin' glasses...' Breathing deeply, Peggy decided she might as well tell her friend. 'I'll need more help soon, because I'm pregnant...'

'Peggy! That's a bit of a shock, isn't it – or have you been trying?' Anne looked startled.

'Let's say it was a surprise – but a pleasant one,' Peggy said. 'I thought there was no chance of it happenin' after all these years...'

'It must have been the change of air,' Anne said, clearly thinking that Laurie was the father. 'It's given him a new lease of life...'

'Yes...' Peggy didn't meet her friend's eyes, because she couldn't tell Anne the truth. Anne knew nothing of her brief affair with Able and Peggy thought it better that only those who had to know were told the truth. She hadn't even told Nellie that it was Able's child, though those wise old eyes saw more than most and she knew Nellie would never condemn her. 'Perhaps. Anyway, I'm happy about it. Janet's husband will be comin' home in a few weeks and as soon as they can get a house of their own they will move out...'

'You'll miss her company,' Anne said, 'but I doubt they'll be lucky enough to get anything around here for a while.'

'One of my customers was tellin' me the government are goin' to build some temporary houses – prefabs they're callin' them. They go up quick and don't cost much, because they're not bricks and mortar...'

'Yes, I've heard about them,' Anne agreed. 'They will be further out I expect, in the suburbs. Janet wouldn't want to go out there, would she?'

'I doubt it. Nellie says she wouldn't have one if they paid her,' Peggy said with a laugh. 'She's been lookin' for weeks, though I've told her she can stay with me for as long as she likes. I've got a room here you could have, Anne, but Mavis would probably let you have two if you wanted. You could have a sittin' room and bedroom, and make your own tea on a gas ring...'

'I've got an electric kettle; it's one of the new Russell Hobbs ceramic kettles and works really well,' Anne said and hesitated. 'I might only need a room for a while, because I might move into my uncle's flat. As you know, my uncle is ill and they've taken him into the infirmary. I don't know what will happen to his place if he never comes back – and I don't really see how he can. He's had a woman in to clean for him since my aunt died, but she says he doesn't eat properly and she doesn't have the time to look after him... so I might move in to keep things right until he asks someone to sell it.'

'Percy was the same after Mum died. I went round and did what I could for him, but it's the loneliness – men aren't good at copin' alone. Women manage it much better, or most of them do. Mavis is bearin' up well at the moment. Why don't you pop in and see her before you go home, Anne? It would be nice havin' you in the lane – we could see each other more often.'

'Yes, I will,' Anne said, 'and don't forget I'll help out with Shirley so Maureen doesn't have to give up her work and come back...'

*

Peggy stared at Laurie's letter for a full five minutes before opening it. Her stomach clenched as she considered what she would do if he told her he wanted her out of the pub. The relief flowed over her as she read the rather cold, controlled letter.

> *What do you expect me to say? I can't pretend to be anything but angry, but I suppose it isn't the end of the world and I know there is no point in asking you to get rid of the child. So we shall just have to make the best of things. Fortunately, I'm not likely to be around much for a while, though I'll come and see you when the baby is born if you let me know – and, naturally, I expect you to keep the truth to yourself. If we're going to live together it's the only way. Of course, we'll stick to separate rooms.*

He'd signed his name without any form of affection and Peggy understood that he was seriously upset, but she hadn't expected anything else. She'd thought he might want her to leave, but it seemed that Laurie valued her as a landlady and a cook if nothing more. It sounded as though he was reconciled to living separate lives as long as she was discreet and didn't tell anyone that she was carrying the child of her American lover.

Peggy felt the chill at the back of her neck. Somehow she would rather Laurie had gone for her than write a letter like this, because it was just too cold and remote. Once he would have flown into a temper and they would have both felt better for a good row, but this made her feel as if she were in the wrong. Laurie had let her down so many times but it seemed that she was being forced to bear all the blame for the breakdown of their marriage. Yet common sense told her that this was the best outcome for her – at least for the time being. She would've found it hard to move her life at this moment, because of the baby in her womb. Besides, Janet and Nellie were both relying on the pub for accommodation. Eventually, they would find new homes and perhaps Peggy would too, when the war was over and things got back to normal – if they ever did.

Throughout the spring and summer the news had been bad from overseas; the Russians were fighting desperately against superior odds and the Allies had one setback after another, though the air force was building up its strength again under Bomber Harris, the new chief in command. They were now preparing fresh attacks on German cities, partly to cause chaos and give Hitler pause, and partly in revenge for the attacks against London, Coventry, Birmingham, Liverpool, and many other ports, towns and cities across Britain. In June, it became necessary to ration the purchase of new clothes, but until the new ration books were printed people were advised to use margarine coupons: sixteen for a raincoat, two for gloves, seven for a pair of men's boots. However, a lot of women were buying from the market without coupons and selling their clothes that no longer fitted them.

The WRVS had set up centres for women to exchange clothes their children had grown out of, because the coupons allowed just weren't enough for growing children. Families who lost everything through an air raid were told they would get two years' coupons to buy new, but, despite the hardships, the V for Victory sign was beginning to appear everywhere in shops and on buses and people refused to admit defeat. Everyone was being cheerful and saying that the tide had to turn soon – if only the Americans would come into the war.

The newspapers were filled with tales of small victories on the ground one day and terrible defeats another, the Allied troops making a hurried exit from Crete after a spirited defence, but in the air there were daily triumphs as the thin blue line continued to hold firm. No one was certain which way the war was going, and at this point there seemed no end to a war on so many fronts...

Given the state of the world in summer 1941, Peggy knew it could be years before Laurie was able to return to the pub. He needed her to hold it together for him as best she could, and she would do her utmost to make sure that he had a business to come back to when he finally returned. Most of the extra stock he'd bought before the war had been used and it wasn't easy to buy more, though she'd continued to purchase what she could. To have done otherwise might have aroused suspicion that she was dealing on the black market, and had the bottles of American bourbon been discovered in the cellar she might well have been accused of it, but they were long gone and Able wasn't around to bring her any more...

Peggy's eyes stung with tears as she thought of Able, but she brushed them away impatiently. She wasn't the sort to feel sorry for herself. She'd had a good time with Able and she wasn't sorry for any of it. She was strong, she knew that, and nothing was going to break her spirit – even though she sometimes cried herself to sleep.

Yet there was always someone else worse off. At the moment, Peggy's thoughts were with the young lad in the hospital. She and Maureen's gran had visited him in the intensive care ward, but he'd been under sedation and she wasn't sure he'd even known they were there, because the nurse would only let them peek at him.

'Tom is going to be with us for a while,' the nurse had told Peggy. 'Next time, please telephone first and you'll save yourselves a wasted trip.'

Peggy had left the hospital feeling more determined than ever that she was going to do something about Tommy's dad. Most people in the lanes had signed her petition, even though they thought she was mad.

'They'll never let Jack Barton out,' Harry Jackson told her, 'but I'll sign yer petition, Peggy. Tom's not a bad lad and I feel sorry fer 'im stuck in there and his ma ain't been near...'

'He's not ready for visitors yet,' Peggy told him, even though she thought privately that Tilly was behaving badly towards her son, 'but we've got to try and get his father home, even if it's only for a few weeks...'

'Right, leave a copy 'ere on me counter,' Harry said. 'I'll get a few signatures for you if I can...'

Peggy thanked him and left a sheet of her petition for his customers to sign. She could only hope it would be enough, because Tilly was getting worse day by day. The last time Peggy went over with a meal for her she'd just left it uneaten on the side, and she would swear that Tilly hadn't changed her dress or washed in weeks.

Peggy might have her own troubles, but this terrible war had caused so much pain and suffering all round. She was determined that whatever life brought next, she would keep smiling – because she had good reason to smile. No matter what happened, she was having Able's child and that meant she had something to make her life worthwhile.

Chapter 24

Maureen read Peggy's letter when she came off shift late that night. Anne had promised to help look after Shirley until after the war when her father came back, and Peggy said there was no need to return to London just for the girl's sake. She should stay where she was while she was needed and not feel guilty.

Maureen folded the letter and tucked it away in her drawer. It was good of her friends to rally round like this, because she knew it was too much for Gran to have permanent care of the little girl. Maureen had tentatively broached the subject of transferring to London to work and live with Rory. They'd met one night after her return to Portsmouth, and he'd been furious with her for considering it.

'You wouldn't come back to London when I was in hospital and needed you,' he said, his eyes glittering with temper. 'Your job was too important, so I came down here for you – but now you say you should give it up and run back to take care of a kid that means nothin' to you...'

'I'm fond of Shirley. She used to be a spoiled brat, but she's had a hard lesson living on that farm and I feel sorry for her. Besides, I wouldn't have to give up nursin' – just take my turn when I'm off duty...'

Rory's eyes flashed with temper. 'You've fetched her back, now let that be the finish of it. Her bloody father can ask for leave and come home and see to her – he should pay someone to take her on or put her in a kids' home…'

'No!' Maureen cried. 'That's a horrid thing to say, Rory. None of us would let that happen to her – she's one of us.'

'And I'm not…' He looked sullen. 'It didn't matter that I needed you when I was in hospital. Oh no, you couldn't leave your bleedin' job for me – but you'll run back for Hart's brat. Are you sure it's not him you're after?'

'Rory! How could you?' Maureen stared at him, feeling hurt, but also a little guilty, because perhaps she was considering Gordon's feelings too much. 'I'm just being a good friend, looking after a neighbour's child while he can't…' Yet a little voice in her head told her that Rory had some right on his side. She enjoyed writing to Gordon and receiving his letters and perhaps she did feel closer to his daughter than the situation called for. Once again the doubts crowded in on her. She'd loved Rory when she was a young girl working in her father's shop; he'd represented freedom and a new life to her, but he'd changed, or she had, and she wasn't certain that she still felt the same.

'Supposin' he doesn't come back ever?' Rory glared at her and Maureen was silent, because she knew what was coming. 'Well, I'm not havin' the brat in my house, so you'll make your choice, Maureen. If you go back to London for her sake we're finished…'

'Don't say things like that – you know I love you…' But did she? There were times now when Maureen wondered if what she felt for him was the kind of love that would last. It was good when they were together in bed and Rory was happy, but he soon turned sulky if things didn't go his way and they argued too often for Maureen's liking. She'd begun to realise that she'd never truly known him. When they went anywhere it was always where he chose and it seemed that he didn't bother whether or not she wanted to visit the pub or the picture house.

Rory's expression remained hard. 'I thought you did once – but you put your father first and broke my heart. I married Velma because of you and that was a mistake, but now you're still puttin' other people first – and this time it's a kid that doesn't even belong to you. I mean it, Maureen. It's me or the kid...'

'But I promised to care for her...' Maureen felt a sinking sensation inside, because there was no talking to him when he was like this.

'Break your bloody promise then,' Rory said and turned away.

Maureen caught his arm. 'Where are you goin'? I thought you were takin' me to the pictures tonight? I was lookin' forward to seein' that Bing Crosby film.'

'Go on your own or take one of your friends,' he said harshly. 'I didn't want to see it anyway and I dare say there's half a dozen come way before me...' He stalked off and Maureen stared after him, too choked to call him back.

He couldn't mean they were finished? Surely it wasn't the end? She felt the pain of his rejection strike her and it hurt so much. Rory was selfish and he lost his temper easily. She loved him, but sometimes she wondered if she was a fool, because he seldom seemed to consider her feelings. It was always what he wanted, never what suited her best. Yes, he'd come with her to fetch Shirley but he'd hardly spoken to the girl or her on the way back to London. He'd left them at Gran's and gone straight back to Portsmouth and his job, leaving Maureen to catch a train the next morning. It was as if he was punishing her for being a caring person... but she couldn't help the way she was; her nature was always to help others, but it seemed as if Rory didn't want her to bother about anyone but him.

She'd gone back to her home in the hut at the hospital after their row that night and had a good cry, but she hadn't spoken to Sister about a transfer, because she believed it would be the end for her and Rory if she did. Her conscience over Gran and the others nagged at her, but Peggy's letter made it easier. She hadn't written to Rory to tell him she wasn't going back to London. He was the one that had flown into a temper and he ought to apologise. Why should she always be the one to give in...? Yet, she didn't want to lose him. Torn this way and that, she felt as if she were caught on thorns and whatever she decided would cause her pain.

After a week of crying herself to sleep, Maureen overcame her pride and wrote to Rory. He didn't reply for several days, and then he sent a message through one of the guards that he'd be waiting for her that evening when she got off shift.

I'll wait for half an hour, his note said, *but if you don't come I shan't bother coming back...*

Maureen screwed the note up angrily. She was furious herself now and thought it would serve him right if she didn't bother to go, but that would mean it was over between them and she couldn't bear that, so she decided she would give it another chance. However, they had an influx of wounded patients that afternoon, and Sister kept her running round the whole time. She didn't get her tea break and she knew that as the clock hands moved towards seven she wasn't going to get away on time.

She asked Sister if she could leave at twenty past seven, which would just have given her time to meet Rory outside the gates, but Sister shook her head and looked annoyed.

'You can see for yourself that it isn't possible, nurse. I know it's the end of your shift but we all have to make sacrifices.'

'Yes, Sister,' Maureen whispered. 'She dared not ask again, even though the clock crept round to eight and past as she was kept busy handing bandages, bringing fresh dressings, emptying bedpans and changing drips. When she was eventually told she could leave, it was gone nine.

Maureen didn't even bother going to the gate, because she knew Rory wouldn't be there. She was way over time but he wouldn't care that she'd had to work. He was too angry with her to care how she felt about anything and Maureen was numbed and miserable. Rory would think she'd stood him up, but what could she do – you didn't walk out on Sister Martin even if your boyfriend had given you an ultimatum.

Maureen undressed and got into bed, but she didn't sleep immediately. She was awake when Carol crept in much later, but she didn't sit up because the girl hardly spoke to her these days.

She'd felt weepy for a bit, but now she was just resigned. If Rory could just break things off like that, he didn't love her. Perhaps it was best that she'd discovered it now and not when it was too late...

*

Carol was packing her things into two suitcases when Maureen got back from breakfast the next morning. She turned and glanced at her, but then carried on packing without speaking.

'Are you goin' on leave?' Maureen asked, feeling that she ought to make the first move in healing the breach, though she didn't really know what she'd done to cause it.

'I'm leaving the service,' Carol said, though she didn't turn her head to look at her. 'I'm getting married...'

'Oh?' Maureen was startled, because she hadn't even known that Carol was courting. 'That's nice for you – have you known him long?'

'Long enough, not that it's any of your business...' Carol said rudely.

'Sorry, I just wondered.' Maureen turned away to sort out her clean uniform.

'It's your fault...' Carol said suddenly and she sounded angry, resentful. 'If you hadn't stood him up all those times because you were working we shouldn't have gone out so much and...'

Maureen whirled round and looked at her, seeing the other girl's red face and accusing eyes. 'What are you talkin' about – you can't mean Rory? You can't be marryin' him? I don't understand...'

'He has to marry me, I'm pregnant,' Carol said and her eyes filled with self-pitying tears. 'My parents are going to kill me. I've let them down and they'll never speak to me again – he's not the sort of man they wanted me to marry...'

'Rory is goin' to marry you, because you're havin' his child?' Maureen was trying to get her head round the girl's startling announcement, because it was just too shocking to take in. She couldn't have heard right! 'But you hardly know him...'

'We've been out six times,' Carol said defensively. 'He got fed up waiting for you – and I liked him, so he took me to the pub and the pictures, and we made love a few times in the back of a car he borrowed...'

'Are you in love with him?' Maureen was fighting an overwhelming desire to be sick. Surely Carol was lying? She had to be! This couldn't be happening again. He'd gone with Velma in a temper and caused Maureen years of regret and heartbreak; surely he wouldn't do it again? Yet, if she believed Carol, he had. Her thoughts were going round and round as she tried to make sense of things. Rory had taken Maureen away for that weekend and they'd fetched Shirley together. On both occasions they'd slept together and made love several times since. Maureen had thought they were a couple and been sure Rory loved her – but he'd been sleeping with Carol at the same time, even before they quarrelled! He'd been taking the younger girl out when Maureen was working, making love to her in the borrowed car and blaming Maureen for trying to do her best for an innocent child and for the breach between them, when all the time he was cheating on her. Carol had to be lying, because if she wasn't Rory was a cheat and a liar. It was as if Maureen were on the edge of a deep chasm and one step would send her over the edge. 'When did this start?' she demanded fiercely.

Carol took a step back as if she were nervous, but looked at her defiantly. 'Right from the first night you weren't off duty when you should've been. He was outside the gate when I went to tell him and he persuaded me to go with him – we've been out a few times since...' Carol choked back a sob. 'I swear I didn't plan it – it just happened. My father will kill us both if he finds out I'm pregnant before we're married.'

'You stupid little fool,' Maureen said, but then, quite suddenly, she discovered she wasn't upset, just disgusted with Carol and with Rory. It was like being outside of a window and looking in, watching a play unfolding. 'How could you let him? You went out a few times and you let him make love to you. I've known him for years and we were engaged…'

'I know and I'm sorry, I really am, Maureen. I didn't mean to break you up, but he was so lovely to me, telling me about his life in the Army – and it just happened, and now he has to marry me.' Carol's face was white now and tears trickled from the corners of her eyes. She probably didn't even want to marry him, but she had no choice because she wasn't the kind of girl who could go home and tell her parents the father of her baby wouldn't marry her.

'Yes, he does need to marry you,' Maureen said and closed her eyes. 'I shan't stand in your way.'

'I feel awful about you,' Carol faltered. 'I know he was yours and I've been horrible to you, because I was jealous…'

'No, he was never really mine.' Maureen opened her eyes to look at her, and it was as if the scales had fallen off and she was suddenly seeing things clearly. 'I loved him once or I thought I did – but, to be honest, you're welcome. I hope he makes you happy…'

Carol burst into noisy tears, but Maureen ignored her and walked out of the hut. She wasn't going to offer comfort to a girl who had deliberately gone with another girl's man. It was her own fault if she was in trouble and she was lucky Rory was prepared to stand by her – because if Maureen hadn't quarrelled with him he probably wouldn't have.

Maureen went for a walk around the grounds, deep in thought. She'd had her heart broken by Rory once, but this time it wasn't going to happen. Maureen was older and wiser now and she knew Rory for what he was – a flirt and a womaniser. He'd known what he was doing and he'd taken advantage of a silly young girl's blind adoration. Maureen knew now that if she'd wed him, it would've happened again and again over the years, making her wretched. He was the kind of man who would always cheat and make excuses.

Rory had used her, just as he did any girl foolish enough to let him. Had Carol not opened her eyes to the truth, she would've let him draw her into a trap; Maureen might have been tied to him for life and miserable every time he let her down. She'd forgiven him for going with Velma, thinking it was partly her fault, but for all she knew it had been going on before she'd broken it off with him. Knowing Rory he would probably come crawling back and blame it all on Carol, but this time she would refuse to listen. Maureen had grown up and she had other, more important things in her life.

*

Maureen thought she must be in trouble when Matron called her to the office later that afternoon. She knew Sister Martin was a bit cross with her for asking if she could leave on time the previous evening, but she couldn't think of anything she'd done to necessitate a lecture from Matron. However, when she knocked and entered the office, Matron smiled at her and invited her to sit down.

'Ah, Nurse Jackson,' she said. 'I've asked you to come and see me this afternoon for two reasons. The first is rather distressing I'm afraid, so perhaps I shall tell you the good news first. You are being transferred back to London. They have a chronic shortage of nurses at the London itself and asked us if we could spare any of ours – and Sister Martin recommended you, nurse. It appears that she thinks you have the makings of a fine nurse, and though she doesn't want to lose you, we are up to full staff here and must help others less fortunate than ourselves. I imagine you won't mind being transferred back home?'

Maureen swallowed hard as she looked at her. It seemed Fate had taken a hand in her destiny and she would be glad to go back to the people she knew cared for her.

'I have no objection, Matron. I am ready to go wherever I'm needed most.'

'Ah, just as Sister Martin told me. Good.' Matron looked at her in silence for a moment. 'I fear that my other news is not good – indeed it is a terrible blow for you, my child. There is no gentle way of breaking it to you – your father has had a stroke and has been rushed into hospital...'

Maureen was glad she was sitting down, because for a moment she felt faint. 'Dad is really ill? Last time I heard, he was fine...' Her father had traded on his weak chest for years, but this sounded more serious.

'These things are often sudden, as you know,' Matron said. 'I am so very sorry, nurse. You will of course be granted compassionate leave of eight days and you will report to your new posting at the end of that time...'

'Thank you, Matron. I should like to see him...' Maureen felt a lump in her throat. Her father had not always been kind to her but she still cared that he was ill and knew that she must go home as soon as possible.

'Naturally – and there will be things to arrange, of course. At least if you're posted in London you won't have to keep going back there in your free time. It has worked out quite nicely for you in the circumstances, though illness is never pleasant. I've informed Sister Martin and she will not be expecting you on the ward.'

Matron had tried to be calm and reassuring, but Maureen felt her eyes prick with the tears she couldn't hold back as she walked to her hut and began to pack her things. She felt odd knowing that she was unlikely to return and a little bewildered by the way things had changed so suddenly.

'Gosh, I'm glad I caught you,' Rita said, coming in just as Maureen was fastening her suitcases. 'I'm going to miss you – and Sister told us about your father. I'm sorry he's ill, Maureen. You've had your share of bad luck recently, haven't you?'

'It's bloody awful.' Maureen looked at her, eyes brimming with tears, and Rita held open her arms and they went into a fervent hug that helped a little. 'It's all happened at once,' she said emotionally. 'I've lost so many friends and...' Maureen shook her head because she hadn't told anyone at the hospital about Rory and what he'd done to her. 'It isn't as if my father and I got on all that well – but he's family...'

'Yes, I know...' Rita looked at her with sympathy and Maureen wondered if she'd heard about Carol and Rory from somewhere, but she didn't ask. She couldn't take any more just at this moment. 'It's rotten luck, love – but at least you'll be back with people you know...'

'Yes.' Maureen smiled and lifted her head. 'They're a decent lot in Mulberry Lane. I shall be fine when I get home, Rita – but we'll keep in touch. I'll write to you and tell you what I'm doing and you can visit if you come up to town now and then...'

'I'd love to,' Rita said; she hesitated, then, 'And I'm sorry. I should've told you when I first suspected what Carol was up to, but I didn't want to hurt you.'

'Not your fault,' Maureen said and managed a wobbly smile. 'Besides, she's welcome to him. He's not worth cryin' over.'

'Plenty more fish in the sea,' Rita agreed. 'He was good-looking, charming, but I thought he had a roving eye when he came looking for you. I refused to go out with him a couple of times. He would've been the same if you'd married him.'

'Yes, I know,' Maureen said and this time she was able to smile properly. 'I'll get over him, Rita.'

'Maureen love,' Peggy said when she walked in the pub that September evening. 'How's your dad?'

'About the same,' Maureen replied and sighed. 'He's really ill, Peggy. All those times he played up and I got so cross because he did it just to stop me going out – but he hardly knew me when I visited him just now. He looked so poorly lyin' there in that hospital bed – and he tried to smile and say somethin'. I think he wanted to say sorry...'

'I'm so sorry, love,' Peggy said and lifted the end of the bar so that she could come behind it. 'Janet and Anne can manage here. We'll go into the kitchen and have a cup of tea – unless you'd like somethin' stronger?'

'Could you manage a drink of some sort?' Maureen said. 'I've had tea at the hospital with Violet and more with Gran at home. I could do with somethin' a bit stronger.'

'I'll get you a port and lemon in the kitchen. I've got a half bottle left that I keep for when you come. I know it's your favourite.'

'Thanks,' Maureen said and shivered. It was a cool, wet night, which made her aware that the summer had almost gone. She could hear the faint sound of Vera Lynn singing on the radio somewhere and the sentimental words made her think about the last time Rory had taken her dancing.

Tears stung her throat but she choked them back. 'I just need somethin' to warm me up.'

'Yes, it must be a shock to see your father that way. I think your gran was more upset than she let on. I know she makes out she's cross with him for marrying Violet and pushing you out of your own home, but she only has the one son...'

'Yes, of course she's upset; we all are. I was surprised at how hard it has hit Violet. I thought she was after money when they got married, but I think I misjudged her. She seems heart broken now that he's really ill...'

'Yes, that's only natural,' Peggy agreed, 'and she's probably frightened you'll throw her out on the street if anythin' happens...'

'It's not my property, it's Gran's. I don't know what she'll do with it. She asked if I would like to go back there after the war but I said no. I'd rather she sold it to someone and had the money for herself. I'm not sure what I'll do in the future, but I shan't go back to standin' behind a counter. I prefer nursin'...'

'I thought you were going to marry Rory when things settled down a bit?' Peggy was surprised as she handed Maureen her glass of port and lemon. It was warm and comfortable in the big kitchen and the smell of apple pie was still lingering in the air. 'Could you eat a slice of this? I've only just taken it out of the oven...'

'I'd love some.' Maureen said and smiled. 'No one cooks like you do.'

'What happened?' Peggy asked, frowning as she sliced into the crisp pastry. 'No cream I'm afraid...'

'Fine as it is.' Maureen sniffed appreciatively. 'I love your apple pie... but I don't love Rory.'

'What did he do?'

'We quarrelled over something, but then I learned the truth – what kind of a man he really is. He got a junior nurse pregnant and she told me he was goin' to marry her – I hope he does for her sake, because her parents will be furious. She's young and from a decent family, and madly in love with him.'

'Not again!' Peggy shook her head in disbelief. 'What kind of a man is he?'

'I don't know,' Maureen said and her throat was tight, because it still hurt no matter what she told herself. 'Not what I believed him to be anyway. I knew he could be thoughtless and selfish, but I thought he really loved me. There were times he made me feel so special – but he'd been havin' sex with her ever since he came down to Portsmouth. They met every time I worked late. I feel such an idiot for not knowin' – for fallin' into his trap. He was just using me, Peggy, and if I'd married him he would have gone on doin' it.'

'A lot of people wouldn't have taken him back after the first time,' Peggy said. 'I'm sorry, love. Wait until I see him again. He'll get the rough edge of my tongue if he ever dares to come in here!'

'Poor Rory,' Maureen said and smiled wryly. 'Don't be upset for me, Peggy. I think I've probably been lucky to discover the truth before it was too late.'

'He hurt you...' Peggy looked sympathetic.

'No, it doesn't really hurt so much this time. I feel all kinds of a fool for trustin' him, but I'm not breakin' my heart over him. It's anger and, yes, some hurt, but I'm glad I found out now.'

'Good! It's best just to get angry, love. That's how I felt when Laurie had an affair – but we'd been driftin' apart for years and I found my happiness in Able. I thought you'd found happiness at last.'

'I have – in my work and my friends,' Maureen said. 'I'm glad to be back here with Gran and you – and Janet, Anne and Nellie – and I can take my turn with Shirley. She was so pleased to see me when I got back this afternoon. She threw her arms round me and hugged me so I kissed her and she told me she loves me.' She'd been surprised how happy it had made her to feel the child's love as she'd held her close.

'I'm glad you're back,' Peggy said. 'And I've got some news to tell you – I'm havin' a baby…'

'You're havin' a baby? But I thought…' Maureen was startled and then saw the sparkle in her eyes. 'It isn't… It is his! Oh, Peggy, that's wonderful. You thought you'd lost Able but now you'll always have the child to remind you…' The two women moved together and hugged. 'I think it's lovely…'

'Keep it to yourself, love. I haven't even told Anne that it's Able's child, though Nellie knows. She doesn't say much but she knows – and Janet, of course.'

'Yes, of course I'll be discreet. You don't want people gossipin' over it. Does Laurence know?'

'Yes. He wants people to think it's his, so…' Peggy shrugged. 'I have to let him have his way, Maureen. I'm not ready to move out yet and – I suppose it's the best. Laurie's a good father most of the time; if he really accepts Able's child and can live with it, then so can I – but I'd leave if he couldn't. For the moment, he wants to carry on as we are – separate lives but still married.'

'I think that's pretty decent of him,' Maureen said thoughtfully. 'As long as he's not horrid to you or the baby…'

'I wouldn't stand for that and he knows it. Besides, he's not blameless…'

'No.' Maureen smiled at her. 'Is Janet all right with it?'

'Yes...' Peggy's smile faded. 'Pip hasn't written to me since I told him – not that he often does. It's usually just a postcard, but... he was angry that I'd been away with Able. I know he will reject the idea of my havin' a baby – and he won't forgive me easily.'

'He'll come round,' Maureen said. 'He's very young, Peggy. I expect he's upset for his dad, but he'll get used to it, because he loves you.'

'Janet says the same,' Peggy said and sipped her port and lemon. 'Do you fancy another, love?'

'No, thanks, one is enough for me,' Maureen said. 'I wanted to see you and talk to you, but I should get back now. Gran is tryin' to be brave, but she's a bit weepy – and I think she's getting frail. This has been a blow to her. She calls Dad names and grumbles about him, but he's her only child.'

'You get back to her, Maureen. You know I'm always here when you want me. I'll pray for your dad but there's not much anyone can do except wait and hope...'

'No, I'm afraid there isn't,' Maureen said. 'They were quite open about it at the hospital; they don't know how much of a recovery he'll make. Even if he comes through this he may be partially paralysed. He certainly won't be able to manage the shop...'

'You won't go back there?'

'No, I shan't do that, Peggy. I've got my nursin' and a life of my own – but I'll find someone to look after it for him. If Tommy hadn't had that accident I'd have persuaded Dad to give him the job...'

'Yes, he's a good lad, but it will be a while before they let him out of hospital,' Peggy said. 'It never rains but it pours...' She hesitated, then, 'I'm trying to get his father out on compassionate leave.'

'They'll never let him come home – will they?'

'Doctor Blake says there's a good chance in the circumstances. Tilly Barton is ill, Maureen. I think she's losin' her mind. She doesn't eat and most of the time she just sits and stares at the wall. Doctor Blake told me that he may have to send her away for special treatment if she doesn't snap out of it – and Sam's body is still at the undertaker's.'

'But it's weeks since...'

'Yes, I know,' Peggy nodded. 'I've tried tellin' her, askin' her to make a decision, but she just stares at me and doesn't answer. Sam's father needs to come home, if only to sign for the body to be buried. And Tom is going to need someone when he does come home. I'd have him here, but...' Peggy sighed. 'It's such a mess. I've been told that unless we get his father home the hospital might send Tom to an orphanage when he's ready to come out – though that's not for a while.'

'You don't need all this worry, Peggy. You should be lookin' after yourself and the baby.'

'I'm all right,' Peggy sighed. 'I just want to do what I can for Tom...'

'Yes, of course you do – we all do,' Maureen agreed. 'If I can be of any help, you know you only have to ask.'

'You can sign the petition, love. Doctor Blake is fetching it in the morning. We've got three hundred signatures. He says he thinks he knows someone who can help. Of course Jack Barton will have to go back to prison and finish his sentence when his wife and son are better but just a few weeks now could make all the difference to his family...'

'Yes, well, we'll do all we can,' Maureen said. 'And now I'd better go along and see how Violet is managing. I feel sorry for her. They haven't been married very long and now Dad is ill and she has to cope with him in hospital and the shop, as well as her own business.'

'I hope she won't have to close the shop – I mean, if your dad can't work or...'

'I suppose that's up to Gran in a way,' Maureen said. 'It belongs to her and she only rented it to Dad. She said that whatever happens she wouldn't put Violet out of the flat until she finds another place – but they don't get on well... so we'll just have to see...'

*

'Well, I hope you're satisfied with yourself,' Violet said as she led the way upstairs to the sitting room. 'Now you can see what you've done – goin' off and leavin' your poor father to cope with the shop alone.'

'Violet, I know you're upset,' Maureen said, holding her temper in check. 'I'm upset my father is ill and I'm sorry you've been landed with everythin', but I think I did my duty for years. You married Dad and it's your job to manage until we can sort somethin' out for the shop. He won't want to give it up and I can't look after it – but I will help to find someone to work for him and if there are any small things I can do to help you, a stock list or visitin' the wholesaler when I have a free period...'

Violet dabbed at her eyes with a lace handkerchief. 'You and your grandmother have made it plain what you think of me. Well, I've got my own business to look after so the shop will stay shut – unless Hilda wants to open it up for a few hours.'

'You're being a bit unkind,' Maureen said. 'Gran isn't

completely well herself and she couldn't manage it – she has more than enough to do at home...'

'She can look after that girl for you...' Violet sniffed, 'but when it comes to helpin' her own son and me...'

'Gran has helped Dad for years and so have I,' Maureen said. 'I'm sorry, but emotional blackmail isn't going to work, Violet. I'll put a card up in the corner post office and see who turns up...'

'Well, I've told you I don't have the time,' Violet said. 'It's up to you, leave it shut until your father comes home – or look after it yourself.'

'I think I should leave,' Maureen said. 'I'm goin' to talk things over with Gran this evenin', but you may as well accept it: I shan't be workin' in the shop now or in the future...'

She got up and left without bothering to look back. Violet had thought she could force her to take over the shop but that was something Maureen wasn't prepared to do.

Reaching the bottom of the stairs, she had a sudden little turn and put out her hand to stop herself falling. Just for a moment she felt really faint, but it passed quickly and was gone by the time she'd crossed the street. It was just all the rushing around and the upset over her father. She was perfectly well, and she would join her new posting in a week's time as she'd been told. In the meantime she should be able to sort something out...

Chapter 26

'Peggy, can you come?' Alice said, rushing into the bar the next morning. 'Only it's Tilly and we can't do anythin' with 'er...'

'What do you mean?' Peggy asked. She glanced at Janet. 'You can manage while I find out what's goin' on?'

'Of course I can, Mum. You go...'

Peggy listened to Alice's rather garbled tale as she hurried across the road to Tilly Barton's house. The front door stood wide open and there was a pile of clothing on the pavement outside, shoes, a man's work boots and an old Army overcoat.

'She's throwing all Jack's things out of the door,' Alice said. 'Some of them have been ripped up. I tried to reason with her, because 'e'll need 'is things when 'e gets 'ome.'

'Yes, of course he will,' Peggy said and bent to pick up the clothes and boots, taking them into the house. Tilly was in the middle of cutting up one of her husband's shirts, but stopped and glared at them. 'Tilly, think what you're doin', love. Jack will need these...'

'What the bugger needs ain't nothin' ter me,' Tilly said bitterly. 'Jack ain't comin' 'ere. He left me in the lurch when he was arrested and I blame 'im fer what happened to me boy...'

'Tilly, I know he did wrong, but he's paid for it – and Sam was his son too...' Peggy saw the fury in her eyes as Tilly snatched an official-looking letter from the table and thrust it at her.

'I know I've got you to thank for this,' Tilly snarled and brandished the scissors at her. 'They're sending the bugger 'ome on compassionate grounds. Well, 'e comes in this 'ouse over me dead body!'

'Tilly...' Peggy eyed the scissors warily. 'You need help and so does Tommy. And you have to bury Sam.'

'Don't you tell me what I need, Peggy Ashley!' Tilly said and flew at her with a stabbing motion with her scissors. 'Sam ain't goin' in the ground. Me boy's frightened of the dark...'

Peggy caught her wrist. For a moment Tilly's eyes were wild with grief and a kind of madness as they struggled, but she'd neglected herself for weeks, hardly eating or drinking, and Peggy was stronger. The scissors clattered to the floor, where Alice quickly retrieved them and thrust them in the sideboard drawer out of harm's way. Tilly gave a little cry of frustration and then collapsed into Peggy's body, all her strength seeming to ebb away.

'Help me get her on the sofa,' Peggy said and, taking most of Tilly's weight, she led her to the ancient sofa with its stained upholstery and sagging springs. 'She won't be very comfortable here, but we need the doctor. I'll stay with her if you go across to the pub and ask Janet to telephone Doctor Blake.'

Alice nodded, casting a knowing eye over Tilly. 'I reckon she's just about done fer, Peggy. She needs puttin' away fer 'er own sake and others'.'

'That's not our decision, but I think it might be the best just for a while. If she had another bout like this she might kill someone without truly meaning to do it; she doesn't know what she's doin', Alice.'

'She knew what she was doin' just now. If she could, she would've done you mischief, Peggy – and after all you've done to 'elp 'er an' all...'

'Anyone would've done the same,' Peggy said. 'Get off quick, Alice. She needs a doctor – and if Janet can't get Doctor Blake, tell her to ask for an ambulance. I don't like the look of Tilly's colour...'

Alice went and Peggy bent over Tilly, placing a hand to her brow. She had a fever and the words she began to utter were a jumble that made no sense. Although Tilly appeared to know what she was saying, Peggy thought the woman very ill. Her mind couldn't cope with her pain and she'd abused her body. It looked as if she would have to be admitted into hospital – but Peggy had no intention of telling anyone about the attack on her. Tilly needed medical attention, but she didn't need to be shut up in a secure unit. Mental hospitals were much better than they had been years ago, but most people still thought of them as places of incarceration for hopeless wretches that society couldn't cope with, holding little hope of release or a cure, and Peggy wouldn't wish such a thing on her worst enemy.

Tommy needed his mother to be home and well, which she might be after a stay in hospital. Peggy knew he'd started to recover from his head injury and the last thing he needed was to be told that his mother had been sectioned as mentally unstable.

*

'How are you feeling, Tommy?' the nurse asked as she took his temperature that afternoon. 'Your fever has gone at last – so I think you could have a visitor, if you feel up to it?'

'Who?' Tommy croaked. His arm still hurt like hell and he was only just starting to focus on what had happened to him. 'Is it Sam – or Mum?'

'It's someone who wants to see you very much,' the pretty nurse replied with a smile. 'It's your dad…'

'Dad?' Tommy tried to lift himself up to see, but his head fell back, because it was spinning. They'd told him the headaches would pass, but he still felt dizzy if he tried to get up. 'Where's me dad?'

'I'm here, son…' Tommy's eyes misted as his father's face loomed into vision and his lips touched Tommy's brow in a light kiss. 'How's my brave boy then?'

'I'm all right, Dad. How did you get 'ere?'

'They let me orf fer good behaviour,' his father said and smiled. 'It's partly cos of what 'appened to you and yer brother, son…'

Tommy saw the sadness in his father's faded blue eyes and fear gripped him.

'They won't tell me what 'appened to Sam…'

'Sam didn't make it, Tom. They told me you went after 'im, tried to keep him clear…'

'I'm so sorry, Dad – it's all my fault. I should've stopped him sooner.' Tom's eyes filled with tears.

'It's my fault not yours, son. I should've been at 'ome to take care of you all – but I'll be around now, for a while anyway…'

'How? You've got another two years to go…'

'It's compassionate leave, see,' his father said gently. 'I've been given parole fer good behaviour. Yer ma can't cope, so they've given me a chance. I'm on probation fer a while

– it's cos I weren't a hardened criminal, see, and it was me first offence. They've let me out to take care of you and yer ma...'

'Good...' Tears trickled down Tom's face. He didn't really understand why they would let his dad out but he was glad they had, because he'd missed him, even though he was angry with him for robbing that post office. 'I tried to stop Sam but 'e wouldn't listen – 'e wouldn't listen...'

'I know,' his father said and touched his face, wiping away the tears with his fingers. 'I should've been 'ere to take care of you both, Tom – but I'm going to look after you now, I promise. I'll get a job until...' He shook his head. 'Just you rest and get better, son. Don't worry about yer ma. I'm takin' care of everythin'. All you've got to do is get better. Peggy and Alice were askin' after yer – and Maureen Jackson wrote a lovely letter to yer mum. It was Peggy and a few others what got me my parole. You've got a lot of friends and they're all thinkin' about yer, Tom.'

'I think that will do for the first visit, Mr Barton,' the pretty nurse said, coming back then. 'You can see him another day, but Tom needs a little rest now...'

'Yeah, thanks for comin',' Tom said and closed his eyes, because he was feeling very tired. 'You tell Peggy I'll be in to finish papering that bedroom soon as I can...'

'Yes, I'll tell her,' his father said and turned away. 'You just get better, son – that's all I ask...'

*

'Peggy, I want ter thank yer fer all you've done for my family,' Jack Barton said later that afternoon as he sat in the pub kitchen and drank the tea she'd poured him. 'I don't know how yer managed ter get me out – but I'm glad yer did; that boy needed someone to visit and give 'im a bit of 'ope.'

'I only did what you or Tilly would've done for me if I'd needed it, Jack,' Peggy said and smiled at him. 'Doctor Blake was concerned about Tilly's state of mind and he suggested we might be able to swing your release if we put her case to the right people. He's the one with connections to the prison parole board. All I did was collect signatures...'

'You've done a lot more than that,' Jack said. 'Alice told me how you gave Tom little jobs so he could earn money and help 'is mother. You looked after 'er when the accident 'appened and you took 'er a meal over every day, even if she didn't eat it.'

'I wish I could've done more,' Peggy said. 'There was no comforting her. She refused to bury Sam – told me he was frightened of the dark.'

'So he was as a young boy,' Jack said and his face twisted with grief. 'He's my son too and I'll do right by him. I shall arrange the funeral as soon as I can. There's no point in waitin' for Tilly: no tellin' when she'll be well enough to face it. Sam needs a decent burial and then perhaps his mother will come to accept he's gone.'

'She became very ill in her mind,' Peggy said. 'Some of your things – she cut them up. I don't think she realised what she was doin'.'

'Tilly knew all right. She blamed me for goin' ter prison, blamed me for what Sam did, and she's right. I know that none of it would've 'appened if I'd been 'ome. It was my fault for lettin' me family down, tryin' ter rob that post office, and making a muck of it.'

'Why did you do it, Jack?'

'I wish I knew,' he confessed. 'I was desperate to pay the bills after I lost my job. I thought if I could just get straight once – but I was a damned fool. Thievin' never does anyone any good.'

'Yes, well, I suppose anyone might make the same mistake.' Peggy gave him an understanding look and refilled his cup.

'Not my Tom. I'll never forget 'is face when the coppers took me away, Peggy. I swear I'll die before I let my boy down again.'

'Good. In that case, you can finish some of the jobs your Tom started while you're out – and I could do with a hand in the pub now and then.'

'You don't 'ave to give me charity, Peggy. I'll find a job somehow – there's more work now for men ready to turn their 'ands to anythin'.'

'Well, the offer is there,' she said and smiled. 'Finish off that pie, Jack – and you're welcome to have your dinner with us any time you like.'

'You're a good woman, Peggy Ashley. I'll eat the pie – and then I'm back off to the hospital to see how Tilly is gettin' on. I'll look fer work tomorrow.'

'Right, but remember my offer if you get stuck…'

'Thanks, I certainly will…'

Peggy watched him leave. Jack Barton was like his son Tommy, a tall. loose-limbed man with large hands and feet. He had rugged good looks and a nice smile, but she doubted if any of that would help when it came to finding a job round here. The people of the lanes might accept he'd made a mistake and they'd signed for him to come home for his family's sake, but when it came to giving him work, most would think twice about offering a job to a man with a prison record. Peggy had offered because she liked Jack and she was fond of his son, and she wasn't sure that anyone else would offer him a decent job.

*

'So the funeral is on Tuesday,' Maureen said as she called in to see Peggy that Friday morning. 'I start work that evening so I'll be able to come with you – and so will Gran, because Shirley is at school.'

'Janet says she'll stay and look after things here. She doesn't know Jack as well as we do, so it's best this way. We thought we'd all club together to buy some flowers for Sam, and help pay for the funeral, though Jack says he's been given a small grant for that. Just a small wreath from everyone in Mulberry Lane – that way no one needs to contribute more than they can afford.'

'I saw the box on the bar,' Maureen said. 'I'll put in half a crown. It's a rotten shame that poor kid had to die – and Tommy is still in hospital, Tilly too. They've had a terrible time of it as a family...'

'Tom is gettin' better his father says. I'm goin' to see him one day next week.'

'Good. Give him my love,' Maureen said. She got up from the kitchen table, pushing back her chair. Then, as the room started to spin madly, she sat back down with a bump. 'Oh... that's weird...'

'What's wrong, love?' Peggy asked in concern. 'Did you feel faint?'

'Yes, just a bit...' Maureen closed her eyes for a moment. 'It happened the other night after I left Violet. I thought I'd been rushing around too much...'

Peggy gave her a long considering look. 'Is there any chance that you might be pregnant?'

'What?' Maureen stared at her in shock. 'No – I mean, I suppose I could be, but I think…' She looked into Peggy's eyes. 'It never occurred to me. Rory said he was careful but – I haven't had a period since two weeks before we fetched Shirley home…'

'You didn't realise that you were late?'

'No, I didn't even think about it,' Maureen said. 'I'm only a few weeks late.' She counted up in her head. 'Yes, it can't be longer than five, but with the long hours we work I'm not always regular…' She met Peggy's worried gaze. 'Could the faintness be a sign?'

'I've never had it take me like that,' Peggy said, 'but some women react in different ways. It could be just that you've been working hard and then the worry over your dad – any number of things. I think you should go to the doctor, Maureen love. It might just be tiredness – unless you've noticed anything else?'

Maureen shook her head. 'I haven't even thought of myself, Peggy. I've been visitin' Dad at the hospital and helpin' Gran with Shirley, and I went to the wholesaler for Violet.'

'I thought you weren't goin' to let her drag you back?'

'I've told her I'll help where I can, but I'm not goin' in the shop.'

Peggy nodded, looking at her thoughtfully. 'Do you think your dad would give Jack Barton a shot at runnin' it for a while?'

'Do you think Jack would take it on?' Maureen frowned. 'I could ask Dad – sound him out, if he's well enough.'

'Perhaps you should talk to Violet about it first? If she's desperate enough, she might give him a chance.'

'Yes, perhaps,' Maureen said. 'I don't want to worry Dad – and Violet would be a fool to say no. It would only be for a short while anyway.'

'Yes, Jack only has a couple of months, just to see Sam buried and get Tommy settled. He'll have to go back to prison once his parole is up.'

'It's not a nice prospect for him,' Maureen said. She stood up a little cautiously, but then smiled. 'It's gone; I probably stood up too quickly or somethin'.'

'Go to the doctor in the mornin',' Peggy advised. 'You want to know – whatever it is, Maureen.'

'Yes...' Maureen met her gaze. 'What do I do if I am pregnant?'

'If you'd known sooner you could have written to Rory.'

'No! That's over. Rory doesn't need to know.'

'It's not easy being an unmarried mother round here, love. You know what folk are like. They all pull together in a crisis, but give them the chance to tear your reputation to pieces and they will.'

'Yes, I know,' Maureen said. 'Well, maybe it's just tiredness and overwork – but even if I am pregnant I'm not goin' to run off. If people want to talk about me let them.'

'That's the spirit!'

Peggy smiled and watched her leave. If Maureen were having her lover's child it would be hard for her. She wouldn't be the first unmarried girl to have a soldier's child during wartime, but folk would expect him to marry her and, when he didn't, some of the gossips would tear her reputation to bits. Peggy would stand by her friend – after all, she would be in the same boat if Laurie hadn't insisted everyone must think her baby was his. Maureen would need some good friends, because her father would be upset and angry, and Violet would seize her chance to moralise. Hilda Jackson would stand by her, but she wouldn't be happy about it.

Peggy sighed. Perhaps it was just tiredness making Maureen feel faint, but she had a feeling that the girl had been very unlucky...

Chapter 27

Janet put her daughter down on the floor, leaving her to play with a truck of coloured wooden bricks she'd bought at the market, as she opened the letter. It was from Mike and her heart gave a leap of excitement as she saw what he'd written.

They've told me I should be able to come home next weekend, Janet. The doctor is having a look at me tomorrow and then I have to wait for some stitches to come out, but after that I can come home for a few days. They say it's just a trial run to see how we cope. I shall be brought back in an ambulance, because you don't drive and there's no available car, but I'll let you know exact details next week. I shall telephone to make the arrangements so that you're expecting me. I hope this is all right and won't be inconvenient for you or your mother?

Janet's eyes stung with tears, because Mike's letter sounded so unsure. He ought to be filled with joy that he was at last being allowed to come home and it hurt that he wasn't sure of his welcome, despite her visits to the hospital and her assurances that she would welcome him back.

'Something the matter, love?' Peggy asked as she walked into the room and saw that Janet was crying. 'Letter from Mike?'

'They're sending him home next weekend for a few days, Mum. It's a trial run to see how we cope...' She handed her mother the brief letter and Peggy read it, nodding and looking sad.

'Yes, I see why you're upset, love, but this is a big moment for Mike. He has accepted your marriage, but still doesn't know who he is – and it must feel so strange to be told you can visit your home when you know nothing about it.'

'Oh, Mum, I want to put my arms round him and kiss it all better like I do with Maggie...' Janet sniffed and scrubbed at her eyes with a hanky.

'Well, that's probably the best thing you can do, love,' Peggy said. 'Mike will at least know that he's loved and wanted here. We'll do all we can to make him comfortable and happy – and for now that's the best we can hope for.'

'Yes, I'm so lucky that he's coming home to me,' Janet said and flicked away the tears. 'I wasn't sure it would ever happen.'

'Well, now it has and that's wonderful, my love.'

Janet looked at her. 'Are you all right, Mum? Not feelin' tired or sick or anything?'

'I'm fine,' Peggy said stoutly. 'At least, I shall be when this funeral is over. I can't help thinkin' how lucky I am to have my family around me – and poor Tilly's lying there in the hospital while they bury her Sam.'

'You've done all you can, Mum.'

'Yes, I have – and Maureen has got Jack Barton the chance of a job in the shop. Violet Jackson says she'll see him and if she thinks he's all right she'll give him a chance just until Henry gets home.'

'Do you think Mr Jackson will ever be able to run the shop again?'

'I'm not sure, but Maureen says *she* won't and Violet maintains she can't – but Henry is gettin' a bit better. Maureen told me his left arm doesn't work properly and he was having difficulty in gettin' his words out, but they're givin' him some therapy for that. He'll be in the hospital for weeks yet, but he should make it – providing he doesn't have another stroke.'

'Well, I'm glad for him and for Maureen,' Janet said. 'Yesterday she brought me a little bonnet she'd made for Maggie. It was very pretty and warm for the cooler weather.'

'Maureen loves kids,' Peggy said, looking thoughtful. 'You like her, don't you, Jan? You wouldn't turn against her if people said things about her?'

'What do you mean?' Janet looked at her, puzzled. 'What are you hintin' at, Mum?'

'Oh nothin',' Peggy said. 'I'll leave you to look after things here, Jan. I'd better leave now or I'll be late at the church. I shall tell Jack there are a few sandwiches here if he wants to bring anyone back.'

'I doubt he's got many relations to bring back,' Janet replied. 'I'm going to put Maggie down to sleep for a while and then I'll open up. Nellie will give me a hand...'

'Yes, I don't know what we'd do without her.'

Janet watched her mother leave. What had she meant about Maureen? A little frown creased her brow as she puzzled over it and then she nodded, a smile creeping over her lips. There had been something in the way Maureen looked at Maggie yesterday – a sort of tender wistfulness.

Janet would never blame her friend for getting into that kind of trouble, but she knew a lot of others in the lanes might...

*

Janet was serving a woman with two coffees and rock buns when a soldier entered and came up to the bar. Looking up, she saw it was Gordon Hart and he was wearing a new stripe on his uniform sleeve.

'Hello,' she said. 'Congratulations on the promotion, corporal. Are you on leave?'

He nodded. 'I've been on a training course and I did well so I got the promotion and a couple of weeks' leave. I wondered if you knew where Maureen or her grandmother was, please? I went to Mrs Jackson's house but it was empty.'

'They've gone to a funeral with my mother,' Janet replied. 'I don't know if you knew that Sam Barton was killed in an accident on the bomb sites?'

'No, I hadn't heard about that,' Gordon said. 'Poor lad. I expect Maureen has probably written but I didn't get her letter...'

'Mum has made some sandwiches and a sponge for anyone who wants to come back afterwards. I expect Maureen and her gran will. Shirley stays to lunch at school and Anne brings her home in the evenings. We've all been lookin' out for her, Mr Hart.'

'Yes, I know. Mrs Tandy told me when I saw her outside her shop just now,' he said. 'I have to be grateful to a lot of friends – but mostly to Maureen...'

'Well, here she is,' Janet said as the door opened and about ten people entered. 'It looks as if a few turned up to say goodbye to young Sam then...'

Jack Barton walked up to the bar and handed over a pound note to Janet. 'It's all I can afford,' he said. 'If you can give people tea or coffee or a soft drink. I don't have enough to pay for sherry I'm afraid.'

'That's all right; Mum put out a half-bottle,' Janet said. 'She couldn't spare any more, but it will go round once I think. The sandwiches are under the tea towel if you want to hand them round...'

'I'll do that,' Maureen said, coming up to the bar. She smiled. 'Hello, Gordon, it's good to see you back. I hoped they would give you leave soon. We'll have a talk later, but Shirley is fine. Janet, your mum said will you ask Nellie to make tea for everyone please.'

Janet nodded and went to the door leading into the kitchen, calling out to Nellie. She walked back to the bar and started to pour sherry into small glasses, setting them on a tray on the bar.

'Maureen, I'm so pleased you're here,' Gordon said. 'Mrs Tandy told me you were back in London, and Janet here said you were at the funeral, but I must have missed your last letter.' Janet noticed that his smile was a caress as he looked at Maureen. 'I can't thank you enough for what you did when Mum died – fetching Shirley back straight away. I'd have been out of my mind with worry if I hadn't known you would look out for her.'

'Shirley was never really happy down there,' Maureen said, seeming to dismiss her part in Shirley's rescue, as if she were a little embarrassed. 'I know you didn't want her to be here in the Blitz, but I think the worst is over – for the moment anyway.'

'Can you spare me half an hour or so when this is over?' Gordon glanced towards the funeral guests.

'I'm afraid I've got to leave in a few minutes,' Maureen said. 'I've been transferred to the London Hospital and I start my first shift this evening, but I want to visit Dad first. Where are you stayin'?'

'I've taken a room in a boarding house. I've got three weeks' leave and it's my intention to take Shirley out as much as I can while I'm home, make a fuss of her. I'd hoped we might see somethin' of you?'

'You've heard about my father?' He nodded. Maureen hesitated, then, 'Yes, I'll come when I can, but I don't have much time between visitin' Dad and my job,' she said. 'Look I'm goin' to take the food round, Gordon. Come to the house at about three tomorrow afternoon, after I've had a couple of hours' sleep, and we'll talk. In the meantime, you could have tea with Gran and Shirley when she gets home from school this afternoon. You're welcome to visit her whenever you like...'

Janet thought that Maureen seemed a little evasive, as if she felt awkward about something, her eyes not meeting Gordon's embracing gaze.

Maureen picked up two plates of sandwiches and started the rounds. Janet watched Gordon's eyes following her and smiled inwardly. It was very obvious to her that he thought that Maureen was wonderful...

Chapter 28

'We are very pleased to have you, Nurse Jackson,' Sister Morrison told her when she reported for duty that evening. 'I know Sister Martin very well and she has highly recommended you to us. We can certainly do with a capable pair of hands.'

'Thank you, Sister,' Maureen said. 'It suited me very well to be transferred to London for personal reasons. I shall try to help you as much as I can.'

'Good. You will be on the medical ward for the moment, which may seem a little strange since you've been used to dealing with wounds and soldiers. However, nursing is made up of all kinds of work, and we've got our most senior nurses looking after the injured. You will be handing out medicines, making up beds and treating lesser problems on a women's general ward. I hope you won't miss the glamour of working in a military hospital?'

Maureen thought there wasn't much to call glamorous about treating young men who cried with the pain of their burns and wet the beds because they couldn't get up.

'I don't mind what I do, Sister. The senior nurses are needed for those in greatest need.'

'Well said, nurse.' Sister Morrison gave her a tight smile. 'This morning I'm going to throw you in at the deep end,

I'm afraid. Mrs Titmarsh has an ulcerated leg that refuses to heal. I want you to dress it for her and make her comfortable. I'm afraid she also has an incontinence problem.'

'Yes, Sister,' Maureen kept her expression bland as she went off to fetch the trolley with the things she would need. It seemed that whenever she went on a new ward the Sister in charge was determined to test her by giving her all the unpleasant jobs. Not that it mattered to Maureen; one bedpan was much the same as another, and nothing could dim her happiness today.

Her pregnancy had been confirmed by her visit to the doctor. Doctor North had told her that he was certain that she was having a baby, though he would be doing the usual test to confirm it; he was a little concerned by the fainting but inclined to think it might be a combination of overworking for months and the hormonal changes in her body.

'When a woman conceives, her body decides it must protect the foetus,' he'd explained to her gently. 'Therefore, it may be trying to tell you that you must not do quite so much.'

'I'm a nursing assistant,' Maureen told him with a smile. 'I am on my feet for hours on end and I'm often asked to work double shifts.'

'Well, that may have to change,' he'd replied and patted her hand in a fatherly way. 'Your fiancé must marry you and then the problem will be solved I imagine.'

'Yes, doctor. I'd like to keep working for a while. I don't want to let anyone down and waste my trainin'.' Maureen turned her face aside, because she couldn't tell him that she had no intention of marrying the child's father after what he'd done.

'Once you become pregnant I think you must accept that you have a duty to your baby and everything else will take a back seat, especially as the pregnancy advances. You are only a few weeks so far, but the fainting is a concern – it may be that you will need to rest if you are to produce a healthy child.'

'Yes, I see. Thank you for your advice,' Maureen said and smiled as she left, her feelings mixed even though she'd always wanted her own children. She was happy that she was pregnant, but concerned at the thought of the future.

It would be awkward if she fainted on duty, because the nurses were not blind and her condition would soon be suspected. Had she still been more or less engaged to Rory, she could've left to get married, but in the circumstances she needed to earn a wage for as long as she could. Maureen knew that her grandmother would never turn her out, but she would be upset once she discovered there was no hope of Rory marrying her, and an unmarried mother was looked down on in close-knit communities like the lanes.

Maureen sighed but dismissed her own problems as she greeted the elderly patient assigned to her. Mrs Titmarsh was a plump, cheerful lady and apologised to her immediately.

'I'm sorry, nurse. I've messed meself again, and my leg stinks somethin' awful today. I'm afraid you've drawn the short straw gettin' me...'

'Not at all, Mrs Titmarsh,' Maureen said cheerfully. 'I was on bedpan duty at the military hospital for months and I'm quite used to it...'

However, after she'd changed the woman's nightdress and her sheets, Maureen opened the bandage on her leg and caught a smell she'd come to dread in the military hospital. The ulcer was suppurating and, by the looks of the pus oozing from it, it had become infected, and, Maureen suspected, gangrenous. Her heart sank as the woman peered at it and asked if the leg was getting any better.

'It looks rather sore,' Maureen said, because it wasn't up to her to break the terrible news; a doctor would do that once it was confirmed. 'I'm goin' to fetch Sister and ask her if we should use a different cream.'

Leaving the leg wound open to the air, she went in search of Sister Morrison and found her speaking to a young doctor. She hesitated, because experience had taught her that doctors did not relish being interrupted, but Sister looked at her in annoyance.

'What is it?'

'I'm sorry to interrupt,' Maureen said, 'but I think Mrs Titmarsh's leg is infected – perhaps with gangrene.'

'Nonsense!' Sister glared at her. 'It is just a nasty ulcer.'

'I don't think so, Sister…' Maureen swallowed hard as she saw the anger in the senior nurse's eyes. 'I've seen it before…'

'Have you indeed?' Sister's eyebrows shot up in disbelief.

'Perhaps we should just take a look,' the young doctor said and smiled at Maureen. 'Better to be safe than sorry…'

Sister barged past Maureen, striding down the ward with Maureen and the doctor in tow. As the curtain was swept aside, the sickly-sweet smell of gangrene hit them and Maureen saw the doctor's nostrils twitch. He looked at her with respect in his eyes and nodded once.

Following the doctor into the cubicle, Maureen pulled the curtains to give the patient some privacy. The doctor was bending over Mrs Titmarsh, gently examining the leg.

'Well, this is unfortunate for you, Annie,' he said in a voice as soft as his hands. 'I imagine you've been in pain all night with this?'

'Yes, doctor. I did tell the nurse and she gave me a pill, but she was busy, poor girl. It's bad, isn't it, Doctor Phillips?'

'I'm afraid we're going to have to take the leg off up to just below the knee,' he replied. 'I'm sorry it has come to this. I did warn you last year not to leave it so long before you came in, Annie. We performed small miracles on the infection presented back then, but I'm afraid it's the leg or your life this time.'

Maureen drew a shocked breath because he was so direct, but Doctor Phillips knew his patient well. Her trusting eyes remained unflinching as she looked into his face.

'You'd better 'ave the bugger orf then,' Annie said. 'My Alfie can't manage without me. I'll use them crutches yer give me the last time.'

'We'll probably have you in a bath chair for a start,' he said. 'You'll cause a sensation in that, Annie.' He touched her hand and gave her his warm smile. 'Trust me, you'll be as good as new afterwards and once you get fitted up with a new leg there will be no stopping you.'

'Yer can fit me up wiv a new engine an' all if yer like,' Annie said and cackled with laughter. 'Orf wiv yer then, Doc. I'll be all right...'

'Thanks to the quick eyes of this young nurse,' he said and went out, followed by Sister, who gave her a quick nod.

'That was quick thinking, Nurse Jackson. Not every trainee nurse recognises the symptoms. Mrs Titmarsh was sent in by her doctor for an infected ulcer late last night and was not examined by a doctor. She has been in many times before with ulcers and no one thought it particularly urgent. What made you suspect it?' Sister asked when Maureen reported to her later.

'I've smelled it before. Some of the wounded men came in with it at the military hospital, and I knew it could mean an amputation,' Maureen said, 'And that suppuration was a clue that something was badly wrong, as well as the discolouration.'

'Unfortunately, it must have been happening for a while before she was admitted, but her doctor didn't report it to us. Well done!' A thin smile touched her lips. 'It seems that we were luckier than we realised to get you, nurse.'

'Thank you, Sister.' Maureen drew a breath of relief. She'd passed her first test and perhaps her time here need not be as unpleasant as she'd feared – for as long as she was able to work.

*

'I can't believe the change in Shirley,' Gordon said, when Maureen poured him a cup of tea the following afternoon. 'She is so much happier here than she was on the farm, and yet she loves animals...'

'I think Mrs Hunter was rather strict,' Maureen said. 'Children need discipline but...' She shook her head and smiled at him. 'No, it doesn't matter. That is all over, Gordon. Gran looks after her and I'm goin' to be around to do my bit – so whatever happens you don't need to worry, because we'll all look after Shirley.'

'I know and I'm more than grateful,' Gordon said, his gaze bringing a blush to her cheeks. 'I know you always said you would look after her if anythin' happened to Ma, but you're a nurse now – and you've got Rory. What does he say about you taking responsibility for Shirley?'

'Rory wasn't too pleased over it,' Maureen said, deciding that the truth was best. 'However, his opinion doesn't matter, because we're over.'

'You didn't quarrel because of my daughter?' Gordon looked startled.

'We did, but that wasn't the reason we split up...' Maureen drew a deep breath. 'I discovered that he'd been seein' another nurse when I was workin'. She was very young and she was dazzled by him, thought he was a war hero...'

'He cheated on you? After all that fuss he made about you leavin' your job to get married? The stupid fool!' Gordon looked furious. 'Do you want me to thrash him for you?'

Maureen laughed and declined. 'He finished himself in my eyes, Gordon. I thought the first time it happened it was Velma's fault and partly mine. I should've known then that he was a liar and a cheat, but I thought I was in love with him – and when he was injured I couldn't let him down. He claimed he loved me and I thought perhaps I still loved him...'

'Now you know you don't?'

'Yes.' Maureen lifted her head and looked into his eyes. She had to be straight with him now even though it was hard to say the words. 'I was an innocent fool. Stuck in the shop, I knew nothin' of life. I've learned so much since I took up nursin', Gordon. I've lost so many friends and I've seen death and sufferin' – and it's made me realise that people are human and they have lots of failings. Rory is just that sort of man. He says he loves me and perhaps he does, but he can't be faithful – and I'm lucky I found it out before I married him.'

'Yes.' Gordon looked serious. 'I'd be lyin' if I said I was sorry you'd broken up with him. I'm sorry you were hurt though, Maureen. I care for you deeply – I think you know that?'

'Yes...' Maureen looked at him and saw how intent he was. Her heart gave a little flutter. 'When you first spoke to me about Shirley I knew you wanted a mother for her but I thought that was all...'

'It probably was at the start. I grieved for my wife, Maureen, but as I got to know you better I felt more and more for you. I've wished so many times I could go back and start at the beginning – ask you out and court you.'

'Well, you can if you wish,' she said a little hesitantly, because she wasn't sure how he would feel when she told him her news, and if he turned from her it was going to hurt. 'I'm willin' to go out with you and with Shirley, as a family... and just see how we go on.'

'Maureen, you know I want to marry you – the sooner the better.'

Maureen met his fervent gaze steadily. It was now or never and her nerves fluttered as she met his steady look. 'I'm goin' to tell you somethin' that may change your mind,' she said and took a deep breath. 'I thought Rory loved me and I expected we would marry one day – so I slept with him. I'm havin' his child, Gordon. I intend to keep the baby, but I've finished with Rory and I don't intend to tell him about the child – ever.'

Gordon sat looking at her, a maelstrom of feelings rushing through his expressive eyes. She saw it all: shock, anger, sadness, compassion and disappointment, but in the end there was just a gentle kindness as he reached out to take her hand.

'You are certain it's over with Rory?'

'Quite sure. I feel nothing for him now – not even anger.'

'Then marry me, Maureen. You know I love you. It's the perfect solution, my dearest, and would make me very happy.'

Maureen looked at him sadly, because she knew that her news must have hurt him. 'Are you sure you wouldn't resent the child, Gordon? I'm goin' to keep my baby.' His offer was so generous and loving, and it would mean so much to her, but was it selfish of her to take advantage of him?

'I wouldn't expect you to do anythin' else,' he said and held her hand tighter. 'I know you don't love me, but I think we could be happy. Shirley would be delighted to have you as her mum, and it's all I want. I mean it, Maureen. I'm not just comin' to the rescue. I want you for my wife.'

'May I think about it for a few days?' Maureen asked, though she felt a little breathless and believed she already knew what she wanted. Yet would it be fair to him when she was pregnant with Rory's child? 'If we can spend as much time together and with Shirley – get to know each other a little better. I'm not workin' such manic hours at the London. I get three nights on and one night off. It means I can take Shirley to the zoo with you on Saturday or Sunday... and we can go somewhere on my evenin' off. Talk about things...'

'Yes, of course, but it would be so much better for all of us,' Gordon said. 'I'm not goin' to throw stones, Maureen love, but others will. If we're married, only the most spiteful ones will count the days.'

'I know and I have thought of it, because it would make me happy,' Maureen said. 'You're a lovely man, and I do like you a lot – perhaps more than that if I'm honest. If Rory hadn't come back into my life and you'd asked me again I might have said yes before this... but I want to be fair to you. I want to be sure that I can make you happy.'

'Think about it, my darling,' he said. 'Your letters have meant so much to me and it would mean the world if you became my wife. I never thought I would be happy again after Shirley's mother died, but then there was you... You and Shirley – you're my reason for comin' back after this horror is over.'

'You must come back,' Maureen said and squeezed his hand. She leaned towards him and kissed him softly on the mouth. 'If we marry it will be a proper marriage, Gordon. I want to be your wife and to share everythin' – if you'd been in love with me I think I might have married you in 1939.'

'I've wasted nearly three years because I didn't know my own heart,' Gordon said ruefully. 'If I bought a special licence we could get married before I report back to my unit.'

'Yes, I know,' Maureen agreed. 'I'll give you my answer on Sunday. Is that all right?'

'Yes, of course it is. You know I'd wait forever – I want you to be sure, love. Your happiness means everythin' to me. You mustn't say yes just for me and Shirley. What you want matters too.'

'You're the nicest man I know,' Maureen said, acknowledging in her heart how much his letters had meant to her all this time. It was Gordon she'd written to when she was coping with Sally's death, and his letters that had comforted her. It was he she'd turned to when she'd been uncertain how to respond to Rory's demands that she return to London. Why hadn't she realised how much she'd come to respect and rely on him? 'And now you have to leave. I need to get ready for work. One of my patients had her leg off this morning. She will have been transferred to a surgical ward, but I want to visit her and I need to be on my toes on Sister Morrison's ward…'

*

Maureen slept well despite the decision she had to make. It was a big step to take, because she wasn't the kind of girl to break a promise once it was made; marriage was forever and she had to be sure that she could make a life with Gordon.

Shirley was no problem these days, and Maureen liked Gordon for himself. He was a little slow making up his mind at times and some years older than she was – but those things were not a barrier to happiness. Maureen had been very much in love with Rory and she was aware that she didn't feel anything like that for Gordon, but she did feel something; it had been growing for some months now without her realising it – and perhaps it would grow into the kind of love she'd hoped she had with the man whose child she was carrying.

Maureen had made up her mind that Rory would never know she'd had his child. Her love for him had died when Carol told her they'd been sleeping together. It was such a cruel, careless betrayal and it had hurt for a while, but the pain had soon eased and become just a nagging ache of regret. Why had she ever loved a man who took cheating and lying in his stride?

Well, that was over. Whether or not she married Gordon, her affair with Rory was finished. Even if she'd wanted him to wed her it was too late, because he'd gone home with Carol and was probably already married to her...

Busy on the ward, caring for her patients and tending their boils, ulcers and upset stomachs, Maureen's mind kept going over and over Gordon's proposal. It hadn't come as a surprise. She'd known when she told him the truth that he might ask her, because although it might hurt him to know she had conceived another man's child, he really did want her to be his wife. A part of it was Shirley, of course. He was grateful for what she'd done, and he wanted a mother for his daughter – but he did love her? His letters had told her that time and time again, even though he didn't always write the words. She'd known it instinctively the last time they'd met briefly in Peggy's pub – and it made her feel wanted and quietly happy.

Yet something nagged at the back of her mind, making her hesitate. Gordon deserved love. Could she ever give him the kind of loving warmth any man was entitled to find in his wife?

*

Maureen left the hospital at ten o'clock on Sunday morning after a busy night on the wards. Two new patients had been admitted with vomiting and stomach pain and she'd been late coming off shift. As she emerged into the cool of the autumn morning, Maureen didn't see the man until he put himself in her way, obstructing her passage along the pavement.

'Maureen. Rita told me I'd find you here. She didn't want to, but I told her I had to see you...'

'Rory!' Maureen stared at him in surprise. 'I should've thought you would be on your honeymoon. Carol told me you were goin' to marry her.'

'Don't look at me like that!' Rory pleaded. 'I know you've every right to hate me – but it was only once. I was in a mood and I got drunk...'

Maureen looked at him and felt nothing. He was lying again. His eyes couldn't meet hers. Why hadn't she seen him for what he really was all those years ago?

'I'm sorry, I don't believe you,' she said. 'Carol told me it happened several times – besides, once is enough. She's havin' your baby and her father will kill her if you don't wed her.'

'No, that was a mistake,' Rory said. 'The doctor says she's anaemic because she hasn't been eatin' properly and she's not havin' a baby at all...' He looked at her pleadingly. 'You know I love you, Molly. I'm a bloody fool. I've got a wicked temper and I do stupid things when I've had too much to drink – but she didn't mean anythin' to me. I hardly remember touchin' her...'

Maureen stared at him in disbelief, feeling the anger mount inside her. Did he think she was such a fool? Whether the story about Carol's anaemia was true or the baby story had been a deliberate lie on the girl's part she had no idea, but what she did know was that she wasn't interested. Nothing on this earth would make her trust Rory again.

'Go away, Rory,' she said coldly. 'What makes you think I'm interested in your sordid little problems? I don't care whether you marry Carol or not – she's as bad as you. I'm finished with you. I never want to speak to or hear from you again.'

'Maureen...' Rory grabbed her by the upper arms, glaring at her fiercely as his fingers dug into her flesh. 'You can't just brush me off like this... I love you.'

'Take your hands off me, Rory. I meant it. We're finished.'

'No... I shan't take that answer!' He started shaking her and Maureen tried to fight him off, but he was hurting her and she cried out in pain. 'You love me, you know you do!'

'No. It's over...'

'Are you all right, Nurse Jackson?' Doctor Phillips asked, stopping to investigate.

She shook her head at him and he moved forward, laying a firm hand on Rory's arm.

'Now then, sir. I think you should allow Nurse Jackson to pass, don't you? She's had a long night and she's tired.'

Rory glared at him and then Maureen. 'All right, bitch,' he said. 'I don't know what I saw in you anyway...'

He strode off in a rage, leaving Maureen shaken and feeling unwell. For a moment she swayed and the doctor held her steady. He looked at her in concern.

'Did that brute hurt you?'

'No, it's all right,' she said as the faintness passed. 'He has a nasty temper, but I don't think he will bother me again.'

'If he does, you should go to the police,' Doctor Phillips said. 'I have my car here; may I give you a lift – save you catching a bus?'

'No, that's fine,' Maureen smiled at him. 'You've already helped me, sir. I shall be perfectly all right now – I know exactly what I want to do...'

*

'Can we feed the monkeys?' Shirley asked as they passed a man selling buns. 'Can we, Mummy?'

'Yes, I don't see why not,' Maureen laughed, feeling happy because Shirley had called her mummy. She bought a sixpenny bag of buns and passed it to her. 'Mind your fingers, Shirley.'

'She's so happy,' Gordon said as the child skipped off to push pieces of bun through the wire of the cage holding different kinds of chattering monkeys.'

'Did you tell her I was going to be her new mummy?' Maureen asked, looking up at him.

'No, I think she's just assumed that herself,' Gordon said, smiling down at her. 'But you are, aren't you?'

'Yes, I am.' Maureen said, looking up at him, unable to hide her pleasure. 'You're sure you want us to marry this leave? You don't want to think about it or wait until the baby...?'

Gordon reached for her, pulled her close and kissed her so sweetly that Maureen subsided. Two soldiers passing by laughed and called out something ribald, but neither Maureen nor Gordon took the least bit of notice.

'I've got the licence,' Gordon said and tapped his jacket pocket. 'As soon as you say the word, I'll arrange it.'

'I get next Friday and Saturday off,' Maureen said, feeling excited as the realisation that she was getting married came over her. 'I can't ask for any longer than that, because I've only just been transferred here. We could get married on Friday, have Saturday and Sunday together – and then I have to work Sunday evenin'...'

'I'll arrange it,' Gordon said and touched her cheek with one finger. 'We'll have two nights in a posh hotel up the West End and save the honeymoon for when I come back next time.'

'Yes. Lovely,' Maureen said and smiled. 'You haven't asked me why I don't just give my notice in.'

'Why should you give up a job you love?' Gordon said. 'You'll know when you're ready – or they'll decide. It's ridiculous that nurses can't marry and remain in the service, especially now. We need all the nurses we can get.'

'Some hospitals turn a blind eye these days,' Maureen said, tears stinging her eyes because he was so thoughtful and kind. 'I'm not allowed to wear jewellery on the wards, so I'll wear my ring on a chain round my neck under my uniform. I'll have to tell them in time... but there's no sense in givin' up while I can work.'

'We'll have to decide where you and Shirley will live. My house was let for the duration, but I could find somewhere for us... somewhere to come back to when I'm on leave.'

'Why don't we just stay with Gran until you're home for good?' Maureen said. 'She's happy havin' Shirley and me there – and she'll make you just as welcome, Gordon. I think she's guessed already, because I've seen a knowin' look in her eye.'

'Whatever makes you happy,' Gordon said. 'I'm not sure where they're shippin' me off to next time – but I've heard it might be quite hot.'

'You couldn't tell me even if you knew,' Maureen said. 'I know our men are fightin' all over the place and I know you have to go – but don't let's think about it. We have another two weeks before you leave, and I want to spend as much time as I can with you before then...'

'Maureen, my love.' Gordon kissed her and then realised his daughter was watching them. 'I think perhaps we should all have some ice cream at Lyons, don't you?'

'Yes, why not?' Maureen held out her hand to the child. 'Come along, darling. Did the monkeys like their buns?'

Listening to Shirley's chatter, Maureen tucked her arm through Gordon's. Her feelings for Gordon were still a little new and uncertain, because until now she'd thought of him as a friend, but his letters had been nurturing this warmth inside her for a long time, a warmth she'd just begun to realise could be love.

Chapter 29

'It's very quick, isn't it, Maureen?' Gran switched off the radio and looked at her after Gordon had taken Shirley up to put her to bed. 'I like Gordon and I'm glad if he makes you happy – but what about Rory?'

'Rory let me down, Gran. I've realised that I would've made a big mistake if I'd married him, and now I've decided that I want to marry Gordon.'

'It isn't that you have to get married quickly?'

Gran's shrewd eyes met hers and Maureen's cheeks heated. 'Yes, I am havin' a child and Gordon does know. He has accepted it and it's over with Rory. I shan't ever tell him...'

'Is that right or fair?' Gran asked, giving her a long, hard look. 'I never did think much of Rory and I'm glad you've chosen Gordon Hart – but even a cheat has the right to know his child.'

'No! I've made up my mind, Gran. Rory will never know. I can be happy and I can forgive him in time – but I shan't forget what he did, and I won't give him the chance to ruin my life or my child's.'

'Well, it's your decision, my love,' Gran said, but the doubt was in her eyes. 'It may prove harder to keep the secret than you imagine, but you must be the one to choose.' She smiled and kissed Maureen on the cheek, the smell of lavender soft and sweet in her clothes and hair. 'You're my girl and I just want you to be happy – have you told your dad yet?'

'No. We'll visit him before next Friday together and tell him, but I shan't tell him about the baby until I have to. It's best if everyone thinks it's Gordon's. He thinks that's for the best and so do I.'

'Well, as I said, it may prove harder to keep the secret than you imagine, but as long as you're happy that's all that matters... and that child of his loves you.' Gran smiled. 'She was a right little madam when you first had her to tea, but she's changed completely.'

'I suppose Mrs Hunter had a lot to do with that,' Maureen looked thoughtful. 'Shirley hasn't said much about her life on the farm but Mrs Hunter told me herself that she'd taken a hairbrush to her. I'm just glad that Shirley's here with us now.'

'Well, you'd best be off to work then,' Gran said as Gordon came down the stairs. 'Have you two thought about where you'll have the wedding?'

'It will be a registry office – and I thought I'd ask Peggy if she'd do us a small reception at the pub,' Gordon said. 'Maureen doesn't want a church weddin' and there isn't time to arrange anythin' fancy.'

'I would have my weddin' at the pub anyway,' Maureen said. 'It's where we live and all our friends are here in the lanes, Gordon. I don't know if you have any Army friends you want to ask?'

'None of them are on leave just now,' Gordon replied. 'I'll probably ask Jack Barton to be my witness. We used to be good friends and there isn't anyone else – and your friends are mine, Maureen.'

'I'll tell Peggy for about twenty then; I'm goin' to ask her to do a buffet like she does for her Christmas party,' Maureen said. 'Everyone enjoys that and it's easier to arrange than a sit-down meal these days.'

'As long as you're happy,' Gran said and nodded. 'What will you wear, love? Your mum's dress is in the wardrobe, but it's a bit old-fashioned...'

'Maureen will have a new dress,' Gordon said, giving her a look filled with love and pride. 'We'll go up West and get it...'

'No, you won't,' Maureen said and laughed. 'The groom doesn't see what the bride wears until the day. Leave it to me, Gordon. I know just what I want...'

*

Peggy looked at the bride as she stood in her bedroom at Hilda's in the pretty yellow full-skirted dress and jacket. Maureen's hair had been done earlier that morning by Ellie from the shop in Mulberry Lane; she'd opened early specially for her. Maureen had a tiny hat that was made of yellow and white silk flowers and fine veiling on the back of her head, white leather court shoes and white lace gloves, and she carried a posy of yellow roses tied with satin ribbons.

'You look beautiful, love,' Peggy said, her eyes moist with affection. 'Really lovely. And that hat is gorgeous with the veiling just over your eyes – perfect for a wartime bride.'

'That's what I thought,' Maureen said. 'It would've seemed wrong to marry in a long white dress for several reasons, Peggy. I feel special in this dress and I was lucky to get it. I knew what I was looking for but not sure I would find it – but there it was in the first shop I tried.'

'That's a pretty brooch, Maureen. I haven't seen you wear it before.'

'It was my mother's,' Maureen said and touched the pearl and gold brooch pinned to her jacket. 'It's too special for every day – and Dad bought it for her as her wedding gift.'

'It's a pity your dad can't come to the wedding, Maureen.'

'Yes, but he did manage to wish us luck and told Gordon he was pleased. He told Violet to give me ten pounds to buy myself something nice, and she has. I shall put it away for later.'

'You'll be all right now. Gordon has a few bob put by I dare say.'

'Well, he owns his house, but that's let for the duration. He's had the money paid into a bank account for Shirley in case anythin' happened to him, but there isn't very much put away otherwise. He really only has his Army wages; that was one of the reasons he decided to let his house while he was away.'

'Well, that's as much as most have,' Peggy said.

'Oh, I wouldn't want him to be rich. I'm not marryin' him for money.' Maureen smiled. 'Besides, I can work for a few months and I've always been good at managin'.'

'I can see you're happy,' Peggy nodded. 'I hope everythin' goes well for you, love. Janet wanted to come and see you married, but Mike is home today. She'll be there at the reception, Mike too if he feels able. You won't mind that?'

'Of course not,' Maureen said. 'Knowin' you, there will be loads of food and it will be lovely.'

'I couldn't manage an iced cake,' Peggy said regretfully. 'I've made a sponge though and some other treats... but you'll see.' She glanced at her watch. 'The car should be here any minute now. We'd better go down...'

Gordon looked very handsome in his best uniform. Shirley was wearing a pretty white voile dress that Maureen had made for her recently and carrying a little basket of rosebuds tied up with yellow ribbons. Gordon had asked her to be one of his witnesses and she looked nervous but proud to stand behind her dad as the brief ceremony took place.

It seemed like the blink of an eye before they were out again in the October sunshine and Maureen had a wide gold band on her finger. The wind was cool and she shivered a little in her thin dress and jacket, but the smiles and jokes, the hugs and presents, and silver horseshoes tied with ribbons given her by Mrs Tandy and Alice Carter helped to keep off the chill. Maureen blinked back the foolish tears, because she knew she was happy – far happier than she'd expected to be. Marrying Gordon might have been a marriage of convenience, but it wasn't, because she felt her new love growing stronger all the time. Within a few minutes, everyone had piled into the borrowed cars and they were all driven back to Mulberry Lane.

Outside the pub, someone had tied a big bunch of colourful balloons and some silver ribbons and another horseshoe. A large hand-drawn sign welcomed Mr and Mrs Gordon Hart on their wedding day, and when they walked into the pub, the bar had been dressed with white and silver ribbons and a large card stood on the table by an impressive sponge cake. Looking inside the card, Maureen smiled to see it had been signed by everyone in the lanes.

Quite a few presents had been placed on a table near the splendid buffet and there were telegrams to read when the cake was cut and the toast drunk, one of them from Violet and Henry Jackson. Violet hadn't come to the wedding, because she was visiting her husband in hospital, but she had given Maureen a lace tablecloth as a gift and wished her happiness.

Peggy tapped a glass to gain everyone's attention. 'As you all know, Mr Jackson is unfortunately ill and cannot be with us today, so I've been asked to say a few words. It should have been Hilda, but she thinks I'll do it better...'

Smiling, Peggy told them all what a good daughter, granddaughter and friend Maureen had been. She congratulated Gordon on finding himself a wonderful wife and then spoke briefly about Maureen's selflessness in working as a nurse.

'So I ask you to please raise your glasses and wish them well... Gordon and Maureen. May their lives together be long and happy...'

There were cries of hear, hear, and then everyone raised his or her glass to toast the bride and groom, who smiled and looked suitably pleased as they sipped the delicious wine.

It wasn't champagne but it was sparkling and everyone said how nice it was, before they all fell on the food. Peggy had done the best she could with the coupons she'd been able to beg, borrow or steal, as she put it with a wicked smile, and if there were any sense of it being a wartime wedding, neither the bride nor the groom was aware of it.

'Mike wanted to say hello,' Janet said to Maureen when everyone was on their second or third drink. 'He didn't quite feel up to a weddin', but he says he'd like to say hello to you and Gordon – but he won't remember you. He knows he should know you, but nothin' is clear to him yet.'

'We'll come through to the kitchen,' Maureen said and took Gordon's hand, giving him a shy smile. 'I was pleased when Peggy said he was home for you, Janet. How long will he be able to stay?'

'They suggest three days for a start,' Janet said and Maureen thought her smile was a little forced, though when she introduced them to Mike her smile became natural. 'Mike love – Maureen and Gordon just wanted to say hello...'

The man who stood up to greet them looked nothing like the healthy, strong and handsome man Janet had married in 1939. What a difference two short years had made – and that was this wretched war.

'It's lovely to see you home,' Maureen said and kissed Mike's cheek. His scars were not that bad really, more just brown skin than puckers or deep gashes, but he looked thin and weary and his eyes had lost their sparkle. 'I expect you're happy to get out of hospital for a few days.'

'Yes, I am, very much so,' Mike said, sounding like a polite stranger. 'May I wish you and your husband a very happy life ahead.'

'Thank you, Mike,' Gordon said and offered his hand. It was a firm handshake and the two men exchanged a few words, and then Gordon said they had to return to their guests. 'We'll look forward to seein' you in the future, Mike...'

'He looked so ill,' Maureen said as they left Janet with her husband and returned to the bar. She'd been shocked to see the change in him and it brought home the realisation of what war could do as never before, making her cling to her new husband's arm in sudden fear, because she didn't want to lose him. 'It must have been terrible for him – and Janet. I thought he must be gettin' better if they let him out, but he looks exhausted.'

'Poor devil. It must be bewildering. Bad enough if you knew you were home but when you can't even remember your name...' Gordon shook his head. 'We see mates gettin' shot, Maureen, but we don't often see them in hospital or the way these illnesses drain them of strength and life... I imagine he has a long way to go yet.'

'Yes, poor Mike.' Maureen looked at her husband. 'Promise you'll come home safe to us, Gordon.'

'I haven't gone yet,' he teased but then saw the expression in her eyes and touched her hand. 'You know I shall if I can, love. I want to be with you until we're old and grey...'

'That's all right then,' Maureen said and the shadows lifted. Seeing Mike that way had upset her, because she knew how much both he and Janet must be suffering – and it had made her very aware of how much she too had to lose.

Shirley ran up to them as they returned to the bar and threw her arms around Maureen. She looked up at them, her eyes wide with wonder.

'Are you really my mummy now?'

'Yes, Shirley, I am. I'm your daddy's wife – but I was always your friend, and I always shall be.' She bent and kissed her, laughing as Shirley's arms clung for a moment.

'Gran says you're goin' to a posh hotel for two nights – can I come?'

Gordon swooped down and picked her up, kissing her cheek. 'Not this time, sweetheart,' he said. 'One day when we have longer, we'll take you to the seaside – how's that?'

Her eyes widened at the prospect of the treat. 'To the real seaside?' she asked.

'Yes, darling, the real seaside.' He put her down. 'Have you had something to eat?'

'Yes, but Gran says I can have a piece of sponge cake if I like...'

'Run to Gran then,' Maureen said. 'You'll be good for her while we're away, won't you?'

'Yes,' Shirley said, then, 'Will you bring me some sweets when you come home?'

'I might if you're good,' her father said and smiled as she ran off. 'I shall feel so much better about her when I go back, Maureen. I never was quite happy about that woman on the farm.'

'She's quite safe with us,' Maureen assured him. 'I think you should give your speech now, Gordon, just to thank our friends for comin' – and for the lovely gifts they've given us.'

Peggy had given them a six-part tea service and the reception. She'd insisted that she wouldn't accept a penny for the reception, because Maureen was like a sister to her, and the tea service wasn't new.

'We found it in the attic when Tom Barton cleared it out,' she'd told Maureen. 'It's perfect but not new – but I think you will like it.'

Maureen thought it was lovely, as were the gifts of two cotton towels from Mrs Tandy and the glass vase from Alice; that too wasn't new, because she'd bought it down the Portobello, but it was crystal and better than anything in the shops at the moment. Anne had given her a silver-plated teapot that had belonged to her aunt and a pretty wooden tray. Quite a few of Maureen's old customers had bought small gifts; things like a quirky corkscrew, some beautiful silver coffee spoons in an old leather case, also probably bought in the Portobello, and tea towels, a breadknife and board, a china jam dish, two slightly yellowed lace hankies and a lavender-scented case to keep them in.

The gifts, so thoughtfully and lovingly given, were all accepted gratefully. In wartime it was difficult to find anything worth buying for wedding gifts and most people had chosen to give something from their dresser drawer or from a second-hand stall. However, everything had been well meant and Maureen accepted the gifts with smiles and hugs and thanked the people who showed their feelings for her in kind acts.

She didn't think she would have changed anything even if she could, and when the car came to take them up West, she kissed her friends goodbye with tears in her eyes.

'Happy tears,' she said as Peggy wiped them from her cheeks. 'It has all been so lovely and everyone is so kind – I really didn't expect so many people to come or so many gifts.'

'Well, you know the Mulberry Lane crowd,' Peggy said and laughed wickedly. 'Anythin' for a free drink…'

Maureen smiled but shook her head. 'It was the best wedding ever – thanks to you. I don't know how you managed it, Peggy.'

'Nellie gave me some of her coupons and she helped me scour the markets for anything we could use. When the war is over I'll bake you a two-tier iced cake for your anniversary, Maureen.'

'I'm happy with what we had,' Maureen said and hugged her. 'I'll see you on Sunday. Bye for now…'

'Bye, love…'

Maureen looked back out of the car window as they were driven away, then she turned to Gordon and saw that he was watching her.

'Are you all right, love?' he asked.

'Yes, of course – and you?'

'Happiest man alive.'

'Me too,' she said and leaned against his shoulder. His comforting strength made her feel secure and loved in a way she never had, opening up a new vista for her. 'Thank you for today, Gordon.'

'I haven't even given you your gift yet,' he said and took a small box from his pocket. 'Like a lot of the presents you were given today, it's not new – but I think you will like it.'

Opening the black velvet box, Maureen saw the ring. Shaped like a daisy, it was made up of platinum and small diamonds that sparkled against the soft velvet.

'Oh... I've never seen such a pretty ring,' she said, looking at him in delight. 'I never expected anythin' so beautiful...'

'I wanted you to have an engagement ring, even though we were never engaged, but one day the diamonds will be a lot bigger. After the war, I'm goin' to get us a lovely home and give you nice things, Maureen. You've given me so much and I want to make you happy.'

'Just always be the same as you are now,' she said and leaned in to kiss him on the lips. 'I'm not bothered about material things, Gordon – just be kind and lovin', that's all I need...'

Chapter 30

Janet and Nellie finished the washing up together. Mike had gone upstairs to rest for a while after Maureen and Gordon's visit. He said he was tired and wanted a lie-down before they had dinner, but Janet knew he was feeling mixed up and uncertain.

Seeing him in clothes that hung on him had made her aware of how thin he'd become. In the hospital he'd always worn pyjamas and a dressing gown and it hadn't been so noticeable. Beside Gordon's slightly tanned complexion and his strong body, Mike's pallor and weakness had seemed more noticeable and she thought it had made him realise just what he'd lost.

'Why don't you take Mike a cup of tea up?' Nellie suggested. 'It must have felt awkward for him with a wedding goin' on 'ere, Janet. He's been used to bein' quiet at the hospital – leastwise, all the other men are like him. They've all suffered and known terrible pain. Normal life must come as a bit of a shock.'

'Yes, I think it upset him to see Gordon and Maureen,' Janet said. 'I know he wanted to and he would've liked to join in more – but it does make you realise just how different his life is now.'

'Yes, well, it's a good thing you understand,' Nellie said

and smiled at her approvingly. 'Not all wives stick by their 'usbands the way you have, love.'

'I love him,' Janet said and put the small teapot, two cups and a jug with a little milk on the tray. 'Maybe he'll drink it if I have mine with him.'

'You go on up then, love. It's 'ard fer you, but it must be a lot 'arder fer 'im.'

'Yes, it is, I know.' Janet smiled at her, picked the tray up and carried it upstairs. Her mother and Anne were clearing up in the bar, getting things ready for the evening opening. She would've helped more if she could but Anne had got the afternoon off to attend the wedding and help Peggy, and Mike needed her.

He was sitting on the side of the bed staring at the wall, but smiled as she entered the room. He watched as she set the tray down and then poured their tea and brought the cups to him, sitting down beside him to sip her tea.

'Is it all right?'

'Lovely. A darn sight better than we get in the hospital,' he said. 'I'm sorry, Jan. This can't be easy – havin' a stranger in your home...'

'You're not a stranger to me, Mike,' she said and put her cup down on the bedside cabinet. 'You are my husband and I love you very much.'

'I'm a shadow of the man you married,' he said and set his cup down next to hers. 'I was thinkin' when I saw Gordon, it isn't fair on you to be stuck with me for the rest of your life. I don't know when I'll be able to take you dancin' or out for a meal – or make love to you...'

Janet leaned towards him and kissed him on the lips. His arms went round her and he held her pressed hard against him, a little shudder running through him. Looking into his face, she saw tears on his cheeks as he released her and sat back.

'I do love you, Jan,' he said in a choked voice. 'I love the girl you are – the way you care for our child and the way you are with me – but it isn't fair to you if I can't remember, if I can't be a proper husband to you. I wanted to come to the weddin' with you, but I couldn't manage it...'

'You're still not well...'

'No, I think I could do most things,' Mike said seriously, 'but I can't bring myself to be with strangers – even your mum is difficult for me, and she's lovely. I have to make myself talk to her.'

'It will get better,' Janet said. She reached for his hand and held it. 'I'm just glad to have you here, Mike. All the rest will come in time...'

'I thought we might go for a little walk in the dark,' he suggested tentatively. 'Just for a start, Jan. Just you and me – look in the shop windows and, if I can face it, stop for a drink...'

'Just as we used to,' Janet said and leaned in to kiss him again. This time he didn't try to hold her, but he touched her cheek. 'I should like that, Mike. I'll do anythin' you want. You don't have to do anythin' you don't feel up to – I don't mind...'

'How did I get so lucky?' Mike asked and she saw tears hover even though he refused to let them fall. 'Some of the chaps – their wives have found other men. They've been carryin' on while their men were away, and they just walk out when things get rough – but you stuck with me, even when I was rotten to you.'

Janet nodded, because she'd seen it herself. Ellie Morris, from the hairdressers', was always having drinks with soldiers, and had let them take her home when she was more than a little merry.

Pressing her face to his shoulder, Janet held back her tears. She loved Mike and always would, but he would never know how close she had come to having an affair with Ryan. That was all over now. Ryan had gone away and Mike would soon be able to come home for good, and he would never need to know that she had once thought she might love someone else.

'Let's go for that walk after dinner,' she said. 'I'm goin' to help Mum get cleared up. Have a rest and then come downstairs when you're ready...'

Blinking back her tears, Janet took the tea tray back to the kitchen. She wasn't brave or perfect and she was finding this much harder than she would admit to anyone else, but she would find a way to make things right. Mike had to be sure of his place here, to be sure he was loved, and then perhaps he would be able to face the future.

*

'Well, Maureen looked happy, didn't she?' Peggy said when she and Janet were sitting alone in the kitchen in the lull just before the pub opened again. 'When Gordon first asked her to be his wife I didn't think it was a good idea. I thought she would come second to his daughter, but you can see he really loves her.'

'Yes, I noticed it the other night, when he saw her in the bar. You'd been to Sam's funeral and Gordon couldn't take his eyes off her.'

'Well, I'm glad everythin' has worked out well for her.' Peggy's gaze narrowed as she looked at her daughter. 'Where is Mike? He seems so tired. I think he's findin' this harder than he'd expected.'

'Yes, he is tired; that's why I took his tea up to him on a tray. He has to get used to everyone, Mum. It's horrid meetin' people that you should know and just can't remember.'

'Of course, it must be uncomfortable for him. It will take time for Mike to get back to normal again, Janet.'

'We're goin' for a little walk later...'

'Yes, get a breath of fresh air...' Peggy looked at her daughter sadly. 'What about you, my love? This is hard for you, too. You've been married a couple of years and yet you've really had hardly any life together.'

'I'm all right, Mum. I'm lucky I've got him home. I can wait for all the rest of it – besides, there's no choice. Mike can't help being ill.'

'No, he can't and he will get better – but you did have a choice, Janet. You could have chosen another life if you'd wished.'

Janet shook her head. 'Ryan is a good friend and if... But no, I shan't even think about it. Mike is the man I love. He's my husband and I want to stick by him, even if it takes forever.'

'Good. I'm proud of you, my love.' Peggy smiled at her. 'Now, there's some good news for a change. Jack Barton told me that Violet has given him the job in the shop. It's just for a couple of months while he sorts out his family – but...' She hesitated, then, 'I know you won't say, Janet. Jack told me in confidence they've given him a choice: he can return to prison when his parole is up or sign up for the Army...'

'He has a chance to go into the Army rather than return to prison?'

'Apparently the parole board think he isn't a habitual criminal and they seem to believe that given the opportunity to go straight he would not reoffend. Jack says it's the last thing he would do, because he bitterly regrets what he did. He told me that he thinks he will join up. His family would get half his wage paid direct and they could probably manage fine on that – and stuck in prison he can't do anythin' for them.'

'I think it's a wonderful chance for him,' Janet said. 'If he hadn't been in prison when the war started I'm sure he would've joined then anyway.'

'Yes, that's what he says. Once Tommy is out of hospital he will tell them he's ready to serve his country – and he asked me if I would keep an eye on his son. He isn't sure when Tilly will be well enough to leave hospital, but I said I'd cook a meal for Tom once a day, and see to his washing, though Jack wants him to keep the house for when his mother comes home, of course.'

'Just remember you're goin' to need to take care of yourself in a few months...'

Peggy smiled. 'Yes, I know, but one more dinner plate makes little difference and Tilly may be home by the time I get so ungainly that I can't manage to cook. Besides, I've got you and Nellie to help me.'

'Yes, but you can't take in all the waifs and strays, Mum.'

'Pip hasn't been home for weeks,' Peggy said, her eyes clouded by sadness. 'I know he's angry with me but if he came home I'd feed him and wash his things – so it won't hurt me to give Tom Barton a helping hand while his mum is ill.'

'I'll write to Pip and tell him to stop sulkin',' Janet said. 'I know they're busy, but he must get leave sometimes. It isn't fair of him to hurt you like this.'

'I hurt him – and his father,' Peggy said with a wry look. 'That's how Pip sees it. I don't blame him for taking your dad's side, but it does hurt – especially when I know that what he's doin' is dangerous. He's my son and if anythin' happened...'

'I'll write to him, make him see sense,' Janet said and gave her mother a hug. 'You've been hurt enough and none of this would've happened if Dad hadn't cheated on you.'

'I'm not sure of that,' Peggy said. 'I fell in love with Able. I might have been more careful if Laurie hadn't cheated – but Able was so lovely, Janet; I'm not sure I could have resisted him. He made me feel young and beautiful again.'

'You are still young and beautiful,' her daughter said loyally and Peggy laughed.

'Well, the other good news is that the hospital has told Jack that Tom will be coming home by the end of next week at the latest. His head wound has healed and he's gettin' better, though his arm is still in a sling. At first they thought he might lose it, but they managed to save it. However, he has to have therapy on it before he'll be able to use it properly again.'

'Tom won't like that,' Janet said. 'He likes to be busy. I've never known anyone so keen on tryin' his hand at so many jobs.'

'He wanted to leave school and work for himself. Of course he also wants to serve in the Army, but it will be years before he's old enough.'

'What does his father say about that?'

'He blames himself, but says if he's sendin' home a wage there won't be the need for Tom to leave school, but he won't stand in his way if it's what he wants.'

Janet nodded. 'I think Tom likes to work with his hands; he's not cut out for office work. We just have to hope he'll be able to do what he loves and that his arm will heal.'

'His father seems to think it's just a matter of time.' Peggy saw her daughter's smile. 'What is that look for?'

'Jack Barton seems to tell you a lot?' Janet quirked her left eyebrow teasingly.

'No!' Peggy shook her head emphatically at her daughter. 'Don't get daft ideas in your head, Janet. Jack is a friend and Tilly is also a friend. There's nothin' funny goin' on and there won't be.'

'Just teasin', Mum,' Janet said. 'I think Jack is an attractive man, but he has a wife and son, and I know you loved Able. It's just my little bit of fun.'

'Good,' Peggy said seriously. 'I had an affair with Able, but that was special. Besides, I'm hardly in the right condition for conductin' torrid affairs, am I?'

Janet met her gaze and started laughing, and then Peggy joined in. It was a release for all the pent-up emotion of the past few months and they were still giggling when Mike walked in. He smiled as he saw their faces and arched his brows.

'What's the joke? Can anyone join in?'

'Janet thinks one of my customers fancies me,' Peggy said and Janet nodded, still laughing. 'Are you feelin' any better now, Mike love?'

'Yes.' He met her look steadily. 'As a matter of fact, I think I am, Peggy.' He turned to Janet with a look of invitation in his eyes. 'Shall we go for that walk now, love?'

Chapter 31

'This is nice,' Maureen said, looking about her at the room Gordon had booked for their wedding night. The bedroom was fitted with cream furniture edged with gold and there was a deep bronze satin eiderdown on the bed, and an elbow chair covered with similar material on the seat. The curtains were gold and cream, and there was a lovely bathroom, which had grey marble tiles and taps that gleamed and gushed piping-hot water, and also a separate shower. 'Real luxury...'

'I wanted the best for you,' Gordon said and smiled as she sat on the edge of the bed, bouncing experimentally. 'I wish we could have gone off to Spain or France or somewhere exotic for our honeymoon...'

'No, this is perfect,' she said and held her hand out to him with a shy smile. 'Everythin' has been perfect all day. I am very happy, Gordon.'

'Are you – truly?' he asked and took her hand in his, holding it carefully, as if he thought she might break. 'To have you as my wife is a dream come true, Maureen. I'm afraid you've got a slow old thing for a husband. I didn't wake up to how much I felt for you until it was too late – but I know it now.'

'You're not old and I don't think either of us was ready back in '39,' Maureen said and held his hand tighter. 'I'm ready now, Gordon.' She said, moving closer and smiling up at him invitingly.

'I love you very much,' he said and leaned towards her. 'I never expected that I would ever know such happiness again, Maureen.'

'I want you to be happy,' she said. 'It isn't the perfect start for us, Gordon, but I plan on bein' a good wife and mother – and I love you too.'

'Maureen...' He hushed her with a gentle kiss. 'You don't have to say anythin'. I've got the most perfect wife I could have and the rest of it doesn't bother me. Why should it? I've been married before and I have a daughter I love. If you can accept that, I can certainly accept that you're havin' the baby of someone you once thought you loved...' He smiled at her. 'I just think I'm lucky to get you.'

Maureen looked up into his eyes and saw that he meant every word. She smiled and put out a hand to trace the line of his cheek. Suddenly, she felt a surge of love and a desire to feel his arms about her. In that moment she realised that she'd come to appreciate and care for him through his wonderful letters and he meant more to her than she'd understood.

'Don't you think you'd better show me then?' she said huskily. 'I'm eager to try out this lovely bed...'

A slow smile started in Gordon's eyes as he saw the teasing light in hers. He pushed her gently back against the pillows and bent over her, his lips moving softly against hers.

'I think that's a pretty good idea,' he whispered. 'After all, we don't have much time to waste...'

*

Maureen lay listening to her husband's steady breathing as he slept beside her. Gordon had made love to her so sweetly, taking care to give her pleasure so that she felt a warm satisfaction in his loving and was able to give herself without restraint, enjoying the touch of his hands and the feel of his smooth, hard flesh against her own.

Gordon was a considerate lover. He'd teased her and they'd laughed together, easy and natural without any of the awkwardness she'd feared might happen when they were in bed. He'd given her a feeling of belonging that she'd never felt before, and together they'd experienced a rare happiness, a surety and content that she knew wasn't given to all. Her heart filled with gratitude and love. She'd been given a second chance and she believed this time her love would be returned and appreciated. Gordon would never let her down. He would never dream of sleeping with another woman just because Maureen wasn't available. She was so lucky to have this loving, considerate and tender man as her husband.

Gordon moved in his sleep and she snuggled up to his warm body, breathing in the fresh, clean smell of him. Her past hurt and disappointment was forgotten. This was all that mattered now, the togetherness and the sharing that came with marriage and loving. Maureen felt passionate love for her new husband, just as she felt motherly love for Shirley. Gordon was the man she'd looked for all her life, never dreaming that he was right there under her nose all along.

She felt like giggling as she nibbled at his earlobe and sensed him respond, his waking smile filling her with a surge of sweet desire and the knowledge that she was both loved and wanted. Something she had never really known before.

*

In the morning when they finally woke, Gordon made love to her again, and it was just as nice, just as satisfying. Afterwards, they took a warm bath together, enjoying the experience of being intimate in a way that made them laugh as they touched and stroked, splashing water on the marble tiles and ending up by making love rather uncomfortably in the bath.

Much later, when they'd had coffee and hot muffins in their room, they went out. It was fun walking round the shops, looking at the luxury goods, which were still available in the more exclusive shops. Perhaps because they were so very expensive they didn't rush out of the shops as everything else did.

It was still possible to buy clothes if you had enough coupons, but very few shops had anything but the plain utilitarian dresses with their short, skimpy skirts that were necessary these days. They lingered outside a shop selling good-quality second-hand clothes, where some rather elegant good-quality silk dresses were on show. Gordon wanted to buy her something, if there was anything she wanted, but Maureen shook her head.

'There's no point until I've had the baby. I wouldn't be able to wear it for long,' she said. 'I think I'll manage with what I have for now and buy something pretty for next summer – perhaps you'll be back on leave again…'

Gordon touched her cheek. 'Don't look so wistful, my love. I know we shan't have long together, but I was lucky to get this much leave. Some of the chaps haven't had leave for over a year.'

'Yes, I know,' she said and squeezed his hand. 'Everyone is in the same boat. This is enough, Gordon. I'm just greedy to want more.'

He laughed and bent down to kiss her there in the street, making a passing sailor whistle loudly. 'Maybe it will be over by next summer, love. I can't see why they have to keep fightin'. Hitler says he wants to make peace but no one believes him.'

'After what he did in Poland and France?' Maureen shook her head. 'We can't let him win, Gordon. This is a wretched war. All the men that have died, the people here who were killed in the Blitz, those brave airmen – and the sailors lost at sea – they can't have died for nothin'. We have to go on until he's beaten.'

'Yes.' Gordon touched her cheek. 'I know it, my love, but I can't help wantin' it to be over. We all feel the same – every man I've met just wants to kill Hitler and get it over.'

'It's a pity no one thought of that at the start. If someone had just shot him then none of this need ever have happened.'

Gordon laughed. 'Unfortunately, things are never that simple, Maureen. Germany was simmering with resentment after the last time and they intended to show the rest of us that they were not a beaten nation.'

'Oh well, we shan't change it,' Maureen said and glanced at a newspaper stand, which proclaimed a jubilant Hitler was close to Moscow. She gave a little shiver and resolutely turned her head, summoning a bright smile. This was her honeymoon and she refused to waste it worrying about the war. 'Gosh, I'm hungry. Shall we go back to the hotel for lunch?'

'Yes, I think so,' he said and slipped his arm about her still slim waist. 'What do you want to do this evenin' – shall we go dancin' or see if we can get into a show?'

'Let's go dancin',' Maureen said. 'I haven't danced for ages...'

'When you get back in the mornin', I'll be gone,' Gordon said as Maureen came downstairs in her nursing uniform. 'I thought three weeks was a lifetime when I was given leave, but it's gone too quickly.'

'Yes, I know,' Maureen said and lingered. She was on the late shift at the hospital, and in the kitchen Gran had got the *ITMA* show on the radio and was chuckling at something Tommy Handley was saying. The warmth and happiness of the last few days had been so wonderful and she was reluctant to leave, knowing that when she returned Gordon wouldn't be waiting for her. Their time together had been so brief, even though he'd been given a generous leave. For a moment, desperation almost overcame her and she said impulsively: 'Should I ring in sick so that we can have one more night together, Gordon?'

He shook his head, moving closer to draw her against him, before bending his head to kiss her softly on the mouth. 'It still wouldn't be enough. I don't want to go, love, but I have to – and you have to work until you choose to tell them you're married and havin' a child...'

'Yes, that's not goin' to be easy,' Maureen admitted wryly. 'They won't be pleased, but it's up to them. I'll go on workin' until it gets uncomfortable, but they won't let me once they know.'

'You don't need to work. I've arranged for most of my pay to come to you, Maureen. Why don't you tell them you're married and let them decide whether you work a bit longer or not?'

'Perhaps I shall,' she said and then put her arms about him, clinging in sudden desperate need. 'Oh, Gordon, I do love you. Take care of yourself, my darling. I want you to come home to me...'

'I will,' he said and kissed her hard, as if giving her his strength. 'I promise I'll come back – and when I do we'll have a proper honeymoon...'

'No, we'll have a family holiday at the sea,' she said and stood back. This was just making it harder for both of them. She made herself smile, catching back a sob that rose in her throat. She wouldn't cry and give Gordon sad memories to take with him. 'I'd better go or I shall be late. Be sure to put Shirley to bed and read her a story tonight. It will have to last her a long time...'

'Yes, I know, but she told me she understands. Her friends all have daddies workin' in the Army. She's being very brave about it and she knows she has to look after you and the baby for me.'

Maureen felt the tears sting her eyes. Gordon always spoke of the child as their baby, and he'd told Shirley she was going to have a little brother or sister. Maureen felt her heart swell. She really did love him. She just wished they'd had months and months to spend together instead of a few short weeks.

'I have to go...' She smiled at him through the tears, forcing herself to put on her coat and leave the house. This was tearing her apart, because she'd had a taste of happiness and now the shadow of doubt would hang over her, broken only by his letters home. Maureen, like so many other women, would have to wait and pray – pray that her man would come home again.

It was easier when she'd closed the door and left him there, as they'd agreed. To prolong their parting to the last moment before she went into the hospital was too upsetting. Both of them had known sorrow and grief, but now they had another chance to find happiness. All they could do was to pray that nothing would happen to snatch it away.